TEARS OF CINDER

BOOK ONE OF THE CONCEALMENT SAGA

BRADY PHOENIX

Tears of Cinder
Brady Phoenix
This book is a work of fiction. All names, places, characters, and events are all products of the author's imagination and are fictitious. Any similarities to actual events, places, people, living or dead, is coincidental.
Copyright © 2025 by Brady Phoenix
Cover Design by Getcovers.
All rights reserved. This book or any portion thereof may not be reproduced or used in any manner without the written permission of the publisher, except for the use of brief quotations for a book review.
First Edition: November 2025
ISBNs: 978-1-7362394-9-0

Also by Brady Phoenix

The Concealment Saga
Tears of Cinder

Standalone
Cardinal Rules
Nun Taken
Troll
Petals of Peril

To Michael:

Thank you for being my guiding light during my darkest times.

Prologue

Once Upon a Time

SINISTER SHADOWS STRETCHED across the blood-orange sunset, their urgency unnatural as the sun dipped below the decaying hills. A heavy fog shrouded the plains, hiding the withered vegetation and the weak sounds of dying screams from the forest. The growing darkness sent horses thundering away, their panicked whinnies a stark counterpoint to the speed of their flight toward distant stables. A growing evil was sensed; there was fear in their wide, frightened eyes reflecting the dimming light of the darkening world.

Stars filled the red hues of the night sky, each one flaring as another soul died. Blood pooled in the gritty soil, twinkling under the dim starlight as the witches' cackles echoed their latest victory. Their laughter drowned out the final cries of the dying as they flew on broomsticks with shredded hemlines trailing behind. From the fog, cloaked figures appeared, their decaying garments sloughing off to unveil grotesque beings. As they stalked the fleeing innocents, their movements were unnervingly deliberate, their limbs twisting and cracking.

A lone sanctuary stood deep in the woods, where a flickering beacon of resistance, wooden barricades and brightly lit torches encircled the stronghold. Along the barricades, guards with enchanted bows and arrows scanned the cursed forest, alert for the encroaching shadows. In white and mustard robes, mages chanted, weaving barriers against the endless tide of evil. Mages' purifying light pierced the chests of the daring dark spirits that ventured too close. A wildfire of light engulfed their skeletal frames, turning them to ash which the wind dispersed. Still, the darkness advanced, the attacks growing fiercer by the hour.

From the barricade's height, a green-cloaked woman, bow sheathed, sprang to the ground with practiced ease. Despite the jarring impact on her knees, she remained steady. Toward the stone sanctuary, she sprinted, brown boots kicking up dirt, where frightened townsfolk huddled within the weathered walls. Faint cries of the dying mingled with the echoing commands from the guards behind her. With her long chestnut hair flowing, she pushed open the heavy door and stepped into the dimly lit sanctuary.

Fear permeated the air inside. Eyes darting to the windows, parents gripped their children tight, anticipating the darkness's intrusion. Their hope of survival against the approaching night sent shivers down their spines. The soft glow of scattered candles illuminated the temple's stone interior, casting long, flickering shadows that did little to comfort the panicked crowd; the shadows against the stone walls caused the children to whimper.

At the temple's far end, an old man knelt before an altar. The glowing candlelight glinted faintly on his lavender cloak, the vivid purple a strong contrast to the surrounding shadows. In the chaotic storm, his tranquil aura was a source of stability as his snowy beard grazed the dusty floor while he whispered chants.

"They're here!" she breathed, desperation coloring her voice as she approached. Her panting breath pushed away the wavy curls of her dark brown hair.

The man offered no response. Lost in thought, he stood motionless, his head bowed low.

"Merlin!" she cried, her voice rising. "The attacks are getting worse! More people are dying, the township is crumbling, and we're running out of time. We have to do something!"

Despite this, Merlin still didn't speak. The candles flickered and danced in response to his calm, measured breaths.

"Answer me, Merlin!" the woman demanded, her voice strained with frustration.

The old man's deep, certain voice, a low rumble, broke the silence. "There is nothing we can do. The prophecy has already been set into motion."

"What prophecy?" A confused furrow creased her thin brow as she asked. Tension caused her fingers to tremble as she fiddled with the voluminous ivory sleeves of her blouse.

"The savior," Merlin answered, his gaze remaining on the altar. "They are not of this world. The spell is already at work, drawing them here. Your task is to lead and safeguard them from the moment they arrive until they are ready to face the darkness. It won't be easy, but this is necessary to restore peace."

The woman's heart sank. "How long must we wait?" she asked, a barely audible whisper escaping her lips. "People are dying every day. The darkness is suffocating what little hope we have left."

"Patience," Merlin urged calmly. "The savior will come soon."

"How soon?" she pressed, tears welling in her eyes.

Lifting his gaze, Merlin's sharp eyes met hers momentarily before drifting back to the dancing flames. Her fists clenched as the woman grappled with warring emotions of fear and anger. The clash of dark magic and the mages' light echoed outside, alongside the ongoing screams. A heavy dread filled her heart as she looked back at the door.

"Soon."

Chapter 1

Dominic

I DON'T WANT TO WAKE up.

It just means that I have to endure another day.

My job sucks. Both of them. The stuck-up and bitchy people I help at this corporate retail job at ChicFabAlliance make it hard to get through each day. This place is neither chic nor fab; it's just another place that sells overpriced goods and calls it stylish. No matter how much I follow the rules, the customers are not always right; I don't care what that stupid phrase says. Also, the amount of time I spent refolding shirts and organizing the stacks that resulted in one person toppling it to the floor within minutes is too much to count. All my hard work is shattered within seconds, and I have nothing to show for it.

I'm sick of people.

When I'm not working in that hell hole, I'm making lattes at this small coffee shop that my old friend owned. I struggle at times with wanting to stay there after Ethan died and his partner took over. I really need the money. That trip to the emergency room when I had pneumonia last month drained all my savings, especially when I missed out on a week of work. I feel like living paycheck to paycheck has aged me a decade.

I feel trapped.

Even when I'm working my butt off, my boyfriend and I struggle with paying the bills in our studio apartment. It's us against the world from our little home in Brooklyn. Marcus is the only family I have ever since I moved out of the orphanage in Nebraska. I met him a couple years ago when he was a customer at Ethan's coffee shop. It was one of those cute hookups that didn't involve any apps; felt like it came straight from a movie. I yearned for some love to give; and luckily I found him, regardless of our ups and downs. What made it even more worthwhile was when I found my cat, Calypso wandering outside our door. Having both of them in my life gives me a sense of purpose. I don't know what I would do without them.

BUZZ! BUZZ! BUZZ!

Well, here goes; the third alarm has gone off, and it's time to get out of bed. If I let it snooze any longer, Marcus would probably kill me. Time to get up and endure another day. This is my life until I can either win the lottery, retire, or die; whatever happens first. At this rate, it will be the third.

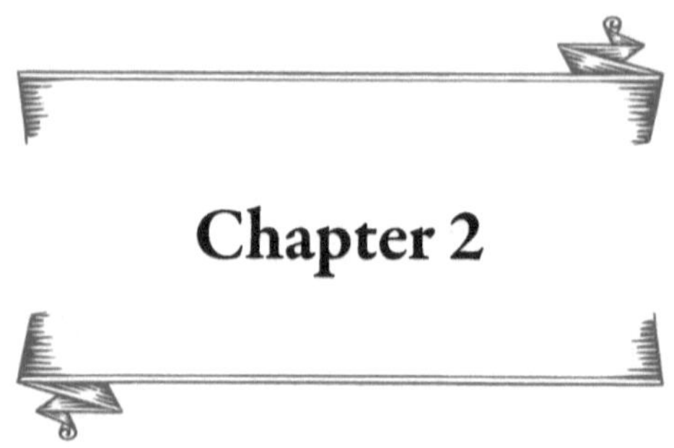

Chapter 2

The streets swelled with people as the first wave of workers began their shifts. Block by block, the streetlights transitioned from red to yellow to green, creating a Christmas tree effect. The vehicles' exhaust fumes mingled with the fresh air. With the morning light dim, Dominic struggled to pour the last of the coffee into his chipped mug, his eyes squinting. Cracked blinds let in harsh white light from New York City streetlights, creating long, skeletal shadows on the futon.

He stroked his greasy black hair, observing his sleeping boyfriend's chest rise and fall in their bed; his envy of those still asleep was profound. With a loud purr, Calypso rubbed against Dominic's ankle while he stirred the murky brew.

"You just know how to keep me going, don't you?" he whispered to him, crouching down to scratch behind his cat's black ears. He blinked slowly, his eyes an emerald green in the light; Dominic perceived an awareness in his gaze.

From his bed, Marcus mumbled, his auburn locks covering his eyes, "Dom, you're going to be late," his voice drowsy.

Seeing the time, Dominic felt his heart plummet; he had fifteen minutes to get out the door to avoid being late. He wished he could vanish as he frantically clipped his paisley bow tie, the ChicFabAlliance shift looming before him. His job had become a dull, repetitive routine under harsh fluorescent lights, filled with interactions with people who hardly noticed him. The constant pressure of maintaining the store's image, despite customer's carelessness, and having to smile while doing so, has become a strain for him.

The chill November air nipped at him as he hurried along, worried he was running out of time. Shielding himself from the cold with his denim jacket, he ducked his head and navigated the bustling streets to the subway entrance. The gritty mix of gasoline and smoke mixed with the cold air, which had brought its unwelcoming second kick with his coffee.

The subway doors slid open, and Dominic was swallowed by the crowd that rushed into the car. Amidst the diverse crowd, he held onto the railing, observing the contrast between the business suits and the sweatpants. With feet tapping a rhythm against the metal floor, each person absorbed their own music, headphones providing their escape. In the crowd, Dominic squinted, trying to identify a cloaked figure; such attire was nothing unusual in the luminous city.

He quickly climbed the stairs after exiting the train, allowing the rude people next to him to pass him by in their rush as their nose pointed higher in the air. Hotdog steam swirled around his face as the enthusiastic vendor hawked his wares from the kiosk. Near the store's glass doors, a few shopping carts, filled with scavenged possessions, lined the brick building, a silent symbol of those longing for a home. As he entered, the lights were so bright they blinded him; it felt like entering another world, his dread pulling him toward the time clock.

The day passed in a blur of retail monotony. Many argyle sweaters needed to be folded flawlessly. Tables with jeans were ready to be organized by size. Besides maintaining the store's appearance, the constant flow of customers needing checkout prevented employees from cleaning because they were always at the register. As his break approached, Dominic's feet throbbed, his mind felt overstretched and the continuous returns from unpleasant customers were wearing him down.

And that was when she walked in.

Approaching his counter was a woman in a large, fur coat, her eyes wide and scrutinizing, a deep frown etched on her face. A plastic bag swung like a tetherball at her hip. Her intense focus made Dominic's coworkers flee. Dominic attempted to secure his till, but the sound of her heels diverted his attention. On the counter, she tossed a pair of pumps. He didn't recognize them from the sales floor.

"I want to return these," she said without preamble, voice sharp and grating.

Dominic glanced from the scuffed shoes to her, his confusion evident as he eyed the damage, noticing the logo had faded. "I'm sorry, ma'am, but I don't believe we sell this brand."

"Excuse me?" she asked, perturbed. "They're from here."

"Did you have a receipt, then?" Dominic asked, his hands fiddling with each other under the counter.

With a scoff, she pulled her coat tighter around her, asking, "Are you calling me a liar?"

Dominic held his ground. "No, ma'am, just saying that I can't process a return on these. If you bought them somewhere else, I'm happy to help you figure out where they came fro—"

"No excuses! I want to speak to your manager!"

Heads turned. A sharp, poisonous voice hung in the air. Dominic felt a familiar fear rising, mingling with his frustration. Before he could intercede, his supervisor appeared from behind a nearby rack, her face expressing utter resignation, which caused his heart to stop pounding.

"Hi, ma'am," the manager politely said, her hands resting calmly. "How can I help you?"

"Yes, this degenerate was so rude and unhelpful!" the woman said, her voice laced with a light, petulant tone.

Degenerate? That's harsh!

"I offered my help, Sarah," Dominic stated, his heart now racing. "I just asked if she had a receipt."

"These were bought from here."

Sarah noticed the intense focus in the woman's eyes. Her penciled eyebrows drew together as the blue in her eyes grew darker. To calm her nerves, the boss clenched her fists in her pockets, the keys jingling.

"I'll handle that for you," she offered, calmly reaching for the gift card beside the register.

The swiping plastic in the machine felt to Dominic like a knife piercing his chest. Witnessing management prioritize customer satisfaction over employee well-being angered him. His knuckles cracked as he made a fist, her victorious smirk making him clench his jaw.

"How much did you pay for this?"

"These were a gift."

She doesn't even know if they came from here!

"You're not going to check where they came from?" Dominic asked, causing the woman's lip to curl further with each word, until the supervisor cut him short.

"Here you go, ma'am. I hope you have a nice day," Sarah said, her hand trembling as she handed her the card.

"You are *very* kind, thank you," the customer said lightly. "And I hope for the sake of this store that you do something about this incompetent fool. I would hate to see this happen again to someone like me."

It wouldn't happen if you brought the receipt. This isn't Nordstrom!

With a swish of her coat, the woman strutted away from the register. As she walked past Dominic's colleagues, her hips swayed, and the colleagues retreated behind the stacks of sweaters. The supervisor's eyebrow arched in disdain as the glass door closed once again.

"You and I both know that they didn't come from here," Dominic said, his face flushed.

"You should know by now that you need to do whatever it takes to make our customers happy. We have survey scores to maintain."

"So we bend over backwards and hand them money for crap we don't sell? How do we even resell this?"

A rapid pulse made Dominic's temples pound like a drum. Sarah's frequent interventions to always override the system to appease them, churned his stomach. Preventing a corporate call was crucial to keeping her job. He didn't have the authority to do so since he wasn't in any position of authority; it was a lose-lose situation.

"You know I will need to write you up this time," she said with remorse. "We've had this talk with you many times before."

"But I'm on corrective action! If you write me up, then I'll be fired," Dominic said, tears welling from his honey-colored eyes.

With an air of indifference, Sarah shrugged. Their year-long friendship evaporated after her promotion; he became a total stranger to her. Her job took precedence. Her sorrowful eyes hinted at the manager's actions, who avoided him as much as possible. The sight of the store manager made him apprehensive, as if a fast-moving taxi was about to strike. Management found him repulsive, and for whatever reason, each of his shortcomings became grounds for disciplinary action.

"Well, I guess this is it, then?"

With a disappointed nod, Sarah acknowledged the unfortunate turn of events. Extending her hand, she waited for him to put his badge on it. As Dominic looked around, he saw the shame on everyone's faces as they bowed their heads in mourning for a fallen comrade, causing tears to run faster.

"Can you at least say I quit so my record doesn't show that I was fired?"

"Sure."

Dominic scuffled his feet on the tiled floor as he passed the male mannequins, one of which had a raised arm, seeming to wave goodbye. In the home goods department, he noticed the general manager, their smile stretching as they observed Dominic's downcast expression. As the supervisor followed, he went upstairs to his locker, saying goodbye while gathering his belongings. Not a single excuse for her justification was enough for him to forgive her. Fearful thoughts about his ever-growing debt filled his mind, leaving him with no solution on what to do next.

THE CITY LIGHTS SHONE as the sun dipped below the horizon, bringing in the early evening shadows. The faint buzz of people around him would stop, lives bustling on without him as they carry on with their lives; clocking out of their jobs to head on to the next or heading home to their families. As he passed Central Park, the children ran to their parents, laughing with joy on their carefree day. Their eyes held no worry; they didn't need to fake smiles to compromise their morals for mere survival, only to be discarded by their employers at will.

He struggled with the idea of how to break the news to Marcus. Unemployment was never something he wanted to have as a part of his identity. The anxiety forced him to go back home early, waiting for the time to pass so he could think of what to do, and for Marcus to not catch wind of the firing just yet.

As a horse-drawn carriage rounded the corner, Dominic sneered at the haughty young woman inside, who regarded the citizens with a disdainful air of royalty. The young woman looked down on the hot dog vendors, despising their livelihood. Seeking to evade observation and the clamor, Dominic turned down a quieter street, burying his hands in his pockets. The phone's vibration was subtle, and he only registered it when he heard the soft ring. A familiar name appeared on the screen, making his heart flutter with excitement.

Penelope Prell.

It had been almost a year since Dominic had last heard from Penelope. Growing up together in the Nebraska foster system, they ended up at a small orphanage near the Kansas border. Penelope was his closest family member despite him knowing nothing of his biological family. Many imaginative adventures that would bring their storybooks to life would overcome their loneliness. Conquering castles and pillaging pirate ships were among his most cherished memories.

"Hey, Pen!" he said, trying to keep his voice steady.

"Dominic," a soft, trembling voice said. "I'm so sorry to call you out of the blue like this. I didn't know if you'd even answer, but I thought you should know something."

A man in a business suit crashed into him, rolling his eyes as he came to a halt, his heart thudding with anticipation. "Know what?"

"Dominic, Miss Reed passed away. It happened last night."

He felt the words like an icy grip on his heart, transmitted through the phone. Miss Reed was the woman who came closest to being a mother to him. Despite a life of strictness and adherence to old ways, she remained devoted to each child and nurtured their greatness as best as she could. Miss Reed was the only one who took him in. Whenever a family adopted a child, she reassured the others of their worth. Dominic believes the children in her care avoided trouble because of her guidance and compassion.

Dominic spoke in a barely audible whisper. "How?"

"They said it was her heart. Peaceful, they think. She went in her sleep." Penelope's voice wavered, as if she were on the edge of tears. "They're holding a service for her next Saturday. I...I know you're far, but if you could make it, I think it'd mean a lot to her. I know it would mean a lot to me and Alex."

Leaning against a lamppost, Dominic watched the city blur around him as his gaze fell on the cracked pavement below. "I...don't know, Pen. I'd have to figure things out here first."

"She always asked about you, you know. Even after you left. She always wanted to know how you were getting along in the city." Penelope paused, her voice softening. "But I get it. Just wanted you to know."

More conversation followed, interspersed with reminiscences and quiet moments, each word further disconnecting Dominic. Each shared laugh made his reluctance to return stronger. As the phone call concluded, a profound weight of memories settled upon him. Miss Reed's rocking chair creaked as her worn hands turned the pages of an old book in the dim light of a single floor lamp. Her quiet laughter followed each time he or Penelope snuck her sweets from the kitchen, and she'd sometimes give them a piece.

It was a simpler life, even if it had felt small and stifling back then.

Taking a deep breath, he walked on, striving to leave the memories behind him. Having left Nebraska for a different life in New York, it felt like a world away. Going back, even just for the funeral, was like stepping into an unfamiliar past. In the city's chaos, he built a new life and strives for happiness amidst its challenges. He wasn't that lost kid anymore; he'd worked so hard to leave that behind. Yet the thought wouldn't leave him alone. Miss Reed was gone. One of the last links to his past, gone.

He crossed into a quieter part of the city, a dark alley lined with grime. An unfamiliar heaviness filled the space as the shadows lengthened. The feeling was that the world tilted, and the air was thick. He perceived a subtle, nearly imperceptible humming sound, as though an unseen current coursed below the streets.

A shiver went down Dominic's back, and he froze. For a moment, he felt like he wasn't alone. He glanced over his shoulder, but only saw dark windows and metal doors. Yet the feeling persisted, creeping along his skin with the lingering thoughts battling against him.

DOMINIC FELT THE LINGERING chill as he returned, but Marcus's activity in the kitchen snapped him back to reality. Calypso, perched on the counter, watched Marcus intently as the chicken ramen simmered, filling the air with its stale scent. A rumbling purr filled the kitchen as he landed, sprawling in the center, belly out for a rub.

"Hey," Marcus said, a soft smile lifting his gaze. "I thought I'd start dinner. I thought your shift ended hours ago, but I guess I beat you home."

"Yeah, work was..." Dominic paused, searching for the right words, a strained smile on his face. "Work was a day."

Marcus chuckled, his broad shoulders bounced. "Isn't it always?"

"Look, I know we don't usually go out until the weekend, but I thought we could try that new Italian place on the corner tonight. You know, act like New Yorkers for once."

Marcus, grateful for the suggestion, nodded in agreement. "Sounds perfect. I think we could use a break from the noodles once in a while."

With a soft kiss on Marcus's cheek, Dominic headed for the closet. As he unbuttoned his shirt, his hand shook at the prospect of breaking the news. Despite the minimum wage barely covering his expenses, he avoided admitting to losing his job. After all that had transpired, he only hoped to be carefree with the one closest to him.

As Dominic removed his dress pants, Calypso rubbed against his exposed ankles. Ignoring the pleading grins, he pulled his fresh pair of jeans up. Donning his Good Charlotte tee and denim jacket, guilt washed over him for neglecting his pet. Marcus put his purple NYU sweatshirt over his black dress shirt, untucking the hem over his khakis before putting on his tennis shoes.

As they walked a short distance to the restaurant, the couple held each other close against the November cold. They passed smokers puffing on their stoops, cigarette smoke drifting in their wake. Nearing the block's edge, the lights flickered, transitioning from green to yellow.

In the restaurant's corner bay window, candlelight flickered. Upon opening the door, the soft sounds of an accordion playing from the speakers met them; a pesto-filled welcome. Warmth filled the space once they removed their coats; the waitress presented menus and water at their table. With a quick sip of water, Dominic observed Marcus's stressed expression as he perused the menu.

Marcus looked up, offering a tired smile. "I'm happy we're doing this," he said. "I needed a break today. Work's been a mess. They cut two shifts, so I had to cover part of their work on top of my own. And they don't pay us more for that, you know?"

Though guilt gnawed at him, Dominic offered a sympathetic nod. Marcus's job change and Dominic's lack of pay from ChicFabAlliance, coupled with weeks of unpaid bills, left them precariously close to a financial crisis. But still, he hadn't found a way to break the news yet. His hidden truth caused a nauseous guilt to grip him.

"Tell me about it," he began, "I had a customer today..." His words escaped before he could restrain them, then he stopped, hoping Marcus wouldn't ask for more.

Marcus put down his glass, his chestnut eyes narrowing before he said, "Dom, what happened? Did someone give you a hard time again?"

A shrug from Dominic preceded him reaching for a breadstick. "You know how it is. They were just difficult. Got into it with my supervisor, and she didn't appreciate that."

A heavy silence separated them. Dominic pretended to be engrossed in the menu to avoid looking at Marcus. Marcus's look was piercing; he seemed to perceive the underlying message.

"Dominic, did something happen with your job?" Marcus asked, his hand reaching out to his partner's. "Aren't you on corrective action?"

Dominic sighed, realizing there was no way around it now; it was time to commit to the truth. "Yeah. There was this woman, making up some story about a return. Supervision tried to smooth it over, but...the customer wasn't appreciating my help. They forced me to quit," Dominic explained, though his light tone veiled his underlying distress.

A look of dismay crossed Marcus's face as he exhaled shakily. "Dom, why didn't you tell me sooner?"

"I didn't want to make it worse," Dominic explained, his hold on Marcus's hand strengthening as he felt his pulse speed up. "Look, I'll find something new, okay? ChicFabAlliance was just a job. I didn't even want to be there forever."

"But it was the job that paid our bills. What about them?" Marcus's voice was very faint. "We've got rent coming up, and Calypso's vet bill is still sitting there. And my shifts...they're cutting hours, Dom."

Dominic gave his hand a steady, firm squeeze. "I know. I know it feels like we're backed into a corner right now, but I swear, we're going to be fine. I'll start looking tomorrow. I'll find something better."

Marcus's hand trembled in his, and Dominic could see the fear in his eyes. He felt that same deep-seated fear, but tonight, he wanted to suppress it. "Let's not think about all that right now," Dominic murmured, leaning closer. "Let's just have a good time tonight, yeah?"

With a sigh, Marcus's shoulders eased. "You're right. You're right. It's just...sometimes it feels like the universe is throwing one thing after another at us."

Dominic gave a steady nod, eyes unwavering. "That's why we're taking tonight off from all that. We'll face it tomorrow, but tonight we get to pretend it's just us, nothing to worry about."

With a smile from Marcus, the tension between them lessened. Their worry faded, replaced by a delicate warmth; a feeling as if they each held a tiny piece of the world.

"Just us," he reiterated, smiling wider, his freckles becoming more defined in the candlelight. "All right, Dom. Just for tonight. And please, stop keeping shit from me."

They let the conversation drift back into easier topics with memories of their first nights in New York, to plans they'd made and forgotten. As their dinners came, shared laughter and tenderness dissolved their tension. Though they laughed, a dark shadow of Dominic's secret grief hung over him.

Having settled the bill, they went back to their apartment. The cold air couldn't cool his racing heart; his guilt was consuming him. He glanced at his reflection in the passing windows, seeing the strained smile mirrored on Marcus's face.

Calypso greeted them with a familiar purr as they entered their apartment, winding around their legs and waiting all evening for their arrival. They tossed their jackets on the futon and gradually removed their clothing to just their underwear while making their way to the bed. As the TV flickered to life with *Modern Family*, they embraced, their cat squeezing between them. His body grew heavy as he drifted off to dreamland once more. For a moment, the darkness lifted, replaced by the comforting familiarity of his cherished place. Though finding a job to survive might be an adventure, the security of his family is what strengthens him to move forward into another day.

Chapter 3

A dim, grayish light filtered through the grimy windows into the kitchen as the sun rose. Dominic watched Marcus get ready as he slowly got out of bed, pulling on his black dress pants over his Calvin Klein boxer briefs. With a shared, tense grin, and his pewter shirt buttoned, they both waited for the other to speak. Dominic's only wish was for another hour of cuddling, with Calypso joining in their blanket pile next to his pillow. Even with Marcus's arm around him, the embrace felt distant.

Steam from Marcus's coffee, carrying the scent of Columbian grounds, roused Dominic from his grogginess. Dominic's black t-shirt, hanging down to his mid-thighs as his feet felt the cold kitchen tiles. A cloying mix of stale dinner and strong coffee hung heavy in the air, a tangible weight. Marcus sat opposite, worry etched on his face; his jaw clenched, his hands fiddling with a placemat's frayed edge as he sipped from his cup.

"So..." Marcus started, the silence heavy as dust on forgotten furniture. "You didn't try to talk them out of it?"

Dominic remained silent, his gaze fixed on the dark liquid. He didn't have to; he knew the flicker of disappointment that crossed Marcus's face. After digesting the chicken parmesan from the previous evening, he had to face the music and provide an explanation.

"Dom, bills don't just stop coming because you lost a job." Marcus said, adjusting his comb over away from his forehead. "We're barely scraping by as it is. Rent's due and you know we already missed last month." He caught himself, swallowing back what he didn't say. Instead, he sighed. "You've got the café job, but that's not even close to enough."

Looking up, Dominic nodded, his eyes unfocused. To comfort Marcus, he tried to speak, but no words emerged. What could he say that would make it all better? That he was sorry for something he had no control over? That he'd find a way, somehow, despite the odds?

"That place wasn't the greatest anyway," Dominic muttered.

"If it wasn't the greatest, then why haven't you found something different?" Marcus continued. "You could've found something better when we're not on the verge of eviction."

It's not like I planned on the woman coming to the store.

With his arms crossed, Marcus leaned back. The worry lines on his face softened, replaced with regret. "I'm not mad, Dom. But I'd be lying if I said I didn't have a hard time falling asleep. I just wish you'd talk to me about this right away instead of shutting down yesterday. We're in this together, remember?"

"But it wasn't my fault!" Tears welled in Dominic's eyes as he yelped.

"You could've read the writing on the walls sooner and made an exit strategy. Instead, you waited to get let go and then you waited to tell me."

A dull ache of guilt pressed on Dominic's chest. He didn't intend to exclude Marcus, yet he found himself unable to speak, overwhelmed by frustration and helplessness. Whatever he could even think about couldn't convince him; It wouldn't convince himself with how overwhelmed he was and no idea on where to start fixing the problem.

"I will make this work," he said, the sounds thick and empty, even to his own ears.

Marcus's hand covered Dominic's as he reached across the table. "You don't have to do it alone."

Although Dominic nodded and squeezed Marcus's hand, his thoughts drifted to a troubling darkness he wished to avoid. Withdrawing his hand, he finished his coffee in one long, bitter gulp. "I need to get to the café," he mumbled, pushing back from the table. "I'll try to pick up extra hours. That'll be a start. I'll see you later."

Though wanting to add more, Marcus remained silent, only nodding. His smile was small and forced. Pausing as he grabbed his messenger bag, he gave Dominic's doe-like eyes a final look.

Dominic offered a weak, forced smile to lighten the heaviness between them. But as Marcus stepped out into the cold, the knot in his chest only tightened, threatening to choke him. A wave of nausea washed over Dominic as he struggled to pour another cup. His defenses left him drained. A growing financial debt trapped him, and he couldn't find a solution. He didn't have it in him to do anything outside of his comfort zone; he had no idea what other skills he possessed with his work ethic besides folding clothes and making drinks. All he could hope for was to win big just to catch up in order for a better life.

THE STREETS WERE UNUSUALLY empty for a Wednesday morning. Pulling his jacket closer, Dominic eyed the surrounding buildings with suspicion. The city had always been strange, filled with shadows that moved just a little too much, alleys that seemed to stretch longer than they should, doors that sometimes appeared where none had been before. But today, the oddities seemed more pronounced, like the city was holding its breath, waiting.

He hurried toward the café, trying to ignore the unsettling feeling creeping over him. But as he rounded the corner, he froze. A distant figure, cloaked and obscure, stood at the street's end. He felt the figure's gaze upon him; its pose was static. Dread washed over Dominic, a spine-chilling whisper slithering across his skin. A taxi speeding past on the adjacent road caused him to glance away; his heart pounded, and when he looked back, the figure had vanished.

"It's all in my head," he mumbled, hastening his steps. A lingering unease, a prickling at the back of his neck, told him he was being watched.

Dominic hurried around the corner, his eyes on the café's withering green awning, battling a fierce wind down the narrow street. Though yesterday's layoff was painful, he tried to remain optimistic. Lattes and pastries weren't glamorous, but the job helped keep him afloat and connected to the world.

Reaching the café at last, he found the warmth and bustle a temporary refuge from the shadows that pursued him. He entered and nodded to the other barista, engrossed in their work. A strong, almost harsh coffee smell filled his lungs as he took off his jacket and went to the back to get his apron.

However, as he fastened it around his waist, he noticed his reflection in the kitchen's small mirror. A pale, tired face stared back at him, but something else in the mirror held his gaze. A shadow flickered, moving behind him. He whipped around, but the room was empty.

"Dominic, you good?" called one of the other employees, her voice muffled from the kitchen doorway.

With a swallow, he nodded. "Yeah, just a rough night."

With an uneasy grin, his coworker gave him a pat on the back, her jaw clenched. Dominic took in a deep breath, trying to remind himself of the mission to make the money he needed to make a living. Above all, his priority was to avoid disappointing Marcus again.

The shift flew by in a whirlwind of orders, hot steam, and the incessant whirring of the espresso machine. But no matter how many drinks he poured, or how many times he wiped down the counters, he couldn't shake the feeling that something was wrong. There was the feeling that the shadows clinging to him were waiting, watching, closing in and teasing him with the cacophony of anxiety.

Dominic saw each customer as a chance to earn more money. The smile he tried to put on his face was a hope for a tip; anything to help him in his time of need. Even with the customers that weren't the most pleasant, he found the inner strength to swallow his pride and provide the best service; at least if there was management that needed to intervene, there wouldn't be anything to worry about with the boss not caring much.

He finished the end-of-day deposit as the last hour ended. On his way to the office, he felt a looming, ominous presence, like a dark cloud settling over the place. The broom's bristles brushed the hardwood, collecting debris just as the door swung open. Victor appeared, his hands displaying a white poster board with four fearsome words written in black marker.

"Closed Until Further Notice."

"Victor," Dominic said, his voice tight, "what's going on? Are we—?"

"It's over, Dominic," Victor said, his tone devoid of hope and emotion.

Dominic struggled to make sense of the words, a bitter taste filling his mouth. "Over? What do you mean, over?"

A long sigh escaped Victor's thin lips as he slumped his lanky form against the counter, his shoulders heavy. "We're closing for good. I can't keep this place running. Not without Ethan."

Dominic felt a sharp pain in his heart when Victor mentioned his deceased partner. The café thrived because of Ethan, whose warmth and joy touched everyone he served. When he died, the café had lost more than just a barista—it had lost its heart and soul. Every child smiled when a parent brought them in. His customer service was above and beyond with doing whatever it took to provide satisfaction. After his passing, Dominic attempted to salvage the situation, maintaining the place to honor Ethan's legacy while balancing a second job.

Grief-stricken, Dominic's anger simmered, his fists clenched. "Victor, I've been doing everything to keep this place going! Ethan left us a successful business, a place people loved."

"I know," Victor said, the tape strips ripping apart. "Times have been tough since he passed."

"Times weren't that tough," Dominic said, his pulse racing. "You just let it fall apart. I don't even think you cared that much about his heart attack."

Defiance flickered in Victor's eyes, which grew dark. "Watch your tone, Dominic. You have no idea what it's like to keep something like this afloat. I did my best."

"Your best?" Desperation edged Dominic's voice higher, making his words sharper. "Victor, we practically ran this place for you. You ignored every idea we suggested, every chance we had to make it work. Ethan built this café from scratch. You didn't care about it then when the money went missing and the bills were due. His health paid for it then, and now you're giving up his hard work."

You won't even give a free cookie for the kids like Ethan did.

A softer, more despairing expression replaced the anger on Victor's face. "I know you guys tried, Dom. And I'm sorry…I truly am. But without Ethan, I can't. I can't keep this place open. It was his dream, not mine."

"Please, Victor. I have no idea how badly I need this job. I've carried this store with all my free time and can dedicate more if you need it," Dominic pleaded.

The finality hit Dominic like a physical blow. He felt his resolve weakening, hope fading away like smoke in the freezing air. With no job and no prospects, he felt utterly helpless. He looked at Victor's face, searching for mercy or hope, but saw only tired resignation.

Victor mumbled a quick "Good luck, Dom" before leaving Dominic alone in the emptying café, his last bit of hope vanishing with his departing, defeated coworkers who were processing their losses.

Stepping back outside, the frigid air hit him like a slap, his mind racing as he tallied his meager tips and considered how to make it until his next gig. What was he supposed to do now? Rent needed to be paid. Two jobs were enough to stay afloat—barely. But now? The empty streets offered no solace as he wandered, his heart pounding from panic fueled by overdue bills, rent, and the memory of Marcus's worried eyes.

A strange, unsettling silence greeted him as he cut through a narrow alleyway, hoping to get home faster. A sharp voice cut through the air behind him before his tingling senses could alert him to react.

"Hey, you got any cash?"

He whirled, only to have a firm hand seize his shoulder and force him back. Tripping, he fell against the cold brick wall as two more figures emerged from the shadows, surrounding him. Though hidden, their faces glowed in the darkness. Their disheveled clothing craved a wash; the holes in their pants were desperate for repairs. The decay on their teeth needed care.

"Let me go," he stammered, fear thickening his voice as rough hands dug into his pockets.

One man smirked, stepping closer. "What is this? Only thirty dollars?"

Dominic's stomach lurched. A constant, uncontrollable blink accompanied his pounding heart. The desire to fight back was brewing within, but the confidence in his strength made him scared. Surrounded by so many people, he became cowardly, his body curling into a fetal position.

"Here's a quick donation, buddy. Won't take long."

A swift punch to the gut rendered Dominic breathless before he had a chance to respond. Searing pain coursed through him as they searched his pockets for his wallet. A blow to his side followed, leaving him gasping as they completed the robbery and added a last kick.

Dominic was left bruised and bleeding on the cold concrete as they retreated into the shadows, their laughter ringing in the air. For a moment, he lay there, his vision blurry, the weight of his situation crushing him. His job and money were gone, and the bitter truth became more clear with each painful breath. For a moment, he thought about staying there, waiting for death to take him away and put the stress and misery behind him; but then who would feed Calypso?

With a wince, he dragged himself home. Each step sent waves of pain through his battered body, but his internal numbness was far worse. He received no acknowledgement of his agony from anyone he passed. As he neared his apartment building, the setting sun cast long, ominous shadows across the broken pavement. Climbing the stairs to his apartment, a warm bath was all he craved to calm his frazzled nerves and regain his composure. Being surrounded by his loved ones in the comfort of his home would restore his peace of mind.

But when he reached his door, his heart sank even further.

Taped to the door was a bright red notice; his worst fear, written in bold black letters.

"Notice of Eviction."

A shudder ran through him as he touched the paper, his fingers tracing its surface, his mind numb with shock. It felt as though a cruel fate had robbed him of all he held dear, leaving him adrift and despondent. He wanted the chance to rise above and prove to himself and to Marcus that he could make things right and pull his share. He knew he could dig deep and find a job to make a living and keep them afloat.

Not anymore.

He pushed open the door, his hands trembling, then stepped inside and softly called out, "Marcus?"

A suffocating silence fell upon him without delay. He realized something wasn't right as his vision cleared in the dim light, the apartment feeling oddly empty. The living room was bare, containing only a few belongings. Only the outline of the bed frame remained indented in the carpet, with cat hair marking its former space. The items they collected on their urban adventures had vanished; every snow globe, every bobblehead.

Entering the kitchen, he stumbled, his stomach in knots at the sight of a piece of paper on the counter. Tears welled in his eyes as he picked up the letter, blurring Marcus's familiar handwriting.

"Dom,

I can't keep doing this. We've been running on empty, and I can't watch you destroy yourself, which has put a strain on us. I've taken my things, and I'm staying with my parents. Take care of yourself. I wish you the best. I will always love my time with you."

A sob choked him as his eyes fell upon the note; its words felt like daggers. He was alone—truly, completely alone. His love and companionship, his sources of comfort and solace, vanished, as did everything else. Marcus had left with his meager possessions, leaving behind an empty apartment and an eviction notice.

Waves of exhaustion from the day's events overwhelmed Dominic, and he collapsed to the floor. He buried his face in his hands, his shoulders shaking as the last threads of his resolve unraveled. A darkness deeper than any he'd ever encountered enveloped him, despair tearing at him as he rocked, lost in a sea of grief and hopelessness.

Gentle warmth touched his side as soft paws padded against him, easing his anguish. He looked down to Calypso gazing up at him with wide eyes. His head rested on his arm, the rhythmic purring a calming counterpoint to his sadness. As his tail dragged across Dominic's chin, the cat's fur soaked up his tears.

Reaching to stroke the fur, he whispered "Calypso," his voice cracking. He pressed closer, curling up beside him.

"You're all that's left," he whispered, his tears unceasing as his fingers played with his soft fur. Calypso, nestled against him, purred more intensely, offering comfort and reminding him he wasn't alone.

The steady rhythm of his breath calmed him as he rested his head against Calypso, eyes closed. The soft warmth of his cat was his only companion in the silent apartment as he surrendered to his feelings. Calypso's warmth was his anchor against the enveloping darkness, preventing a complete fall into the abyss. Clinging tightly, he used his blood-caked hand to retrieve his phone from his hidden pocket. Swiping up, he pulled up his recent contacts to call an old friend. As they answered, his voice grew with certainty; he had no other choice but to do it.

"Hey, Pen. I'll see you at the funeral."

Chapter 4

Dominic

THIS WEEK HAS BEEN too much.

I've lost both of my jobs.

My boyfriend left me.

I have no home.

And my foster mother passed away.

It took so much out of me to sell all of my belongings for as much cash as I could to afford a car to get out of New York. The small collection of Hardy Boys books had to go. When the only friend I made at the café, Justice, fell ill, she gave me her small collection of crystals; I couldn't keep those, either. I had little to begin with, but part of my soul left me when I worked so hard to get these belongings. All the memories I made with the possessions I worked very hard for are now someone else's treasures. To have them taken away from me brought so much shame. It was like I wasn't good enough to thrive in this world.

And now I'm sleeping out of this beater with Calypso by my side, his eyes trying to encourage me to hold on and not have a breakdown.

At least someone believes in me.

All these hours on the road to Everside Valley have given me time to reflect on what I should do with my life. I know I've been looking for some sort of adventure, some sort of change when I wanted to get out of my mundane life in retail. But I was too scared to step out of my comfort zone. I didn't fathom that it would come to this.

I guess beggars can't be choosers, right?

Well, I'm in Nebraska. Part of me missed the open plains since I've been dealing with the congested streets. The buildings aren't stories high and crammed together. There are more houses rather than run-down apartment buildings.

Here goes nothing, I guess.

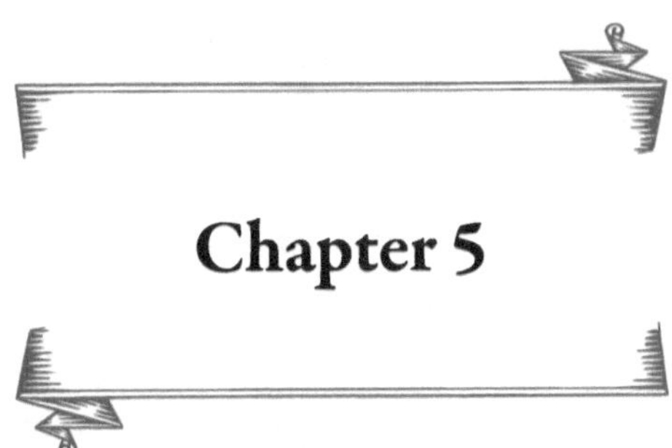

Chapter 5

Only the engine's hum filled the Honda Accord as Dominic's gaze remained fixed on the road, the passing scenery a hazy blend of grays and browns. His knuckles shone white against the wheel he clutched desperately, his only anchor to reality. The incessant radio static and jammed tape player did little to distract him from his overwhelming feelings of failure.

It was too much. He couldn't escape the truth, the thought a relentless pulse in his mind, a mantra. The immense pressure on his chest made breathing difficult. Marcus was gone, disappearing into the night with their shared memories and what little they'd built together. The last words exchanged were an assumption of him not trying hard, and now Marcus believed he had no ambitions or drive. His job at ChicFabAlliance was a casualty, but he hadn't thought the café would go under too. He poured his heart and soul into that place. And now, evicted. The sting of it still felt raw, like the tearing of old wounds he thought had long since healed.

Beside him on the passenger seat, Calypso lay curled in a tight ball on the worn blanket he'd thrown next to his carrier. Those emerald eyes observed him with a still, unreadable feline compassion, his very being a small, warm island amid the vast, cold expanse of the man's thoughts. He'd been his one constant through this dark turn, never wavering, never leaving, even when he felt like he was unraveling from the inside out.

A slow breath escaped Dominic's lips as he looked down at his cat. "Just you and me, pal," he murmured, his voice barely a whisper. "Guess we're heading back to where it all started, huh?"

With a soft purr, the cat stretched his paws out before tucking them back in, his eyes blinking slowly. Even with the heaviness of recent losses, he found comfort and grounding in the sound. The pain in his chest grew sharper, more insistent and raw.

It wasn't supposed to end like this. He arrived in the city, full of dreams, goals, and ambitions, hoping to build a life he could be proud of, free from his past. And for a while, he'd been close. He and Marcus had shared late nights full of laughter and quiet mornings over coffee, a life stitched together with love and hope. Now, though, it felt like everything had turned to ash, slipping through his fingers no matter how tightly he tried to hold on.

Bitterness gathered at the back of Dominic's throat as he let out a soft scoff. It was always the same to him. People came and went in his life, leaving him to pick up the pieces on his own. He thought he'd found a partner, someone who understood the best and worse in him. But in the end, Marcus had turned away.

The road ahead was long and empty, causing Dominic to tighten his grip on the wheel and narrow his eyes. This wasn't the future he had imagined, but it was the one he was left with. And now, for the first time in a while, he was heading back to the place he thought he'd escaped forever.

A strange mix of emotions washed over him as he reflected on Penelope and Alex, his only two friends who felt like family. They'd been his confidants, his protectors, his partners in crime. The three had faced foster care's challenges and the system's apathy together, forging a bond through loss and survival. The memories warmed his heart, piercing the profound gloom that had consumed him after life's cruel rejection.

Penelope's laugh—bright, innocent, full of life—echoed in his mind as he imagined being swept into her next crazy adventure. Alex, on the other hand, was the quiet one, the grounding force in their little trio. He'd been the one to patch them up after their adventures, always prepared with a wry smile. His inner strength was something that became instilled in Dominic, his athleticism was needed for protection when the other kids teased him.

He felt like he hadn't seen them in an eternity, years since they last sat together on the orphanage's dusty couches, whispering their hopes and dreams. Penelope wanted to help people just like how Miss Reed helped them, and Alex wanted to create with his hands. Their contact, maintained through infrequent messages and calls, eventually faded as their lives diverged. Now, though, with nowhere else to go, he was heading back to them, to the only real family he'd ever known.

A roadside sign flashed by, signifying another hour of his long drive. The exhaustion was setting in, a bone-deep weariness that went beyond physical fatigue. Sleepless nights had taken their toll; his mind was muddled, heavy with grief over what he'd lost mixed with the anxiety of reuniting with ones he cherished. His makeshift bed in the backseat wasn't ideal; Calypso's affection, while appreciated, made it worse.

He glanced at Calypso again, his soft purr a steady reminder that, for now, he wasn't completely alone. "I really hope they show up, pal," he whispered, a hint of uncertainty slipping into his voice. "I don't know what I'd do if they weren't."

Calypso yawned, stretched his legs, and curled back up, implying, "One way to find out."

A soft chuckle escaped him, but it lacked warmth. He didn't know what he would do if Penelope and Alex weren't there. They'd been the only people who had seen him at his most vulnerable, the ones who had witnessed the quiet desperation he'd hidden from everyone else. If they were gone from this world, he wasn't sure how he'd pick himself up again. Regret flowed through him; he wasn't available enough to call them more. He couldn't take a couple of minutes to send a text or reply to theirs.

The orphanage loomed in his memories like a spectral figure, equal parts comforting and haunted. The building was already neglected in his youth; its walls showed the toll of many shattered lives. Yet, it was there that he'd found something safe, a space where he could escape the relentless feeling of abandonment that had trailed him like a shadow his entire life. Penelope and Alex had been his family, his haven, a constant in a world that seemed determined to strip everything else away from him. Lost in thought, he barely registered the remaining miles, wondering about the changes in their faces compared to his own. Dominic felt a pang of longing for their friendship, for the uncomplicated bond they'd shared before life tore them apart.

"I hope they've been happy," he whispered, his voice lost in the engine's hum.

The familiar Nebraska roads gave way to the township, a large, looming silhouette of dilapidated houses against the darkening sky, as the car rounded the final bend. Pulling into the gravel driveway, memories washed over him, his heart pounding, leaving him breathless. He sat still, eyes fixed on the buildings, a mix of anticipation and fear consuming his thoughts. This place had been his sanctuary once, but could it be that again?

As Calypso purred and rubbed against his elbow, he felt grounded and remembered to breathe.

"Here goes nothing, pal," he murmured, taking a sip of his gas station soda. He eased up on the gas, feeling the past and present blend, their pain and hope merging as he neared the place he once called home.

Chapter 6

The township of Everside Valley hadn't changed much in the years since Dominic had left. Driving through the narrow streets, he saw the same small, sleepy shops, their paint chipped and their signs faded. Decades of neglect were evident in the Main Street grocery store's appearance, mirroring the diner where Penelope worked as a teenager, its neon "Open" sign still faintly buzzing. The place felt timeless, a treasure chest of dusty memories and dreams almost lost to time.

Calypso sat on the passenger seat, eyes wide as he watched the rural scenery pass by. The steady purr was a comfort, a silent promise everything would work out, that he wasn't facing his past alone. Every citizen that went about their day brought back the need for his cat to provide assurance.

Reaching the town's edge, the orphanage came into view. The building was just as he remembered, a large, aging Victorian house with peeling white paint and a sagging roof that seemed to sink a little lower with each passing year. Overgrown trees crowded the front yard, their branches heavy with the last of autumn leaves clinging for life, casting long shadows that stretched across the yard. He could almost hear the echoes of his childhood, laughter and whispered secrets drifting on the wind as he sat in the car and took it all in.

The Nebraska evening's familiar chill settled over him as he parked and got out. Calypso followed him to the front door, his steps silent as he hopped down beside him. Just as Dominic raised his hand to knock, the door flew open, and he found himself face-to-face with a woman whose face he'd have recognized anywhere. Her breath was heavy, fogging up the lenses of her thick, square spectacles.

"Dominic!" Penelope said, her smile lighting up the dim entryway. With her long red hair falling over her shoulders, her glasses gleamed as she studied him, her warmth filling the space; a warmth he'd been missing.

"Penelope," he said, smiling as she hugged him tight. Her embrace, both firm and comforting, revealed a strength he'd underestimated.

When she finally let go, her darf green eyes glistened with joy. "I can't believe you're really here. Alex didn't think you were going to come, but I knew you would."

Dominic's heart fluttered, a tear glistening on his face. "I didn't think I was going to come either. It's been way too long."

Just as he began to speak, a tall man's scruffy beard glistened by the diminishing daylight. Alex grinned, his hands in his pockets as he gave Dominic a playful look.

"About time you got here," Alex teased softly, his blonde hair fluttering. With a strong hug and a firm clap on the back, he greeted Dominic, his toned muscles tensing. "Good to see you, man. You don't look half as bad as I thought you would."

Dominic laughed, shaking his head. "Thanks...I think."

Alex's gaze shifted to Calypso, who had followed Dominic inside with quiet confidence, his sleek black fur blending into the shadows. He knelt down to pet him, chuckling as he purred and rubbed against his hand. "So, you brought a friend. What's their name?"

"His name's Calypso," Dominic answered, observing their mutual admiration. "He's been keeping me grounded lately."

Penelope joined to scratch Calypso under the chin. "He's adorable. And anyone who's a friend of yours is a friend of ours."

In the old living room, Dominic's gaze swept across the aged furniture, battered coffee table, and old sepia-toned photos decorating the walls. It was both exactly the same and yet entirely different, layered with years of change that somehow hadn't erased the memories etched into every corner. He could almost see their younger selves here, sprawled across the floor, whispering dreams about the future they had all imagined. A faint echo of a nearby bouncing ball creaked in the empty corridors.

"So, what happened to the orphanage?" he asked, finally finding his voice. "It still looks like it's running, but where's everyone?"

Alex's face fell, while Penelope's softened. Before speaking, they exchanged a glance; Penelope's voice was laced with sadness.

"After you left, things were fine for a while," she began, her gaze drifting over the room as if she could see the memories playing out in the air. "But shortly after we left, Miss Reed took a break and lived the last couple years alone before she passed."

Dominic felt a pang in his chest. Miss Reed had been more than just a caretaker; she had been their guide, their protector. A constant presence in their lives. She always wore her thick, gray hair in a bun and had sharp but kind eyes. She was the one who had read them stories at night, bandaged their scraped knees, and listened to their fears with patience and understanding. The meals she cooked were hearty and made with love, pouring her heart into caring for each child as if they were her own.

"How did she pass?" he asked, his voice barely a whisper.

"She'd been struggling for a while, you knew that," Alex said softly, looking down. "But she never told anyone. She was always so stubborn, so determined to be there for us. We all thought she'd live forever."

"Like Superwoman," said Dominic.

Penelope sighed; her gaze was distant. "When she passed, things started to unravel. The orphanage lost funding, and with Miss Reed gone, no one knew how to keep it going. The state was going to shut it down, but members of the community tried to step in to keep it going, just barely. But it's not the same without her. They're going to shut it down."

The weight of those words hit Dominic hard, a dull pain in his chest reminding him of Miss Reed's comforting presence and how she'd been their anchor during difficult times. She had been their mother in every way that mattered, and now she was gone, leaving behind a void that nothing could fill.

Dominic surveyed the room, noticing the worn couches, dusty bookshelves, and empty spaces that once held laughter and life. "She was the best of us," he said, his voice thick. "I don't know where I'd be without her."

A comforting hand rested on his arm as Penelope reached over. "She'd be glad you're back. She always believed in you, Dom."

A lump formed in Dominic's throat as he blinked back tears, swallowing with effort. "I wish I'd come back sooner," he whispered.

After a long, quiet moment, Penelope rose, brushing the dust from her olive, prairie skirt. "Come on. Let's take a walk. I think we could all use a little fresh air."

Grinning, Alex nudged him, and then the three of them went outside, followed by Calypso. They followed a familiar path that led away from the house and into the open fields behind the orphanage, a place they'd explored countless times.

As they walked, the long grass caressed their legs, while the setting sun painted the landscape in warm, golden hues. A cool, crisp breeze wafted the aroma of autumn leaves and rich earth. They didn't speak much, the silence between them comfortable as they walked side by side, lost in memories. In their quest to conquer the kingdom, Alex acted as their knight, Penelope as their wise mage, and Dominic as their newbie squire. The amount of sticks broken from the sword fights on the knoll brought the three closer together, their arms locking around each other.

They reached a clearing surrounded by more tall grass. It was a little hollow, hidden from view, where they'd once dreamed up stories of adventure and escape, where they'd made promises to each other that had carried them through the hardest moments of their young lives. During moments of vulnerability, Alex would bare his soul to Dominic, sharing his biggest fears and insecurities. Their secret spot was a place of beauty, a place of love.

Penelope settled on a fallen log, inviting Dominic to join her, with Calypso jumping onto her lap, appreciating her embrace. With his elbows supporting him, Alex lay on the grass, his deep blue eyes fixed on the twilight sky.

"It seems like ages ago," Dominic murmured, his eyes taking in the well-known clearing.

"Yes, it does," Penelope agreed wistfully. "But some things never really leave us, you know? Like this place, and us."

Alex chuckled, glancing over at them. "This was our kingdom. Out here, we could be anyone we wanted. Remember when we all wanted to be heroes?"

Dominic smiled, reminiscing about their jointly created narratives of knights, adventurers, battles won, and kingdoms claimed. Out here, they'd been fearless, dreaming of lives far beyond the dusty walls of the orphanage.

"Do you ever miss it?" Dominic asked, looking at Penelope and Alex with curiosity. "The way things were?"

Penelope nodded, a yearning look in her eyes. "Sometimes. But what I miss most is how sure we were back then. How certain we felt about everything."

"Yeah," Alex responded, his eyes drifting to the stars appearing above. "But we're still here, right? Maybe a little bruised, a little older, but still us."

Dominic felt a warmth settle over him, a quiet sense of belonging he hadn't felt in years. Despite everything he'd lost here, with Penelope and Alex, he felt a flicker of hope, a reminder that he wasn't as alone as he'd feared.

Penelope reached over, taking his hand in hers. "Whatever happens next, Dom, just remember—you have us. You always will."

AS THEY MADE THEIR way back through the fields after a good hour of reminiscence, the sky deepened into shades of twilight. Faint silver light from more stars illuminated the landscape. Calypso stayed close, his dark form blending with the ground, as Dominic found comfort in Penelope and Alex. The nostalgia of the evening had lifted his spirits, filling him with a sense of adventure he hadn't felt in years. The fuel in his soul has become something he wished he had taken with him in the city.

"You guys remember the old mayor's mansion?" Alex asked, his eyes gleaming mischievously. He gestured toward a hill overlooking the town, where a large, shadowy mansion stood in stark contrast to the sky. With its sharp angles, gabled roofs, and tall chimneys, the building cast a fortress-like silhouette against the fading light.

"Oh, that place," Penelope said with a shiver, pulling her sweater tighter around her shoulders. "I hated it when you dared us to go up there."

A soft chuckle escaped Dominic's lips as memories of those tense nights came rushing back. "I think I lasted all of five minutes before I bailed. Something about those hedge mazes. I kept thinking we'd see something staring at us through the leaves."

"Creepiest place in Everside Valley," Penelope agreed.

"It's the *only* place in Everside Valley," Alex said sarcastically.

"The only rich looking place," Penelope said. "But I heard that after Mayor Hawthorne passed away decades ago, it was left empty. No one's wanted to buy it because of the rumors that it's still haunted and his spirit still lingers here."

Penelope looked at the mansion and shrugged. "That, or it's cursed. After he passed, they say strange things started happening in town...odd noises, shadows moving in empty rooms. People avoided it for years, and now it's just sitting there, abandoned."

A mischievous grin spread across Alex's face. "So, what I'm hearing is that we should check it out for ourselves. You know, just for old times' sake."

Dominic's hand rose as the exhaustion from his long drive washed over him. "Guys, it's been a long day. I'm not exactly in the mood to go poking around some mansion."

Penelope elbowed him playfully. "Oh, come on, Dom. You can't come all the way back to Everside Valley and not try to relive a little of our old childhood mischief."

A sigh escaped Dominic's lips as his eyes flickered between Penelope and Alex; their eager faces, identical to those of their roguish youth, spoke of impending forbidden fun. Calypso rubbed against his ankle, wanting to get back to the orphanage for some sleep and cuddles. Against his better judgment, Dominic felt a flicker of excitement spark in him, too. He had come back to escape the darkness of his life in the city, and a little harmless thrill might be exactly what he needed. Maybe this was the time to revert to some adventure to spark happiness back into him after this week. A little distraction to detox his heart from his grief.

"All right," he said, shaking his head with a reluctant smile. "But if we get caught, I'm blaming both of you."

"Deal!" Alex said, clapping him on the back.

With Calypso trailing, his eyes gleaming dimly, they set off for the mansion. Twisted trees clawed at the night sky along an overgrown, winding path, their branches like skeletal fingers. Walking closer, the mansion's details became clearer to them. The misshapen wrought-iron gates resembled splintered bones with their sharp protrusions. Stone statues stood on both sides of the entrance, the cracks in their foundations like spiderwebs. The maze of tall hedges leading to the front door was untamed.

A stark difference existed between the mansion and the modest township beyond. The building's imposing shadow-filled windows and dark stone front gave it an air of majesty, as if it belonged to a realm beyond Everside Valley's small-town existence. Once home to Mayor Hawthorne—a man who had been both admired and feared in town—the mansion had always felt like it held secrets, its walls bearing witness to a wealth and power that most people in Everside Valley could hardly imagine. The man that once ran the town was only a person who was told in stories as a child; they'd never met the person, nor had anyone in the town.

They paused by the hedge maze, looking up at the massive structure that loomed over them. At the entrance stood weathered statues, their faces twisted into almost lifelike expressions by years of neglect and the half-light. A chill ran down Dominic's spine as he watched the stone figures, half expecting them to turn and follow them.

Alex turned to them with a grin. "Well, here we are. Ready to see if the rumors are true?"

With a nervous glance at the mansion, Penelope summoned her courage. "We made it this far. Might as well see what's inside since it's the farthest we've gone."

A calm, almost indifferent expression from Calypso met Dominic's glance. Taking a deep breath, he went after his friends through the bushes. Towering walls of green rose above them, leaves whispering softly in the breeze. As they moved deeper into the maze, he could feel the familiar thrill of fear bubbling up. Their recollections of childhood dares and the unsettling quiet were interwoven. Every turn revealed more of the mystery; moonlight elongated shadows, creating illusions. At long last, they exited the maze and arrived at the mansion's entrance. Before them loomed a large, dark, weathered wooden door, its ironwork adding to its intimidating presence. Alex reached out, testing the handle, and to their surprise, it turned with ease, the door creaking open as if it had been waiting for them.

"See?" Alex said, amused. "Nothing to it."

A musty air, thick with the smell of decay and dust, enveloped them upon entry. Before them extended a grand entryway, illuminated by the weak moonlight seeping through dusty, cracked panes. A vast, opulent interior featured high ceilings and walls adorned with dark wood paneling, tarnished mirrors, and faded tapestries, contributing to its eerie ambiance. A grand staircase, its carpet worn and faded, held the room's attention.

A shiver ran through Penelope as she looked around. "I always wondered what it looked like in here. It's even creepier than I imagined."

"Feels like we're stepping into Dracula's house," Dominic whispered, his voice echoing faintly in the empty hall.

Their footfalls became absorbed by the carpet the further inside they went, the only sound in the heavy silence. Through the entryway, glimpses of the rooms were caught—a parlor with a piano under a sheet, a long table in a dusty dining room, and a study with a dead fireplace. Every corner displayed cobwebs; delicate strands hung down from the ceiling like fringe. Dominic's pulse quickened as he followed his friends, every instinct telling him to turn back, to leave this place that felt so wrong. But the thrill of exploring, the sheer excitement of sharing this moment with Penelope and Alex kept him moving forward.

"Let's check out the library," Alex murmured, gesturing to a door down the hall with a nod.

A distant sound shattered the silence as they approached, causing them to freeze. A low, haunting moan, similar to wind whistling through a broken pane, filled the air, but an underlying element sent a surge of intense fear through Dominic.

"Did...did you hear that?" Penelope asked, her eyes wide.

Dominic nodded, his mouth dry. "It's probably just the wind."

But even as he said it, he didn't believe it. From a moan, the sound intensified into faint, urgent whispers echoing through the empty halls. They struggled to breathe under the weight of the thick air. They began to leave, but a sudden, high-pitched scream stopped them in their tracks, a sound both terrifying and sharp.

"Run!" Alex hissed, grabbing Penelope's arm and pulling her toward the door. Dominic didn't need any further encouragement; he spun on his heel, stumbling over his own feet as he raced after them. Calypso darted ahead, his sleek form a black blur as he streaked toward the exit.

An eerie scream trailed them as they fled through the entryway, out the door, down the front steps, and back into the hedge maze. Calypso's high jump ended with him in Dominic's arms, claws deeply embedded in his skin. Terror spurred their speed as they raced through the twisting path, every shadow seeming to grab at them in their sprint toward the township's safety. Upon exiting the maze and reaching the open path, their running didn't cease. With ragged breaths, they hurtled down the hill toward the reassuring lights of Everside Valley. Only when they reached the edge of town did they slow down, their hearts pounding as they doubled over.

"W-what the hell was that?" Penelope gasped, eyes wide with terror, looking back up the dark hill, the mansion now hidden.

"I don't know," Alex replied, shaking his head, his face pale. "But whatever it was, I don't think we were supposed to be there to hear it."

A lingering scream echoed in Dominic's mind as he glanced back, causing him to shiver. He felt Calypso press against his chest with eyes wide and alert, as if he, too, had sensed the darkness in that place.

"Let's just get back," Dominic murmured, his voice shaky. "I think we've had enough excitement for one night."

As they walked back into town, a heavy silence fell over them, the thrill of their adventure replaced by a lingering fear. They'd spent their childhood daring each other to explore the mansion, to face their fears. But now they understood why they had always turned back. Some adventures were meant to be kept in the past, buried within their childhood. Some places were meant to be left alone. And whatever haunted the mansion on the hill, it was best left undisturbed.

Chapter 7

As Dominic, Penelope, and Alex walked home from the mayor's mansion, the lights of Everside Valley offered comfort despite their racing hearts and the night's fright. The searing scream echoed in Dominic's memory, a persistent prickling sensation on his skin. He couldn't shake the feeling that something had followed them, that a darkness lingered just beyond the edges of their vision, but the warmth of his friends beside him kept him focused.

Their quiet return through the familiar streets stirred up memories, and Dominic felt himself pulled back to a time long ago, to the days when they had shared the orphanage with a mix of other kids. He felt like a kid again, back in the warm, golden days when their biggest worries were scraped knees and sneaking cookies from the kitchen.

No bills to pay or people to impress to survive in the adult world; just their imaginations and innocence running free.

DOMINIC HAD ALWAYS been one of the quieter children, content to sit alone under the shade of the big sycamore tree, his nose buried in a thick book. While the other kids ran wild through the orphanage's backyard or huddled in noisy groups, he found comfort in the pages of his well-worn fairy tale books, immersing himself in worlds far beyond the small, dusty township. For

Dominic, the stories weren't simply words on a page; they were living worlds, and he could spend hours imagining himself as one of the heroes.

"Look at him," Jasper sneered one day, standing over Dominic as he sat under the tree, deeply engrossed in a tale about knights and dragons. "Still reading those baby books? Off in your land of make believe again? Tell me, are you a prince or a princess this time?"

Few people understood Dominic's fascination with books and fantasy. One boy in particular seemed to make it his personal mission to remind Dominic of just how different he was from the others. Compared to other kids, Jasper was burlier and taller, with a mean streak. With brash confidence and a loud voice, he commanded attention, gathering others around him. And whenever he caught Dominic with his nose in a book, he would take it as an invitation to ridicule him.

"Oh, look at the little prince," Jasper repeated, his voice raised for the other children to hear. "He's got his head so far in the clouds, he probably doesn't even know which way is up."

Though his cheeks flushed, Dominic pretended not to hear, his eyes fixed on the page. He had learned that ignoring Jasper was sometimes the easiest way to make him lose interest.

As Jasper towered over Dominic, a few younger children fidgeted and nervously laughed. Jasper's presence commanded attention, leaving most kids too scared to defy him. But Dominic knew he wasn't alone. He saw Penelope and Alex standing nearby, watching with disapproval out of the corner of his eye.

Penelope approached, her red hair tousled from running, glasses on her nose, and arms crossed. "Leave him alone, Jasper," she said firmly, her voice steady. "Just because you're too lazy to read doesn't mean Dominic has to be."

Beside her, Alex stood, his jaw a tight, determined line. "Yeah. At least he's doing *something*, unlike you."

Jasper rolled his eyes, scowling. "Oh, look, the prince has his army here to defend him. How cute."

Before any of them could respond, the sound of approaching footsteps silenced the group. Miss Reed appeared, her tall figure framed by the afternoon sunlight. Her gray hair was neatly pinned back, and her stern expression could calm even the most unruly child with a glance.

"What's going on here?" she asked, her voice steady, her gaze sharp as she looked from Jasper to Dominic and back again.

"Nothing," Jasper mumbled, avoiding eye contact, his shoulders drooping as he dragged his foot along the ground. Miss Reed had that effect on him; no matter how much bravado he tried to put on, he knew better than to mess with her.

Miss Reed studied him before her expression softened as she turned to Dominic. "Dominic, are you all right?"

Dominic hugged his book tighter and nodded, saying, "I'm fine, Miss Reed. Just with my book."

She smiled gently, bending down to meet his gaze. "And what are you reading today?"

He held up the book for her to see, pages eager to flutter in her face. "It's about a knight who saves a village from an evil dark lord," he said, his voice growing more animated as he spoke. "But he's not a normal knight. He's different from everyone else. He reads a lot too, and that's how he learns how to fight the evil."

Miss Reed's eyes gleamed with understanding, and she placed a reassuring hand on his shoulder. "That sounds like a wonderful story, Dominic. I'm glad you're reading it. You have a beautiful imagination, and that's a gift. Never let anyone make you feel bad about that."

She shot Jasper a meaningful look, her expression hardening. "And you, Jasper, if you spent a little more time reading and a little less time making trouble, you might learn something useful, too."

Jasper huffed, his face reddening as he glanced around, aware of the eyes on him. With a scowl, he turned and stalked off, muttering under his breath. The surrounding kids dispersed, leaving Dominic with Penelope, Alex with Miss Reed.

Miss Reed squeezed Dominic's shoulder before standing up. "Never lose that curiosity, Dominic. It's one of the most important things you have. This world is filled with wonders, and those who are brave enough to imagine them can do incredible things."

Dominic smiled up at her, his heart swelling with gratitude. "Thank you, Miss Reed."

She returned his smile, her gaze softening. "You're welcome. Now go enjoy your book. And don't let anyone take that joy from you."

With a final, reassuring nod, she turned and walked back toward the house, leaving Dominic with his two closest friends.

Penelope plopped down beside him, crossing her legs as she adjusted her glasses. "You know she's right, Dom. You got an imagination I wish I had."

Alex flopped down on his other side, grinning. "Yeah. One of these days, you'll write your own story, and people like Jasper will be begging to read it."

Dominic chuckled, the embarrassment from Jasper's taunts melting away under the warmth of their friendship. "Maybe. But you two are the heroes of the story, not me. I'm not as brave as you two."

"Nah," Penelope said with a smirk, nudging him playfully. "You're definitely the hero. We're just along for the ride."

Settling beneath the tree, the three laughed, their sound filling the quiet yard. Taking turns, Dominic and his companions read the story aloud, each adding their unique style. In those moments, everything else faded away—the loneliness, the uncertainty, even the fear of what lay beyond the orphanage walls. As one, they built a unique world, a haven where they could be themselves, unshackled by reality's limitations. A world perpetually bathed in light, spreading joy and happiness to everyone.

DOMINIC FELT THE PAST echo as he walked with Penelope and Alex through Everside Valley's dimly lit streets. Throughout his life, Miss Reed's belief in him and her encouragement had been a constant source of strength. She had seen something in him that no one else had, and she had nurtured it with patience and kindness. Once he left the orphanage, he forgot about her words and let his imagination fade and reality drive him. There was no time to let his mind wander once the training wheels were off; he was on his own and life had to continue at one-hundred miles per hour. Double shifts took over his urge to read. Stress clouded over his urge to immerse in his imagination.

"You're thinking about her, aren't you?" Penelope asked, sensing the shift in Dominic's smile.

Dominic nodded, his throat tightening. "I am. I still remember how she stood up for me when everyone else thought I was strange. She was the only one who made me feel like it was okay to be different."

Alex gave him a gentle nudge. "That's because it was okay. And she was right about you, Dom. You've always been braver than you think."

"I don't think I'm as brave as you guys give me credit for," Dominic said, shoulders slumping.

"I don't think you're giving yourself enough credit!" Penelope said, slapping the back of his shoulder with frustration.

Smiling gratefully, Dominic was thankful to have his friends there; they alone understood Miss Reed's importance and the weight of her words. She hadn't just been their caretaker; she'd been a mother, a protector, someone who had believed in their potential when no one else had.

Pausing at the town square's edge, they gazed back at the hill, silhouetted against the moonlit sky, where the mayor's mansion stood. Their initial fear had subsided, replaced by a mix of exhilaration and melancholy as they reflected on their trip.

"She would've told us not to go poking around that place," Penelope said with a rueful smile.

"I guess we're not so well-behaved after all," Alex said sarcastically.

For a moment, they lingered, the quiet space between them filled with unspoken understanding. Dominic felt a quiet resolve settle over him. He didn't know what the future held, but he knew he carried a piece of Miss Reed's wisdom and kindness with him wherever he went. And with friends like Penelope and Alex by his side, he knew he had the strength to face whatever lay ahead.

"Is anybody hungry?" Alex asked. "I could use some food after all that running."

AS THEY ENTERED THE Everside Valley Diner, its warm glow enveloped the three, and the familiar bell above jingled a welcome. The place hadn't changed a bit: worn vinyl booths, scratched checkered floors, and the scent of burgers sizzling on the grill, mixing with the faint aroma of stale coffee. An old jukebox playing

Elvis Presley, the needle lightly scratching the record every thirty seconds. It felt like slipping back into a favorite old sweater, comforting and safe.

Taking a window booth, Calypso collapsed onto Dominic's lap, purring contentedly after overworking his four legs. Dominic couldn't remember the last time he'd felt so at ease. Spending time with Penelope and Alex distracted the harshness of recent weeks. A waitress with gray-streaked hair and a friendly, tired smile came over, taking their usual orders from when they were younger: burgers, fries, and three root beers.

"So, Dom," Alex said, relaxing in the booth with his arms outstretched. "What made you want to come back? For a second, I thought you weren't coming."

After the waitress served their sodas, Dominic examined his root beer, swirling the dark liquid as the ice cubes danced within. "New York didn't turn out like I thought," he admitted. "If I'm honest with you guys, I lost both my jobs, and to top it all off, Marcus walked out. He left a note, took his stuff, and that was that. Then came the eviction notice, and, well...coming back here just felt like the only option left."

Reaching over, Penelope squeezed his hand, a gentle expression in her eyes. "Dom, I'm so sorry."

Dominic forced a small smile, appreciating her sympathy. "Thanks. But honestly? I think I needed it. I don't know why, but being here feels right for some reason."

Penelope gave him a reassuring smile. "You're back where people care about you. That counts for something."

They fell quiet for a moment, a comfortable silence hanging between them as they sipped their sodas, each lost in their own thoughts. The jukebox switching to "Surfin' Bird" with only one patron bobbing their head in the booth behind them.

"So, what about you?" Dominic asked, looking at them both. "What's been going on with you two?"

Penelope exchanged a glance with Alex, then sighed. "Well, funny enough, things haven't exactly gone smoothly for me either," she admitted. "I was working at a non-profit in St. Louis, helping with community outreach, but they lost funding and had to lay off half the staff. I tried finding something else, but everything was a dead end."

Dominic felt a wrenching pain in his chest as he listened. He'd always seen Penelope as his successful friend, someone who'd triumph over every hardship. "Damn, Pen. I'm so sorry."

Penelope shrugged, her eyes soft with vulnerability. "I guess I didn't want anyone to know. I wanted to handle it on my own, especially after my boyfriend was killed six months before. But here I am, back in Everside Valley. Sometimes you just have to start over."

Alex let out a short, dry laugh. "Seems like I'm right there with you both."

Penelope and Dominic turned to him, surprised. Alex had always been the stable one, the grounded one who kept everything together. Noticing the sadness in his face was not one that they were used to.

"I was working construction out on the coast," he explained, scratching at his stubbled jaw. "But my supervisor started cutting corners, and I wasn't about to let him get away with it. We argued, things got ugly, and I ended up quitting. Figured I'd get work somewhere else, but turns out that word spreads fast. No one wanted to hire the guy who 'caused trouble.' So here I am, back here to take some time to think about my next step."

As they picked at their burgers and fries, the unspoken struggles between them hung heavy. Dominic couldn't help but feel a strange sense of relief, knowing he wasn't the only one who had ended up back in Everside Valley searching for a second chance. They were all starting over, bound by fate and history.

"So, what now?" Penelope asked, glancing between them. "Do we just...try to make a life here?"

Alex shrugged, dipping a fry into a small pool of ketchup. "Could be worse places to figure things out. At least we've got each other."

Dominic nodded, feeling a surge of gratitude for his friends. Despite everything, he felt grounded here, like he'd found a bit of himself again.

Just then, the bell over the door jingled, and a figure walked in, the clink of keys and heavy black boots echoing across the quiet diner. Dominic looked up, and his heart gave a jolt. His black leather jacket crunched as he adjusted his sleeves. His long, blonde locks were disheveled as he shook his hair. The man stood near the counter, looking around with a hard, tired expression. Something softer replaced the confidence that had once bordered on arrogance, more subdued. He glanced around the diner, his gaze catching on their table.

Penelope's eyebrows shot up. "Is that...?"

Dominic swallowed, nodding. "Yeah. Jasper."

A moment's hesitation followed Jasper's recognition, then he walked over, hands deep in his pockets. He looked different—older, a little worn around the edges. Now he looked more like someone trying to find his way.

"Well, look who's back," Jasper said, his voice carrying a hint of his old confidence, but without the edge Dominic remembered. "The old Everside Valley gang."

Penelope crossed her arms, a wary look in her eyes. "Jasper. It's been a while."

"Yeah," Jasper replied, his gaze shifting between them, lingering on Dominic for a beat longer. "Heard you were back in town. Funny how life brings people back, huh?"

There was an awkward silence, the memories of Jasper's old taunts hovering in the air. Dominic remembered every shove, every mocking comment, the way Jasper had always seemed to pick on him for reading too much, for being different. But as Dominic looked at him now, he could see a different person standing there—a man who seemed as lost as any of them.

"What about you?" Alex asked, his tone neutral. "Back for the funeral too, I'm guessing?"

Jasper shrugged, glancing down at the counter as if avoiding their eyes. "I guess." His eyes flicked back to Dominic. "Hey, look...I know I was a jerk to you back then. I didn't get it, you know? I thought you were just weird." He sighed, shifting on his feet.

Dominic felt a flicker of surprise, a warmth that hadn't been there before. "Thanks, Jasper. I appreciate you saying that."

Jasper nodded, looking like he had more to say but could not find the words. Finally, he gave a small, awkward wave and turned to leave, the bell jingling behind him. As the door closed, Dominic let out a breath he hadn't realized he'd been holding. The interaction felt surreal, like a loose thread finally tied off.

"Did that just happen?" Alex asked, giving Dominic a wide-eyed look.

Penelope laughed, shaking her head. "I think it did. Who would've thought he'd come around?"

Dominic leaned back in the booth, a strange sense of closure settling over him. He'd spent so many years thinking of Jasper as an enemy, a ghost from his past that still haunted him. But maybe people could change. Maybe he wasn't the only one here trying to start over.

As they finished their food, the conversation turned lighter, laughter and jokes filling the booth. The three friends talked about the old days, about their dreams for the future, about the possibility of finding something meaningful in the town they'd all tried so hard to escape. For the first time in a long time, Dominic felt a spark of hope—a feeling that maybe, just maybe, he could rebuild his life with the people who'd known him best by his side.

Chapter 8

Dominic

TODAY WAS THE DAY I didn't think I would dread. But now that it's here, I can't bear it.

The day we put Miss Reed to rest.

So many memories are going through me right now. The time she cheered for me at the community softball game was one of my fondest memories. At the beginning of the game, I couldn't hit or catch the ball to save my life. I became the joke of the game, and everybody on my team thought so too. Once Miss Reed showed up after the third inning, it was like there was a change in me. Her cheering brought out a sense of confidence; it was as though I was a completely different person. I was hitting the ball left and right, and even made a couple of home runs. For someone who isn't the most athletic, I was doing pretty damn good.

It was like magic!

There was this other time that Penelope, Alex, and I were scavenging in the attic. We found old outfits that were baggy on our little bodies, but we felt like we were Laura Ingalls Wilder trying to survive in the harshest of winters in our rickety old cabin. Twirling in the prairie skirts was so much fun until we got dizzy and wanted to throw up the tater tot hotdish we had for dinner. When we put the frocks away, I found a pendant at the bottom of the chest. The intricacy of the bronze metalwork holding the sapphire jewels brought beauty to my eyes. The roaring lion heads guarding the center gem; a tear shape, inspired bravery. The piece was beautiful, and I felt like I saw it somewhere before, but could never point out where. When Miss Reed caught us upstairs, she wasn't too enthused about our little adventure. She let us off the hook as long as we helped with the dishes. After she noticed me putting the pendant back, Miss Reed stopped me and had this strange smile on her face. For some reason, she let me keep it as long as I didn't tell anybody, and that I always kept it in a safe place.

And that's what I did.

That necklace stayed deep in my sock drawer until I left. In New York, I stored it at the bottom of an Adidas shoebox in my closet. And today, I brought it with me. It was the one thing I needed to have with me. With all the chaos in my life, I couldn't sell that to survive even if I had a gun pointed at my head. It was one of the reminders of her any time I felt alone in this world. The reflection of the sunlight in the blue was like calming water. The wink of its shiny surface gave me a reminder to keep pushing through even the worst of times.

This is my inner strength.

This is what I need today.

Chapter 9

The three walked up the winding path to the small cemetery, under gray and suffocating air. The sky hung heavy with low-hanging clouds; the morning was damp, and a faint, cold drizzle left a fine mist clinging to the gravestones.

A small crowd had gathered by the time they arrived, townsfolk who had known her, grown-up orphans she had raised, and a few local families who had felt her kindness over the years. Dominic recognized most of the faces, each etched with lines of grief and reverence. The oak tree, its branches like outstretched arms waiting for a hug, sheltered the simple wooden casket from where the three stood in a circle. Dominic felt a pang in his chest as he looked at the casket; it seemed so small, so unassuming, for a woman who had held so many lives in her hands. Those whose lives she had shaped came back to honor her sacrifices in giving them a better life.

The three found a place near the front. Dominic felt the first sting of tears that came with his heartbreak. He hadn't expected this day to come so soon, or maybe he had never thought it would come at all, as he felt like Miss Reed was invincible. Every kid wished that their parents would live forever, to be around for all the memories in one's life, from successes to be proud of to failures they could uplift them from with encouragement to overcome adversity. That was no longer the possibility for Miss Reed. Her body was now one with the earth, another child under the care of Mother Nature.

In a low, steady, and calm voice, the minister started telling the story of Eleanor Reed's life. She had taken over the orphanage after her husband's death, whom Dominic had never met. She devoted herself to the children who had no one else, giving each of them the sense of family they so desperately craved and deserved. Miss Reed raised dozens of children, many of whom now weeping around her casket, holding flowers or small mementos in their trembling hands. The little ones they now raised watched their parents in mourning, so young, not understanding the loss of someone so influential.

As the minister continued, a few people stepped forward to share their memories of Miss Reed. An older woman spoke about Eleanor's unwavering kindness, how she had always kept a pot of tea ready for any visitor who needed a sympathetic ear. A man who had once lived at the orphanage remembered her gentle scolding when he'd tried to run away, how she had brought him back with understanding rather than punishment, promising him he would always have a home with her. The owner of the diner spoke about the time the power was out during a horrid blizzard. The two of them cooked many batches of beef stew with the help of his backup generator to give to the community, providing hope and warmth in the frigid cold.

Penelope sniffled beside him, dabbing at her eyes with a handkerchief she pulled from her olive cardigan. Dominic reached over, giving her hand a gentle squeeze. Looking up at him, she offered a small, unsteady smile.

"She always knew what to say," Penelope whispered. "No matter what we were going through, she'd sit us down and make everything feel better."

Dominic nodded, his throat tight. "She saw the best in all of us. Even when we couldn't see it ourselves."

Alex cleared his throat, stepping forward to share his own memory. His voice was rough with emotion as he recounted a time when Miss Reed had found him, Penelope, and Dominic trying to sneak out after dark. She had caught them just as they were about to leave to sneak out to the mayor's mansion, standing on the porch with her arms crossed, a knowing smile on her face.

"We thought we were so clever," Alex said with a half-smile. "But she just shook her head and told us to come back inside. She didn't yell. Didn't even raise her voice. She just said that if we were going to break the rules, we'd better be smart enough to not get caught."

A few quiet chuckles punctuated the silence before Alex continued, his voice thick with reminiscence. "She wasn't just a guardian to us. She was...well, she was a mother, in every way that counted. Miss Reed taught us how to be good, how to be kind, how to believe in ourselves. I am who I am today because of her."

Dominic felt his heart pounding as Alex stepped back, the unspoken words heavy on him. While he hadn't planned on speaking, the sight of those whose lives Miss Reed had impacted made silence impossible. He took a shaky step toward the crowd, nerves jangling, hands trembling.

"Miss Reed," he began, his voice catching, "she was the one person who never gave up on me. When I was just a quiet kid with his head stuck in books, she was the one who told me that it was okay. It was okay to dream, to imagine. She made me feel like I had a place in this world, even when I didn't feel like I fit in anywhere."

He paused, his throat constricted, gazing at the casket as tears flowed down his face. "I don't think any of us would be here, standing together like this, if it weren't for her. She was our rock, our anchor. And no matter where I go from here, I'll carry her with me."

Stepping back, he let Penelope put her arm through his, her head finding comfort against his shoulder. In the quiet aftermath of his words, they felt Miss Reed's comforting presence, a solace in their sorrow. He held the chain around his neck, his hand hidden beneath his denim jacket. The sapphire pressed against his palm, feeling like an actual tear with his heartbreak.

Following a closing prayer from the minister, mourners approached the casket to place flowers. A single white rose, placed by Dominic, helped bring him a sense of peace despite his grief. He knew that Miss Reed's influence, her kindness, and her love would stay with him, woven into the very fabric of who he was. As the small crowd dispersed, Penelope, Alex, and Dominic lingered by the grave, reluctant to leave. The drizzle had turned into a soft rain, and they huddled together, each lost in their own memories.

"Do you think she knew?" Penelope asked softly, her voice barely audible above the rain.

Dominic turned to her, his brows furrowing. "Knew what?"

Penelope wiped a tear from her cheek, looking at the grave with a bittersweet smile. "That we would all end up back here. That we'd be here, together, when she was gone."

Alex nodded slowly. "I think so, Pen. She always had a way of seeing what was coming, even when we didn't. I think...maybe she trusted that we'd find our way back to each other."

Dominic saw a sliver of light through the parting clouds above. It was as if, even in death, Miss Reed was watching over them, guiding them as she always had. They left the cemetery together, walking in silence back to the orphanage. The old house loomed against the gray sky, its familiar shape a reminder of the years they had shared within its walls. Inside, the rooms felt empty, as if Miss Reed's absence had drained the house of its warmth. But Dominic knew that her spirit was there along the very walls and strong in the memories they had made, and the lessons she had taught them.

Chapter 10

Miss Reed had hosted many meals, celebrations, and gatherings over the years in the orphanage's dining room, which was where the reception was held. Mismatched cloths covered the tables, with simple platters of food arranged in the middle. Steam rose from the crockpots plugged into several outlets throughout the kitchen with entrees gifted from the community. Soft words of remembrance and comfort filled the room as people shared memories, their faces reflecting both sorrow and cherished recollections. But for Dominic, the room felt stifling, the air too thick, every breath weighed down by a suffocating sense of loss.

Dominic stood near the back wall, clutching a lukewarm cup of coffee, staring blankly at the surrounding faces. His thoughts returned to the burial, and the crushing finality of the casket's lowering. Miss Reed was gone, and without her, a part of his own identity felt lost, slipping away into a void he couldn't hope to fill. He felt a painful emptiness in his chest from her absence, a void he couldn't disregard.

The quiet chatter in the room turned into a loud buzzing in his ears, everybody around him blurring as he tried to gather his thoughts. Penelope and Alex were somewhere nearby, talking to some of the other people who paid their respects. Although he longed for the comfort of their company, a profound sense of loneliness weighed heavily upon him.

And then he saw Jasper.

Seeing him again made the numbness vanish, replacing it with a fresh wave of discomfort. Jasper was standing across the room, talking to a group of people, his face solemn but familiar. Even with the passage of time and his weathered look, Jasper's confidence remained as Dominic remembered. It was a confidence that had always made Dominic feel like he was less, like he was unworthy to coexist in this world. Even when he was a kid clutching his books and lost in his own world of stories, he felt like the peasant getting tormented by entitled royalty.

Dominic's chest tightened as a flood of memories washed over him—memories of the day he had left Everside Valley, the day he'd turned eighteen and escaped everything that had haunted him here. He'd been holding on to his bus ticket, his ticket out of this small town, and all the insecurities he'd carried with him. He didn't care about who he left behind, whether it was Penelope, Alex, or even Miss Reed, he'd been ready to leave, to start fresh in New York, to become someone he could be proud of.

But on that day, Jasper had found him, standing alone outside the orphanage, ready to leave without any farewells. Dominic's heart soared with the promise of a new beginning. He could remember the words Jasper said to him, echoing with pain.

"Running off to the big city, huh? You think that's going to make you better than us?"

"The big apple isn't like those dumb castles."

"Good luck, kid. You'll be back here in no time. People like you? They don't make it out there."

And now, here he was, back in Everside Valley, haunted by the feeling that he'd failed to prove him wrong. No matter how much he sounded like he'd come around, there was something about him that was off. The pain in his heart couldn't bring down his guard. Something about him brought the feeling that Jasper won.

Dominic set his coffee cup down on a nearby table, his hands trembling. He needed air. He felt claustrophobic, the party's noise amplifying until his thoughts became muddled. Hoping to make eye contact, he scanned the room, only to find Penelope engaged with the diner owner. Alex was across the room, talking with one of the other former orphans. Their faces were etched with grief surrounded by familiar faces, comforted by the memories of Miss Reed and the legacy she left behind.

A powerful urge to flee overwhelmed Dominic as his heart pounded; a sense of inadequacy, as old as his memories, fueled his desire to escape. He turned on his heel, striding toward the door, his footsteps quickening as he made his way outside.

Standing on the orphanage porch, he felt the sharp, cool air clear his mind with a sudden shock. Each familiar, worn wooden step creaked under his foot—steps he'd fled down when leaving Everside Valley years ago. But now, instead of freedom, all he felt was the weight of everything he'd tried to leave behind pressing down on him, suffocating him. He took a few deep breaths, trying to steady himself, but his mind kept circling back to the idea of leaving. Calypso sat beside him, his tail curling around his ankle.

Right before he walked down the steps, the door behind him creaked open. Turning, he saw Penelope standing there, worry etched on her face. The hem of her calf-length skirt billowing in the wind as she cradled her arms.

"Dom?" she asked softly, stepping closer to him. "Are you all right?"

Dominic forced a smile, but it felt hollow, forced. "I just needed some air," he said, his voice barely above a whisper.

Penelope studied him, her eyes full of understanding. "I know this is hard for all of us. But you don't have to go through this alone. Alex and I are here. We always have been and always will."

He felt her words like a blow to the stomach. Despite longing to trust her and recapture their bond, his insecurities overpowered her compassion. He looked away, unable to meet her gaze.

"It's just…seeing him here," Dominic admitted, his voice choked with bitterness. "It's like I'm right back where I was when I left, as though nothing's changed. I thought I'd moved past all of this, but it's still here, eating at me."

Penelope's warm, grounding touch rested on his shoulder. "Dom, you have changed. You've grown, and experienced life outside of this place. Jasper doesn't know the life you've had since you left. And he doesn't get to define who you are. He never did."

Dominic wanted to believe her, but the knot of shame and self-doubt in his chest wouldn't loosen. He felt like that same scared kid again, the one who had clung to stories to escape the world that didn't understand him. He took a step back, shrugging off her hand, feeling the walls closing in again.

"I just need a minute, Pen."

Without another word, he turned and walked down the steps, his footsteps quick and determined, his heart pounding as he left the orphanage behind him. He didn't look back, not even to stop to see if Penelope was still watching. He simply kept walking, his mind racing with eager thoughts to escape.

Calypso padded alongside him, his small black form weaving through the tall grass. The sun hung low in the sky, the soft amber light brushing the fields with an ethereal glow. The breeze was cool and crisp, carrying the faint scent of earth and rain. Dominic shoved his hands into his jacket pockets, his breath forming soft clouds in the air as he walked.

They reached a small rise in the field where the land dipped down into a hollow, and Dominic stopped, letting the stillness of the moment wash over him. The whispers of the grass and the distant rustle of leaves were a balm to his frazzled nerves. A momentary lightness replaced the weight of the day, filled with bittersweet recollections of his childlike sanctuary.

But his peace was short-lived.

"Didn't think I'd find you out here," a voice cut through the stillness, rough and familiar.

A sharp turn revealed Jasper's approach across the field, filling Dominic with dread. A smirk on his lips, he strolled with ease, his hands shoved in his leather jacket. Behind him trailed a large Briard, its shaggy coat rippling in the wind as it trotted at Jasper's heels, causing Calypso's body to freeze.

"What do you want, Jasper?" Dominic asked, his voice sharper than he intended.

A few feet away, Jasper shrugged, his calculating gaze unnerving Dominic as it had when he was a teenager. "Saw you leave the reception. Thought I'd see if you were okay. But now that I'm here..." He tilted his head, a mocking smile curling his lips. "Looks like the city didn't toughen you up much after all."

Dominic felt his chest tighten, his fists clenching at his sides. "I'm not doing this with you," he muttered, turning away. "Besides, I thought you changed?"

But Jasper didn't let up. "What? Don't tell me you're still sore about the past. You always were so sensitive. Guess some things don't change."

The words hit harder than they should have, stirring up memories Dominic had spent years trying to bury. The teasing, the cruel jokes, the constant feeling that he didn't belong. And now, here was Jasper, dragging it all back to the surface.

"Why are you even here?" Dominic demanded, his voice low and angry. "You didn't care about Miss Reed, and you surely didn't follow her rules. You just came to stir up trouble, like always."

Jasper's smirk faltered, a flicker of something unreadable crossing his face before his grin returned, sharper this time. "Careful, Dom. You don't want to make me the bad guy here, like you've always done." He gestured toward the horizon. "Besides, you were the one who ran off to the city, thinking you were better than the rest of us. How'd that work out for you?"

Anger simmered beneath Dominic's surface, churning his stomach. The urge to lash out was strong, yet Jasper's every word seemed to worsen the insecurities he'd carried since Everside Valley. His hands shook with the effort of keeping his composure whenever Jasper's green eyes blinked.

Before he could respond, a sharp bark cut through the tension. Jasper's dog had perked up, its ears twitching with piercing brown eyes. It barked again, louder this time, and Calypso froze mid-step, his fur standing on end as she turned to face the dog.

"Control your dog," Dominic snapped, stepping protectively in front of Calypso.

But Jasper just chuckled. "Relax, he won't hurt anyone. Harley just wants to play."

The dog lunged forward, barking and growling as it raced toward Calypso. The hissing cat's swift escape into the tall grass caused Dominic's heart to leap. A wave of panic washed over Dominic as he yelled, but the cat already ran off, the feline's instincts propelling him away from the chaos.

"Calypso!" Dominic yelled, running after him.

"Hey, Harley, get back here!" Jasper called after his dog, but the animal ignored him, bounding after the fleeing cat with unrestrained excitement.

With Calypso in his sights, Dominic sprinted through the grass, his pulse throbbing. He ran across the never-ending fields, tall blades whipping at his legs, his voice raw from shouting his name. Harley's barks echoed in the distance, growing fainter as they both disappeared over the next rise. He pushed himself harder, his lungs burning as he crested the hill—and then he saw it. The mayor's mansion loomed ahead, a dark silhouette against the golden fields and sky.

Dominic's stomach sank, the memories of his childhood fears and the dark stories that surrounded the mansion keeping him away. Screams echoed in his mind from last night, terror shaking his bones. But now, Calypso was running straight toward it, his body darting through the overgrown hedge maze that surrounded the building.

"Damn it," Dominic muttered under his breath, his fear for Calypso outweighing his hesitation.

He followed their path, pushing through the thick, tangled hedges that marked the entrance to the maze. The air grew colder as he entered, the shadows of the tall walls swallowing the last light of the setting sun. Behind him, Harley's barking echoed.

Dominic's heart hammered in his chest while he called out Calypso's name in the maze's winding paths. As he ventured further, the hedges enveloped him, their leaves caressing his arms and shoulders. He could feel the weight of the mansion looming just beyond the maze, its presence heavy and unwelcoming. He burst through the last row of hedges and into the clearing at the center. Before him, the mansion seemed to watch, its dark windows like eyes. The building was even more imposing up close, its stone walls cracked and weathered, its iron gates rusted but still standing. Calypso was nowhere to be seen.

"Calypso!" Dominic shouted, his voice echoing off the stone walls of the mansion. The silence that followed was deafening.

For a moment, the only sound was the wind rustling through the grass. Then, a faint, frightened meow reached his ears, emanating from the mansion's vicinity. Driven by a mixture of fear and determination, he moved closer to the sound, his chest growing tight.

"Calypso! Where are you?"

The mansion's door loomed before him, slightly ajar as if inviting him inside. With a deep breath, Dominic pushed open the door, the hinges groaning in the stillness of the halls. Darkness flooded the opening like a mouth ready to consume the fearful man. Dominic's frantic search for his child fueled his trembling fingers.

"Okay, Dominic. Be brave."

Chapter 11

The air inside the mansion was heavy with the weight of abandonment. The scent of mildew and damp wood hung thick in the air as Dominic stepped over the threshold, his heart pounding in his chest. Every creak of the floorboards under his boots echoed through the cavernous hall as though the building itself were groaning in protest of his presence. The dim light from the setting sun piercing the cracked and dust-coated windows, leaving the grand interior cloaked in murky shadows.

"Calypso?" he called, his voice trembling. The result was softer than intended, as if the walls themselves resented his presence. A faint whisper of wind through unseen cracks in the stone walls was the only response.

Dominic advanced, his gaze sweeping across the desolate room. The once-grand entryway was in ruins: a broken chandelier lay shattered across the floor, its crystals scattered like fallen stars. Tattered tapestries hung from the walls, their vibrant colors faded into muted grays. Dust coated every surface, undisturbed for what felt like centuries.

Somewhere deeper in the mansion, he thought he heard a faint, plaintive meow.

"Calypso!" he shouted again, louder this time.

"Meow!"

He turned toward the sound, his feet carrying him down a long corridor. The shadows seemed to thicken as he moved further from the door, each step taking him deeper into the mansion's suffocating gloom. The hairs on the back of his neck prickled with every instinct screaming at him to turn back. But he couldn't leave without him. Apart from Penelope and Alex, Calypso was all he had left.

The hallway opened into what had once been a parlor, the remnants of opulence scattered across the floor. In a corner sat a broken piano, its remaining keys yellowed and warped. A grand mirror hung crookedly on the wall, its surface cracked into a spiderweb of distorted reflections. Dominic avoided looking at it as he passed.

"Meow!"

Another cry broke the silence, closer now. It came from the direction of a large, carved door at the end of the parlor. His pulse quickened as he approached, his hand trembling while he reached for the brass handle. The door creaked as he pushed it open, revealing a vast library bathed in an eerie orange glow. Initially, Dominic believed the sunlight caused it. His breath hitched when he entered. The library fireplace held a soft, crackling fire, recently stoked. The fire's warmth was a stark contrast to the building's chill, adding to Dominic's unease.

And there, curled up on the edge of a tattered rug in front of the fire, was Calypso. His sleek black fur glistened in the firelight as he stretched, unbothered by the strange circumstances. A wave of relief washed over Dominic, causing him to rush forward and embrace him.

"Calypso, you scared me half to death," he murmured, burying his face in his fur. He purred softly, his green eyes blinking up at him with calm indifference.

But his relief was short-lived. As he straightened, he noticed something else in the room—someone else. A figure sat in the high-backed armchair that faced the fireplace, their silhouette stark against the flickering flames. Dominic's stomach clenched, his grip tightening on Calypso.

"Who's there?" Dominic demanded, his voice trembling.

The figure didn't move for a moment, then slowly turned their head to look at him. The firelight couldn't illuminate its face, which was covered in a black hood. Their orange eyes were dark and piercing, like twin voids that drew him in despite himself.

"You came," the figure said, their voice smooth and velvety, yet carrying an undercurrent of something ancient and primal. "I wondered if you would."

Dominic took a step back, clutching Calypso tight. "W-What do you mean? Who are you?"

The figure tilted their head. "Names are of little consequence here," they said. "But if it comforts you to call me something, you may call me Brone."

Dominic swallowed hard, his instincts screaming at him to leave, to get as far from this place as possible. "What do you want?"

Brone's eyes seemed to glimmer with amusement as they leaned forward, resting their elbows on their knees. "It is not what I want, Dominic. It is what you want, or perhaps what you need."

The mention of his name sent a shiver down Dominic's spine. He hadn't introduced himself, and yet Brone spoke it with ease, as if they had known him all his life.

"I don't know what you're talking about," Dominic said, his voice strained. "I'm just here for my cat."

"Ah, yes. The loyal companion," Brone said, their gaze flickering to Calypso. "But you are here for far more than that, whether you realize it or not."

Dominic shook his head, backing toward the door. "I don't have time for this. I'm leaving."

Brone's smile revealed in the shadows of his hood, widening, but there was no warmth in it. "Leaving? To go where, Dominic? Back to a place that doesn't understand you? To a life that has already fallen apart?"

The words struck him like a blow, raw and cutting. He froze, his heart hammering in his chest.

"I see your heartbreak," Brone continued, their voice softening into something almost comforting. "I've been following you for quite some time. The pain you carry. The abandonment. The failure. You are drowning in it, Dominic, and yet you continue to fight it. Why? Why not let it go? Why not let the darkness take it from you?"

The sapphire pendant glowed brighter underneath Dominic's denim, its light casting shifting patterns across the walls. Dominic felt a strange pull, as if the pendant's light was drawing out his very thoughts, exposing his deepest fears and sorrows.

"Darkness? I—I don't want the darkness," he stammered. "I just want to live my life. To find some kind of peace."

"Peace?" Brone echoed, voice dripping with disdain. "There is no peace in this world, Dominic. Only struggle. Only suffering. The sooner you accept that, the sooner you can free yourself from it."

Dominic shook his head, his breath quickening. "No. That's not true. I won't—"

"Why resist?" Brone's voice grew harsher, cutting through Dominic's protest. "The darkness is not your enemy. It is your salvation. It is the only thing that will ever truly understand you."

The sapphire trembled against his chest. The chain rattled as though it had a beat of its own, synonymous with his own heart. As the light grew brighter, Brone's black gloved reach retreated to his cloak like it was touching a blazing fire.

"No!" Dominic shouted, clutching Calypso tighter as he stumbled back toward the door. "I don't want it!"

Brone's expression twisted into something monstrous, their eyes blazing with a terrible light. They rose from the chair with an inhuman grace, their presence filling the room like a storm about to break. The bottom of the cloak fluttered with no feet to support its stance.

"Foolish boy," they hissed. "You cannot run from what you are!"

Then Brone let out a scream—a primal, guttural sound that shook the very foundation of the mansion. The flames in the fireplace roared higher, casting grotesque shadows across the walls. The air itself seemed to vibrate with the force of the sound, and Dominic felt as though the entire building might collapse around him. Panicked, he turned and bolted from the room, Calypso clinging to his chest. He sprinted through the hallways, the echoes of Brone's scream following him like a lingering beast. The walls closed in, the shadows stretching and writhing as though trying to grab hold of him.

He shoved it open and burst into the setting sun, gasping for air as he stumbled down the front steps and into the maze of hedges. The cold air stung his lungs, but he didn't stop. He ran until his legs burned, until the mansion was nothing more than a dark blot on the horizon behind him. Tears ran down his face, realizing that the scream would never leave his memory. No story he'd ever read had been as horrid as what he'd witnessed. No page had given him this amount of goosebumps. When he reached the edge of the orphanage grounds, he collapsed onto the grass, his chest heaving. Calypso meowed, nuzzling his chin, his small body trembling against him.

"Dominic!" a voice called out, and he looked up to see Penelope and Alex running toward him, their faces etched with concern.

"What happened?" Penelope demanded, kneeling beside him. "Are you okay?"

"The mansion," Dominic gasped, his voice shaky. "It-it wasn't right. There was someone—something—inside."

Alex exchanged a confused glance with Penelope. "The mansion?" he asked, frowning. "Dom, the mansion's been abandoned for decades. There's no one there."

"You didn't feel it?" Dominic asked, his voice rising in desperation. "The ground was shaking, the air—"

"Nothing shook," Penelope said, placing a hand on his shoulder. "Maybe you just—"

"No," Dominic said, standing abruptly. He looked toward the orphanage, then back at the distant silhouette of the mansion. "I'm leaving."

Penelope's eyes widened. "Dom, you can't just...there's a storm coming. Look at the sky!"

Dominic glanced up, his heart sinking as he saw the dark clouds swirling overhead, the distant rumble of thunder echoing across the fields. But he shook his head, his resolve hardening.

"I can't stay here," he said. "Not after...that."

Alex stepped forward. "Dom, whatever you think you saw—whatever happened—we'll figure it out. Together. Let's just get inside."

But nothing could sway Dominic. With trembling hands, he turned and headed back to the orphanage to grab his bag. Penelope and Alex followed, their protests falling on deaf ears as Dominic packed the few belongings he'd brought with him inside his messenger bag.

As he stepped out into the storm, the wind whipping around him, he glanced back at his friends one last time, drizzle tickling his cheek. "I'm sorry," he said, his voice barely audible over the rising wind.

He turned and stepped into his Honda. Calypso crouched low on the seat in terror as he drove away. Leaving his friends behind with the orphanage, the clouds darkened around him with thunder rattling the steering wheel. Dominic looked back at the mirror, catching one last look at Penelope and Alex as they huddled closer in sadness, with their family fleeing in fear.

THE ROAD STRETCHED out before Dominic, dark and winding under the brooding sky. A low, ominous rumble of distant thunder made his heart skip a beat. As he pulled onto the empty road, the drizzle had become a steady rain, pattering against the windshield as the lights of Everside Valley faded in his rearview mirror.

Dominic's knuckles whitened with each mile, his grip on the steering wheel growing stronger. The day's grief pressed down on him like a weight he couldn't shake. Miss Reed's absence loomed in his mind, pulling him back into the despair he'd been trying to outrun. The memory of her voice, of her gentle smile, of the comfort she'd offered during his hardest moments—they were gone now, just ghosts haunting the edges of his mind.

Beside him, Calypso lay on the passenger seat, his small body curled tightly into a ball. The feline watched him with wide, worried eyes, his tail flicking as he sensed the tension radiating from him. Every time the thunder rumbled, he flinched, his ears flattening against his head.

Dominic reached over, running a shaking hand over his fur. "It's okay, Calypso," he murmured, though his own voice sounded hollow, barely holding it together. "It's just a little storm."

As if in answer, a bright flash of lightning split the sky, followed by a booming clap of thunder that seemed to shake the entire car. Calypso yowled, pressing himself against the seat as the storm intensified, rain hammering down on them with renewed force. The wind began to pick up, rattling the car, and Dominic's heart quickened as he realized just how quickly the weather was turning.

He drove faster, squinting through the rain that lashed against the windshield, barely able to make out the road ahead. The storm loomed, black and furious, swirling above him as if it were alive, as if it knew he was there and wanted to consume him whole. The wind whipped against the car, and he felt the tires shift on the wet gravel. Panic flared in his chest, overriding the grief and exhaustion that had been weighing him down. He couldn't afford to lose focus, not now, not with the storm closing in around him.

"Come on, just keep it together," he whispered, clutching the steering wheel with both hands, his voice trembling as he fought to keep his mind clear. But the road was slick, and the gusts of wind were relentless, howling through the darkened landscape. Every crack of thunder, every flash of lightning sent Calypso into a frenzy, his claws digging into the seat, his body trembling.

The radio crackled, the static giving way to a shrill, urgent warning: "Severe weather alert. Tornado sighted, moving northeast at high speed. Residents are advised to seek shelter immediately."

A chill ran through Dominic as the words sank in. He hadn't seen any shelters along the road and his opportunity to find protection was long gone when he left Everside Valley. He was in the middle of nowhere, surrounded only by open fields and the occasional tree bending under the force of the wind. With his eyes darting between the road and the ominous clouds overhead, he pressed down on the gas pedal, desperate to outrun the approaching storm.

Rain poured in sheets, reducing his visibility to near zero. The road became a blur of dark lines and waterlogged reflections as the wind howled louder, a terrifying, guttural roar that drowned out even the sound of the car's engine. Dominic's pulse thundered in his ears, his hands shaking as he gripped the steering wheel, trying to keep control.

"Hang on," he said, his voice a strained whisper as he struggled to remain calm for him. "We're going to be okay. We just have to get out of here."

But as he drove, he could feel the storm closing in, the air thick with an eerie stillness that sent a chill down his spine as the rain stopped abruptly. The world outside was suddenly quiet, like the silence before a scream. Dominic's breath caught as he saw it—a dark, swirling funnel descending from the clouds, twisting violently as it touched the ground and tore across the fields toward him.

A primal fear gripped him, overriding every other thought as he slammed his foot on the gas, the car lurching forward as he tried to outrun the monstrous force bearing down on him. But the funnel was gaining, growing larger, darker, an unstoppable force that seemed to consume everything in its path. The car shook, the wind tugging at it like a giant hand trying to rip it from the ground. Dominic's vision blurred with tears, and he clenched his teeth, fighting the terror that clawed at him, the sense of helplessness that threatened to drown him.

"It's okay, it's okay..." he whispered, though he was saying it more for himself than for Calypso now. He didn't know if they would make it, didn't know if there was any escaping the fury of the storm.

Suddenly, the wind picked up with a force unlike anything he'd ever felt. The car reeled sideways, the wheels lifting off the ground before slamming back down. The funnel was on top of them, the air vibrating with an intense pressure, the deafening roar filling every corner of the car.

And then, with a shuddering thrust, the car lifted off the ground.

For a moment, everything seemed to slow, a surreal, weightless sensation overtaking him as the tornado pulled the car into its grip. A dizzying whirl of gray, black, and flashing lights spun as the storm hurled them into its merciless grasp. Dominic could feel the car twisting, spinning, his head slamming against the window as he lost all sense of direction.

With the world around him starting to blur, his chest felt the tugging vibration under his shirt. A soft, blue glow emerged from his chest. The pendant glowed, creating a vibrancy blue within the darkness of the car's interior along with a warmth that washed over him.

Calypso let out a panicked wail, his claws digging into Dominic's leg as the car tumbled through the air. Dominic screamed in pain as he reached for him, clutching him to his chest as tightly as he could, trying to shield him from the chaos, from the terror that surrounded them.

And then, as suddenly as it had begun, everything went dark.

WHEN DOMINIC CAME TO, he felt a dull, throbbing pain in his head, his body heavy and sore. It took him a moment to open his eyes, his vision swimming as he tried to make sense of where he was. The world around him was quiet, broken only by the faint patter of rain on the car's shattered windshield. He was slumped over the steering wheel, the seatbelt digging into his chest. His whole body ached, and a trickle of blood on his forehead was sticky and warm. His ears rang, the faint echo of the tornado's roar lingering in his mind.

Slowly, he looked around, his heart sinking as he took in the damage. The car tilted at a strange angle, with its front half buried in mud and debris. Shattered glass glittered on the seats and dashboard, and outside, he could see fragments of trees and twisted metal scattered across the landscape, remnants of the storm's destructive path.

"Cal..." he murmured, his voice hoarse as he reached over, searching for his companion.

To his immense relief, he felt a soft, warm body pressed against his side. Huddled beside him, Calypso trembled, unharmed, his wide eyes looking up at him with a mixture of fear and relief. He let out a tiny, questioning meow, pressing his face into his arm as if to reassure himself that he was really there.

"It's okay, Cal," he whispered, stroking her gently, his own heart calming at the feel of her familiar warmth. "We're...we're okay."

He took a shaky breath, his mind reeling as he tried to process what had happened. The storm had taken them, hurled through the air, and somehow, miraculously, they were still alive. As he looked out at the unfamiliar landscape, an unexpected feeling washed over him—a strange, hollow kind of relief. His head became lighter, his muscles heavier with his consciousness drifting away as he rested on the steering wheel. The storm had torn him away from Nebraska, from the painful memories he'd been drowning in, and left him in a place he didn't recognize, a place with no ties to the past.

Chapter 12

Dominic

SPECKLES OF DIRT TICKLE *my lungs. My throat is raspy, each breath more labored than the last. The skin on my nose burns from the itchy fibers of the uncut blades of grass after I roll out from the seat of my car. All I see is darkness; I'm too pained to open my eyes, too shaken from the howling winds that swept my car off the ground.*

Am I dead?

I can't be alive. There's no way a person survives a blast like that. Part of me even hopes I'm dead. It would free me from the world I've fought too hard to survive. No more scrambling to make ends meet. No more folding shirts for jobs that barely last, only to see them destroyed minutes later. No more managers siding with asshole customers who mock my voice to get their way.

I move my arms under my chest to push myself up; pain radiates sharply through my ribs, stopping me cold. It's unbearable. My gut clenches, tightening to hold back whatever's left from the banquet. The thought of losing the last serving of Miss Reed's chili and cornbread from the reception breaks my heart.

"Shit!" I scream, rolling onto my back, hoping another angle might help me get up.

The darkness behind my closed eyes begins to brighten. I open them, and I'm immediately blinded by a beam of pure white.

Perhaps I did die.

No more men walking into my life, only to give up without trying. No more changing who I am just to make someone else stay. No more fighting to be heard.

What about Calypso?

My poor cat. I dragged him into this life of struggle with me. I hope it was quick for him when the tornado took us. He's suffered long enough, stuck with my whiny company. I'm shocked he never ran off to find a better home—maybe a family with kids who'd adore him the way he deserves. Even now, I can almost feel his tail brushing my ear, his fur tickling my earlobe. His purr rumbles deep inside my eardrum.

A tear slips from the corner of my eye, trickling slowly down the side of my head.

The sandpapery sharpness of a wet tongue flicks away the moisture from my cheek. A whisker pokes the corner of my eye. I stay still. I remain under the hypnosis of chirping birds wisping softly through my mind. I try to focus on them—on anything but the pain and the trauma. The faint whisper of wind nudges through the tall grass, swaying the blades until they gather close together and bend toward the earth.

Then, I feel a small weight on my stomach—a familiar pressure, as if my body remembers what it's like to support fourteen pounds of comfort. Back when I came home from brutal shifts, I'd sprawl out on the living room floor with Paramore playing, trying to decompress. I'd barely get a few minutes to myself before my partner in crime came demanding attention.

I open my eyes. Paws knead against my damp shirt, claws curling rhythmically into the fabric. It was the relaxing massage of biscuits being made.

"Calypso," I whisper, breathless with relief. My voice is hoarse, my throat aching for a sip of water.

I stare into his green eyes. His lids droop halfway, lazy and loving. His purring grows louder, a low, steady rumble like a small engine revving to life. The tips of his back claws poke through the thick denim of my jacket, grazing the skin of my stomach.

I don't care. Dream or not, dead or alive, none of it matters. He's here. The only thing I truly need. He inches closer to my face, purring like a storm. The side of his face rubs against my chin, and his whiskers graze the cracked skin of my lips.

"I'm so happy to see you, Dominic," a voice says—soft, gentle—slipping from the mouth of my cat.

My body jerks forward. My heart slams to a stop, then races, forcing all focus onto the impossibility before me.

What the hell?

Chapter 13

"Did you just talk?"

Dominic's voice cracked as his trembling hand clutched the side of his head, his other arm struggling to push himself upright. Blood pulsed back into his extremities, a tingling sensation rippling through his limbs as the world slowly came into focus.

Calypso paused mid-step, his sleek black tail curling as his eyes narrowed. His head tilted to the side, and Dominic's gaze landed on the off-colored toe beans of his otherwise flawless coat.

"I guess I am," Calypso replied, his voice measured and calm, though tinged with disbelief. He paced in small circles, his tail trailing behind him like a curious shadow. "This is unexpected."

Dominic blinked hard, his mind fumbling to piece together reality. "I have to be dead," he muttered, his voice barely above a whisper. "This has to be some kind of afterlife."

"No, you're not dead," Calypso said with assurance, the words crisp and clear as though it were the most ordinary thing in the world. "I was awake the whole time."

"What do you know? You're just a cat!" Dominic snapped, his tone sharpening as his head throbbed. "You only know how to eat, sleep, and poop! What could you possibly know about any of this?"

Calypso stopped pacing, his piercing gaze locking onto Dominic's. "Well, for starters, us cats are a lot smarter than you think. We only make you humans think that's all we do. Also, I don't think we're in our world anymore. Look around."

Groaning, Dominic hunched his body forward, his ribs protesting every movement. His denim jacket bore a tear at the elbow, the fabric stiff with dried mud. The strain in his ankles wobbled his balance as he forced himself to his knees. The floaters in his vision faded, revealing a vibrant green that stretched in every direction. The grass reached up to the middle of his calves, blades swaying gently in the breeze, unlike the brittle, browning terrain of Nebraska.

Dominic's heart sank as he surveyed his surroundings. His car, battered and crumpled like a discarded piece of paper, rested on its side. The impact shattered the back window completely, and it looked like enormous hands had wrenched the hood apart. The vehicle was unrecognizable, a sad skeleton of what it once was.

Beyond that, nothing familiar greeted him. No bustling streets, no honking horns, no polluted haze clinging to the air. The oppressive weight of New York was absent, replaced by an eerie tranquility. The endless horizon betrayed no signs of life—not a single building, car, or human figure.

"See?" Calypso pressed, gesturing with a paw to the endless expanse. "This isn't our world."

"Don't be ridiculous," Dominic grumbled, though unease curled in his chest. "This is just an open field. This could be Kansas for all we know."

Calypso fell silent, his tail flicking as he stepped around shards of glass that glinted in the grass. His feline elegance contrasted starkly with Dominic's ungainly struggle to stand.

"Good lord," Dominic muttered to himself, pressing a shaky hand to his ribs as he rose to his feet. "I'm arguing with my cat about where we are. I need to get to a hospital."

Using the car for balance, he moved to the back seat, yanking at the warped door until it gave way with a protesting groan. Inside, the chaos of the storm was evident. Belongings were strewn everywhere—boxes of knickknacks reduced to mushy pulp, a burst-open duffel spilling its contents across the seat, and his messenger bag shoved beneath a seat cushion. Dominic's heart strained; the last of his life's mementos lay reduced to rubble.

Dominic grabbed the bag, brushing off shards of glass and bits of debris. A slight discoloration marred the navy-blue canvas, but otherwise, it was intact. He shoved in essentials: two black shirts, two pairs of jeans, a couple pairs of socks, and a pack of black Calvin Klein underwear. His teal canteen rattled empty in his hand, a regretful reminder of his lack of preparation. He crammed a half-full bag of Meow Mix at the bottom, Calypso's ears perking with interest.

"Not now," Dominic said, zipping the bag shut with wide eyes as he argued with his pet. "We need to ration. Who knows how long we'll be stuck out here."

"I'll bite you if I have to," Calypso said matter-of-factly.

"Yeah, yeah," Dominic muttered, slinging the strap of his bag over his shoulder and clutching a photo of Miss Reed and the other orphans. His throat tightened as he stared at their smiling faces, memories flooding him in painful clarity. A chill crept through his jacket as dark clouds gathered overhead, blotting out the sun and signaling an impending storm.

"Not again," Dominic said, shouldering his bag. "We have to move."

"But where?" Calypso asked, glancing toward the expanse. "There's nothing out here. We'll wander for hours."

"It's better than waiting for someone to find us," Dominic replied, gesturing toward a faint blur of trees in the distance. "We need shelter."

Calypso eyed the far-off speck of green and brown and groaned. "That's so far away! Can't you carry me?"

Dominic sighed, biting his lip while adjusting his bag. "Are you going to be as annoying in this so-called-world as you were in ours?"

HOURS PASSED AS THEY trudged through the open fields, the wind tugging at Dominic's jacket and whipping the tall grass against his legs. Calypso's frustration grew with every step; his sleek coat barely peeked above the grass, and his grumble was incessant.

"Can we eat yet?" Calypso asked, his tone agitated.

"In a little bit," Dominic replied, his stomach growling in agreement. "Let's reach the trees first."

"Come on, I'm starving!" Calypso whined, his tail twitching.

"So am I!" Dominic snapped, his voice strained. His legs wobbled with exhaustion, the endless walk through uneven terrain draining his energy. "You're not the only one struggling here!"

The back-and-forth bickering continued as the distance to the trees closed. Dominic's patience wore thin, every quip from Calypso poking at his already frayed nerves. The weight of his bag dug into his shoulder, his ribs throbbed with every step, and the faint rumble of thunder behind them spurred him forward despite the pain. Finally, the forest came within reach. Towering trees shaded them as they entered, the scent of pine and damp earth filling the air. Dappled shadows stretched across the forest floor as the sunlight dimmed. Crunching twigs and rustling leaves mingled beneath Dominic's shoes, contrasting the stillness with the fields' chaos.

"You complain more now than when you meowed," Dominic said, his voice laced with exhaustion.

Calypso sniffed indignantly, striding ahead with a newfound confidence. "I know my truth."

Dominic groaned, his fist clenching at his side as hunger and fatigue gnawed at him. Before he could retort, a distant sound pricked his ears—a gentle but steady murmur, like the hum of a song carried on the wind.

"Do you hear that?" Dominic asked, his breath catching.

Calypso froze, his ears twitching. Then his eyes widened, his tail shooting straight up. "Water!" they both exclaimed in unison.

The sound grew louder as they hurried forward, dodging branches and weaving through thick undergrowth. Dominic's heart raced, the thought of fresh water giving him a renewed burst of energy. Calypso bounded ahead, his sleek form darting between tree trunks with the grace of a panther. At last, they broke through the foliage and into a clearing. A narrow stream cut through the forest, its crystal-clear water bubbling over smooth rocks. Dominic dropped to his knees at the edge, plunging his canteen into the stream as he slurped from cupped hands. Beside him, Calypso lapped at the water, his purring almost drowning out the sound of the rapids.

For a moment, the world stilled. The cool water soothed Dominic's parched throat, and the tension in his chest eased. He reached into his bag, pulling out a handful of kibble for Calypso, who devoured it with haste the moment they landed on the stones. Dominic glanced at his reflection in the water. His face was pale and drawn, streaked with dirt. His hair stuck to his forehead, and the weariness in his eyes was unmistakable. But as he stared, something shifted in the reflection—a shadow, dark and fluid, moving behind him.

The crunch of branches snapped him back to reality.

Dominic spun around, his heart hammering in his chest. Calypso hissed, his fur bristling as a figure emerged from the shadows of the trees. Cloaked in black, the figure stood motionless, their presence radiating an unnatural stillness that sent a chill down Dominic's spine.

"Who's there?"

Chapter 14

The forest closed in around Dominic, its thick shadows clinging to the fading daylight. His breaths came in shallow, uneven gasps as he stared at the figure before him, a flicker of desperate hope igniting in his chest. Surely, someone had found him. Someone who could help. Someone who could guide him back to the place he knew, where roads led somewhere and phones worked.

He allowed himself a moment of imagined relief. Perhaps this was one step closer to finding someone who could fix his mangled car, one step closer to a hot shower to wash away the layers of dirt and muck from the storm that had swept him to this new place. One step closer to food—warm, filling, comforting food—to soothe the gnawing emptiness in his stomach. And finally, maybe, one step closer to sleep. Real sleep, in a bed where he wouldn't have to keep one eye open, waiting for whatever new nightmare might crawl out of the woods.

Calypso brushed against his ankle, and Dominic glanced down. The cat's eyes glimmered in the dim light, as if sensing his thoughts. He let out a low, rumbling purr that Dominic found oddly reassuring. "I bet you'd like that too," he murmured, though his voice cracked with exhaustion.

He cleared his throat, straightened his shoulders, and forced himself to speak. "I'm so glad you're here," he said, his voice trembling as he addressed the figure.

The person remained silent. Their silhouette was stark and haunting, framed by the skeletal trees and the faint glow of twilight. The fabric of their cloak billowed in the wind, the frayed edges flickering like shadows against light. A hood obscured their face, creating an unsettling impression with no features to distinguish, nothing to acknowledge.

Dominic took a hesitant step forward, crossing his arms tightly over his chest to stave off the biting chill. His skin prickled beneath his jacket, damp from the remnants of the storm and the sweat of exertion. "Do you know where we are?" he asked, trying to sound steady. "The storm...it swept me away from the roads. I haven't seen a single sign of anybody."

Calypso, who had been pacing at his side, paused and raised his voice. "The storm didn't just take you. It took *us*."

"Shh!" Dominic hissed, glaring down at the cat.

He didn't need this stranger to focus on the impossibility of a talking cat. The last thing he needed was someone questioning his sanity when all he wanted was directions—or, better yet, salvation.

To Dominic's unease, the figure didn't react to Calypso's outburst. In fact, they didn't react at all. Their stillness was unnerving, the absence of even the smallest movement unsettling against the backdrop of a restless forest. The air felt charged, heavy with the tension that made the hair on the back of Dominic's neck stand on end. Though the figure said nothing, he felt their gaze—or the weight of something—bearing down on him. It was as though they were peeling back his layers, staring not at him but through him, right into the core of who he was.

Dominic's patience began to fray, the cold gnawing at his resolve. "I don't mean to be rude," he said, his voice wavering as he tried to keep the desperation from seeping in. "But we're tired and hungry. If you can point us toward a road, or somewhere we can find shelter, I'd really appreciate it."

The figure remained motionless, the void of their hood fixed on him. Dominic's nerves began to unravel, his breath quickening. This was supposed to be the part where they responded—where they offered help, or at least acknowledged his presence. The silence was unbearable.

"I'm not asking for much," Dominic pressed, the edge in his voice betraying his frustration. "Just some help. Anything. Please."

Still, nothing.

Dominic's exhaustion, hunger, and fear boiled over. "Look, I don't know who you are or what your deal is, but we're not playing games here!" He took a bold step forward, his foot slipping on the wet stones beneath him. "Can you at least tell me where we are?"

As he moved closer, the figure seemed to grow. It wasn't a movement—there was no shifting of their form—but an unsettling change in perception. What had appeared to be a person of average height now loomed tall. Dominic blinked, his head tilting back as he realized the figure towered over him, easily a full foot taller. The air seemed thicker now, colder. The shadows cast by the trees stretched unnaturally, dark tendrils creeping toward him like the edges of a dream he couldn't wake from.

Dominic's heart pounded in his chest, his breath coming in shallow gasps. "Please," he whispered, his voice cracking. "I...I just need help."

The figure remained still, but something shifted in the air between them. Then, from beneath the hood, a pair of eyes ignited like coals stoked by an unseen fire. Bright, searing orange light cut through the darkness, piercing straight into Dominic's own gaze. He stumbled backward, his knees giving way as the heat of those eyes seemed to burn away any pretense of courage he had left.

Suffocating emptiness extinguished the hope that had fluttered in his chest moments earlier. It was as though the warmth in his heart, the fragile remnants of his resolve, were being pulled from him by an unseen force. His legs buckled, and he fell hard onto the stones, pain radiating up his spine.

"What...what do you want?" he gasped, his voice barely audible. "Brone?"

The figure leaned forward, the folds of their cloak shifting like smoke given form. One hand emerged from the darkness, its fingers long and thin, the skin blackened as though charred by fire. For a brief, naïve moment, Dominic thought they might help him up—might offer some kind of reassurance.

But then the hand closed around his ankle.

Pain erupted through Dominic's leg, a searing, unbearable heat that tore through his body like wildfire. He screamed, thrashing against the figure's grip, but their hold was unyielding. The skin beneath their touch blistered and bubbled, the stench of burning flesh filling the air. Dominic clawed at the ground, his vision swimming with tears.

"Please!" he begged, his voice raw with agony. "Stop!"

The pain ceased, leaving him gasping and trembling. He clutched his ankle, the skin scorched and raw beneath his fingers. His vision blurred as he looked up at the figure, who now staggered backward, clawing at their shoulders as though something unseen had attacked them.

A flash of black darted across Dominic's field of vision, and a feral hiss split the air. Calypso leapt onto the figure's back, his claws sinking deep into their cloak. The cat swiped furiously at the hood, his growls resonating with an intensity Dominic had never heard before. The figure roared—a guttural, otherworldly sound that shook the trees and the very ground beneath Dominic. He scrambled backward, his hands scraping against the jagged stones as he tried to put distance between himself and the horrifying visual before him.

"Calypso!" Dominic shouted, his voice breaking. "Get down! Let's go!"

The cat turned his glowing eyes toward Dominic, then sprang off the figure's back in one fluid motion. He landed beside Dominic, his fur bristling as he hissed once more at the figure before retreating into the safety of Dominic's arms.

Branches whipped against his face and arms, the sting of cuts barely registering as he sprinted through the forest. The pain in his burned leg was excruciating, every step sending sharp jolts of agony through his body. But he didn't stop. He couldn't. As he stumbled by each tree trunk, every nerve in his body was alight with pain and exhaustion. His breaths came in short, labored gasps, the air clawing at his throat like shards of glass. Calypso clung to his shoulder, his claws digging through the thin fabric of Dominic's jacket as the cat hissed at the unseen creature pursuing them.

"Are you okay?" Dominic rasped, the words were hard to escape between gulps of air.

"I'm fine," Calypso replied, his voice calm despite the situation. His eyes remained fixed on the dark shadows behind them, his ears twitching with every snap of a branch and rustle of leaves. "But I suggest you ditch this son of a bitch! That thing isn't slowing down."

Dominic didn't need to be told twice. He pushed forward, the sharp branches of low-hanging trees tearing at his sleeves and cutting into his exposed hands. Every step sent fresh jolts of agony through his leg, the burn creeping steadily upward to his knee. The incline of the terrain grew steeper, his calves screaming in protest as he scrambled up the uneven path with the dirt becoming moistened by the drops of falling rain.

Ahead of him loomed a small ravine, its walls lined with exposed roots that jutted out like skeletal fingers. He pressed forward, ignoring the sharp sting of snot trickling to his upper lip and the grit of dirt clinging to his tear-streaked cheeks. His vision blurred with sweat and exhaustion, but he forced himself to keep going.

"Pain is just weakness leaving the body," he told himself, the mantra hollow and bitter now.

The earthy hues of the ravine surrounded him, the dense greenery overhead casting heavy shadows that only added to the suffocating weight around him. The air reeked of damp soil, thick and gritty in his nostrils, as if the earth itself was trying to choke him. He dared a glance back and spotted his pursuer, its dark form closing the gap with unnerving ease. It was no longer fifty yards away. It was gaining fast.

His leg screamed for a reprieve. The skin felt raw, the pain radiating upward like a spreading fire. Looking at it, the bubbles on his wound were eager to pop. All he wanted was to collapse, to give his body a chance to rest, to stop fighting. But stopping wasn't an option. Not now.

He swallowed hard, his throat clicking painfully as his mouth ran dry. His lungs burned, each breath a fresh reminder of how woefully out of shape he was.

"Should've joined a gym," he muttered bitterly.

The roots lining the ravine became his only lifeline. He grabbed at them, his knuckles blistering from the friction as he heaved himself upward. His sweaty palms slipped on the rough, slick bark, and every misstep felt like a potential death sentence. Calypso, still perched on his shoulder, dug his claws deeper with every lurch forward.

"Keep going!" Calypso urged, his voice sharp and commanding.

Dominic gritted his teeth, swallowing down the groan of pain that threatened to escape. His forearms trembled with exertion, his biceps screaming as they endured his weight. The strain on his shoulders was unbearable, but he couldn't afford to stop. Not with the crackle of branches below signaling that the creature had begun its ascent.

Dominic risked a glance downward and regretted it. The figure was climbing effortlessly, its movements fluid and predatory, as if gravity were a mere suggestion to it. Panic flared in his chest, a sharp, cold spike that threatened to freeze him in place.

"What the hell is he?" he gasped. "A damned Olympian?"

"Less complaining, more climbing!" Calypso shot back, though Dominic could hear the faint tremor in his companion's voice.

The final stretch loomed above him—just ten more feet. His forearms burned, his fingers slipping on the muddy terrain. Loose stones tumbled beneath his feet, each one sending him lurching backward before he caught himself on another root. A guttural grunt escaped his throat as he clawed his way upward, his determination outweighing the sheer agony coursing through his body.

At last, Dominic's hands found solid ground. He collapsed onto the flat ridge, his knees buckling as he tried to stand. Mud caked his fingers, staining his hands as though he'd been digging through wet ash. His body trembled, his muscles rebelling against any further exertion.

But there was no time to rest.

The creature's clawed hands appeared over the ridge's edge, digging into the soil with terrifying precision. Dominic's breath hitched as the thing pulled itself up, its movements unhurried and deliberate. Its hooded face tilted upward, the burning orange orbs of its eyes locking onto him like twin suns in the dark.

Dominic staggered backward, his balance faltering as the weight of his bag pulled him toward the edge. His breaths came in sharp, shallow bursts, his lungs on the verge of collapse. Calypso leapt from his shoulder, landing on the ground in front of him. Dominic's knees buckled as he forced himself back on his feet; the tingling sensation of his heels and soles were fading away as the blood flow was rushing back. His weight teetered towards his toes, becoming unsteady as the villain was now less than five feet away, ending their climb. Dominic's breath became shorter, gasping for regulation.

The force of gravity pulling him back relentlessly; the weight of the bag was working in their favor. His strength had reached its fullest capacity; he couldn't fight the strain of his body any longer. If this were indeed a dream, what harm would it do if he just gave in? And if this was real life, perhaps death would be better than the endless amount of pain that continues to pile up.

The air rushed around his face, providing a cooling sensation as it combated against the drenching perspiration all over his skin. Calypso spread his limbs out crazily; the webbing in between his stretched-out paws spread out. His screeching meow wasn't too agonizing since Dominic's mind was focused on the peace he was feeling facing the inevitable, real or not. The shadow became smaller with each passing second the further he went down, staring deep into his soul as he submitted to his premature death.

Here it comes, my big landing. Dominic thought to himself as he caught his breath.

He could just feel it coming.

And he did.

Dominic's insides thrashed. His spine cracked slightly. The thought that death would be much more painful, but it wasn't. He felt an itch, and the urge to scratch grew stronger, yet he was too tired to move.

He turned his head to look for Calypso; the sudden prick of straw irritated his eye.

Damn.

He landed in a bed of hay. He indeed didn't die or wake up from this fantasy. A horse let out a communicative nay before picking up the pace. The ground was moving, at least what was supporting the straw was. Wooden wheels endured the slight bumps from the rocks that they drove over, bumping Calypso closer to him.

"Dominic, you're okay!" he said, sniffing his master's forehead before gifting him with a couple of grateful licks.

The semi-moistened sandpaper texture of Calypso's tongue, for some reason, brought comfort for the first time since he got to this place. It brought him back to when he would relax out on his couch; itchiness and all. The ease of checking out from all the chaos in his life and only having his fur baby being in his presence when Marcus was unavailable. Dominic looked at the clouds that were clearing up, with only a few that gave the impression of cotton candy. The silence diminished with the birds chirping harmoniously like they were before. The humming of the wheels screeching became a soft lullaby with the blanket of mist coating his face.

No more moving for the day.

His eyelids became heavier, succumbing to the exhaustion his body was feeling.

He didn't care.

He gave in.

It was time for sleep.

Chapter 15

Dominic

HOLY CRAP!

What is going on?

All I see is darkness, and right now there's no place I'd rather be. A part of me misses the hypnotic chaos of New York—the constant noise that became a strange comfort. The blinding lights were better than this endless black sky. I'd trade this silence for the polluted cocktail of cigarette smoke, restaurant scraps, and car exhaust. Even the absence of strangers, each rushing toward their own destination without giving a damn about me feels like something I long for. At least they weren't chasing me with hands that felt like lava.

Not anymore.

Whatever the hell was after me is no longer my problem. My time of roughing it in the wilderness is probably over, even if it only lasted a day. Still, I appreciated the cool stream, the refreshing touch of glacial water trickling down my throat and filling my stomach was pure bliss. For a moment, it felt like heaven—right before my body went through the gauntlet from hell. And let's be honest, I've endured worse. Retail taught me pain. Holiday season shifts, twelve-hour days, screaming customers—I thought my legs could withstand anything.

Not this time.

I'm glad that I'm no longer in agony with the pain in my foot becoming more of a pain in my ass. My ankle no longer burns. And pain doesn't just vanish like that... not without something surreal going on.

I knew this was a dream!

For the first time in what feels like forever, I feel like me again. Not the me who got swept up in a tornado. Not the me who crumbled when Miss Reed died. No—this feels like the version of myself from long ago. The kid whose heart fluttered with joy, running wild with imagination, chasing Penelope and Alex through our backyard.

God, I miss those days.

We never listened when Miss Reed warned us not to wander too far. She always said that the woods were dangerous. Easy to get lost in. She wasn't wrong.

But we loved it.

We darted through the hedges that marked the line between our structured lives and our imagination. We were wild when we snuck into the wooded wonderland. One of our favorite adventures was going on pirate adventures to escape from prison and living in the wilderness. There were times that we could get lost for hours, usually on Sundays when Miss Reed had other engagements with the community. There were a couple of nights that we would sneak out after lights out to go hunting for treasure.

There were even nights we snuck out after lights out—flashlights in hand, eyes wide with anticipation—hunting for treasure in the shadows.

There's one night the three of us sneak out after the town's Fourth of July party. The fireworks have finished showing off their spangled glory, leaving behind a blanket of intoxicating smoke that makes it hard for anyone to see more than a few feet ahead.

That was our chance.

That, and Miss Reed has had one too many mixed drinks with her hotdogs. I guess even she needs a splash of vodka in her fruit punch to take the edge off from her daily routine of rules and responsibilities.

We run deep into the woods. Alex says he heard from one of the older kids that there's treasure scattered across the ten-acre lot behind the yard.

I know. It sounds ridiculous now. But when you're eight and your world is just school, storybooks, and chores, you'll believe just about anything. And trust me, I've read every book within reach. Every fairy tale. Every fable. If it had a hint of magic or mystery, I devoured it.

The honking horns of downtown celebrations fade behind us the farther we go. Owls dive for field mice darting through the brush, desperate to escape into a safer burrow.

"Are you sure there's treasure out here?" Penelope asks, a flicker of hesitation in her voice.

"Of course there is!" Alex replies, parting a branch with practiced ease and pushing forward like a boy on a mission.

I don't know why Penelope suddenly wants to back out. She's usually the one dragging us on these wild adventures. She once swore she'd find some antique chachki and make it a trophy—proof to the others that she had pride in something, that she found something worth showing off.

Then I see her.

A woman's form blends into the trees. Her shape moves with the forest, the curves of her body sculpted into the lines of bark and trunk. The only thing that stands out is her hair, black and long, shimmering in the low light. Her clothes are camouflaged, covered in bark and leaves like she's grown from the forest itself. There's something maternal about her. Calming. Alluring.

And then I blink.

She's gone.

"Let's split up," I suggest. "We can cover more ground before it gets too dark."

We spread out, our feet crunching over the dried foliage as we cross the small hump surrounding the tallest pine tree in the clearing. I veer toward the dry creek bed about ten yards from our usual meeting spot. My hands scrape through the carpet of pine needles, their tips prickling my skin. I'm focused—determined. I want to find something. I need to.

I just wish Penelope felt the same.

Finding treasure would mean something. It would be proof that magic does exist. That stories can bleed into real life. Right now, the only meaningful thing I own is the sapphire pendant hidden deep in my sock drawer—my secret, my only heirloom.

The woods darken around me. Shadows stretch long and wide. I approach a hollowed-out tree trunk. Everything feels still. Even the rustling leaves have fallen silent. The hum of distant cars fades into nothing. It's just me and the woods. I press my fingers against the bark. The flakes crumble beneath my nails. Each touch chips away the years, the layers. There's something satisfying, almost sacred, about peeling back the tree's skin, hoping to find what's behind.

The ground is squishy. My palm sinks into the muddy dampness inside the hollow trunk. My shoulder cracks as I contort my arm, reaching deeper into the nook than I probably should.

I feel something.

It's cold. My knuckle taps against it with a hollow clink—metal. I curl my fingers around it and pull it free. It fits perfectly in my palm. A circular object with a sapphire gem winking back at me.

At the top is a loop, a thin chain still threaded through it.

"Sweet," I whisper to myself, heart racing with a rush of excitement. My fingers tremble, still buzzing from the discovery. This is the kind of moment you wait your whole childhood for.

The silence doesn't bother me. I've grown used to it over the years. Maybe that's because my days have always been filled with noise from other kids and their laughter and chaos. And where there's excitement, there's always noise.

But it doesn't stay silent for long.

There's a flutter—fabric caught in the breeze. It sounds like a pair of pants being snapped straight from the dryer. Crisp. Sudden. My neck strains as I try to glance behind me. For a second, I catch a glimpse of something—a tattered, triangular hem and frayed at the edges like the ripped flags on a pirate ship. My breath catches, choking slightly on my own spit as panic spikes in my chest. I scramble back from the tree, branches scratching at my arms as I push through them. But once I clear the foliage, it was gone.

I don't have time to piece it together, that flutter of cloth. It looks similar to the one from my dream. The same kind of shadow I saw all those years ago. It feels the same. This, of course, is based on the small piece of fabric that I saw. What was even more strange was that the next day when I had a chance, I run like a bat out of hell to the same spot to look for the item.

The object was gone. Whatever I held... vanished. Like it had never existed at all.

And now, as if summoned by memory, the pain flares back. It feels hot and vicious as it's pulsing under my knee. My leg seizes. Throbs. My body remembers what my mind hasn't caught up to yet.

Damn.

Chapter 16

Though the mattress felt firm and scratchy, Dominic sank into it gratefully, unlike the worn one he was used to back at home. The faint scent of straw confirmed his suspicion that it was stuffed with something far more utilitarian than comfort. Even so, the limited lumbar support was better than no support at all, especially after the arduous last few days. His body ached, a dull reminder of the trials he'd endured.

The air sneaking through the withered shutters was crisp and invigorating, rushing into his lungs and awakening his senses as he stirred. For a moment, he wondered if this was still part of the dream—the bed of hay, the field, the fiend-like figure chasing him through the woods. But as his vision cleared and the shapes around him became more defined, he realized this was no dream.

Dominic froze. Shadows loomed over him, but as his eyes adjusted to the dim, flickering light of the room, the forms took shape. They weren't monsters, but people—several of them. Though their faces were darkened, their simple, loose-hanging, tattered clothes caught his eye. One woman wore a bonnet, the fabric tied tightly under her chin in a way that screamed a time long past.

Amish? he thought, though the word seemed absurd. His mind scrambled for context as his body retreated under the thin muslin sheet.

A dull ache lingered in his ankle, but the pain was much less intense. A woman dabbed at it with a sponge soaked in a liquid that stung sharply before fading into a cooling numbness. Dominic flinched, noticing a glittery sparkle in the liquid when it was being rung out. Whatever they were using, it seemed to work.

The man standing nearest to him caught his attention. His presence was tall and broad, with a chest that revealed through the loose fabric of his blouse. His beard, streaked with silver, glimmered in the candlelight, and the bald crown of his head shone faintly. Everything about him spoke of hard work and quiet strength.

"W-where am I?" Dominic croaked, his voice hoarse.

"Now, now, my child," an older woman said gently as she fluffed the pillow beneath his head. Her voice was gentle, her hands practiced. "You're safe now."

"Safe?" he murmured, his throat dry as he tried to make sense of his surroundings.

"Yes, you're safe with us," said the younger woman with red hair.

The man stepped closer, his deep, resonant voice chiming in. "You were passed out when we found you. You were lying on top of a batch of straw headed for the stable outside of Mynnshire Village."

Dominic blinked as he pinched his arms. "The stable? Mynnshire Village?"

The man nodded. "We brought you here immediately. You were hurt—badly. You've been unconscious for three days."

"Three days?" Dominic sat up too quickly, groaning as a sharp pain flared through his back. His muscles protested the sudden movement, and he sank back against the pillow. "What is Mynnshire Village?"

The group looked together in confusion. They hesitated more with each opportunity to explain further until the elder spoke. "Mynnshire Village is here in Golponia."

"Golponia?"

"Yes," the man said. "Like I said, you were out for three days."

His thoughts raced. Three days? That wasn't possible. His body, already battered and sore, felt the strain of lying dormant for so long.

"My cat," he said, panic flashing across his face. "Where's Calypso?"

The older woman smiled with reassurance. "Nothing to worry about. He's outside, chasing the field mice."

Dominic exhaled, relieved, though he couldn't help but roll his eyes. "Of course he is. Where was that enthusiasm when there were mice in our apartment?"

The man chuckled. "He's quite the talker, that one. Told us to help you. Explained everything."

Dominic froze. "He...told you?"

The man nodded earnestly. "Yes. He spoke clear as day. Cried out for us to save you, then complained about being hungry. He did that a lot." He smiled as though this were the most natural thing in the world. "Finished a saucer of milk in no time."

Dominic's lips parted in disbelief. *At least I'm not the only one who hears him talking*, he thought.

Before he could dwell on it, the woman by his bedside interrupted. "Now, if you don't mind answering a question for us. What happened to you? How did you end up on our farm?"

"Did...Didn't Calypso already tell you," Dominic stammered, trying to deflect.

The woman's expression hardened, her patience thinning. "Not how you got here," she said, her tone clipped. "Where you're from. You're clearly not from around here."

Dominic glanced down at his clothes, suddenly aware of how out of place they must look. His faded jeans and black t-shirt were worlds apart from the rough linen and coarse wool the others wore.

The man picked up Dominic's jacket, running his hand over the fabric with admiration. "This material is very fine," he mused. "Even on a stable boy's pay, I couldn't dream of affording something like this."

"Stable boy?" Dominic echoed, distracted.

"Yes," the man said. "I'm a stable boy for Queen Ella's former home."

Dominic blinked, the words taking a moment to register. "Queen?"

The man raised an eyebrow. "You *really* aren't from around here, are you?"

"No," Dominic admitted, his heart pounding. "I'm not."

The room seemed to shrink around him, the air thickening as questions swirled in his mind. "Queens? Stable boy? Where the hell am I?" His brain scrambled to reconcile the words with reality. There hadn't been princes or princesses for centuries—at least, not like the ones in Miss Reed's fairy tales.

He swung his legs over the side of the bed, ignoring the rush of blood to his feet that made him dizzy. His injured winced from the movement, but he didn't care. The need for answers outweighed the pain. Dodging a woman carrying a basin of liquid, Dominic slipped his shoes on hastily and stood. His balance wavered, and he stumbled straight into the broad chest of the stable boy.

"Whoa there," the man said, steadying him. His hands were strong, his grip firm but gentle. The faint scent of sweat and campfire clung to him, intoxicating in a strange, earthy way.

Dominic flushed, stepping back quickly. "Pardon me," he mumbled. "I just need some air."

He pushed past the man, ignoring the curious stares of the others as he flung open the wooden door. Warm sunlight poured over him, blinding after the dim interior of the room. The heat kissed his skin, and for a brief moment, he closed his eyes and let it wash over him.

"Wait," the man called, following him outside. "I didn't mean to offend you. If I did, I deeply apologize."

"You didn't," Dominic said quickly, blinking against the light. A tear slid down his cheek, the result of squinting too hard against the sun.

"I only meant..." The man hesitated. "We didn't want to disrespect royalty."

Dominic froze. "Royalty? I'm not royalty."

The man looked puzzled. "Then who are you?"

Dominic sighed. "Dominic. Just Dominic."

The man's expression softened. "Pleased to meet you, Dominic. I'm Sebastian."

Dominic's breath caught as he got his first proper look at the man in the sunlight. His olive skin glowed, kissed by years of working outdoors. His angular face was framed by strong, defined brows and a warm smile that seemed impossibly kind. For a moment, Dominic forgot his questions, his fears, and even his situation.

"So," Dominic said, forcing himself to speak, "you're a stable boy?"

Sebastian nodded. "Yes, I work at Queen Ella's farm. She moved to the castle after meeting the king at the festival.

"Festival?"

"Oh, yes! That festival last year was the first one that invited all the maidens in the land, and Ella was blessed to go."

Dominic's heart stuttered. "Ella? Does she have a stepmother? Stepsisters?"

Sebastian frowned. "Yes, they were so horrible to her. We were all elated that she found the king and banished those rotten folks from her property. Why?"

The realization hit Dominic like a freight train. His knees weakened, and the world spun.

This isn't just a strange farm, or a forgotten corner of another state in the Midwest. I know this place. I'm in one of the stories from Miss Reed's books. The tornado didn't just take me to another place—it did indeed take me to another world!

"Cinderella," Dominic whispered, his voice trembling. "I'm at Cinderella's farm."

Chapter 17

FROM THE PAGES OF THE STORYBOOK
Ella

ANOTHER DAY BEGINS on the farm. The sun hasn't yet risen, and the air is still heavy with the lingering dampness of the early morning dew. My breath fogged in the chill, and for a moment, I remain under the thin muslin blanket, hoping to soak in what little comfort it offers. But the day waits for no one—not even me—and certainly not for my grief.

It has been many years since my mother's passing, but her absence never feels any less acute. She was a remarkable woman, beautiful, yes, but her beauty paled in comparison to her kindness. She was the sort of person who could see the good in anyone, even in those who probably didn't deserve it. Her compassion was her greatest strength, even when others tried to crush it.

I often think about the stories she used to tell me about her sister, my aunt—a cruel and bitter woman. My aunt seemed to delight in belittling her, mocking her talents, and making her feel small. And yet, my mother never let the bitterness take root in her heart. Instead, she chose to fight back with compassion, vowing to rise above the pettiness and hatred.

I try to live by her example, though some days feel impossible.

I remember one story in particular. My mother once crafted a dress by hand, a masterpiece of chiffon and embroidery so intricate that even the most downhearted soul couldn't help but admire it. She worked tirelessly on it, pouring her heart and soul into every stitch, despite not even owning a proper sewing machine. The rest of her family, of course, dismissed it as frivolous, mocking her for wasting her time. But my mother never let it break her. Instead, she wore that dress proudly, knowing it symbolized her strength and resilience.

I wish I could've seen that dress on her.

She used to say that evil thrives on acknowledgment, that it feeds on sadness and reaction. Her mantra was simple: fight back with love and kindness. But now, as I sit here in the cold attic that now serves as my bedroom, her words feel more like a cruel joke than wisdom. How can I fight back with kindness when my life feels like a constant battle against cruelty?

Last night was the worst of all.

A man arrived at the farm just after sunset. His face was lined with the sorrow that only comes from delivering bad news. And oh, what news it was. My father, my last pillar of strength, had taken ill while on the road. He didn't make it. The words hit me like a storm, and for a moment, I thought I'd collapse right there in the doorway.

My father is gone.

I don't know how to process it. The grief is a weight on my chest, heavy and suffocating. Both of my parents are gone now, and I'm not even grown—not truly. How am I supposed to carry on? The farm was already a struggle with my father here. Without him, it feels impossible.

When my father remarried, I thought things would get better. Mirelle, my stepmother, was no substitute for my mother, but I accepted her with open arms in hopes she might bring some stability to our lives. She brought her two daughters, Evangeline and Aurelia, into our home, and I gave up my own bedroom so they could settle in more comfortably and possibly be in their good graces. It was Mirelle's idea that I take the attic, but I didn't mind at first. My mother would've been proud of me for making that sacrifice.

But now? The attic has become a symbol of how far I've fallen in this family. The cold seeps in through the cracks in the roof, and when storms rage outside, the rain drips onto my bed. Still, I tell myself that I'm lucky to have a roof over my head, even one that leaks.

My stepmother's adjustments didn't stop there. She dismissed all my friends—Sebastian, most painfully of all. He was like a brother to me, always there when I needed comfort or someone to share a laugh with. I used to meet him by the stables, and we'd talk for hours, playing with the horses and escaping the weight of reality for a little while. But Mirelle said friends were a distraction we couldn't afford, so she sent them all away.

I miss him. I miss all of them.

Now, I'm left with nothing but the endless cycle of chores that consume my days. Cooking, cleaning, scrubbing stains from Evangeline and Aurelia's clothes—tasks I endure for the scraps of food left on their plates. My hands are raw from scrubbing floors and washing dishes, and my back aches from hauling firewood and tending to the animals.

I wake before dawn every day to care for the chickens, gather eggs, and feed the horses. Sometimes I think they're the only ones who see me as a person, the only ones who greet me with warmth instead of disdain. Evangeline and Aurelia certainly don't. They treat me like I'm beneath them, like I'm a servant rather than their stepsister.

I tell myself that it doesn't matter, that kindness will win in the end. My mother's voice echoes in my mind:

"Always fight back with love and compassion."

But it's hard. So hard.

This morning, I made my way to my mother's grave, hidden in the shade of the old oak tree at the edge of the farm. I sat there in the damp grass, letting the tears flow freely as I whispered to her. I told her how much I miss her, how much I miss the warmth of her embrace and the sound of her voice.

Every time I go to visit, my tears bring the sparrows over for a visit. I know their chirping is their way of telling me life will be okay. I also hear a woman's soft humming. I get startled every time. What scares me every time is that there is nobody else there, just me and the tree. If I squint, the swirl of the base looks like a nose with two little holes appearing like eyes. I know it's not them; I believe in the magic of the land, but not here.

The grave is overgrown now, but I refuse to let it fall into neglect. I'll tend it, just as I tend the farm. It's all I have left of her, and I'll honor her memory no matter what. I let my tears soak into the earth, telling myself they'll help the grass grow and flowers bloom. Maybe, in some small way, my grief will nourish something new. And now my mother won't be alone with my father put to rest next to her.

But my stepmother won't care. Mirelle doesn't see me as anything but a burden. She says as much when she raises her cane to strike me, claiming it's to "beat the complacency out of me." The bruises fade, but the ache lingers. Still, I endure it. Maybe if I work hard enough, if I prove myself enough, she'll see my worth.

That hope is all I have left.

I know Evangeline and Aurelia laugh at me behind my back, mocking my threadbare clothes and calloused hands. They drape themselves in fine fabrics while I make do with patched dresses and aprons I created myself, thanks to my mother teaching me how to sew. I don't care about the clothes, not really. What I want is their love—or at least a shred of respect.

I'm not asking for much. I just want to feel like I belong somewhere, like I matter to someone.

For now, I tell myself that today is just another day. I'll cook, clean, and scrub as I always do. I'll endure Mirelle's sharp words and Evangeline's sneers. I'll remind myself of my mother's teachings, even when the weight of grief feels too much to bear.

But I'll keep going. What else can I do? I have no choice.

And maybe, just maybe, I'll find the strength I need to believe in myself again.

Cinderella *needs to believe it, according to my stepsisters.*

Chapter 18

Sebastian

I DON'T KNOW HOW TO take all this in. Earlier this week, everything was normal. Just another day on the farm, with my horses. Nothing brings me more joy than taking care of them. Yes, there's Petunia and Giselle that keep me company during our down time, but they're busy being there for each other. The only other human interaction is when I help the others with market days and go into town to help make a living, even though Ella has taken good care of us since her reign as Queen. She always makes sure we have the resources and time to make warm meals, and have a roof over our heads, which was far better before Mirelle let us go.

And that's enough for us.

Some nights her stepmother kicked us out in the rain after a long day of keeping up with the work. When she was going broke, we were removed from our jobs and became decimated by the day. After my guardian was let go, I still made time to check in on Ella. She needed a friend when nobody else was there for her.

I miss seeing her every day.

She was so heartbroken when her father died. He was the only one that nurtured her kindness and believed in her even when she didn't believe in herself after her mother died. She was so lost in this world, with nobody to have her back.

I see the same in Dominic.

It's as though he feels like I'm not real, or this entire place isn't real.

How can he feel like this is make believe? I don't feel that way about him; no matter how goofy he looks with those clothes. He clearly doesn't know a thing about manual labor since I don't see a speck of dirt under his nails or a callus on his hands. I want to see him work the farm for half a day and then come talk to me about hard work. It's not like I have a problem with the life I have. I just don't like it when people don't feel what I feel and take our work for granted.

I love my life.

I just want more.

Something new.

The monotony of this place has driven me a little crazy, like a bee constantly buzzing in my ear. I can see the same voice annoying this helpless soul in front of me. I know I just met him, but I see so much misery in his eyes. He looks so lost, yearning for somebody to be there for him. So much loss has been wrecking his soul. The only one that cares about him is his cat.

But who am I to judge? I have my horses.

His jaw rolled close to the ground when I told him where he was. Does he have any idea where he is?

This land is plentiful with history and full of life!

At least it was.

Darkness has flooded the land. Happiness is fading into depression. Life is wilting closer to death.

We need someone to save us.

Is he the one?

I hope so.

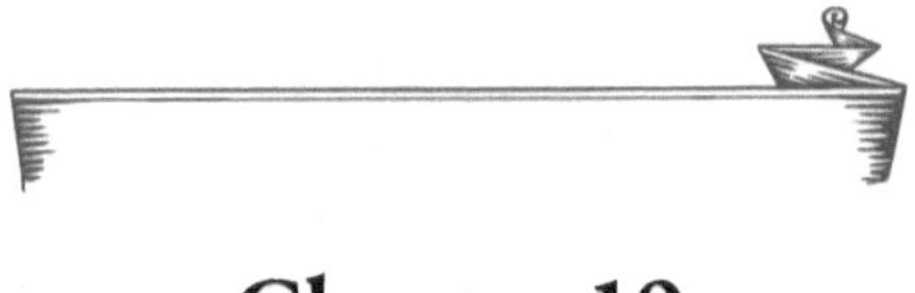

Chapter 19

Sebastian watched as Dominic's expression twisted into something between disbelief and dawning realization. His question lingered in the air, hanging heavy with incredulity.

"Did you say I'm at Cinderella's farm?" Dominic asked, his voice tight with a mixture of wonder and unease.

Sebastian nodded, though his jaw tightened at the name. "Yes, but we don't call her that," he said firmly, his gaze steady on Dominic. He noticed how Dominic's eyes shimmered as if holding back a tide of emotion. "There's too much hate tied to it."

Dominic blinked, clearly surprised. "But that's how I've always known her—since I was a child."

Sebastian tilted his head slightly, confusion flickering across his face. "You knew her too?"

For a moment, Dominic hesitated, his lips parting as though to say something, but whatever thoughts had formed seemed to retreat just as quickly. He glanced away, looking uneasy. "Something like that, I guess," he muttered, avoiding Sebastian's gaze.

Sebastian studied him for a beat longer, puzzled but unwilling to press. There was something unusual about this stranger—something unspoken that Dominic seemed desperate to keep hidden. But for now, Sebastian let it lie. He gestured toward the back of the barn, where the horses whinnied softly, their ears flicking in response to the rustling tall grass.

"Come on," Sebastian said, leading the way. The two men moved quietly, their steps punctuated only by the swish of grass and the occasional snort from the nearby horses.

Sebastian's boots were heavy on the ground, their weight pressing down on the resilient blades of green beneath him. He glanced back at Dominic, who seemed distracted, his eyes darting between the barn and the horizon as if seeking answers in the wide-open sky.

When they reached the top of the small mound that overlooked the sprawling field beyond, Sebastian stopped. He turned his face toward the wind, closing his eyes to feel the sun's warmth on his skin. The vibrancy of the grass stretched endlessly, punctuated by yellow patches where the sun had kissed the earth too fervently. Beyond the field stood a patch of trees, their leaves trembling in the breeze.

Sebastian let out a low sigh, murmuring a quiet thanks to the land, a habit he'd picked up from the countless days spent working this farm. This place held beauty, yes, but also a sharp edge of wildness. It demanded respect, as much for its generosity as for the hidden dangers it harbored.

Dominic, however, didn't seem interested in the view or the moment. His pace quickened, his strides growing longer as though compelled by an unseen force. Sebastian watched as the stranger's silhouette grew smaller, his form cutting across the hill like a dark shadow.

"You shouldn't be running on that leg!" Sebastian called out, his voice laced with concern. He took a step forward, frowning as Dominic ignored him. The man was favoring an injured limb, yet he moved as if pain were nothing but an afterthought. He acted without a care for the consequences, a reckless abandon in his behavior.

He hesitated, glancing down at the spot where the hill rolled into the field. The tall grass rippled in the wind, masking the uneven ground beneath. Dominic didn't know the lay of the land, and Sebastian knew all too well the hidden dangers that lurked—holes, brambles, and worse things that didn't show themselves until it was too late.

Sebastian's frown deepened as his thoughts turned to Ella. She'd once been like that—driven, distracted, and constantly running from something unseen. The thought stirred a pang of regret in him, but he quickly shoved it aside. This wasn't about Ella. Dominic needed someone to keep an eye on him, even if he was too stubborn or prideful to admit it.

With a soft sigh, Sebastian continued walking after him, his strides deliberate but unhurried. He spotted the faint flick of Calypso's black tail, the cat trailing after Dominic as if the two were tethered by some invisible thread. Calypso, at least, seemed to know his way through the chaos.

"Oh, Dom!" Calypso exclaimed, his body skipping with glee. "I'm so glad you're okay!"

The breeze picked up, carrying with it the scent of sun-warmed grass and distant rain. Sebastian quickened his pace, his boots crunching against the ground as he followed. The field ahead seemed peaceful on the surface, but he knew better. Dominic was a stranger here, and strangers always misjudged the farm's tranquil facade.

Sebastian's voice broke through the quiet again, firm but tinged with a note of care. "Dominic, wait! You don't know what's out there."

But Dominic didn't stop. Whatever drove him forward was stronger than reason, and Sebastian could only hope he'd catch up before the land—or something worse—taught Dominic a lesson the hard way once again.

Chapter 20

The trees seemed to thicken the farther Dominic wandered from Sebastian, their shadows growing deeper and more oppressive with every step. He had no intention of being rude—Sebastian and the others had saved his life, after all—but the weight of everything that had happened was crushing. He needed space, a moment to collect himself. The overwhelming kindness shown to him only sharpened the surreal edges of his reality.

Dominic's hands trembled as he walked, the tips of his fingers brushing against his sides like they needed grounding.

How did I end up in a storybook? How is this Golponia place even real?

He tried to shake off the thoughts, but they clung stubbornly to his mind, looping like a song he couldn't forget. The trees creaked in the breeze, their gnarled branches shifting against one another like old bones. The sunlight pierced through the canopy in sporadic bursts, lighting patches of the forest floor with an earthy glow.

And then, almost as if fate itself had nudged him, he saw it.

A stone jutted out of the ground just ahead, bathed in a golden shaft of light that slipped through the branches above. Its surface was smooth and inviting, its earthy tones flecked with moss and lichen. Around it, vibrant flowers bloomed, their petals soft hues of purple and yellow, shaped like delicate bells and tiny hearts. The shape of a silhouette appeared through the foliage. The soft hum from the leaves brought his pulse down. Giggles echoed in his ear, bringing the joy of his childhood back to his mind.

Dominic stopped, taking in the sight. There was something magical about it—a purity he'd never seen back in New York. He wondered if Cinderella had ever come to a place like this, seeking solace from her misery. The thought made his chest tighten, making him miss Nebraska more, looking at the foliage that was like Miss Reed's property.

If I lived her life, I'd need this kind of peace, too.

He lowered himself onto the stone, wincing as his muscles protested. The smooth surface was cool beneath him, but not uncomfortably so. His gaze drifted to a small pond nearby, its surface reflecting the flowers and the swaying trees like a mirror. A group of frogs perched on the lily pads, their slippery skin glistening like sequined fabric. They moved lazily, their soft croaks blending with the rustle of the leaves and the occasional chirp of birds.

Dominic smiled faintly. *Imagine living like that,* he thought. *No stress, no pain—just hopping around, sunning yourself, and catching flies.* For a moment, he envied their simplicity, their innocence.

One frog jumped closer, its small body landing on a lily pad just feet from where Dominic sat. Its beady eyes blinked at him, unbothered by his presence. He extended his hand, curious, and almost touched its warty skin before it leapt again—only this time, something incredible happened.

Wings unfurled from the frog's back, delicate and shimmering like butterfly nets, catching the light and scattering it in tiny specks of gold. Dominic's jaw dropped as the creature took to the air, fluttering like a bird learning to fly for the first time. It circled him once, twice, and then hovered in place, water droplets flinging off its tiny, webbed feet.

"What the hell?" Dominic whispered, stumbling back as his heart raced.

The frog darted closer, its wings humming as it circled his head. Dominic flinched, his hands swiping at the air as he tried to back away. His heel caught on a root, and he tumbled backward, his jeans scraping against the damp earth as he scrambled to put distance between himself and the bizarre creature.

His hand hit a cluster of flowers, their stems bending under the force. To his shock, one of them snapped upright and hissed, "Watch it, you clumsy oaf!"

Dominic froze. "Did you just—"

"Ass!" snapped another flower, its bell-shaped bloom trembling with indignation.

"Sorry!" Dominic stammered, his head whipping between the flying amphibian and the flowers. The entire forest seemed to come alive. Vines slithered up tree trunks, their leaves swaying rhythmically like they were dancing to some unheard tune. High above, tiny blossoms tinkled like bells, the sound growing louder and louder until it felt like the chimes of a gothic cathedral.

"This has got to be a dream," Dominic muttered, his voice trembling.

"It's not!" a voice barked from behind him.

Before he could react, firm hands clamped around his armpits and hoisted him to his feet as if he weighed nothing. He gasped as his back bumped against the solid warmth of Sebastian's chest, his hand inadvertently brushing against the man's stomach. Hard muscle flexed under his touch, and Dominic quickly pulled his hand away, his face flushing.

Sebastian's brow furrowed as he steadied Dominic. "Are you okay?" he asked, his deep voice laced with concern.

"Y-yeah," Dominic stammered, trying to catch his breath. His heart raced, though he wasn't sure if it was from the frog, the flowers, or the sudden closeness of Sebastian. "W-what was that?"

Sebastian's lips twitched into a faint smile. "This is our land," he said simply. "And those are flue frogs."

Dominic gawked at him. "That's not normal. It's like...magic."

Sebastian chuckled, his green eyes glinting with amusement. "That's because it *is* magic. And you're lucky you weren't greeted by something more dangerous."

Dominic groaned and ran a hand through his hair. "This isn't real. It can't be. I must be dreaming."

Sebastian frowned, his head tilting. "Why do you keep saying that? This isn't a dream. I'm just as real as you are."

"I'm sorry," Dominic said, shaking his head. "But where I'm from, there's no magic. No flying frogs, no talking flowers. Just...reality."

Sebastian's curiosity deepened. "Where are you from, then? By the sea?"

Dominic snorted despite himself. "No. New York."

Sebastian's brow furrowed. "What's New York?"

Dominic opened his mouth, then closed it again, unsure how to even explain. How could he describe skyscrapers, subways, and constant chaos to someone who didn't even know the concept of a city? He hesitated before saying, "It's like...an overpopulated Emerald City."

Sebastian's face lit up with recognition. "Camelot?"

Dominic bit back a laugh. "Sure. Close enough."

Sebastian's smile widened. "It sounds busy. You must not be used to all this peace and quiet."

"Not in a long time," Dominic admitted, glancing around at the forest. "But I could get used to it again."

Sebastian's grin grew, his teeth bright against the glow of his skin. "I know you will. Come on. Let's head back. You should rest more. Maybe tonight you can join us to watch the fireflies. They light up the fields after dark. It's quite a sight."

"I'd like that," Dominic said, a warmth blooming in his chest. "Maybe we can have a drink, too. Do you guys have White Claw?"

Sebastian blinked, confused. "White bears? No. The mountains of Ungdor are too far for us to reach the ice beasts."

Dominic laughed, shaking his head. "Never mind. Let's just get something to eat. I'm starving."

Sebastian chuckled as they started walking. "I'd imagine so. Three days without food will do that. Maybe it's what's making you think this is all a dream."

Dominic smirked, though he couldn't quite deny it.

Maybe it was.

Chapter 21

Dominic tilted his head toward Sebastian, his brows furrowed with mild confusion as they entered the clearing. "So, what's this shindig you were talking about?" he asked, his tone light but tinged with curiosity.

Sebastian raised an eyebrow, the sharp arch meeting the shine of his smooth, sunlit forehead. His open shirt revealed just enough of his chest to catch the light, making the tiny beads of sweat glisten. He gave Dominic a perplexed look, his confusion reflected in his eyes.

"Shindig?"

"Never mind," Dominic muttered, shaking his head.

Sebastian's confusion faded, replaced by a faint smile as he caught on. "Ah, you mean the gathering we're having tonight?"

"That's the one," Dominic replied. "You said it's a get-together of sorts?"

Sebastian nodded. "It's nothing formal. Every so often, some workers bring food and we all share a meal and be merry. It's nice to unwind."

"That's something I can get behind," a voice chimed in from below. Calypso trotted through the tall grass beside them, his tail cutting through the golden stalks. His claws, however, dug into Dominic's sneakers when he cut in front of him, pricking his toes as he leapt up. "What's on the menu?"

Sebastian chuckled, his eyes twinkling with amusement. "We'll see what everyone can contribute. It's whatever people bring."

"Well," Calypso growled, "if there's salmon or chicken involved, I'll be sure to help clean the plate."

Dominic gave the cat a gentle nudge with his shoe and rolled his eyes. "You're lucky anyone feeds you at all."

As they walked, the barn came into view, its wooden siding blending with the muted tones of the workers' clothing. Despite the heat that reddened their faces, a group of women greeted Sebastian and Dominic. The older woman, dressed in a simple homespun dress with a faded floral pattern, studied Dominic. Every stitch of his denim ensemble caught her eye.

"I think we need to take him into town," she said to Sebastian. "He needs clothes that suit the rest of us."

Dominic frowned, brushing dried dirt from the knees of his jeans. "What's wrong with what I'm wearing?" he asked defensively, his hands clenching the fraying hem of his jacket.

"Everything," the woman said bluntly, though not unkindly with her salt-and-pepper eyebrow raised. "You'll stick out like a sore thumb."

"Agnes is not wrong," Sebastian agreed, his expression softer. "You'll need to blend in."

Dominic bristled at the suggestion. The idea of conforming to yet another set of expectations irritated him, dredging up memories of his days working as a receptionist for a law firm when he first moved to New York. Back then, no matter how neatly he dressed, how much he tried to fit in, he was always treated like an outsider—a young man without a college degree, looked down on by his more privileged coworkers. The thought of altering himself to fit in again left a bitter taste in his mouth.

"Do I really have to?" he asked, his voice strained. "I thought you said I needed rest."

"If you don't," Agnes interjected, "people will ask questions. You don't want them wondering where you're from. Not when you don't even know why you're here."

"Agnes is right. I guess rest will have to wait. If they find out how you got here," Sebastian added, his tone serious, "they might think you're crazy."

"Or worse," Agnes said, her voice dropping to a conspiratorial whisper. "They could lock you up in a tower, like that one girl."

Dominic's mind immediately flashed to the story. Rapunzel.

THE RIDE TO MYNNSHIRE Village was rougher than Dominic had expected. Uncomfortable on the horse, he held on to Sebastian's waist, his fingers digging deep into the man's shirt. The constant bumps and jolts caused him increasing pain, his groans evolving into exasperated yelps.

"Jesus!" Dominic exclaimed as the horse trotted over an uneven patch of ground. He winced, shifting in the saddle. "How do you deal with this?"

Sebastian glanced over his shoulder, his brow furrowed in confusion. "Deal with what?"

"I mean, there may be a time when I'd like to have kids someday, and this feels like a step in the wrong direction!" Dominic shot back.

Petunia and Giselle, two other servants riding beside them burst into laughter. Even Sebastian allowed himself a quiet chuckle, though his gaze remained focused on the road ahead.

"Don't have horses in...New York, you say?" Petunia teased, her cheeks appeared through her red hair and became rounder when she smiled.

"No," Dominic grumbled. "We have cabs and subways."

"Cabs?" Giselle repeated, her tone curious as her long, brown hair fluttered behind her. "Subways?"

Oh crap, I forgot!

"Don't worry about it," Dominic said, shaking his head. "Let's just say the horses smell better."

"Those things must be horrid beasts to ride!" Giselle exclaimed, horrified with her pale skin becoming lighter.

Depends on who's riding with you.

"Well, Sebastian has been a great trainer," Giselle said, winking at him. "He taught us how to ride when way back when we were young."

"It's the only way to get around," Petunia said sarcastically.

Passing by a field, Dominic's eyes widened at the sight of a bird that appeared close to an ostrich. Their feathers were a gradient blend of aqua and fuchsia. A young man waved at the three, holding the reins behind the animal as its foot-long beak clenched a tiller to slice up the tall grass.

"I'm going to guess that you haven't seen roxogals before either?" Sebastian asked with ease, the horse's trot causing no struggle for him.

"I guess I haven't," Dominic said, leaning closer to grab tight as his balance teetered to look at their neon yellow eyes. "I think we used horses to do this where I come from."

Giselle gasped, "You couldn't do that to these poor creatures!"

"They don't deserve that kind of treatment!" Petunia agreed.

"Sebastian, is this person still your friend after hearing about how they would treat your babies?" Giselle asked, biting her lip as she held on tight to Petunia.

"It's not like I had a say in what we did with them," Dominic defended, blood rushing with the buildings getting closer in sight.

The small group arrived in town not long after with silence taking over the rest of the trek. Dominic dismounted with difficulty, his legs wobbling like a newborn fawn as he tried to regain his footing. He grimaced, rubbing his thighs and glaring at the horse as though it had wronged him. They tethered their horses to a post near the marketplace with Giselle shedding a grin toward Sebastian as his focus remained with his fingers combing through their mane.

The marketplace was a sensory overload. Vibrant fabrics fluttered in the breeze, their rich colors a stark contrast to the muted tones of the workers' clothing. Vendors shouted over one another, advertising everything from fresh-baked bread to handmade jewelry. The scents of roasted nuts and honeyed pastries wafted through the air, mingling with the earthy aroma of the packed dirt beneath Dominic's boots.

"Ever seen anything like this?" Sebastian asked, his tone casual but curious.

Dominic shrugged. "Bodegas?"

Sebastian's brow furrowed in confusion, and Petunia and Giselle exchanged puzzled glances.

The group moved through the bustling crowd, weaving between clusters of townsfolk. Dominic's stomach growled as they passed a stall selling sizzling meat skewers. He tried to ignore it, but Calypso's muffled voice from the bag on his back made that impossible.

"We need food," the cat whined. "Now."

Dominic rolled his eyes, patting the bag. "We'll eat later."

"You're torturing me," Calypso grumbled dramatically. "It's been three days! I'm practically wasting away."

"Liar! They've fed you plenty while I was out!"

"They're the liars!"

"We'll figure something out," Petunia said, overhearing the exchange. "There are always favors to trade."

"Favors?" Dominic asked skeptically.

"Ella wanted to ensure no one went hungry," Sebastian explained. "People help each other out here. No one takes advantage of it."

Dominic nodded but didn't comment. The concept felt different to him—strangers helping one another without ulterior motives. It was hard to reconcile that kind of community with what he knew of the world. Not a single person in sight that would take advantage of someone for their service or possessions out of greed is something that he couldn't believe.

Dominic was nudged between two identical young men. Their strut reeked of arrogance as they turned back to him. Sunlight winked from the slicked surface of their blonde, polished hair. Their lips curled when they scoped Dominic's appearance, letting their sheathed swords trail behind them. It was just like being in high school all over again with jocks feeling like they run the hallways, their shoulders standing tall allowing the contours of their muscles to create tension through the seams of their coral suitcoats.

Townspeople approached Dominic one by one, each with their items to sell. Tight, desperate smiles were used to sell in order to support their families. The foods were tempting, and the animal hides were repulsive to him; not even in New York did he find that appealing. Through the middle of the crowd, a woman stopped him, her black hair glistening in the sunlight with curls that cascaded down her chest. The pea-colored blouse fluttered with the stems resting in her hands. Rose petals fell to her wooden clogs, saddened to part ways with the rest of their counterparts.

"Flowers for sale. Flowers for sale," the merchant said. "Would you like to buy some flowers?"

Dominic's smile was weak, looking at the beautiful arrangement of plants on her wagon. "These are so nice," he said, causing the merchant to nod with heightened energy. "I don't have any money, though."

"Oh, well that's unfortunate," the merchant said, her smile straightening.

"I really am sorry, though. I wish I could help you out."

The woman's cheeks flushed on her porcelain skin. Her brown, textured skirt brushed the ground when she walked back to her wagon. Placing down the roses, she picked up one of her carnations, her hands cradling over the petals with delicacy.

"How about a gift?" she asked, her shoulders relaxed with ease. "Because of how sweet you are."

Dominic's hands retreated from him the closer the flowers inched toward him. The beauty in the yellow and pink petals was so simplistic, it was something he could remind him to breathe even during times of uncertainty. He struggled as he looked at the citizens around her, passing by without a care to stop and admire nature's beauty that she'd taken the time to show.

"I don't think so," Dominic said softly. "Thank you anyway."

"I Insist," she said as she placed the plant in his hand with force. "You were so sweet to take the time to talk to me. And for that, I thank you."

"Okay," he said, his hand pricked from the edge of the stem when he grasped it.

"Have a lovely day."

The woman walked back to her cart, leaving him one last smile. The petals trembled each time the wheels of her wagon hit an uneven level of the cobblestone. Children stopped chasing each other to admire the plants, only to be stopped by their parents who kept them focused with not conversing with strangers. Dominic's smile tightened, placing the flower into his bag, tucking it into his shirt for safety before joining the rest of the group as they waited at the end of the street.

As they passed a jewelry shop, something caught Dominic's eye. A ruby pendant glinted in the sunlight, its gem refracting the light into tiny pools of scarlet that danced across the windowpane. He barely had time to admire it before a blur of movement crashed into him. Dominic stumbled backward, his arms flailing as he tried to catch himself. His palms hit the ground hard, and he groaned, brushing dirt and pebbles from his hands.

A young woman darted past him, the frayed threads of her embroidered skirt trailing behind her like a banner in the wind. She wore her hair in two buns, loose strands flying as she sprinted into an alley. She disappeared before Dominic could get a proper look at her face, though the icy blue of her eyes lingered in his mind.

"Stop her!" shouted the shopkeeper, bursting out of the store and pointing angrily in the direction the girl had gone.

Dominic glanced at Sebastian, who was already helping him to his feet. "Who was that?"

"No one knows her name," Sebastian said, his expression grim. "But she's been trouble for a while now."

"She has been the talk of the town for ages," Petunia added.

"Not a girl you want to be associated with," said Giselle, flourishing her comment with a wink.

"A thief," said Petunia.

"A killer!" said Giselle.

As the shopkeeper ranted about the girl's mischief, Dominic's gaze drifted back to the alley. A chill crept down his spine. Something about the girl felt familiar, though he couldn't place why. He brushed the thought aside as Sebastian gave him a gentle nudge.

"Come on," Sebastian said. "The seamster is waiting."

Dominic nodded absently, following the group but glancing back at the alley one last time.

"Please, be careful out there," the shopkeeper called after him. "Darkness has been creeping in, and it's closer than you think."

Chapter 22

A haze of dirty film on the windows obscured some of the sunlight, making the air heavy. Anticipation was felt in the muffled chatter of women passing by the stone walls. Dominic stepped into the shop, the weight of his body causing the floorboards to groan. He felt a fleeting surge of insecurity the lower the wood buckled.

Am I really that heavy? Or is this place just old?

He pushed the thought aside with a wry smile.

Gay culture's really messed with my head.

The anxiety of stepping into a clothing store brought him back to ChicFabAlliance. He anticipated that one customer to be at the counter ready to cause drama. One person had to be there to jeopardize his future with selfish behavior. Every world, even those without cars or skyscrapers, includes entitled people.

His musing faded as the space opened up before him, and his breath caught. Color exploded in every direction. The fabric bolts lining the shelves glowed, every shade of the rainbow represented in rich textures and intricate patterns. Silks glistened like moonlight shimmering from under water, brocades gleamed with threads of gold and silver, and velvets begged to be touched by admiring hands. Dominic's eyes widened. It was like stepping into a dream—or maybe heaven.

The possibilities overwhelmed him. Gone was the neutral monotony of his wardrobe back in New York. No more jeans and understated shirts designed to avoid offending anyone's sensibilities. Here, every piece was loud, unapologetic, and dripping with personality. It was as if every pride parade had manifested into fabric.

Dominic let out a quiet, awestruck, "Wow."

"Beautiful, isn't it?" Petunia said, stepping beside him. She seemed just as enraptured by the textiles, her fingers grazing the edges of a vibrant floral print.

"If only we could afford it," Giselle said flatly, her tone dropping like a stone and killing the mood.

"I would love to make a dress out of this," Petunia whined, her hand caressing the yellow chiffon, imagining the red hair to compliment the sunny delight.

"That would look so beautiful on you, Petunia," Sebastian said with a smirk.

"I would kill for a new dress!" Giselle said.

Dominic's stomach sank. Giselle wasn't wrong. He didn't have a dime to his name—not here, anyway. Even if he emptied his pockets of every bill and coin, he doubted these people would accept American currency; these people probably had no idea who George Washington was. He let out a heavy sigh, a mixture of longing and resignation.

Just once, he thought as looked at the textures of the tulle fabrics. *Just once, I'd love to wear something like this. Something bold, something that feels like me. Something that lets me show the world who I really am.*

He dragged his gaze away from the bold fabrics, folding his arms across his chest. "Guess I'll keep dreaming," he muttered under his breath.

Sebastian, standing nearby, cleared his throat. "Good afternoon, Mister Gloomis," he said, addressing the tailor at the counter.

The tailor looked up from his work, his thick spectacles glinting in the sunlight streaming through the window. "Good afternoon," he replied, his voice smooth and measured. "What can I help you with today?"

Sebastian gestured toward Dominic. "This young man here needs some clothes. Anything you could spare would be greatly appreciated."

Dominic's lips twitched into a small, grateful smile. *Young man? Bless your heart, Sebastian.*

"Anything to help get him out of this would be fantastic!" Giselle said, her hand brushing a clump of dirt from the jacket.

The tailor turned his attention to Dominic, his eyes narrowing as he took in his appearance. Dominic immediately felt self-conscious with his body locking up, standing there in his well-worn denim jacket and scuffed sneakers. Gloomis moved closer, his inspection as intense as a jeweler's assessment of a rare diamond.

"Son," Gloomis said at last, his voice tinged with confusion, "what on earth are you wearing?"

Dominic hesitated, unsure how to explain modern fashion to someone who clearly lived in a pre-industrial world. He wasn't sure that discussing *Vogue* or *Elle* magazine with people that churned butter out of their windmills would make sense. Before he could respond, Gloomis reached out, his hands brushing over the denim of Dominic's jacket. His fingers trailed along the seams, lingering on the stitching like a scientist studying an alien artifact.

"So immaculate. So brilliant!" Gloomis exclaimed, his eyes widening. "Where do you get such fine clothing?"

"Isn't it weird?" Petunia added, her head popping over Dominic's shoulder, interrupting Gloomis's admiration.

"It's a long story," Sebastian interjected. "But do you think you can help us? He needs something more suited to...this place."

Gloomis's expression brightened, his grin stretching so wide it made Dominic take an instinctive step back. There was something unsettling about the way the tailor looked at him—as if Dominic were both a mystery to unravel and a prize to claim.

"I think I can spare a frock or two," Gloomis said finally, his tone dripping with faux magnanimity.

"For a price," he added.

Dominic's stomach twisted. *Here we go,* he thought. *What's the catch?*

His mind raced through worst-case scenarios, from being overcharged to being asked for something far less savory. His fingers fidgeted as he blurted, "What do you want?"

"The jacket," Gloomis said simply.

Dominic stiffened, clutching the hem of his beloved jacket. "Not my jacket!" he exclaimed. "I worked hard for this—it's like armor for me! I don't want to give it up."

"Please, get rid of it," Petunia joked.

"Cut it up! Cut it up!" Giselle added, chuckling.

Gloomis raised a calming hand. "Not to keep, my child. Just to rejuvenate. I can tell that this piece has seen better days and it would be an honor to restore this into something amazing."

Dominic frowned and gazed down at the garment. At first glance, it seemed fine, but as his eyes roved over it, he noticed the damage—frayed edges, small tears in the collar, and a sizable hole near the shoulder seam. His heart sank. The jacket had been with him through so much. It wasn't just clothing; it was a symbol of his resilience, his connection to the life he'd built for himself back in New York.

"What do you mean by rejuvenate?" Dominic asked cautiously. "Can't you just repair it?"

Gloomis's eyes gleamed with excitement. "I'll use the material to create something new—something that allows you to fit in here without losing the essence of this incredible piece."

Dominic hesitated, his hands trembling as they ran over the familiar fabric. Memories flooded his mind: the day his first roommate gave him the jacket, the way it made him feel like he could take on the world, the countless nights it had shielded him from the cold in more ways than one. Walking down the streets for the first time, swaying his hips like a model in Fashion Week was one of the happiest moments of his adult life. Letting it go felt like shedding a part of himself.

"Let it go, Dominic," Sebastian said gently. His voice was steady and reassuring, like the calm before a storm. "It's just a jacket."

Dominic met Sebastian's gaze, the sincerity in those green eyes softening the knot of anxiety in his chest. With a deep breath, he nodded. "Okay," he whispered. "But you better do it justice."

Gloomis's grin widened. "You won't be disappointed."

As the tailor whisked the jacket away, Calypso poked his head out of Dominic's bag, letting out a small yawn. "Make sure you clean it, too," the cat added nonchalantly. "I shed a lot."

Dominic shot him a sharp look. "Now's not the time, Calypso."

Gloomis chuckled and disappeared into the back room, leaving Dominic standing amidst the sea of colorful fabrics. Despite his apprehension, a flicker of excitement sparked in his chest. For the first time in a long while, he felt the promise of transformation—not just in his clothing, but in himself.

Dominic took a breath and stepped forward, fixing his gaze on the tailor as he gathered the courage to ask. "Sir, I have one more question for you."

The tailor, already busy examining the fabric bolts on his counter, turned toward him with a curious raise of his thick brows. "Yes?" he asked.

Dominic hesitated, running his fingers over a nearby roll of rich, woven fabric, its deep jewel hues glimmering faintly in the shop's light. "How much would it cost if you made something more formal for me? From scratch. Something with these kinds of fabrics."

"Formal, you say?" The tailor set Dominic's worn denim jacket aside and walked over, joining him at the shelf of materials. He studied the fabrics Dominic had been admiring and then shifted his sharp gaze back to him.

Dominic couldn't help but compare the man's attention to the fashion designers he'd occasionally glimpsed back in New York—not the big-name elites, but the fresh graduates with unrelenting creativity. There was a similar glimmer in this man's eyes, a spark of inspiration ready to burst forth. One that was ready to follow their creative vision as opposed to compromising to a company for the sake of survival.

"These types of projects are often quite costly," the tailor admitted after a moment, his tone apologetic but firm. "I'm afraid I couldn't do this free of charge."

Before Dominic could respond, Sebastian chimed in. "That's okay. Dominic doesn't need something like this at the moment." His voice was calm but definitive, and it made Dominic's shoulders stiffen.

Thanks for speaking for me, Sebastian, Dominic thought sourly, though he knew the man had a point. It wasn't like he had a reason to dress up. The grand festival that had defined Cinderella's story had already happened. Ella was in her castle now, and Dominic was just an outlier in her world, with no prince waiting for him at the end of any party.

But then Mister Gloomis's eyes lit up. "Well, there is the anniversary festival coming up in a couple of days," the tailor said.

"Oh," Sebastian said, his tone casual. "I forgot about that."

"Yes, the anniversary festival!" Petunia exclaimed, clasping her hands together with a dreamy sigh.

Dominic blinked. "Okay, someone's going to have to explain. What is this anniversary festival?"

"It's a celebration," Giselle said with a smile, stepping closer. "A way for everyone in the community to come together and remember how things came to be. A way to start over."

"With their true love," Petunia added, her voice filled with wistful admiration as she noticed Giselle shedding a warm glance at Sebastian.

Dominic frowned. "A party?" Social gatherings had never been his strong suit. Back in New York, invitations rarely came his way, and even when they did, he always felt like the odd one out—too awkward, too unsure of himself to really belong. Not even his beloved jacket, which made him feel invincible, could grant him the kind of confidence required for such events.

"It's okay, guys," Dominic said quietly, his tone laced with resignation. "I don't need to go to this party. I'm not from here and I haven't been invited. And besides, I can't afford anything formal, anyway."

But as he spoke, his hand slipped into his bag, searching for nothing in particular. His fingers brushed against something smooth and cold, unlike anything else he'd packed. He pulled it out carefully, his eyes widening as the object caught the light streaming through the window.

A ruby pendant.

The gem gleamed, its fiery red facets throwing tiny sparks of light onto the walls. Dominic stared at it, dumbfounded. He didn't remember packing anything remotely like this. His mind raced back to the girl who had barreled into him earlier, the one who had fled from the jewelry shopkeeper.

Could this have fallen into my bag during the chaos?

His stomach churned. He didn't like the idea of using something stolen, even unknowingly, to get ahead. But as he looked around at the tailor's eager expression and his companions' hopeful faces, another thought crept in.

What do I have to lose?

It wasn't like anyone knew he had the gem, and the shopkeeper surely assumed the girl still had it. The people don't know of him either, so it may not hurt to use it if his identity is anonymous. Plus, his sapphire necklace was out of the question; there was too much value to it now that the rest of his belongings had been reduced to mush.

"How about this?" Dominic said, holding out the ruby.

The air in the room seemed to still. The ruby's vibrant glow reflected in the wide eyes of everyone present. Mister Gloomis's mouth fell open, and for a moment, Dominic wondered if the man would faint. The tailor reached out with trembling hands, taking the gem as if it were the most precious thing he'd ever touched. He turned it over, inspecting every angle, his grin growing wider and wider until it threatened to split his face in two.

"Magnificent," he whispered. "With this, I'll make you more than just one outfit. Come back tomorrow, and I'll have everything ready."

"My goodness, strange one!" Giselle said, her hand fluttering over her chest. "You do come from money after all!"

Before Dominic could process what had happened, Gloomis rushed to the shop's entrance and flipped the sign to "Closed," shooing away two girls who had just arrived. The disgruntled pair muttered curses—some familiar, others strange—as they stomped away, their ruffled skirts swishing like storm clouds.

"Thank you," Dominic said, his voice a mix of relief and exhilaration. "Thank you so much!"

"Could you share a little of that wealth to buy some of that fabric for my dress?" Petunia asked, her eyebrow raised to a serious point.

But as Dominic turned back to Sebastian and the others, he noticed their expressions. Petunia and Giselle looked uneasy, their excitement tempered by something else. Sebastian's smirk had vanished, replaced by a pensive frown. Dominic thought that people who wanted him to blend in would be supportive of his new venture. Maybe the idea of a look to conform with them would've been something that could've brought ease.

"I'll just need to take your measurements," Gloomis said, interrupting Dominic's thoughts. "Step over here."

Dominic walked to the center of the room with a spring in his step, the excitement of getting a new look erasing his concerns. There was never an opportunity that presented itself where he could have something custom made for him. Items that were too tight or baggy was something he was used to since he was in between sizes. He spread his arms and legs wide, eager to see what the tailor would create. For the first time in what felt like forever, he was excited about something—really, genuinely excited. The opportunity to have something made for him made his heart flutter; this was beyond using the small employee discount at ChicFabAlliance.

The tape measure traced over his arms and chest, Gloomis muttering numbers under his breath for memory. Dominic barely noticed. His mind was already spinning with possibilities, imagining himself in a dazzling ensemble that rivaled anything he'd ever seen in fashion magazines.

Then the tape measure dipped between his legs.

Dominic's enthusiasm faltered as Gloomis knelt to check the inseam, the thin tape brushing against his inner thigh. His knees buckled slightly, and his face flushed a deep crimson as the others stifled laughter.

"There's the moment I was dreading," Dominic muttered under his breath, casting an embarrassed glance at Sebastian, whose mouth twitched in amusement.

"Take it in, you guys," Dominic added with a groan, his voice dripping with sarcasm. "Enjoy the show. I deserve this."

As Gloomis finished and stood, Dominic tried to shake off the awkwardness, reminding himself that the result would be worth it. Whatever the tailor created, it was bound to be spectacular. If he was going to fit in to their society, at least he was going to do it his way.

Chapter 23

FROM THE PAGES OF THE STORYBOOK
Ella

LAST NIGHT IN THE ATTIC was one of the worst I've endured yet. The wind howled mercilessly, pushing through every crack in the walls with icy ferocity. My small frame trembled beneath the bitter breeze. You'd think giving Evangeline and Aurelia my room—my warm, cozy room—would warrant some shred of generosity in return, perhaps even a blanket or a pillow.

But of course, it didn't.

Most nights, I can endure it. The chill cools my body after a long day of scrubbing, hauling, and toiling to keep their lives as comfortable as possible. But last night was different. Last night was a cruel parody of winter—freezing temperatures without the courtesy of snow to soften its bite. Even the birds that usually share my attic fled to warmer nooks, leaving me alone beneath a gaping hole in the roof large enough to converse with the full moon.

I couldn't take it anymore.

I dragged myself down to the kitchen, seeking the fire. The stone floor was rough and unyielding, but it was warm. That was all I needed. I laid myself as close to the embers as I dared, stretching my aching limbs and letting the heat soak into my skin. For a few precious hours, I slept—deeply, dreamlessly. For once, the cold did not jolt me awake. And in those fleeting moments, I could almost feel whole again.

I WOKE FAR LATER THAN usual. The sun was already high, streaming through the cracks in the shutters and highlighting the fading embers of the fire. My body protested as I sat up, every muscle stiff and sore from sleeping on stone. A sharp yawn escaped my lips, musty with the taste of morning breath. Before I could shake the grogginess, the kitchen door burst open with a deafening slam.

Three shadows loomed at the top of the staircase.

Mirelle, clad in a flowing silk, plum nightgown, stood in the center like a queen surveying her kingdom. Her impeccably groomed brow arched high, her lips curling into a sneer. Aurelia and Evangeline flanked her, their coifed hair bobbing as they exchanged theatrical looks of disgust. They were like carrion birds, hungry for a fresh corpse.

"Sleeping on the job now, are we?" Mirelle's voice was sharp, cutting through the silence like a whip.

"No, Madam," I stammered, trying to explain. "It was too cold in my room."

Mirelle hated when I called her by her name. She loathed "Mother" even more. I would never dream of calling her that. That title belonged to one person alone—the woman who gave me life, kindness, and love.

And, lucky for her, she never had to meet Mirelle.

"Don't talk back to me with your excuses, child!" Mirelle hissed, her tone laced with venom.

"Yes, Madam," I murmured, lowering my gaze.

My knees cracked like brittle wood as I rose to my feet, the dull ache in my legs making it clear I'd spent far too long on the hard floor. My stomach churned, both from hunger and nerves.

"Let me fix you some breakfast," I offered hastily, reaching for the kettle. My hands trembled as I filled it with water from the bucket, droplets splashing onto the counter. The burlap sack of flour felt heavy as I hauled it to the table.

"She hasn't even started breakfast!" Evangeline whined, her manicured finger jabbing the air in my direction.

"We're going to starve, Mother!" Aurelia added, clutching her stomach dramatically. "I can't live like this!"

Mirelle descended the stairs with the grace of a predator, her cane tapping the floor with each deliberate step. She came to a stop in front of me, her icy green eyes locking onto mine. I tried not to flinch under her scrutiny, but her gaze was as piercing as a blade.

"Child," she said, her voice low, "what is that on your face?"

"My face?" I echoed, confused.

I reached up, my fingers brushing against my cheeks. They came away dusty with ash and dirt. I glanced at the bucket of water, catching a blurry reflection of myself. Beneath the grime, I saw the dark circles under my eyes, the weariness etched into my features. I barely recognized myself.

"You're filthy!" Evangeline crowed, laughing cruelly.

"I cannot have my servants looking so unpresentable," Mirelle said, her tone dripping with disdain. "What is this?"

Servants? You only have me, so deal with it.

"It must be from the fire," Aurelia offered, snickering behind her hand.

"Cinders!" Evangeline exclaimed with glee. "She's covered in cinders!"

"Girls," Mirelle said softly, waving a hand. "Go set the table for breakfast. We must make sacrifices and serve ourselves just this once, since this ungrateful brat can't manage even the simplest tasks."

Their mocking laughter echoed as they disappeared into the corridor. Mirelle's expression hardened as she turned back to me, her cane tapping with impatience.

"Now listen to me, you ungrateful wretch," she snarled. "I have shown you kindness by allowing you to stay in this house. Given you food, clothing, a roof over your head. And this is how you repay me? With laziness?"

Her words stung, each one a dagger aimed at my heart. My fists clenched at my sides, nails digging into my palms. Kindness? The food I received was scraps. The clothes I wore were threadbare and barely held together by stretching fibers and my sewing whenever I'd had a moment to repair them. The roof over my head was a drafty attic with a gaping hole that continues to get bigger with every relentless storm.

"I will not tolerate complacency!" Mirelle continued, her voice rising. "Do you want me to throw you out into the cold forever? Do you want me to banish you from this house?"

Before I could respond, her hand struck my cheek. Pain exploded across my face, the force of the blow making me stagger. My eyes stung with tears, but I blinked them back, refusing to let her see me cry.

"Do you understand me, little girl?" she demanded, her voice venomous.

"Yes, Madam," I whispered, my voice barely audible.

"Good." Her lips curled into a satisfied smirk. "As punishment, you will sit out this meal and the next three. Finish cooking and make it presentable."

With that, she swept out of the kitchen, her cane clicking against the floor as she ascended the stairs. Triumph filled her parting glance, as though she'd won some unspoken battle.

I turned back to the table, my hands trembling as I kneaded the biscuit dough. The tears I'd held back fell, mixing with the flour and water. Each tear was a fragment of my spirit, another piece of my heart chipped away by her cruelty.

"Stay strong," I told myself. "Do it for Mother."

I slammed my fists into the dough, imagining Mirelle's sneering face with every punch. The satisfaction was fleeting, but it was enough to keep me going. The kitchen echoed with the sound of my frustration, each strike on the table a silent rebellion. Perhaps this was a healthy way of blowing off some steam. Even the sweat trickling down my forehead was starting to clean off the cinders that created my new identity.

I need to make biscuits more often!

LATER THAT MORNING, after my family had ravenously devoured the tea and biscuits I had prepared, I found myself dusting the curtains in the sitting room. Each swipe of the rod sent plumes of dust swirling into the sunlight, revealing the vibrant colors and patterns buried under grime. My arms ached, but at least I could see the results of my labor.

Out of the corner of my eye, Aurelia appeared, sauntering through the room with a plate in her hand. She licked it clean with exaggerated gusto, her tongue sweeping over the porcelain to ensure not a single crumb escaped her.

Taste my tears, *I thought bitterly.* Taste every single one of them.

"Cinderella!" Mirelle's voice cut through the moment like a blade.

"Cinderella!" Evangeline echoed, her high-pitched whine grating on my nerves.

The peace of the morning shattered as their commands began piling on, each more demanding than the last.

"Cinderella, my sheets need to be washed!"

"Cinderella, help me tighten my corset!"

"Cinderella, polish my shoes!"

The hollering never stopped. If they weren't bellowing my name, they rang that awful brass bell. I dreamed of snatching it from their hands and tossing it into the fireplace. Or better yet, if I could pocket their voices for just one day, silence would be a sweet reprieve.

But it wouldn't happen. Not in this life.

I moved to the grand entrance, kneeling at the base of the marble structure. Grime had dulled the once-beautiful green swirls in the stone, and it cried out for polish. I scrubbed furiously, the rag in my hand becoming blackened with dirt. My knees ached from the hard floor, and I could already feel tomorrow's bruises forming.

As I worked, I focused on the task, ignoring the beauty of the pewter-blue walls and coral accents around me. My reflection emerged faintly on the marble, a ghostly outline of myself staring back. The cleanliness is always a reminder that I'm the only one left in my family in this house.

Then came a sudden, thunderous sound.

THUMP! THUMP! THUMP!

The door reverberated under the weight of heavy knocks, sending vibrations through the quiet house. A lone vase on the mantle trembled, and even the chickens outside went silent, their clucking abruptly cut off.

Pushing myself up, I approached the door. My arms strained as I pulled it open, the heavy wood resisting after years of wear. Two men stood before me, both in resplendent baby-blue military jackets. Their epaulets gleamed in the sunlight, the gold polished to perfection. I caught a distorted glimpse of myself in one man's monocle—a soot-streaked face, the very picture of exhaustion.

"*Good morning,*" *said the other man, whose voice carried the practiced weight of someone accustomed to delivering proclamations. "By the decree of His Majesty the King, we bring joyous news."*

I blinked, unsure of how this involved me. Nothing has been joyous for a long time.

"The prince has decided it is time to find a suitor," the man continued, his voice resonating with grandeur. "A worthy maiden who will join him in ruling the kingdom."

The prince? What did that have to do with me?

"This will not be an ordinary selection process," the man added with a flourish. "The king has decreed that all eligible maidens in the land are to be invited to a grand festival, a celebration of the kingdom and its future."

The word "festival" lit a spark within me. My heart quickened, and I felt a small, long-forgotten thrill stir in my chest. The man handed me a thick envelope, sealed with the royal crest. I hesitated for a moment before accepting it, my hands trembling as I held the weighty parchment.

"Dress to impress," the man said, nodding. "Good day."

As they turned and strode back to their horses, I curtsied, murmuring, "Good day."

The moment they were gone, my heart leapt. A festival! An actual festival! For as long as I could remember, I'd dreamed of something—anything—to break the monotony of my life. A chance to dress up, to leave this house, to dance and forget the weight of my chores for a single night.

I rushed back inside, my excitement carrying me up the freshly polished staircase two steps at a time. My hand slipped along the banister, still slick with the sheen of my work. The hallways seemed narrower as I ran, the walls pressing in, but I didn't care. This was a chance for something wonderful.

At the end of the hall, the discordant sound of a wailing voice shattered my momentary joy. Aurelia was humming a tune, one that nobody could understand with every note being flat and harsh like a torturous screech. Evangeline was practicing her arts—or at least that's what Stepmother called it. Her hand grabbed the paintbrush with hairs pelting the canvas. Her attempt at replicating the fruit basket was a mere blob as though her fingers smeared across the fabric. To me, it was more torture than talent. I proceed further into the room, barely suppressing my annoyance. Evangeline slammed her hands onto the keys, glaring at me.

"Cinderella! We're practicing!" she barked.

"You're interrupting our studies!" Aurelia whined, her face twisted in irritation.

Mirelle rose from her chair in the corner, her expression darkening as she approached. Her cane thudded against the floor, each step like a countdown to punishment. She raised it slightly, her intent clear.

"Madam," I said quickly, throwing up my hands in defense. "I have news! News from the castle!"

Mirelle stopped mid-step, her sharp gaze narrowing. "The castle?"

"Yes, the king," I explained, holding up the envelope. "He's inviting all the eligible maidens in the land to a festival. A grand festival for the prince to find a wife."

The room fell silent for a moment. Then Evangeline and Aurelia erupted into high-pitched squeals, their excitement nearly deafening.

"A festival? For the prince?" Evangeline exclaimed, her voice shrill with anticipation.

Mirelle snatched the envelope from my hands, her eyes scanning its contents with practiced precision. She rubbed her thumb over the royal seal, ensuring its authenticity. Slowly, a sly grin spread across her face.

"Girls," she said, her voice low and deliberate, "this is our chance. You must look your best. The prince will not choose just anyone."

The sisters erupted into a frenzy, rushing to the wardrobe and pulling out dresses, accessories, and anything else they deemed worthy of the occasion. Every outfit that I've repaired has now become a weapon to seduce royalty. The room became a whirlwind of silk and lace, their piercing voices competing as they fought over what to wear.

"Cinderella," Mirelle said sharply, pulling me back into reality. "Go to the seamster. Place an order for three new dresses—one for each of us. And be quick about it."

"Three?" I repeated, my heart soaring for a moment. "Thank you, Madam! I—"

"Not for you, silly girl!" she snapped, cutting me off. "For me and my daughters. Did you honestly think you'd be going to the festival?"

I froze, the weight of her words crashing over me. "But the invitation said all maidens—"

"And you think the prince would waste his time on a servant girl like you?" she sneered. "The very idea is an insult to the kingdom."

Aurelia and Evangeline giggled behind her, their cruel laughter echoing in my ears.

"Now, hurry along," Mirelle commanded. "The seamster will need our measurements."

I turned to leave, clutching the envelope of money as I descended the stairs—my father's money—what was left of it. Their mocking voices followed me, growing quieter as I moved further away. By the time I reached the door, my chest felt heavy, the excitement I'd felt earlier crushed beneath the weight of their disdain.

It was worth a try.

Chapter 24

Dominic

GETTING NAKED AT THE atelier to try on these clothes was about as awkward as I expect—maybe worse. It reminds me of the locker room at the local gym for the small moment when I could afford it, which I've always hated. Too much testosterone, too many egos. The weight room was even worse. There, it was a battlefield of unnecessary competition, with every guy trying to out-lift the others to assert some primal dominance.

It was all about aesthetics—bulging muscles straining against tank tops, veins popping like they were part of the workout routine. For some, it was probably about testing the steroids they'd been taking; for others, it was clearly to show off to someone—and, of course, to get laid.

At one point in my life, I'd found all of that attractive. But over time, it became demoralizing. Watching them parade around the locker room, naked and self-satisfied, lost its appeal. Especially when they would record themselves flexing in their underwear in front of the mirror with other people changing in the background, no matter how illegal or gross it was. The allure of perfectly carved muscles gave way to something else: a sense of disgust, maybe jealousy, and definitely exhaustion.

So, yeah, changing in front of people? Not my idea of fun.

They're all respectful enough to turn away while I undress, but it still feels creepy. The whole time, I can't stop wondering if they're imagining what I look like under my clothes. Even with tight shirts and jeans, which leave little to the imagination, it feels like being under a microscope. My metabolism has blessed me with a bit of a slender build, but it's not perfect. And in a community that can be hypercritical of appearances at times, I've become my own harshest critic.

Gays can be such bitches sometimes.

I could never look like Sebastian, with his perfect balance of muscle and body hair—at least as far as I've seen. Why does this bother me, though? Why do I care what he thinks about my body? It's not like I even know if he's into people like me. But that doesn't stop me from worrying.

I shove my legs into the pants and pull the blouse over my head, struggling a bit with the voluminous sleeves. Looking at myself in the mirror, I grimace. This is...going to take some getting used to. The blouse is a deep plum color—not a shade I'd pick for myself—and the sleeves puff out dramatically before tapering at the cuffs. It gave off a weird "corporate worker from another century" vibe. The pants are slightly better. They're fitted, at least, which is something I'm used to, but the Sherlock Holmes-style tartan plaid makes me queasy.

And then there are the shoes. I'm not ready to part with my sneakers. Like my jacket, they're a part of me, an extension of my identity. Sneakers give me the kind of edge I didn't have naturally, making me look rebellious even if I don't feel it. They're armor for my self-confidence—something I'm trying to build.

I turn toward the group, my shoulders hunched so high they nearly brushed my ears. "So, what do y'all think?" I ask, the fabric of my sleeves sagging in folds, dangling from my arms like loose, unwanted skin.

They all turn to look at me, their expressions unreadable. Silence. Weird, given that the girls always have something to say. But this time? Nothing.

Even Sebastian, who usually seems more open, gives me this strained grin. It was the kind of smile I've seen on my ex's face whenever he pretends to support one of my ideas while silently judging me. It stings.

The only person who reacts genuinely is the seamster. His face lights up the way an artist does when they see their work appreciated for the first time. He practically skips to me, snipping at stray threads hanging from the hem and running his hands over the fabric to check the fit.

Of course, an excuse to get all up in my business again.

This time, though, I don't feel as weird about it. Sure, his hands darting around to feel the seams make me tense, but I can focus on something else: Sebastian.

What's with that smile? It looks so forced. Did I do something wrong? Did I say something to upset him? Or is it that I just looked ridiculous? I can't tell, but it nags at me.

"Perfect fit," the seamster says, pulling back to admire his handiwork. He beams at me, clearly pleased. "You wear it well, my dear."

I try to smile back, but my heart isn't in it. Instead, I glance over at Sebastian again, hoping for something. A genuine smile. A nod of approval. Anything. But he's looking away, talking with Petunia and Giselle.

Maybe I shouldn't care what he thinks. Maybe it doesn't matter. But I do care. And that scares me more than I want to admit.

Chapter 25

Sebastian

SOMETHING ABOUT DOMINIC feels off.

At first, I thought his confusion was endearing. Watching him fumble through our world, the way his brow furrowed with uncertainty—it was captivating. It made him seem so genuine, so refreshingly unpolished compared to everyone else I know. His clothes, strange as they were, added to the intrigue. I'm curious to know what a Calvin Klein is. I'd never seen anything like them before, not on anyone outside the farm, and certainly not here in town. They made him stand out, not just because they were different, but because they seemed to carry a story, a history.

That jacket of his—I don't know why, but it struck me. It made him seem tough, like someone who could take on anything. It's the kind of strength I'd always tried to embody but had never really felt. And yet, when he spoke, when his guard dropped just a little, there was a vulnerability there. He wasn't as invincible as that jacket made him seem. He was afraid, unsure of himself, and that drew me in more than I expected. It made me realize that in some ways, he's a lot like me.

Different from what people assume on the surface.

Petunia and Giselle don't see it. They talk about him when he's not around, their sharp whispers like daggers aimed at his character. It frustrates me, their willingness to judge someone they don't even know. But their words only make me want to help him more. Maybe it's my protective instinct kicking in—after all, it's my job to keep everyone at the farm safe. But with Dominic, it feels personal. Like I'm meant to be there for him, somehow.

Even now, as he adjusts to his new clothing, I can't help but smile—at least, inwardly. He's clearly uncomfortable, tugging at the blouse like it's some kind of troll's garment. Watching him try to blend into our society is almost heartwarming. He's trying, even if it's clumsy, and that effort says a lot about him.

But I can't let my smile show. Not this time.

Because something isn't sitting right.

I know what's in his bag. I saw it winking at me earlier—something I had to do, to be sure he wasn't a danger to the farm or the people on it. The ruby, shining brightly in his clothes, stood out like a beacon. The jewel wasn't in his bag when he first showed up. It wasn't his. I'm certain of it.

I had hoped—expected, even—that he would do the right thing. That he would return it to its rightful owner. He seems so honest, so grounded. We seem alike in that way—humble, hardworking, taking pride in earning what we have. But now, seeing how he used the gem to secure clothes from Mister Gloomis, I'm not so sure. Did he mean to use it as a bargaining chip all along? Was it an act of desperation? Or was there something darker at play?

I can't tell. And that uncertainty gnaws at me.

Part of me wants to believe the best in him. That he got caught up in this unfamiliar world and didn't know what else to do. But another part of me—call it instinct, or caution—can't let it go. I have to protect the farm, the people here, from the dangers that creep into our land. And those dangers don't always come with sharp claws and glowing eyes. Sometimes, they come as strangers with secrets.

Is Dominic one of them? Is he dangerous?

I hope not. I want to believe he's not. But right now, I'm a little guarded. I have to be.

And yet, even with all this doubt swirling in my mind, I find myself wanting to know him more. To understand what brought him here, to peel back the layers of his strange, guarded self. There's a spark of something in him—a kind of honesty, a quiet strength—that I can't ignore.

But for now, I can't let my guard down. Not yet. Not until I know who Dominic really is.

Chapter 26

The ride through the countryside was excruciatingly awkward. Nobody would make eye contact with Dominic. Even Petunia and Giselle, who had never stopped talking since the moment he met them, were uncharacteristically quiet. The thick, uncomfortable silence replaced all the chatter.

"Well, that was fun," Dominic said as he ignored a couple of people passing by.

"Yes, it was," Petunia said, her hand squeezing Giselle's body.

"And that Mister Gloomis guy was pretty nice."

"He is," added Sebastian softly.

The dismissiveness stung, even more than the discomfort of his body being squished against the saddle. His legs ached, his back throbbed, and the saddle still wasn't kind to certain parts of his anatomy. With all his discomfort, he couldn't shake the feeling that he'd done something wrong.

Sure, using the gem as a bargaining chip wasn't his proudest moment, but what choice did he have? He had no money here—or back in his own world, for that matter. They'd been adamant that he needed to look like one of them, to blend in and avoid suspicion. What was he supposed to do? Walk around in his ripped jacket and sneakers while everyone stared? The thought of cutting holes in a burlap sack to wear as a shirt made his skin itch.

He'd done what he had to do.

Still, the heavy weight of judgment hung over him as they rode through the hilly plains, leaving the town behind. What Dominic expected to be a typical countryside landscape quickly transformed into something magical. Gnomes darted through the grass, chattering in a language he couldn't understand. Fae zipped through the air, their wings shimmering like fragments of a rainbow. Even the trees seemed alive—one ancient-looking trunk groaned as it stretched its branches like a sleepy giant, its moss glistened with dew.

Same, Dominic thought, letting out a tired sigh.

Further ahead, windmills spun lazily in the breeze, their hypnotic rhythm lulling him into a near-dreamlike state. His grip on Sebastian tightened as his head nodded forward, dangerously close to dozing off. He forced himself to stay awake, though, biting the inside of his cheek to focus.

After what felt like an eternity of trotting, they finally arrived at their destination. A sprawling gathering had taken shape in the open fields, with groups of people milling about. Sebastian dismounted first and turned back to offer Dominic a steadying hand.

"Careful," Sebastian said, his voice unusually soft.

Dominic accepted the help, grateful for the support. As he slid off the saddle, his legs felt like jelly, and he staggered. Sebastian caught his arm to steady him, his touch firm and reassuring.

"Thanks," Dominic muttered, avoiding his gaze.

Petunia and Giselle had already rushed off, giggling and hugging a cluster of other young women nearby. They exchanged whispers and pointed in Dominic's direction, their laughter carrying just enough to prick his ears. Dominic's stomach twisted.

High school all over again, he thought bitterly.

Children played tag in the distance, their shrieks of joy punctuating the otherwise calm gathering. Calypso, unsurprisingly, made a beeline for a nearby fire where the smell of charred meat wafted through the air, joining a teenage boy who was monitoring the temperature. Dominic watched his cat with envy, his stomach growling, but he couldn't bring himself to join the others. The sting of being an outsider was too fresh.

Instead, he spotted a lone tree atop a hill, its branches wide and inviting. He trudged toward it, passing by Agnes who was preparing the vegetables on the table with a pair of elders who were deep in conversation while enjoying the fiddler's song. As he was taking a swig from his water bottle, the lukewarm liquid did little to soothe his parched throat, but he didn't care. At least up there, he could be alone. As Dominic climbed the hill, he cast a glance back at the crowd. The people below were a cohesive community—cooking, laughing, comforting one another. They were like a family. Dominic's chest ached with longing.

"I want that."

He sank to the ground beneath the tree's shade, leaning his back against the trunk. A gentle breeze rustled the leaves above, and one of the smaller branches swayed toward him, brushing his shoulder like a comforting pat. Dominic let out a shaky breath. The weight of everything hit him at once. He wasn't going home anytime soon. He wasn't even sure if home existed anymore. The thought was a sharp knife twisting in his gut. Tears welled in his eyes and spilled down his cheeks before he could stop them. His limbs felt heavy, his chest hollow.

Maybe it wouldn't be so bad to just...fade away here.

"Looks like you could use some company," came a familiar voice.

Dominic flinched, hastily wiping his face. He turned to see Sebastian approaching, the food on a plate balanced in his hands. The sight of the turkey leg and roasted vegetables made Dominic's stomach twist again, but this time with hunger.

"I'm not hungry," Dominic lied, his voice hoarse and his stomach grumbling.

Sebastian gave him a knowing smile, crouching down beside him. "You've had a rough couple of days. Trust me, this will help."

Dominic hesitated, but the warmth in Sebastian's gaze melted some of his resistance. Reluctantly, he took the plate and held it in his lap. The steam rising from the food was almost intoxicating.

"Thank you," Dominic muttered, picking up the turkey leg.

As he took a tentative bite, the flavors exploded on his tongue—rosemary, thyme, a hint of garlic. His body sang with relief as the nourishment hit his system. He took another bite, then another, until he was devouring the meal like a starved animal.

Sebastian chuckled. "Easy there."

Dominic paused, wiping grease from his mouth. "Sorry," he said, a shy smile creeping onto his face. "I guess I was hungrier than I thought."

Sebastian nodded, his expression soft. "It's good to see you taking care of yourself."

For a moment, Dominic forgot the weight of his insecurities. He felt seen, not judged, not pitied—just seen.

"Thanks for everything," Dominic said, his voice thick with emotion. "I don't think I'd be alive right now if it weren't for you guys."

Sebastian's smirk returned, but there was warmth behind it. "It's my pleasure. I'm glad you're alive. I just need to figure out if you're crazy or not," he teased.

Dominic chuckled, the sound light and genuine for the first time in days. "Maybe a little of both."

Dominic tore into the turkey leg like a ravenous vulture, the savory flavor almost overwhelming his senses. Each bite felt like a victory, satisfying in a way he hadn't experienced in days. Grease smeared across his face, but he didn't care. The sheer act of eating, of indulging, was cathartic.

Now I get why those dudes at the bar go feral over chicken wings during Sunday Night Football, he thought, pausing only to wipe his mouth with the back of his hand before diving back in.

Sebastian watched him with a small smirk. "That's what I like to see," he said.

Dominic glanced up, swallowing hard. *What? Me finally getting nourished, or me losing every bit of table manners I've ever learned?*

Dominic laughed, a little too hard, then let out an unintentional burp. Embarrassment heated his face as he quickly covered his mouth. "Excuse me."

Sebastian chuckled. "I just know a lost person when I see one."

Dominic tilted his head, intrigued. "What do you mean?"

Sebastian's smile faded, replaced by something more serious. "I don't mean you're lost because you're not from this world. I mean, you're in need of a friend. Someone to have your back."

Dominic's heart thudded in his chest. No one had ever said anything like that to him before—not friends, not lovers. He swallowed hard, unsure how to respond.

"Well, you have Agnes and Petunia. And aren't you and Giselle a thing?"

"Thing?" Sebastian asked as they looked at Petunia and Giselle holding hands, skipping along the fiddler playing on the lawn. "Giselle and I were together a long time ago. It didn't work out."

"What happened?" Dominic asked as he took a swig from his water bottle.

"She wasn't interested in me any longer."

"She seems to still be interested in you."

"I don't know why. She was interested in Theo from one of the other farms. I'm not interested in her anymore."

"Hmm," Dominic said, noticing one of the servant men joining in, causing the glow on Giselle's face to lighten up. "I guess you still shouldn't feel lost. You still have them."

"I still do," Sebastian added, his voice softer now, almost wistful.

Dominic raised an eyebrow, leaning in slightly. "What do you mean? Are you from a different world too?" he asked, attempting to lighten the mood with a bit of sarcasm.

Plates clattered along the table. Agnes grunted as the fiddler's song ended, shaking her head at Calypso, who moved from one platter to the next. Dodging the children running beside her caused a flush in her face that the two could notice even from the top of the hill.

Sebastian laughed, shaking his head. "No, not quite. But I don't know who my real parents are. I was abandoned as a baby."

Dominic's heart sank. "Really?"

"Yeah." Sebastian gestured to the tree they were sitting under. "I was found here, actually. Right under this very tree."

Dominic glanced at the gnarled branches above, now taking on a profound sense of significance. "Do you know anything about them?"

Sebastian shook his head. "Nothing. I've spent my whole life trying to figure out who I am. If I'd known something about them, maybe I wouldn't feel so incomplete."

"I'm sorry," Dominic said, his voice barely above a whisper. He reached out, patting Sebastian's back. It was a clumsy gesture, but it felt right.

Sebastian smiled faintly. "Don't get me wrong. I love the life I've had. The people here are kind, and I'm grateful for them."

Dominic nodded, though a pang of sadness twisted in his stomach. "I was left on a doorstep too."

Sebastian's eyes widened slightly. "No kidding?"

"Everything you're feeling, I get it." Dominic's voice cracked, and he cleared his throat, fighting the lump that had formed there.

Sebastian's eyes shimmered with emotion, reflecting the last vestiges of sunlight. For a moment, Dominic thought he saw something more—a connection that went beyond shared experiences. He wanted to hold on to it, to freeze the moment in time.

"Do you want to see something?" Sebastian asked with an eager smile.

Dominic's heart skipped.

If it's what I'm thinking, then yes. A thousand times, yes.

Sebastian's hands moved closer, but instead of toward Dominic, they went to a dead branch sticking out from the tree. Disappointment flared, but he quickly pushed it down, confused by his reaction.

Sebastian's fingers danced over the decaying wood, almost like a magician preparing a trick. At first, Dominic thought it was just a bit of theatrics, maybe an attempt to cheer him up. But then the air around Sebastian's hands began to glow. Green sparks flickered like fireflies, swirling and shimmering until they landed on the branch. Dominic's breath hitched as the lifeless wood trembled. Bark thickened and spread like a protective shield, while tiny buds sprouted along its length, unfurling into delicate white blossoms. The air filled with the faint scent of fresh growth.

"It's magic," Dominic whispered, awe-struck.

Sebastian grinned, pulling his hand back. "Pretty neat, huh? It doesn't always work, but when it does..." He trailed off, his expression a mixture of pride and wonder.

"It's incredible," Dominic said. He wanted to say more, but words failed him. "How did you get that?"

"I don't know. As long as I could remember, I guess. Nobody on the farm knows."

"Why not? I think they would love it."

"Perhaps," Sebastian said with apprehension. "I just feel like Giselle would make a big deal out of it. She doesn't like things to be out of the ordinary. Once word gets out, she would spread the news like wildfire."

They exchanged a look then—one that Dominic couldn't quite describe. It was something raw and unspoken, a tether pulling them closer without either of them moving an inch.

But the moment shattered as the air filled with the sound of screams.

Sebastian's head whipped around, his entire body tensing. Dominic followed his gaze and saw it, the very fear that terrified him in the woods three days ago. Shadows creeping across the field, growing and twisting like living nightmares with the red hues bleeding into the yellowy clouds. Mothers clutched their children, running for the nearest shelter as the darkness consumed the joyous gathering.

"We have to move!" Sebastian barked, yanking Dominic to his feet.

"What's happening?" Dominic asked, his voice trembling.

But before Sebastian could answer, the monster moved swiftly, grabbing a helpless maiden by the throat. Dominic froze, paralyzed as he watched the creature pull a gleaming sword from its cloak. The blade plunged into the woman's stomach, and her scream was a sound Dominic knew he'd never forget.

One shadow was coming in closer to a lone maiden, curling up to the ground helplessly. Her faint mutters of pleading grew louder before the darkness took shape.

"It's them. It's the asshole that attacked me."

The arm of the shadowy cloak seized the maiden by the throat, its darkened grip merciless. Her hands clawed at the assailant's shrouded figure, desperate to break free, but her struggle was in vain. Her gasping breaths, strained and ragged, sent shivers through Dominic's spine. His chest vibrated, and as he looked down a tiny bit of blue glowed underneath the plum fabric.

From within the folds of the cloak, the creature withdrew a gleaming metal instrument.

A sword.

The sunlight caught the blade for a fleeting moment, its reflection a brief, sorrowful farewell, before the weapon plunged into the maiden's stomach. She froze, her body locking in a grotesque tableau of agony. The fiend released her neck, and she crumpled to her knees, blood already soaking through her dress. Her trembling hands pressed against the wound, slick with crimson that spilled onto the dirt in a growing pool of blackened red.

The sword rose again.

And again.

And again.

Each strike was a cruel punctuation to her muffled cries, her pain echoing in the heavy, terrified silence that had fallen over the field. Her final scream, raw and broken, seemed to beg for release—whether through salvation or the end. The fiend gave neither mercy nor reprieve, driving the blade down one last time, straight through her skull. The weapon impaled the ground beneath her, silencing her.

Dominic's stomach twisted violently. He clenched his jaw, fighting the rising bile that threatened to undo the small meal he had just enjoyed. The sight of her crumpled body and the glistening blood pooling beneath her seared itself into his mind. He looked away, swallowing hard, battling the two heaves that wracked his chest.

"Stay here!" Sebastian shouted, pushing Dominic toward the tree.

Dominic didn't argue. The crowd of victims was running around frantically. Families rushed into the doors of the windmills, desperate for safety. Dominic noticed Sebastian rushing toward a child, but it was too late as another shadow beheaded the little girl with its weapon. Giselle ran toward Agnes; their struggle up the incline was frantic as they continued to look behind at the other servants in the ambush.

"Sebastian!" he screamed, but the cacophony of terror drowned his voice.

He stumbled back, pressing himself against the rough bark, his heart pounding like a war drum. His hands clawed at the tree's surface, desperate for something to anchor him as chaos unfolded around him. The flowers around him trembled with petals waving in his face. A soft, womanly giggle floated around him, so hypnotic. Suddenly, a gloved hand clamped over his mouth. Terror widening his eyes with someone yanking Dominic backward.

"Shhh," a soft voice whispered. "If you want to live, follow me."

Dominic nodded, his heart hammering in his chest. Looking over at the huts, doors started to get closed with the fear of faces disappearing into darkness. The woods behind him made his heart race, animal noises growled in the brush with the endless possibilities of what could lurk. Whoever this was, they might be his only chance.

SEBASTIAN'S HEART POUNDED in his chest as chaos unfolded around him. This was insane—unfathomable. They were showing up more often than ever, these dark, cloaked figures bringing destruction and death. He had been enjoying his time with Dominic, sharing a rare moment of peace. But that peace was shattered.

"Damn it," he said.

Sebastian's protective instincts roared to life. He wanted to shield Dominic, to keep him safe from the horrors sweeping across the land. But his people needed him, too.

A piercing scream cut through the air. Petunia's cry sliced through him like a blade. Without hesitation, he sprinted down the hill, his boots thudding against the uneven ground. A mole's burrow almost twisted his ankle, but he pushed on, the need to protect overpowering any thought of his own safety.

He had to save her. He had to save them all.

As he approached, Petunia's screams grew weaker, but more agonizing. He watched, helpless, as one of the cloaked figures plunged its sword into her side. Blood sprayed from her lips, painting her teeth a sickening red. She collapsed to her knees, her eyes wide with pain and disbelief.

The figure drove the blade through her again. Her scream, sharp and piercing, abruptly ceased, leaving only the sound of her shallow, labored breaths. She clenched her fists and grit her teeth, a defiant refusal to succumb to fear. But her strength failed, and with a final, brutal thrust, the sword tore through her spine. Her body twisted grotesquely as she fell, her head striking the ground moments before her lifeless hip tilted to the earth.

"I failed you."

Anger surged in Sebastian's chest, but there was no time to grieve. All around him, his people were fleeing in terror. Families rushed to the windmills for shelter, children tripping and scrambling to escape the chaos. He caught sight of a small child tumbling to the ground just as another figure's sword struck. The blade pierced the child's back, ending the young life in an instant.

Thank goodness it was quick, I guess, Sebastian thought bitterly. A cruel blessing amidst the carnage.

He turned his gaze to another victim—a mother sprawled across a table. The woman's innards were strewn about like a grotesque mockery of the feast they had shared just moments ago. Her fingers let out a weak twitch, as if in a futile attempt to push away the darkness overtaking her.

Rage boiled within him, a fury so consuming it threatened to spill out in ways he could not control. His hands tingled, a sensation that crept up his arms like wildfire. Another child ran past him, their wide eyes full of terror with tears rushing down their cheeks, not for the shadowy figures, but for him.

Sparks ignited in Sebastian's palms, faint and flickering at first. Then they roared to life, transforming into a blazing fireball. The flames danced and crackled in his hand, casting fiery reflections in his green eyes.

This wasn't just sparks anymore.

The fireball hovered in his hand, its heat searing his skin but feeding his determination. He turned his gaze to the child as a shadowy figure lunged toward them.

"Not another life. Not this one."

Sebastian tightened his grip on the fireball, his mind racing. There was only one thing to do. With a powerful throw, he hurled the flaming orb at the shadow. Upon colliding with the figure, the fireball engulfed it in flames, forcing it to recoil. The child took the opportunity to flee toward safety, vanishing into the crowd.

The figure stumbled as its cloak caught fire, the flames tearing away the dark fabric to reveal something unexpected. From beneath the burning shroud emerged a green cape of rich emerald hues. A red feathered cap tipped out from under the hood as the shadow dissolved.

A human.

Sebastian stared in shock as the figure's glowing, feral eyes locked not on him, but on something—or someone—behind him. The human sprinted past Sebastian, heading straight for the tree at the hill's crest. The tree, which had moments ago offered shade and comfort, now shivered violently, its leaves cascading to the ground in fear.

Sebastian's stomach dropped. He turned toward the tree, his chest tightening as he realized what was missing. Or rather, who.

"Dominic."

He was gone.

Chapter 27

Dominic

I DON'T EVEN KNOW WHAT to do anymore.

People in cloaks—these dark, terrifying figures—are taking away innocent lives right in front of me. Who are they? What do they want? Watching them reminds me of the jerks back home, the ones who terrorized people simply for being themselves. Those people would cover their faces with masks, their hands gripping assault weapons, using fear to suppress anyone who didn't conform to their narrow worldview. They came from a place of privilege, unwilling to live with an open mind, unwilling to let others just exist.

Cowards.

And maybe that's what these cloaked figures are, too—cowards. Perhaps they're part of some cult, targeting a certain group for reasons that only make sense in their warped heads. But why servants? Why these people?

It's heartbreaking to see. A mother loses her child; a child loses their parents to murder. The anguish on their faces, the screams that pierce through the chaos, all of it feels too familiar. Back home, I'd seen news reports of families torn apart by violence, but this...this is something else. It's personal, immediate, and relentless.

Not another child without a parent. Please.

None of this makes sense. It just doesn't.

And now I'm running. Running through the woods with this stranger. A person who I don't know, don't trust, and don't even want to trust. But what else am I supposed to do? Sebastian went to protect his people, and I have no one else. No one. Even Calypso has vanished, and my heart clenches at the thought of him out there alone.

Please let him be okay.

Branches whip at my face, paper-thin leaves scratching at my skin. Roots jut out of the ground like nature's tripwires, and my ankles are buckling with every misstep with the burn returning from days ago. My knees ache, and my thighs strain as I try to keep up with the small figure ahead of me. The uneven terrain makes every step a gamble, and my lungs are heaving, desperate for air.

This person—whoever they are—moves with a determination I can't match. It's almost like they're younger, maybe middle school age, judging by their speed and endurance. Their willpower is astonishing, but I hate to admit it, because it's making me feel weak in comparison.

God, I wish I hadn't quit the track team. Maybe if I had stuck with it, I wouldn't feel so useless right now. But I didn't fit in with those guys either.

When are we going to stop? My chest is on fire, and my legs feel like they're about to give out. I need a break. I need answers.

"Do you think we're safe?" I manage to gasp, my words broken between labored breaths.

They don't reply. They just keep moving, dodging bushes and ducking under low-hanging branches like the forest itself is alive and trying to grab them.

"Can you at least tell me who you are?" I call out, my voice rasping from thirst and exhaustion.

No answer. Just the sound of their feet crunching against the dirt, their breathing lighter and steadier than mine.

I can't keep going like this. My arm shoots out, grabbing the rough trunk of a tree to steady myself as I double over, panting. Fog swirls around my feet, thick and eerie, like something out of a horror movie. I glance around, and the further I realize I've gotten from Sebastian, the more I feel exposed. Vulnerable. Lost. I don't care anymore. If this stranger isn't going to talk, I'm not moving another inch.

"I'm not going any further until you start talking," I say, planting my feet. My voice is sharper than intended, but I'm too tired to care.

The figure skids to a stop ahead of me. Their feet scuffle against the dirt, and for the first time, I notice their breathing falter slightly. It's not as steady as I thought.

Finally.

"Thank you," I say, letting out a breath of relief as I straighten up. "Let's start with who you are."

For a moment, there's nothing but silence between us. Then, to my surprise, the figure lifts their hands and pulls back their hood.

What I see stops me in my tracks.

The figure is a girl—dirty blonde hair tucked into two disheveled buns, strands falling loose in greasy, tangled curls. Dirt streaks her lavender undershirt, and her torn embroidered dress reveals a small hint of cropped shorts and stockings that run up to her thighs. Pouches and belts hold weapons and trinkets for a person on the go. She has grime streaking her face, and her sharp, determined eyes pierce through the muck like steel.

It's her. The girl from the marketplace.

"I'm Gretel."

Chapter 28

Dominic stared in disbelief after the girl removed her hood. *Gretel?*

The name rang in his head like an old tune he couldn't place. His chest tightened. First Cinderella, and now her? Another figure pulled from his childhood stories was standing right in front of him. Only this Gretel wasn't quite what he remembered.

She looked slightly younger than him, maybe in her late teens, but her stature was small. Yet, there was a sharpness in her eyes, something hardened and resolute, like she'd seen more than her years should allow. Her outfit, dirty and tattered as it was, suggested survival rather than comfort. Dominic took in her ragged wardrobe, and he thought for a moment how similar she looked to how he felt: out of place but adapting the best she could.

Still, there was something off. The Gretel from his memories was a picture of kindness and light. Pure. Innocent. This girl? She carried daggers at her hips, and her sharp expression warned she wouldn't hesitate to use them.

"You can't be Gretel," Dominic said, his voice filled with disbelief and a hint of disappointment. "Gretel is good. She did nothing wrong."

"I am good," she snapped, her tone defensive but not unkind.

"Oh yeah?" Dominic crossed his arms, eyes narrowing. "What about the jewels you stole?"

Her gaze flickered, momentarily clouded with guilt, but she didn't back down. "I did what I had to," she hissed, lifting her chin defiantly.

Dominic sighed, running a hand through his hair. That sounded familiar. Too familiar. His own actions of late, using a stolen ruby to pay for clothes, mirrored hers more than he wanted to admit.

I did what I had to do to survive.

Maybe she had, too.

"Well, nobody just chooses to be bad," he said after a pause. "Why do it? Why steal?"

"Most of the things you've heard about me are lies," she said, her voice quieter this time. "Rumors spread faster than truth."

Dominic studied her, wanting to believe her but unsure if he could. Before he could press her further, the wind howled through the trees, sounding more like a chorus of wailing spirits than a natural breeze. He flinched as the cries of terrified children echoed faintly in the distance. The anguish clawed at his chest, and he covered his ears, squeezing his eyes shut.

"Enough!" he shouted, the sound muffled by his own hands. "We can catch up later. Who the hell are those things?"

Gretel didn't answer. Her eyes darted to the trees around them, as if expecting the shadows to spring to life. She fiddled with the hilt of one of her daggers, scraping the blade under her fingernails in a way that made Dominic's stomach turn. Finally, she spoke.

"They're the Concealment."

"The Concealment?" Dominic echoed, his brow furrowed. "What the hell is the Concealment?"

"They're a force of pure darkness," she said, her voice trembling despite her best efforts to appear composed.

Dominic scoffed, his nerves fraying. "Yeah, so are corporate lawyers and politicians, but you don't see them murdering people in fields!"

Gretel's lips twitched, but she didn't laugh. Instead, she took a step closer, lowering her voice as if the trees themselves were eavesdropping. "These aren't merely people, Dominic. I mean, they were people once, but they let the darkness consume them. It's like a disease. Once it takes hold, it completely controls them."

"Like cancer," Dominic muttered, more to himself than her.

"Most of them come when the sky turns red—redder than the blood they spill," Gretel continued, her icy blue eyes glistening with fear. "They take what they want, destroy what they don't, and leave nothing but despair in their wake."

Dominic's stomach churned. "Why are they here?" he asked, though he wasn't sure he wanted to know the answer. "And do you know if Brone is one of them?"

"I don't know," she admitted, glancing around nervously. "I don't have all the answers."

Before Dominic could respond, another voice cut through the tension, smooth and mocking. "Perhaps I could assist."

Dominic's blood ran cold. The voice slithered around them, sending every nerve in his body into overdrive. He clenched his fists, his fight-or-flight instincts battling for dominance.

"Where the hell is he?" Dominic muttered under his breath, scanning the trees.

A crack echoed above them, and Dominic's head snapped up just in time to discover a figure crouched on a thick branch. The man leapt down, landing in front of them with ease. The leaves scattered from the impact, swirling like ripples in a pond. His emerald-green vest and pantaloons, tailored and tight, covered him with a billowing taupe shirt underneath. A single red feather bobbed in the red cap atop his head.

Gretel stiffened beside Dominic, gripping her daggers tighter. "Robin."

Dominic blinked, his mouth falling open. "Robin Hood? Are you kidding me?"

Robin smirked, his teeth flashing white against his tanned skin. "That's no way to speak to us. Show some respect," he said, his voice dripping with arrogance.

Dominic's stomach dropped. *Robin Hood, a villain? What kind of messed up storybook is this?* he thought.

Gretel moved in front of Dominic, her shoulder brushing his with her dagger clenched tight. "Stay back," she warned.

Dominic was done. Done running, done hiding, and definitely done being intimidated by a supposed hero-turned-monster. "Screw you!" he shouted, his anger bubbling to the surface.

Robin's smirk twisted into a snarl. "You little brat," he spat. "I'm going to enjoy ripping the light out of you."

Before Dominic could react, Robin lunged. His gloved hands wrapped around Dominic's throat, squeezing with terrifying strength. Dominic gagged, his airways tightening as pain radiated through his neck. His vision became hazy as his hands scrambled desperately for a weapon, for anything. His fingers brushed against something cold and sharp—Gretel's dagger. Gritting his teeth, Dominic ignored the pain slicing through his palm as he gripped the blade. With a surge of adrenaline, he drove the dagger into Robin's side.

Robin's orange eyes widened in shock and pain. Dominic didn't stop. He brought his knee up, slamming it into Robin's groin with all the force he could muster. Robin let go, stumbling back with a guttural groan.

A voice rang out in warning, sharp and urgent. "Watch out!"

Before Dominic could process it, Gretel shoved him hard, sending him sprawling to the ground. His head struck a rock with a dull 'clunk' that reverberated through his skull like a hollow wood chime. Pain radiated outward as his vision blurred momentarily, but not enough to miss the streak of light hurtling past Robin Hood.

Robin leapt aside with uncanny agility, narrowly avoiding the fireball that exploded against the base of a tree behind him. The fireball burst like a water-filled balloon, spraying flames in every direction. Dry brush and pine needles ignited instantly, the fire growing with alarming speed. Smoke and fog mixed into a suffocating veil, and Dominic's eyes stung as he squinted through the haze, coughing against the acrid burn filling his lungs.

A firm hand reached down and gripped his, pulling him up with such strength that Dominic staggered into the broad chest of his rescuer. He blinked rapidly, recognizing the familiar calloused touch and serious face.

"Let's get out of here!" Sebastian's voice was firm, though the panic in his eyes betrayed the urgency of the moment. His focus, however, never wavered.

Dominic nodded, grabbing Gretel by the wrist. Her arm felt alarmingly thin, her small frame jostling as he yanked her along behind him like a child clutching a teddy bear. The three of them raced through the inferno, weaving between trees and leaping over burning branches.

"We should go this way!" Gretel said, pulling Dominic away from Sebastian.

"No, this way!" Sebastian combated, his teeth gritting.

"I know these woods!"

"I do too!"

The heat made Dominic's skin feel stretched. His breath became hitched as the feeling of shadows looming over him grew with every argument the two spewed. Every pull of his arm from each one of them shot waves of pain throughout his body.

"Why would we want to go with you?" Sebastian asked furiously.

"Because I can help you!" Gretel hissed, huffing out a cough.

Sebastian's eyes lit heated anger, "What if you're one of them? I've heard everything about you."

"I'm not," she said nonchalantly.

"I don't believe you."

"You don't have to believe me. You just have to trust me."

"I don't!"

"I trust both of you right now!" Dominic said, his patience dwindling with smoke stinging his eyes. "Can we please just go somewhere other than here!"

Dominic's thighs burned with each frantic step, breaking away from their grasp as he chose the path for them. His breath came in ragged gasps, and he cursed himself for not eating enough earlier—anything to have more fuel for this harrowing escape. Every tree around them looked the same, their silhouettes blurred by smoke and fear. The haze made him uncertain, so he looked to Sebastian to take the lead once again. He prayed Sebastian knew where he was going; if only they'd left breadcrumbs like Gretel did in Dominic's storybook.

His foot snagged on a root, sending him pitching forward. "Damn it!" he yelped as he tumbled, pulling both Gretel and Sebastian down with him. The momentum carried them down a steep incline, the hill seeming endless as they rolled. Rocks jabbed into Dominic's ribs; branches slapped against his face and tangled in his hair. Every tumble was like a punch to his stomach or a slap to his cheek.

For a split second, his childhood flashed in his mind—the desire to spin endlessly on carnival rides Miss Reed could never afford. Except this spinning wasn't fun. This was chaos, pain, and the unnerving screeches of his voice mixing with Sebastian's grunts and Gretel's sharp yelps.

After what felt like the longest minute of his life, Dominic's body slammed into freezing water. The shock jolted him upright. He scrambled to his feet, his boots soaking and heavy as he stumbled into the shallow stream. Water splashed up his legs, soaking his pants, the chill snapping him back to reality. His stomach churned, threatening to reject the dinner he had so desperately enjoyed earlier. He clenched his fists, forcing down the bile rising in his throat.

Gretel and Sebastian surfaced nearby, equally battered and drenched.

"See, I told you not to trust her!" Sebastian said, the force of his legs wading in the water causing massive waves.

"Shut up!" Gretel said, frustrated. "It's not my fault we fell!"

The three of them exchanged weary, wordless glances, the unspoken question hanging between them:

Where's Robin Hood?

Dominic scanned the treeline, his vision blurred with nerves. For all he knew, Robin was tumbling down the hill too—or worse, waiting in the shadows. There was no time to dwell on it. The fire raged behind them, flames licking at the underbrush, creeping closer with every passing second.

A shadow loomed over Sebastian, their arm wrapping over him. Sebastian winced in pain as the constriction quickly seized his airway. Pink flushed his cheeks with the hood of the Concealment revealing one of his peers from the party; a teenager that helped serve Calypso earlier. Dominic jumped toward Sebastian, his hands furiously trying to pry off his fingers from Sebastian's throat.

"G-go!" Sebastian gasped as his balance teetered, his body collapsing closer to the water's surface.

"No!" Dominic said, distracted by the orange glow in the teenager's eyes.

Within a second, the teenager let go. Blood pooled out of his mouth, his body gyrating from pain. Gretel grunted with every stab of her daggers going in and out of the enemy's body. The black cloak slowly sank into the water, life slowly drifting. Sebastian gasped for air, his knuckles crunched with anger creating a fist that knocked a blow into their face. Blood exploded out of the teen's nose, blasting all over their face. As the body became limb, a dark force floated out of its dead corpse like smoke, releasing themselves from their conduit.

"Are you okay?" Dominic asked, his hand caused pain when he touched Sebastian's neck.

"Yes," Sebastian said, his voice dry and raspy.

"Believe me now?" Gretel asked sarcastically as she dipped her daggers in the water to cleanse the blood from her blades.

Dominic's gaze shifted upstream, where a massive boulder jutted out from the forest floor like a fortress. A dark opening was visible near its base, a gaping mouth promising shelter.

"There!" Dominic shouted, pointing toward the cave. "Let's hide in there!"

Without waiting for a response, he grabbed Gretel's wrist again, leading her toward the rocky refuge. Sebastian pushed forward with hitched breaths, his hand resting on Dominic's shoulder as if to guide and protect at the same time. The three of them stumbled into the waterlogged cave, wriggling through the narrow entrance. Rocks scraped Dominic's knees and elbows as he crawled inside, his breath catching in his throat. The space felt claustrophobic at first, tight and suffocating, but then the walls opened into a small chamber just large enough to huddle together.

The cave smelled of damp earth and their fingers felt the fuzz of moss. Drops of water clinked from above, the sound oddly soothing against the chaos they'd just escaped. Dominic leaned back against the wall, his chest heaving. His muscles ached, and his eyelids drooped heavily as adrenaline faded.

Sebastian settled beside him, his solid presence grounding Dominic in the dim, flickering light. The man's arm wrapped around Dominic's shoulders, his touch warm and steady despite the cold seeping into the cave. Gretel crouched nearby, dagger still in hand, her wary eyes darting to the cave entrance as if expecting Robin to charge in at any moment.

For the first time since the chaos began, Dominic felt a glimmer of safety. He looked at Gretel, who seemed to relax ever so slightly, her tense posture softening as she glanced at Sebastian. She didn't have to be alone and go through life in isolation anymore, Dominic realized.

None of them did.

The three of them sat in silence, their breaths mingling in the cool air. The fire roared somewhere far away, but inside the cave, it was quiet. Safe. For now, at least, they had each other—and that was enough.

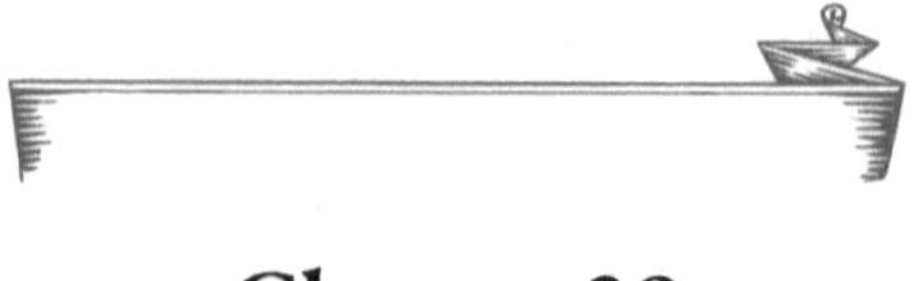

Chapter 29

Gretel

THE SUNLIGHT SPILLS *into the small cave, creeping over the jagged rocks like it's trying to find us. Smoke still hangs in the air, thin and faint, but enough to sting my eyes and stick to my skin. My body aches everywhere—my legs, my back, my arms—everything is sore, but that isn't anything new. Pain is a familiar companion. Running, hiding, surviving—it all comes at a cost.*

At least I'm alive. For now.

I watch Dominic sitting across from me, clutching this carnation from his bag like he's afraid to let go of the pain. Looking at the petals fall from the tension onto the stone, his expression is vacant, completely numb. He looks like someone who's been thrown into a nightmare and hasn't yet figured out how to wake up. I can relate.

I've spent my whole life running. Ever since Hansel and I escaped that witch's cottage, it's been one endless sprint from one danger after another. That day, I saved my brother, got him away from that monster before she could finish fattening him up. But saving him isn't enough. Somehow, I become the villain in everyone else's story.

The whispers, the accusations, the judgment—I can still hear them. They say I brought the witch's wrath upon the town, that I should've been her meal. They say it's my fault. After a while, I stop trying to defend myself. What's the point? No one listens. No one cares. People give up on me, so I gave up on them.

But Dominic? He's different.

When I first run into him, literally, I think he's just another helpless outsider—a lost boy in a world he doesn't understand. He looks so out of place, so fragile in his strange clothes. But then I look closer. There's something in his honey-colored eyes, something that catches me off guard. A glimmer. A light.

It's faint, almost drowned out by the sorrow and fear written all over his face. But it's there. I can see it, even if he can't. And it isn't just light. It's something stronger, something that makes me believe in the impossible, even for a second.

Hope.

I don't feel hope often. Or ever, really. People like me don't get the luxury of believing in things like that. But with Dominic, it's different. I can't explain why, but I feel like he matters in a way none of us do. Like he's the answer to a question none of us have dared to ask.

The Concealment doesn't care about questions or answers. They care about chaos. They're darkness incarnate, feeding on fear and misery, and right now, they're winning. They've already taken so much, turned so many people into hollow shells of who they once were. And now they're here, hunting us, hunting him.

I won't let them have him.

He doesn't know it yet, but Dominic is important. His light—it's rare. Precious. It might be the only thing strong enough to fight back against the darkness swallowing this world. But how do I tell him that? How do I convince someone who looks like they're ready to give up that they're the one we've been waiting for?

I adjust my grip on my dagger, sharpening the blade against a rock to keep my hands busy. The steady scrapes fill the silence in the cave. Dominic's eyes flick to me for a moment, curiosity breaking through his exhaustion, but he doesn't say anything. He just watches me, his expression guarded.

I want to say something, to reassure him, but the words stick in my throat. I'm not good at this—comforting people, offering kindness. It's been so long since anyone offered it to me, I wouldn't even know where to start.

So I stay quiet and keep sharpening. The only sounds are the scrape of the blade, the other man's steady breathing, and the faint crackle of the fire outside. The flames still linger from whatever magic the stable boy unleashed earlier, and it makes me wonder just how much he's holding back. He seems calm now, sitting beside Dominic like a shield, his broad shoulders casting long shadows against the cave walls. But I see the fire in his eyes when he fights. There's something in him too, something powerful. Maybe Dominic isn't the only one with the light.

I sigh and lean back against the wall, letting the cool stone press against my shoulders. The ache in my legs throbs in time with my heartbeat, but it doesn't matter. I'd run a hundred more miles if it meant getting us away from the Concealment. I'd do whatever it takes to keep Dominic safe. I've done it before and will do it again if I have to. Because the truth is, I need him too. I've been running my whole life, and I'm tired. So tired. Maybe Dominic is the light we've been waiting for, but he's not the only one who needs saving. Maybe, just maybe, I can find some of that light for myself.

We need as much light to vanquish the Concealment.

Chapter 30

Sebastian leaned against the cave's entrance as the first tendrils of sunlight clawed through the dense, ash-choked trees. His muscles screamed for relief, every fiber of his being aching from the battles of the previous night. He flexed his fingers, the soot-stained knuckles trembling as they tried to grip the reality of what had just transpired. The charred skin wasn't from handling the firewood back at the farm or tending the stables. No, this was something entirely new—fire conjured from within him, fire that had erupted in his desperation to protect.

The weight of the night pressed heavily on his chest. Friends he'd grown up with, neighbors he'd shared meals and stories with, were gone. Families ripped apart, children slaughtered, innocence snuffed out in a matter of minutes. He didn't think he'd ever be able to close his eyes without seeing the lifeless stares of the people he had failed to save. The blood, the screams, the carnage. It was all too much. His hand brushed the gritty cave wall, grounding himself in the rough texture, trying to tether his mind to the present. But the past lingered like smoke, clinging to him, suffocating.

He glanced at Dominic and Gretel, both still recovering. Dominic's head was bowed, his fingers absently tracing the worn fabric of his blouse. The boy was an enigma. He'd stumbled into their world by accident, yet there was something about him that felt purposeful, necessary. Sebastian couldn't place it, but he felt drawn to him, like a moth to the faint flicker of light in an otherwise endless darkness as the sapphire dangled around his neck.

Gretel's reputation preceded her, the stories of her deeds whispered in the town's alleys and taverns. Some called her a thief, others a murderer. Sebastian wasn't sure what to believe, but he couldn't ignore the fact that she'd saved Dominic from Robin Hood's attack. For now, that was enough.

"Sebastian, what's the plan?" Dominic's voice was hoarse, but it carried an edge of determination. His eyes met Sebastian's, searching for reassurance.

Sebastian straightened, ignoring the protests of his aching limbs. "We head back to the farm," he said firmly. "It's the only place we can regroup and figure out our next move."

Dominic nodded, though his expression was skeptical. "Do you think it's safe? What if the Concealment follows us there?"

"They'll follow," Gretel interjected, her tone flat and devoid of optimism. She tightened her grip on her dagger, its blade still faintly gleaming with blood. "They always do."

Sebastian didn't have an answer for that, so he turned his focus to the task at hand. "We'll deal with that if it happens. Right now, we need to make sure everyone's accounted for."

They emerged from the cave slowly, their movements cautious and deliberate. The forest was eerily silent, as though the trees themselves were mourning the lives lost. The once-vibrant landscape was now a desolate wasteland, the ground littered with ash and the charred remains of plants and animals. Sebastian's favorite tree, the one he'd grown up climbing and resting beneath, stood scarred and bare, its branches clawing at the sky like skeletal fingers.

"Holy shit!" Dominic said. "We're lucky the fire didn't get us too."

The walk back to the windmills was grueling. Each step felt heavier than the last with their boots sinking into the smoldered ash, the weight of exhaustion and grief bearing down on their shoulders. The smell of death lingered in the air, mingling with the acrid stench of smoke. Gretel walked slightly ahead, her small frame deceptively sturdy. Dominic lagged behind, his face pale, his steps unsteady.

When they reached the windmills, the sight that greeted them was both haunting and familiar. The once-thriving gathering place was now a graveyard, the ground stained with blood, the scattered remnants of a celebration turned into a massacre. The door to the windmill was shut tight, the sturdy wood splintered in places where desperate hands had clawed at it for safety.

Sebastian stepped forward, his large frame casting a shadow over the door. He pounded on it with his fist, the sound echoing through the still air.

"Is anyone in there?" he called, his voice rough and urgent.

There was no answer. His heart sank, and he turned to Dominic and Gretel, their faces mirroring his dread. The thought of being the only survivors of having failed to protect the people he cared about, was almost too much to bear.

He knocked again, harder this time. "It's Sebastian!" he shouted. "Open the door!"

Finally, there was movement. A faint rustling sound, followed by the creak of hinges. The door opened just a crack, and a familiar eye peeked through the gap. "Giselle?" Sebastian breathed, relief washing over him.

The door swung open fully, and Giselle threw herself into his arms. Her body shook uncontrollably, a silent testament to her terror with dirt and tears streaked on her face. "Sebastian," she sobbed, her voice breaking. "I thought...I thought we'd lost you."

He held her tightly, his own emotions threatening to spill over. "I'm here," he murmured. "I'm here."

Memories of Robin Hood surfaced, watching him diminishing the light out of even the brightest of people. The thought of Sebastian being taken too soon by his hand, and it has now become something that nobody talks about. Viewing the casualties along the property made him concerned if she would be strong enough to handle it.

Behind her, others began to emerge from a tunnel hidden around bales of hay. Agnes, clutching Dominic's cat, who mewed softly in protest. A few other survivors emerged from the opening, their faces pale and gaunt, crawled out. They looked broken, but alive.

The withered wooden interior was covered in assortments of letters and symbols. Dominic tried to piece them together and couldn't figure out what it could say. The symbols brought back times of hanging out with friends who had an affinity for watching movies involving witchcraft. The only explanation for the structure staying in tact was a spell of some sort protecting the people from darkness.

"What is *she* doing here?" Giselle asked as she huddled closer to Sebastian.

Gretel clenched the handle to one of her daggers. The echo in Giselle's fear shook the foundation of the rickety building. Eyes widened with every second, causing her breath to quicken.

"She's one of them," said one servant.

"She has to be. I saw her kill one of the kids," said another.

"Get the pitchforks!"

"Wait, wait! There's no need to get shit!" Dominic said, his voice filled with impatience. "She didn't do anything to us."

"She saved us," Sebastian added. "She's on our side."

Giselle's hand clenched Sebastian's arm, yanking his head down closer to her face. "Are you serious? You're telling me that this murderer is a good guy now?"

"Yes," Sebastian said with certainty, pulling himself out of her grip. "I don't want to hear anything else about it!"

"Just drop it, Giselle," Agnes said, her voice strained with exhaustion.

"Petunia is dead, and you want me to believe you?"

"If you love him, then you would," Dominic interjected, his eyebrow raised.

Sebastian noticed the twinkle in Dominic's eye when he glared at Giselle, causing him to shed a tight smirk. Part of Sebastian wanted to scold him for using his baggage as leverage, and the other part of him wanted to admire that quick wit.

"Fine," she said, her eyes unblinking as they stared directly at Gretel on her way to a hay bale for a seat.

"This woman saved our lives. She is a good person and deserves to be treated with dignity like everybody else. If anybody else has a problem with that, they will have to go through me."

The rest of the group relaxed their shoulders, their eyes filled with trepidation. Gretel let go of her dagger, her tough exterior fighting the urge to let out a smile. Her nostrils let out a relieving sigh, taking in the courage Dominic exuded to speak up against people he didn't know. She had some hope that perhaps he may be the chosen one after all.

"What do we do now?" Agnes asked, her voice trembling. She held Calypso as though the cat were her last tether to sanity.

Sebastian squared his shoulders, forcing himself to exude a confidence he didn't feel. "We gather the horses and load up the buggies. We head back to the farm. It's the safest place we have."

The survivors nodded, their movements slow and hesitant. They trusted him, even after everything that had happened. That trust was both a comfort and a burden. He couldn't let them down again. The servants he grew up trusting and calling family now held a look of fear, one that may not be of love. His heart strained with the thought that this would be the start of their disassociation because of the people he chooses to align with. The pain in his neck throbbed once again, distracting him from the start of the endless possibilities.

As they began to prepare for the journey, Sebastian glanced at Dominic, who was helping a young girl climb into one buggy. Dominic didn't merely belong here; he was needed here. Sebastian didn't know how or why, but he was certain of one thing. Dominic was their hope, and Sebastian would do whatever it took to protect him.

Chapter 31

Dominic

NOBODY SPEAKS ON THE ride back to the farm. Not a word, not even a whisper. The silence isn't peaceful; it's heavy, suffocating. The kind of silence that wraps itself around you and squeezes until it's all you can hear. I can't even think of anything to say that would bring peace to them. People are mourning, each lost in their own thoughts. Parents who have to face the unimaginable truth that they've outlived their children. Children who are realizing, for the first time, that they're now orphans. The weight of their grief fills the air, pressing down on all of us.

It's sad. So sad.

And here I am, sitting in the comfiest chair in the foyer of Cinderella's farmhouse. The chair, a worn but inviting chesterfield, feels like it's cradling my body. Its plush cushions ease the tension in my spine and my aching backside, sore from the hard ride and rough rocks. Calypso perches on my lap, purring softly. His rhythmic vibrations tap against my thigh, reminding me that at least someone is glad I'm still here.

The moments drag, time stretching into a slow crawl. I watch the servants go about the room, their movements quiet and deliberate as if trying not to disturb the delicate stillness. They carry rounds of tea to small, huddled groups of survivors, all clutching their cups like lifelines. They aren't drinking it to warm up or to quench thirst—it's just something to hold on to. Something solid in a world that has suddenly become so uncertain.

They are survivors. Every last one of them.

But me? I'm not so sure. I don't feel like a survivor. I feel like an outsider, just a bystander who has stumbled into their lives at the worst possible moment. I don't understand this world or the evil that just ripped it apart. The Concealment? I don't know what they are, and honestly, I don't want to. But what I do know is that they're worse than anything I've seen back home. And I've seen plenty.

Back in my world, evil comes in different forms—from muggers in dark alleys to corporate greed that leaves families bankrupt. People hurt others for money, for power, for the sake of their own twisted satisfaction. But this? This isn't like that. This isn't petty crime or unchecked capitalism. This is darkness—real, tangible darkness. And it doesn't just take lives. It devours them.

I look around at these people, the ones who've made it through the night. Despite everything they've lost, they hold onto each other. Their gratitude for simply being alive is etched into their faces. These aren't people who need much. They don't care about Instagram filters or the latest cars. They don't need sprawling lawns or fancy dinners to feel whole. These people cherish the little things, the simple joys of life.

I envy that.

And yet, they carry themselves like this isn't the first time they've faced horror. Like they've lived through something like this before. Is this just their reality? Do they expect this darkness to come back again? And if it does, who will be next?

My stomach twists at the thought. I'm not built for this. I'm not a hero. I'm not even the kind of person who stands up for himself most of the time. I can't imagine taking on this kind of evil, and I hope they don't expect me to. Because if they do, they'll be putting their faith in the wrong guy.

It's too much. Too much pressure, too much responsibility. I've never stood up to a bully, never confronted anyone who crossed me. Hell, I can't even fight back at Jasper! I don't have the strength, the courage, or the skill to fight something as monstrous as the Concealment. If they're looking for a savior, they need to look somewhere else.

As my thoughts spiral, the door swings open, and a harsh light fills the foyer. I blink against it, my eyes struggling to adjust. When I finally look up, two men stride in. Their uniforms gleam with navy velvet, the polished buttons and epaulets reflecting the light from the chandelier. Behind them, a woman follows, and my breath catches in my throat.

Her gown is a flowing cascade of frosty blue fabric, layered and shimmering like a frozen waterfall. The hem barely skims the floor, but the lightness gives it an ethereal quality, like she's floating rather than walking. Her shoes sparkle with crystals, each one catching the light and scattering it like tiny stars. And her face—her face is something I've seen before, in the pages of my childhood books.

Cinderella.

Sebastian excuses himself, stepping away from the group to greet her. Gretel, however, shrinks back into the shadows of the room, her sharp eyes watching the guards with suspicion. The darkness practically swallows her small frame, and I can't help but wonder why she's so intent on avoiding notice. We are in troubling times, and people are more focused on their grief from the Concealment over what she may be capable of.

And me? I just sit there, frozen. My mind spins. I can't believe she's real, standing right there in front of me. The actual Cinderella. She commands attention, yet remains approachable, down-to-earth. Maybe it's the way she glances around the room, taking in the faces of the survivors with a sadness that mirrors their own. Maybe it's the faint crease in her brow, a sign of the burden she carries.

I don't know what's about to happen, but as I sit here, I can't shake the feeling that my life has just shifted in a way I'm not ready for.

Chapter 32

Ella's presence was magnetic. Her beauty demanded reverence as she gracefully floated across the room, every head lowering in deference. Her eyelashes fluttered softly, delicate as butterfly wings, and her movements had an effortless grace. Her hands rested lightly, like a debutante gliding into a ballroom before she ascended the staircase.

Dominic couldn't look away. She was beautiful—not just in the traditional sense, but in a way that made everything else in the room fade into the background. The words he'd read about her in childhood books couldn't begin to describe her. They didn't do her justice. Calypso leapt down from his lap, sliding forward on the polished floor to join the subdued yet reverent crowd. Dominic's heart stopped for a moment as his mind emptied, overtaken by Ella's sheer presence.

"E-excuse me, Your Majesty," Dominic stammered, his neck straining from the sudden, awkward bow of his head. His cheeks burned as he scrambled to remember his manners.

"No worries, dear," Ella replied, her tone full of forgiveness, as though his flustered greeting wasn't a big deal.

Her warmth was disarming. Dominic thought about how different this was from back home, where people in positions of power exuded an air of entitlement that demanded respect. Ones that would get upset if not properly greeted to their liking. Ella didn't.

"You must be new here," she said, her tone as light and kind as a spring breeze. "I'm Ella."

He straightened, fumbling over his introduction. "Dominic, Your majesty. Dominic Graves."

She smiled, an expression so genuine that it almost put him at ease. "I heard what happened last night. It must've been horrible."

"It was," Dominic said, swallowing hard as the memories surfaced. "I've never seen anything like it. So much sadness."

Her eyes softened, glistening as though she truly felt the weight of his words. "I can only imagine."

At Dominic's feet, Calypso wound his tail around his legs. The usually vocal cat was subdued, as though he, too, felt the gravity of the moment.

"I was informed about your arrival, Sir Graves," Ella continued, her voice thoughtful. "I also learned about where you came from."

Dominic raised a brow, intrigued. "Have you been to New York?"

Ella shook her head with a soft laugh. "Of course not. I've never even heard of it. But that doesn't mean it doesn't exist."

She extended her hand, her touch as gentle as her demeanor. "Come with me. I have something to show you."

Dominic's heart raced as her fingers caressed his. He followed her through the winding halls of the farmhouse, passing rooms bustling with helpers boiling water and kneading dough. A refreshing coolness filled the air, a stark contrast to the inviting warmth of the hearth. Flames danced around a massive cauldron, the embers casting golden light across Ella's face. She paused there, her gaze fixed on the fire, and placed a hand over her chest.

"Everything all right?" Dominic asked, his concern genuine.

She didn't answer right away. Her eyes lingered on the flames, as if lost in some distant memory. Finally, she spoke, her voice tinged with nostalgia. "I was just reminiscing about the source of my identity."

Cinder.

He knew her story well enough to understand the weight that word carried for her. It wasn't just a name; it was a scar, a constant reminder of the cruelty she'd endured. To people in Dominic's world, it's a name people spoke freely and embraced with fun and humor, but to her it's her history of pain and trauma.

"I'm sorry, Ella," he said softly. "I know they weren't kind to you. That name means nothing anymore."

Ella turned to him with a bittersweet smile. "On the contrary, it does. That name is a part of me. Yes, it came from pain, from the insults and humiliation my stepmother and stepsisters heaped upon me. But it also reminds me of what I overcame. It's part of my story."

Dominic recalled tormenting words, self-inflicted wounds on his soul. She had a point. You could try to forget, but the scars would always remain. Whether you embraced them or buried them, they became part of you. Time may have passed to allow healing, but the memory and pain would always linger, trying its hardest to sting like before.

"Come," she said, breaking the heavy silence. "There's more to see."

They stepped outside, where chickens scattered across the courtyard, pecking at freshly thrown feed. Dogs, overstimulated and eager, ran up to sniff them both, tails wagging furiously. Ella's face lit up as they passed the horses, her hand reaching out to stroke one of the sleek manes. The sight of her in this setting—so at ease, so happy—gave Dominic a glimpse into what must have been her refuge during her darkest days. He imagined her finding solace in the animals and the farmhands, her support system.

As they moved farther from the farmhouse, the grass grew thicker, brushing against their legs. The cascade of her golden hair bounced all the way to the crook of her back with each step. They approached a towering tree, its branches sprawling like arms that embraced the sky. At its base sat two flat boulders, weathered by time and nature. The sight of them filled Dominic with a quiet reverence.

"This place means so much to me," Ella said, resting her hand on one stone. "I come here often to think."

Dominic nodded, sensing the weight of her emotions. "Is this where—?"

"Yes," she said softly, her fingers tracing the boulder's surface. "This is where my parents rest."

The sunlight caught the tear forming in her eye, and Dominic felt his throat tighten. "I'm so sorry for your loss," he said, his voice barely above a whisper.

"Thank you," Ella replied, her voice steady despite the pain in her cornflower eyes. "For a long time, I dwelled on all they've missed. I wished they could have been there to protect me."

"From your stepfamily?" Dominic guessed.

Ella nodded, her gaze distant. "I've learned that darkness isn't just something external. It's in all of us. Some succumb to it, while others fight it. I made a promise to my mother to always choose kindness, no matter how hard it gets."

"Kindness," Dominic echoed. The word felt heavy, like a shield against an overwhelming force.

Ella's eyes met his, filled with both sadness and strength. "The Concealment is only one form of darkness. There will always be another. We can never truly defeat evil; we can only control it. It's a constant battle, and even when you're scared, you have to fight."

"I don't know if I can fight," he admitted, heart pounding. "I've never fought anyone, let alone something like the Concealment."

Ella smiled, a knowing warmth in her expression. "That's why you're here. Let me take you to the castle. We'll train you. Together, we'll fight this darkness."

SEBASTIAN STOOD NEAR the hearth with the other servants, watching Ella glide through the room. It had been too long since he'd last seen her, and while their time together was limited by her royal obligations, he was glad she'd finally found a family who truly valued her. Her former family had only the bare minimum to tolerate her, keeping her under their roof out of obligation rather than love.

His eyes scanned the crowded foyer, the survivors' shared sorrow weighing heavily in the air. In the far corner, almost obscured by the throng, he spotted Gretel. Draped in a wool blanket, she sat cradling a cup of tea in her hands, her wide eyes darting across the room from the shadows in the corner. She didn't seem to search for comfort—only scanning for judgment. But nobody appeared to be paying her any attention.

"Are you okay?" Agnes asked as she approached him, holding a tray of biscuits.

"I will be," Sebastian said, the steam creeping into his sinuses.

"I just want to make sure that you're not making any decisions that will be costly."

"What do you mean?"

"I mean, you take this kid under your wing, and now her. You don't even know these two."

"You know why Dominic is here," he said, biscuit crumbs falling out his mouth. "He's the chosen one."

"Is he?" Agnes asked. "He hasn't done anything yet. And now we lost Petunia."

The rest of the biscuit crumbled in his hand. He didn't care if the floor became polluted with bits of the baked good. His teeth gritted with heat radiating from the red spot on his neck from the strangulation.

"Petunia's death is not Dominic's fault. You know that," Sebastian hissed. "You've known me since I could walk. Have some faith in me when I put my trust in people."

"Okay," Agnes said, her mouth tight.

"That includes Gretel, too," he added. "She saved my life. Would Concealment help us if they didn't want Dominic to be the one to shut out the darkness?"

"I suppose you're right."

"Please, don't look at me differently because of her. Don't look at her the way others do. She's good."

"Okay."

Sebastian tilted his head in her direction to acknowledge Gretel. She blinked, her expression unreadable, but it was the first sign of life he'd seen from her since morning. He'd heard the stories about her—the whispers of how she'd killed her own family. He had no idea if the rumors were true, but her actions the previous night spoke louder than gossip. She'd saved them, risking her life when she didn't have to. That alone made Sebastian pause. There was light in her, even if it was hidden beneath layers of mischief and whatever troubles she carried.

He resolved to reach out. If someone like Gretel could be steered toward the light, perhaps she could be an ally in the fight ahead.

Giselle gave him a look of concern as he stepped away from the group. Her need for solace grew; she needed a guiding hand through her sorrow and pain. Her lips parted slightly as though she might protest his leaving. But Sebastian didn't stop.

He approached Gretel carefully, not wanting to startle her. "How're you holding up?" he asked.

She shrank deeper into her blanket, her fingers tightening around the mug. "Fine," she replied curtly, her tone colder than the tea she clung to.

Sebastian tried again, his voice sincere. "I didn't get the chance to thank you for your help last night."

Her lips twitched, betraying a hint of emotion she tried to suppress. It wasn't quite a smile, but it was close.

"I mean it. I've heard about you," he admitted, lowering his voice. "I know it must've taken a lot for you to step in and help us."

Her eyebrows furrowed, and she let out a small cough, as if clearing her throat to hold back a retort. "Excuse me?"

"You're Gretel," he said. "One of the most notorious people in the area. I didn't think you were the type to look out for anyone but yourself based on what everybody has said."

Her reaction was swift. Her eyes rolled skyward, and her body shifted as though she might storm off if she had anywhere else to go. "Well then," she snapped, "it looks like you don't know me at all."

Sebastian winced. He hadn't meant to offend her, but exhaustion and worry had made him clumsier with his words than usual. "I'm sorry," he said, his tone softer now. "You're right—I don't know you. But I'd like to get to as we figure this out."

Her posture softened ever so slightly, the blanket slipping from one shoulder. She sipped her tea in silence, but she wasn't shutting him out entirely anymore.

"Look," he continued, his voice earnest, "I'm thankful for what you did for Dominic and me. We differ, yet we're united in wanting to protect him. That's a good place to start, don't you think?"

She remained silent. Then, to his surprise, the faintest smirk curved her lips. "I guess you're right," she whispered, her voice carrying a flicker of warmth.

Sebastian nodded, relief washing over him. Whatever Gretel's past, there was hope for her yet.

The door swung open, breaking the fragile peace. Ella stepped inside, her regal presence commanding attention. Dominic followed behind her, his demeanor a stark contrast to hers. Where Ella radiated confidence, Dominic looked timid, his hands fidgeting and his eyes avoiding contact. Sebastian noticed him picking at his arms.

"Sebastian," Ella said, her voice bright with purpose. "I'm taking Sir Graves to the castle for training. Care to join us?"

Sebastian nodded without hesitation. "Of course."

"I believe Agnes and Giselle can handle the group here," Ella added, her tone firm but encouraging. The two girls exchanged uncertain glances before nodding in agreement, unwilling to contradict her.

"Excellent," Ella said. Her eyes flicked toward Gretel, who was trying to shrink back into the shadows. "You should come too. You look like you could benefit from some lessons, Miss..."

"Bernadette," Gretel interjected hastily, her voice sharp with panic. "My name's Bernadette."

Ella's brow arched in mild curiosity, but she didn't press further. Instead, she clapped her hands, summoning the guards. "Very well. Let's get the carriage ready for you three. We've got a long day ahead."

Sebastian cast a glance at Dominic, who seemed torn between excitement and dread. Then he looked at Gretel, whose defiant smirk had returned, masking whatever uncertainty she felt. And finally, he turned his gaze to Ella, whose confidence steadied them all.

Another long day, he thought. But at least this time, they'd face it together.

Chapter 33

It was early afternoon, and Dominic already wanted the day to end. The sun hung high in the sky, mocking his exhaustion. Days here were longer than in New York. For some reason, it felt like the sun rose earlier and set later, stretching every moment into an endurance test. Back home, he'd complained about life's nonstop grind, but this place was something else. Work here wasn't just hard—it was relentless—and he wasn't even doing the manual labor like everyone else.

He slumped in the carriage, trying to appreciate the small mercy of the cushioned seat. It wasn't luxurious by any means, but compared to riding horseback, it felt like paradise. His thighs still ached from the earlier journey, and the memory of the saddle smashing into his most sensitive areas made him wince. Across from him, Gretel sat stiffly, her arms crossed as if trying to keep her guard up even in her exhaustion. But Dominic could notice the strain around her eyes, the heaviness in her posture. He caught her head nodding forward a few times, only for her to jerk back upright as if she didn't trust herself to relax.

He wished he could close his own eyes, but the weight of everything that had happened pressed too heavily on his chest. The fire, the attacks, the screams—it all played on a loop in his head. He glanced at Gretel again, wondering how she managed to keep going. Despite similar or worse experiences, she remained sharp, agile, and prepared. The situation made him feel soft, like he wasn't built for any of this.

Dominic straightened in his seat as the carriage rattled into town with the last of the roxogals turning to the fields. Cobblestone streets echoed with the clatter of wheels and the rhythmic clop of horse hooves. Upon their entrance, everything froze. Conversations stopped mid-sentence, and all eyes turned toward the carriage. The noise of daily life faded into a hushed murmur as townspeople began bowing, their heads lowering in reverence.

The attention made Dominic's skin prickle. He knew the bows were for Ella, who sat gracefully at the front of the carriage, her poise as effortless as always. But for a fleeting moment, Dominic let himself pretend it was for him. In New York, he'd always been invisible, just another face in the crowd, another body taking up space. Here, people looked, even if it wasn't really at him. It was intoxicating in a way, though he hated himself for thinking about it.

The gates to the castle creaked open, their iron bars scraping loudly as they swung inward. Inside, the courtyard was immaculate. Perfectly trimmed hedges formed geometric patterns, their precision rivaling the work of any high-end landscaper back home. Statues and fountains dotted the space, their marble surfaces gleaming in the sunlight. A team of gardeners worked in the background, trimming every leaf and blade of grass to perfection. Dominic couldn't help but gape at the sheer opulence. It was like walking into a period drama.

When the carriage stopped, Dominic groaned at the sight of the steps leading up to the castle's main entrance. At least a hundred steps rose steeply like a mountain, and he felt unequipped to climb them.

It's fine, he thought. *Maybe I'll just roll down them later, get this day over with faster.*

"Welcome to Mynnshire Castle," the footman said, his cheeks rosy with glee as he turned back to Dominic.

But instead of heading for the grand staircase, they were guided toward a side building. The air inside was cooler, the stone walls absorbing the heat of the sun. They entered a vast, empty room, a few children practicing their dancing in the far corner next to the lineup of knight's armor. Their instructors barked commands with military precision, stepping on their toes with little patience for mistakes. A lone violinist in the back corner scratched out a tune, the droop on his face looking like he wanted to be anywhere else. Dominic envied him.

Ella clapped her hands lightly, drawing everyone's attention. "This," she said, her voice carrying across the room, "is where you'll train."

Dominic blinked as he glanced around the room, his gaze lingering on the bored violinist and the fidgeting children. Somehow, he'd imagined something a little grander. Maybe an armory with gleaming swords or a medieval training ground complete with straw dummies. Not this.

The room's distant door opened, and three men entered. Their boots clicked against the marble floor, their movements perfectly synchronized. Dominic couldn't deny they were impressive—their uniforms were pristine with the elder in glossy mint and the younger two in coral, their faces stern. They looked like the kind of men who had never doubted themselves a day in their lives.

"This is Sir Winston," Ella announced, gesturing to the tallest of the group. "He is one of the finest fencing instructors in the kingdom. And these are his top students, Callaghan and Phineas."

Dominic studied them as they approached. Sir Winston looked like he'd stepped out of an oil painting, every detail of his appearance meticulously groomed. His pale complexion and perfectly waxed curly mustache gave him an almost ethereal air. By contrast, Callaghan and Phineas were younger, their slicked-back blonde hair and sleepy eyes giving them an air of detached arrogance. They were much more cocky than he remembered them back in town, the snarls on their faces when he bumped into them reminded him of the hallways in high school. Their snickering comments echoing down the street reminded him of Jasper's superiority complex.

Ella turned to leave, her gown sweeping behind her in a way that made it seem alive. "I'll leave you to it," she said over her shoulder, disappearing into the corridor.

Sir Winston's gaze landed on Dominic, sharp and appraising. He raised one eyebrow, his lips curling into a smirk. "So," he said, his voice dripping with condescension, "this is the one who's going to save us from the darkness?"

Callaghan and Phineas chuckled, their amusement barely stifled. Dominic's stomach churned, but he forced himself to meet Winston's gaze. The moment reminded him too much of middle school, standing in line as team captains decided who to pick. He'd always been the last choice, the kid no one thought could pull his weight. His determination to work harder resulted from that, hitting baseballs so far that his doubters were left slack-jawed.

"I guess so," Dominic said with a shrug, trying to sound unfazed. "And you're the guy who's going to turn me into a hero?"

Winston's smirk disappeared, replaced by a glint of annoyance. "Grab a foil," he ordered, gesturing toward the rack of weapons.

Dominic hesitated, his palms already sweating. He could feel Gretel's eyes on him, as well as the sneers from Callaghan and Phineas. Crossing the room felt like walking into the lion's den, but he forced his legs to move. The rack of swords gleamed under the dim light, their hilts varying in design and size. He reached for one with a robin's-egg-blue handle, its smooth surface comforting in his grip.

"Let's see what you've got," Winston said, raising his blade with ease.

Dominic stepped forward, his heart pounding. The sword felt awkward in his hand, heavier than he'd expected. He squared his shoulders, trying to ignore the tightness in his chest. For a moment, he thought about charging, but Winston's smug expression made him hesitate. He didn't want to give the man the satisfaction of seeing him falter.

Finally, Dominic lunged. The clash of metal rang out as Winston deflected the blow with ease. Dominic swung again, harder this time, but Winston blocked it without even flinching. Winston met each strike with the same effortless deflection, and the sound of Callaghan and Phineas snickering in the background only made Dominic more desperate. His arm ached, the muscles burning with every failed attempt. Sweat dripped down his temple, stinging his eyes. He swung one last time, but his grip slipped, and the sword clattered to the floor with a deafening crash.

"Pick up your weapon," Winston said, his voice cold and unyielding. "We have a lot of work to do."

Chapter 34

Gretel

TWO HOURS. TWO AGONIZING hours of listening to the relentless clang of swords, the sharp scrape of metals, the grunts of effort, and the dull thuds of Dominic hitting the ground—over and over again. Sir Winston is merciless, and Callaghan and Phineas are even worse, so smug. They don't merely want to win; they want to humiliate us.

I'm holding my own, though. The longer I practice, the more I get the hang of the sword. It's not my weapon of choice—I'd take my daggers over this hunk of metal any day—but I can feel my body adjusting to the weight, the movements. A few times, I even manage to gain the upper hand, usually when Phineas gets distracted with his own arrogance. He's too busy taunting Dominic to notice my blade coming for him.

But Dominic...Dominic is struggling.

He keeps charging, keeps swinging, keeps trying, but it's painful to watch. His movements are clumsy, his attacks easily deflected. Every time Sir Winston knocks him down, Dominic gets back up, only to get knocked down again. I admire his persistence, but even I can see how much this is wearing him down. He doesn't belong in this kind of fight—not yet, at least.

I can't help but see my brother in him. Hansel was like that too, once. So innocent, so hopeful, so determined to prove himself. Back then, I'm always the one to look out for him, to make sure he doesn't get hurt. But Dominic isn't Hansel. He's his own person, and he has his own battles to fight. Still, watching him reminds me of a time when I believed in something—someone—with all my heart.

And now...I'm not sure what I believe in anymore.

The door creaks open, breaking my thoughts. A short man in an oversized fuchsia suit stumbles into the room, panting as if he's just run across the entire castle. His ridiculous outfit is too big for him, the fabric bouncing with every labored breath.

"The queen...invites you...to dinner," he wheezes, barely getting the words out.

Calypso perks up at the announcement. He slides across the floor like an excited child, his tail swishing with anticipation. At least someone's having a good time.

"Enough for today," Sir Winston declares, planting his sword into the rack with a sharp clang.

Dominic immediately collapses to his knees, bracing himself against the instructor for support. Winston shoves him off like he's an insect, and Dominic crumples to the floor. Sebastian rushes over to help, his face full of concern.

"You okay?" Sebastian asks, crouching beside him.

"Yeah," Dominic mumbles, though his shaky breath says otherwise. He isn't okay. Not even close.

Callaghan and Phineas linger by the door, whispering to each other like conspirators. Their smug laughter makes my blood boil. They have the nerve to mock us after hours of showing off? I want to say something, but Dominic beats me to it—sort of.

He tries to stand, wobbling like a newborn deer. "I'm—"

Before he can finish, Callaghan sneers, "You two have got to be the worst students this castle has ever seen."

Dominic's head drops, his shoulders folding inward. I clench my fists. He doesn't deserve this. Sure, he's not great with a sword, but he's trying. That has to count for something.

"Get up," I say sharply, grabbing his arm to pull him to his feet. He's heavier than I expect, and when his knees buckle again, I have to let him go before we both topple over.

"If this is what the queen thinks will save us, we're doomed," Phineas adds with a laugh.

Something inside me snaps. Before I know it, my daggers are in my hands, and I'm on Callaghan. My blade hovers just inches from his neck, my knuckles white from the grip.

"Gr-Bernadette, stop!" Sebastian shouts from behind me.

But I don't move. My eyes lock onto Callaghan's, and for a moment, his smug expression falters. Just a moment.

"What's the matter, little girl?" he says, his smirk returning. "You think that's enough to scare me?"

Phineas steps closer, circling around me. "Careful, you wouldn't want to embarrass yourself even more."

I angle my second dagger toward him without breaking eye contact with Callaghan. "Leave him alone," I hiss.

"Make us," Callaghan challenges, leaning closer to my blade as if daring me to act.

Sir Winston's voice, sharp as a whip, follows the door bursting open. "Enough!" he barks, his glare sweeping over all of us. "They mustn't keep the queen waiting."

Reluctantly, I lower my daggers and step back, sheathing them with a sharp snap. Callaghan and Phineas smirk as they turn to leave, but not before Callaghan leans in close enough for only me to hear.

"Midnight. Courtyard," he whispers. "We'll settle this."

I don't respond, staring him down until he finally walks away. My fingers itch to draw my daggers again, but I force myself to stay still. There will be time for that later. As Dominic leans heavily on

Sebastian, I look over at him. He's pale, exhausted, but his eyes meet mine with a flicker of determination. He's tougher than he gives himself credit for. Maybe not a fighter yet, but he has the heart for it.

Midnight can't come soon enough.

Chapter 35

The walk to the dining table felt more like a jaunt through a museum of unimaginable wealth. Dominic trailed behind the others, wide-eyed as they passed through corridors filled with polished surfaces, gleaming chandeliers, and antiques that looked brand new. Compared to this, his first apartment back in New York might as well have been a broom closet. Even a walk-in closet in this place could make his old home look shabby.

Dominic tried to ignore Gretel's simmering anger. Her boots scuffed against the floor with a deliberate, irritated rhythm as though she were stomping on Phineas and Callaghan. Her anger was justified, but sometimes it's wiser to let things go. They were better armed, stronger, and more skilled. Even if Sebastian could probably take them down, he wasn't about to risk offending the queen by starting a fight. Gretel, on the other hand, looked like she might enjoy it.

"You're not going to fight them, are you?" Sebastian muttered as they passed the knight statues, his low voice bouncing off the metal armor.

"No, of course not," Gretel said quickly.

"Good. Just think about the bigger picture. We can't waste our time and energy on them."

When they entered the dining area, Dominic couldn't help but gawk. Every shade of green imaginable painted the walls, giving the space a strange but regal warmth. A massive tangerine-colored table stretched across the room, laden with antique plates and silverware so shiny they reflected the candlelight.

At the head of the table, Calypso sat like a king, his fur ruffled and his tail swishing lazily. The cat was already halfway through a feast of roasted meats—chicken, duck, salmon—his tiny mouth stuffed with more food than Dominic thought possible.

"There you are," Ella said, rising from her seat at the far end of the table. A warm, gentle smile played on her lips. "Please, sit. Help yourself to anything you'd like."

Dominic didn't need to be told twice. His stomach growled as he lunged for a plate, his hands shaking with eagerness as he battled his heavy muscles. Gretel had beaten him to the food, her nimble fingers already piling corn and duck onto her plate with impressive speed.

She's quick, Dominic thought. *No wonder she was such a good thief.*

The steam rising from the roasted carrots and potatoes hit Dominic's face like a soothing balm, and the rich aroma of rosemary and thyme made his mouth water. The chicken on the platter gleamed with juices, begging to be devoured. He grabbed a fork and knife, barely able to steady his hands long enough to carve into the tender meat.

Dominic didn't bother with manners. He dug in with the fervor of someone who hadn't eaten in days, which wasn't far from the truth. Back home, he'd skipped meals often enough—sometimes to save money, other times because he was too busy to eat—but this was on a whole other level. The food here wasn't just sustenance; it was an indulgence, a luxury he hadn't realized he'd missed so much. The days he went with little to no food was hard on his body, and the loosening waistline on his pants was showing for it.

Ella and Sebastian exchanged amused glances as they watched Dominic and Gretel devour their meals. Even Calypso, now gnawing on a duck leg, seemed less concerned with table etiquette than usual.

"Worked up quite the appetite, haven't you?" came a deep, melodic voice from behind Ella.

Dominic froze, his mouth full of chicken, as the speaker stepped into view. The man was tall, his jet-black hair slicked back to perfection. Bronze buttons, gleaming in the candlelight, adorned his ivory outfit, and the red fringe of his epaulets bounced with each step. He had the air of someone who belonged here, someone who commanded attention without trying.

"Forgive us, King Sawyer," Sebastian said quickly, his cheeks flushing as he stood and bowed. "They haven't eaten in quite some time."

King? Dominic thought, almost choking on his food. *That's the king?*

"Don't worry about it," Sawyer said with a chuckle, waving Sebastian's concern away. "After a long day, I've been known to eat like that, too."

Relieved, Dominic wiped his mouth with his sleeve and took a sip of water to compose himself. "Thank you for understanding," he said, his voice hoarse. "And thank you for your hospitality, Your Highness."

"It's our pleasure," Sawyer replied, settling into a chair near Ella. "Ella tells me you're not from around here."

Dominic swallowed hard. "That's right."

"Where are you from?" the king asked, leaning forward with genuine curiosity.

"America," Dominic replied, bracing himself for the usual confusion.

"I've never heard of it," Sawyer admitted, his brow furrowing. "Is it a small kingdom?"

"Not exactly. It's big, crowded, noisy. People from all over the world live there."

"Fascinating," the king said, his amber eyes lighting up. "And do you have royalty there?"

"Not really," Dominic said with a smirk. "We've got people who act like royalty, though."

Sawyer laughed. "It sounds like quite the place."

"It is," Dominic said, though his tone lacked the usual spark. He wasn't sure he missed it all that much. "You can say something like that. It's a melting pot of all different kinds of people."

"Is there a royal family there?"

Not if you don't count the Kardashians, I guess, Dominic thought.

"Not necessarily. But we do have those who work and those who have people work for them."

Yeah, there are those that benefit from the blood, sweat, and tears of the struggling families.

"Fascinating," Sawyer said in astonishment. "How is that working out there? It didn't really do so well here. Yes, there was an economic system that was functional, but there was no happiness or stability amongst the people. It seemed that there was a group that thrived off of the generosity of others.

Dominic looked through the ornate dining hall, his head spinning from the richness of the food. The golden candlelight flickered off the walls, dancing along with the chatter around the table. As he cut another generous square of butter to spread on a soft roll, he rolled his eyes at himself.

"That's how it's like there," he said, referring to New York, his tone casual but laced with irony. He waved his knife lazily. "Maybe you should come back with me, King Sawyer, and run for president. We could use someone like you."

Sawyer blinked, looking amused but confused. "What's a president?"

"Never mind," Dominic said with a dismissive laugh. He leaned back, rubbing his stomach, which now felt like it was on the verge of bursting. It had been a long time since he'd eaten so much in one sitting, and now the fullness hit him all at once. Sweat dotted his forehead, dampening the hair at his temples. Across the table, Sebastian smirked at him, enjoying his discomfort.

"Ella has done so much for this kingdom since her reign a year ago," Sawyer said, his voice warm with pride. He reached across the table and grasped Ella's hand. "I'm very lucky to have met her at the festival. Without her, the kingdom—and I—would have suffered far longer."

Dominic perked up at the mention of the festival. "Oh, the festival!" He froze for a moment, realizing he might have said too much. "Wait, uh...you know, the one where you met. Everyone talks about it."

Sawyer tilted his head slightly. "You've heard about it? But you said you've never been to this kingdom."

Crap, Dominic thought, his mind scrambling for an excuse. He couldn't exactly tell them that their love story was famous in his world because it was written in a children's book.

"Oh, you know how it is," Dominic said, feigning nonchalance. "Word travels fast. The people here are really passionate about your journey."

Sawyer and Ella exchanged a fond smile, pleased by his answer. "It was a magical night," Ella said, her tone wistful. "I wouldn't be here today if not for my friend. I never dreamed I'd get a chance to attend something like that, let alone survive it."

Dominic furrowed his brow. "Survive it?"

Ella nodded, her expression softening with memory. "My stepmother and stepsisters...well, they weren't the kindest to me. When I returned from the festival and they found out the prince was looking for the maiden who had lost her golden shoe, they did everything they could to keep me from claiming it."

"She was wicked," Dominic said, his voice low, almost instinctive. "I heard."

Ella smiled at his solidarity. "The birds saved me," she continued. "They flocked to my stepmother and stepsisters, blinding them and—well, they did what they had to do."

Dominic felt his stomach twist at the imagery. Birds pecking at eyes and ripping flesh from toes weren't details he remembered from the fairy tale, but Ella recounted it calmly, as though it were simply another chapter in her story.

"That's horrible," Gretel chimed in, her voice low. It was the first time she'd spoken since dinner began. Dominic glanced at her, grateful for the interruption.

"I know," Ella admitted, her tone a mixture of sadness and resolve. "But I've forgiven them. My mother always taught me to forgive those who hurt you."

Dominic tilted his head, confused. "Wait a minute," he said cautiously. "Didn't you just say you banished them from the farm?"

Ella rose from her seat, her graceful movements quieting the room. Her fingers brushed a stray strand of hair back into place as she turned to Dominic, her gaze calm but firm.

"Forgiveness doesn't mean forgetting," she explained. "It means releasing the hold someone has over you. Letting go of the anger, the resentment—that's how you take your power back. But that doesn't mean you allow them back into your life to hurt you again."

Dominic held her gaze, her words sinking in deeper than he expected. She was right. At least, it felt right. He thought back to all the times he'd held onto resentment and let it fester in his mind and heart. What had it gotten him? Nothing but bitterness.

"I guess that makes sense," he said, his voice quieter now. "I've never thought about it like that."

Ella smiled. "You'll learn. Sometimes, strength isn't about fighting battles—it's about knowing which ones are worth fighting."

Sawyer reached for her hand again, his eyes glowing with admiration. "Ella's resilience is the reason this kingdom thrives. Without her, none of this would have been possible."

Dominic smiled faintly, watching the two of them. Their love story had always seemed like a fairytale because it indeed was one. But sitting here, listening to them speak, it felt more real than he ever imagined. They probably weren't perfect—they'd fought their battles and paid their dues—but they'd found happiness together.

"You three must be exhausted after such a long day," Ella said, her voice gentle again. "Let us show you to your rooms."

Dominic nodded, the thought of a bed sounding like heaven. He glanced at Sebastian, who mirrored his relief. They spoke in unison: "That would be nice."

Dominic chuckled, a rare moment of levity easing the tension from the day. As they followed Ella and Sawyer through the corridors, Dominic's thoughts lingered on her words about forgiveness. Maybe there was something to this idea of letting go. Maybe he could learn to forgive himself too.

DOMINIC WADDLED OUT of the dining room, his bloated stomach leading the way like a balloon about to burst. He regretted every bite of the feast, even though he knew he couldn't have stopped himself if he tried. It wasn't every day that a table groaned under the weight of such decadent food, and he'd treated it like a personal challenge to taste every single dish. Now, his blouse stretched tight over his belly, the fabric protesting with each breath he took. He could barely move without feeling like he was going to pop, and the effort to put one foot in front of the other up the grand staircase felt like an Olympic trial. Its elegant marble steps seemed to mock him, each one polished to a high shine that reflected his awkward waddling figure. He winced as his shoes scuffed the pristine surface, his movements slowed by the constant jabs of discomfort in his overstuffed gut.

The castle was opulence personified. Every corridor, every chamber was immaculate, with murals of fruit and bountiful harvests adorning the walls in rich, detailed colors that practically leapt off the surface. Dominic couldn't help but resent them a little. How could anyone live among so much luxury and stay sane? His thoughts returned to his old, cramped apartment with its single, lopsided poster on a wall that was unpainted since the 1980s and stained with cigarette smoke. That dingy place was a palace compared to the orphanage where he grew up. But being in Ella's castle was a completely different universe.

Ella led the way, her presence as calm and composed as ever. She stopped at each guest room, offering a gentle smile as she opened the doors. Gretel was the first to disappear, her face still set in a simmering scowl from earlier. Her boots scuffed the floor, and Dominic didn't need to ask what she was thinking. He'd felt the same frustration, but where Gretel bristled with barely contained energy, Dominic preferred to avoid confrontation. Why poke the bear when you were clearly the smaller animal?

Next came Sebastian, whose room boasted a breathtaking view of the town below. Dominic glimpsed flickering torches lighting the streets, the trees swaying gently in the breeze. It was a calming sight, one that made the harsh realities of the day feel more bearable. Yet it also made Dominic painfully aware of how far from home he was—not just physically, but emotionally. He didn't belong here, no matter how much food he stuffed himself with or how often people called him "Sir Graves."

Finally, Ella brought Dominic to his room at the end of the corridor. The walk felt like an eternity, but it gave her plenty of time to point out the various treasures displayed on polished mantles along the way. Candleholders, vases, trinkets—all pristine and radiating wealth. Dominic could barely nod in response; his eyes glazed over until they landed on the most spectacular artifact of all.

The golden slipper.

It sat atop a navy velvet cushion, catching the light in a way that made it almost glow. The delicate bronze vines curling over the heel and toe seemed too intricate, too perfect to be real. Dominic stared, mesmerized. He thought of the stories he'd read, the ones that described this very object, but no words could have prepared him for seeing it in person.

The temptation to reach out and touch it was overwhelming. He knew it wouldn't fit—unless the shoe could magically expand to a size twelve and accommodate his less-than-slender feet—but he still wondered what it would feel like. The memories of a Halloween party when he first moved to the city bubbled up in his mind. He'd dressed in drag, his first and only time, and strutted into a run-down apartment with all the confidence he could muster. The look on their faces had been priceless. Even with his poorly applied makeup and a pair of wobbly heels that didn't quite fit, he'd owned the night. That memory gave him a small, bittersweet smile as he turned away from the slipper and followed Ella into his room.

The doors swung open, as though pushed by invisible hands. Dominic stepped inside and froze, his breath catching in his throat. The room was massive. Larger than any he'd ever seen, larger than he thought a bedroom had any right to be. The ceiling stretched high above him, painted with an intricate mural of woodland scenes that seemed to come alive under the glow of the lights. Every detail was flawless, from the delicate veins on painted leaves to the shimmering golden light filtering through the imagined trees. He had to crane his neck just to take it all in.

The bed dominated the room, an enormous expanse of plush comfort that looked big enough to fit a family of five. The blush-colored comforter appeared soft enough to sink into forever, and Dominic immediately felt his knees wobble at the thought of lying down on something that luxurious. Calypso, ever the opportunist, had already perched on the bed. The cat kneaded the fabric with his paws, his purring loud enough to echo off the walls.

"This is beautiful," Dominic said, his voice barely above a whisper.

Ella smiled with pleasure. "Thank you. I decorated it myself."

Her voice softened as she ran her hand along the back of an olive velvet chair. "My mother inspired this room. She loved nature—everything about it. She believed every part of the earth had a purpose, even the hardships we face. And her favorite color was pink."

Dominic nodded, though the sentiment didn't sit well with him. He wasn't one to believe in things happening for a reason. Too many bad things had happened to him for that idea to hold any weight. Still, he wasn't about to argue with a queen.

"It's lovely," he said.

Ella perched on the edge of the bed, her hands trailing through Calypso's fur. She tilted her head, looking at Dominic with an expression that was both curious and kind. "What about your mother? Was she like that?"

Dominic hesitated, the question catching him off guard. "I...I never knew my mother," he admitted, his voice faltering.

Ella's face softened. "I'm sorry."

"It's okay," Dominic said quickly, though the familiar ache in his chest told a different story. "I grew up in an orphanage. The woman who ran it—she was the closest thing I had to a mom. And the other kids there. They were my family."

"Oh. Well, I hope she fostered you pleasantly."

"She did," Dominic said, his stomach turning, remembering her recent passing. "She and the other kids were the only family I could claim, even though we weren't related. They were there for me when I needed someone to. They are like a chosen family."

"Chosen family? Like you get to choose who you want? I've never heard of that."

"Chosen family," Dominic explained, seeing the confusion on Ella's face. "It's when you build your family from the people who love and support you, even if you're not related by blood."

Ella nodded slowly, though her expression suggested she didn't fully understand. Dominic tried to clarify, using her own story as an example. "The helpers on your farm—the ones who treated you kindly while your stepmother didn't—they're like a chosen family, right?"

Ella's eyes lit up with understanding. "I suppose they are," she said, her voice thoughtful.

Dominic watched Ella disappear down the hall, her slippers clicking softly against the polished floor. Her graceful movements and cheerful demeanor seemed at odds with how late it had become. Her parting words hung in the air: "Off to bed for you! What am I even doing here keeping you up so late?"

The grand doors to his room shut behind him, their smooth, magical swing still something he wasn't used to. Dominic crossed the room, taking in the sight once again: the sprawling bed, the plush comforter, the swirling woodland mural painted on the ceiling. It all screamed luxury, a far cry from the lumpy mattress in his apartment or the scratchy straw bedding or the rocky hideout since landing in this strange world.

He wasted no time. Stripping off his clothes, piece by piece, he let them fall to the floor without a second thought. Even his underwear joined the pile. He wasn't sure if it was the weight of the day or the indulgence of dinner, but modesty had taken a backseat to comfort. After placing the sapphire necklace on top of his clothing, he caught one final wink of the moonlight reflecting from the gemstone. The sheets embraced him like a cloud, and as his head sank into the pillow, his body released all its tension. His spine let out a satisfying series of pops as he stretched, and for the first time in what felt like forever, Dominic felt at peace.

As his eyes drifted shut, the swirling birds in the mural above seemed to bid him goodnight. The cool breeze from the open window kissed his cheek, a gentle reminder of the world outside. For a brief moment, the puzzling conversation with Ella about family and forgiveness flickered through his mind, but he pushed it aside. The queen could afford to philosophize about it from her gilded throne, but Dominic knew the reality was messier. He had experienced enough of life to know that pain didn't always lead to growth, and forgiveness didn't always mean forgetting.

He was on the brink of sleep, his breathing evening out, when—

TAP. TAP. TAP.

The sound barely registered at first. Dominic rolled onto his side, groaning softly. *Probably just some mice scuttling around*, he thought. It wasn't his problem. *Let them have their midnight fun*; he wasn't about to let a few rodents ruin his long-awaited sleep.

TAP! TAP! TAP!

The noise grew louder, more insistent. Dominic opened one eye, groaning in frustration. "Really?" he muttered to no one in particular. Dragging his hand down his face, he sat up reluctantly. A chill shot up his legs from the cool stone beneath his bare feet as he stood, weighed down by grogginess like a lead blanket.

A soft creak preceded the door swinging open, revealing a dark hallway. Dim light muted the once-vivid decorations and cheerful artifacts, making them seem ominous. The faint rustling of drapes, swaying like ghostly figures, announced a colder breeze through the corridor. From behind the winking shimmer on the golden slipper display, a shadowy figure emerged in the moonlight.

"Gretel," Dominic groaned, recognizing her immediately. "What do you want? I'm trying to sleep here."

She stepped closer, her face illuminated by a stray beam of moonlight. Her usual sharpness was still there, but something about her expression seemed urgent. She held up a hand to shield her eyes and immediately turned away.

"Do you mind?" she snapped, her tone half-irritated, half-mortified.

It took Dominic a moment to realize why. He looked down and froze, noticing he was completely naked.

"Oh crap," he muttered, quickly cupping his hands over himself as his face turned red. His embarrassment hit him in waves, making the cold air on his skin feel even more unbearable. Back at home, this kind of thing could land you in serious trouble. Here, it just added another layer of absurdity to his already surreal situation.

"I'm sorry!" he blurted out, his voice cracking. "I didn't realize—wait, why are you even here?"

Gretel rolled her eyes, unimpressed by his flustered state. "It's time to go fight those bastards," she said, her voice firm and eager. "Let's kick some ass."

Dominic stared at her, his exhaustion battling with disbelief. "What?" he asked, blinking slowly, as though he hadn't heard her correctly. "Are you serious? It's the middle of the night."

"Yes, I'm serious," Gretel said, her eyes narrowing. "You think Phineas and Callaghan are just going to forget about their little challenge? They're probably sharpening their swords right now, getting ready to humiliate us. Are you really going to let them get away with that?"

Dominic groaned again, this time more out of exasperation than sleepiness. He pinched the bridge of his nose, trying to process her words. "Can't this wait until morning? You know, when I'm not like this?" He gestured vaguely at his own unclothed state, still doing his best to maintain some semblance of dignity.

Gretel crossed her arms, her impatience radiating off her in waves. "Dominic, you can't let them think you're weak. If we don't show up, they'll spread rumors all over the castle about how we're cowards. Is that what you want?"

Dominic sighed, his shoulders slumping. She wasn't wrong, but that didn't make him feel any better about the situation. His body ached, his mind was foggy, and the thought of wielding a sword again made his stomach churn. Still, something in Gretel's determined expression stirred a small spark of defiance within him. Maybe it was exhaustion, or maybe he was simply tired of feeling helpless, but he found himself nodding.

"Fine," he muttered. "Give me a minute to...you know, put some clothes on."

"Make it quick," Gretel said, turning her back to give him privacy. "We've got a fight to win."

Chapter 36

Dominic waddled around his room, groaning in discomfort as his overstuffed stomach made every movement a chore. His indulgence at the dinner table now seemed like a terrible idea. The act of bending or stretching sent ripples of discomfort through his body. He shuffled toward her once again, his bare feet sticking slightly to the cold stone floor.

Gretel stood waiting, her foot tapping with impatience. Her small frame seemed coiled like a spring, radiating barely contained irritation. She watched him approach, arms crossed, her face half-hidden by the shadows of the flickering torches that lined the corridor. Her piercing gaze bore into him.

"Can you hurry it up?" she snapped, her voice cutting through the quiet like a whip.

Dominic winced, his exhaustion outweighing his shame. "Do we have to do this?" he groaned, leaning against the doorframe. His arms crossed over his chest as though that could make his vulnerability less obvious.

"Yes, we do!" Gretel shot back, her tone brooking no argument.

"But why?" he whined, the petulance in his voice making her roll her eyes dramatically. "I don't want to—"

"You don't want to?" she said, her eyes narrowing. "After the way they humiliated you? After everything they said about us? They deserve to be taught a lesson."

Dominic sighed heavily, his whole body sagging with defeat. His hands rose in surrender as Gretel marched forward, picked up his tunic, and threw it at him with surprising force. The soft fabric smacked against his chest before slipping to the ground.

Her face flushed with irritation, the dim moonlight catching the fire in her expression. Without missing a beat, Gretel reached into her pocket, pulled out one of her daggers, and began twirling it idly in her fingers, the blade glinting in the faint light.

"If you don't get moving," she said with deliberate calm, her voice low and dangerous, "I'll have to chop something off."

Dominic's eyes widened as his mouth opened and closed like a fish out of water. He swallowed audibly, the sound echoing faintly in the quiet corridor. With shaking hands, he snatched up the tunic and quickly pulled it over his head. His pants followed soon after as he struggled to cover himself, all the while throwing glances at Gretel, who stood watching with an expression of smug satisfaction.

"This is ridiculous," he muttered, tugging at the hem of his shirt. His cat was still curled up on the bed, undisturbed by the commotion. The feline let out a contented purr, blissfully unaware of his owner's predicament.

"I don't think this is necessary," Dominic added, glaring at Gretel.

"It's absolutely necessary," Gretel shot back, her tone firm. "If you let people like them walk all over you, they'll never stop. Trust me on this."

Dominic sighed, shaking his head. "Sometimes you need to pick your battles, Gretel. Not everything is worth fighting over."

Gretel scoffed, spinning her dagger one last time before sliding it back into its sheath. "This is worth it. Now, let's go."

As Dominic and Gretel crept through the castle halls, an eerie quiet filled the air. Long, flickering shadows cast by the faint candlelight danced across the walls. The two moved cautiously, their footsteps muffled by the stone floor. Dominic hesitated in front of one door.

"Should we get Sebastian to help us?" he whispered, glancing at Gretel.

"No," she replied firmly. "This is between us."

"But he could help—"

"He won't support this. And if he disagrees, he will stop us."

Dominic frowned, but said nothing more. Together, they descended a series of winding staircases. The silence between them was heavy, broken only by the occasional sound of the wind whistling through the openings in the castle walls. Gretel occasionally stopped to use the reflection of her blade to check around corners, ensuring they didn't run into any guards.

Finally, they reached the castle's main doors. Gretel pushed one open slightly, and a chilly breeze swept in, biting at their exposed skin. Fog shrouded the courtyard beyond, its thick white mist clinging to the ground like a ghostly blanket. Tree branches swayed in the wind, their rustling sounding like whispers in the dark.

"Now, where are these two jerks?"

CALLAGHAN AND PHINEAS waited in the courtyard, their swords at the ready. The fog obscured much of their surroundings, but the faint glow of the fountain nearby provided just enough light to see. The two boys exchanged cocky grins, their breath visible in the chilly night air.

"I can't wait to beat that little worm," Callaghan sneered.

"And that girl," Phineas added, shaking his head. "She thinks she's so tough. We'll show her where her place is."

Their laughter echoed faintly in the empty courtyard. They peered through the mist, their eyes scanning for any sign of movement.

"There!" Phineas suddenly hissed, pointing to a dark figure emerging from the shadows.

The two boys tensed, their weapons raised as they moved cautiously toward the figure. The fog seemed to swirl and shift around it, obscuring its features. Another figure appeared behind the first, their cloak billowing in the breeze.

"We've got them now," Callaghan said with a wicked grin.

But as they drew closer, something felt off. The figures didn't move, their faces obscured by their cloaks. Callaghan's confidence faltered.

"Why aren't they saying anything?" he whispered.

The first figure reached up, pulling back their hood. Callaghan and Phineas froze, their eyes widening in shock. It wasn't Dominic or Gretel.

It was Sir Winston.

The boys stammered, their bravado evaporating in an instant. "S-Sir, we didn't mean to—"

"Forgive us, please," said Phineas. "We were tricked into coming out here. Those pathetic excuses for saviors are the ones that told us to meet out here."

"Yes. It was them! We're innocent!"

But Sir Winston didn't reply. The enamel on his teeth glistened the further the corners of his mouth crept closer to his ears. He huffed a faint bit of laughter as the irises of his eyes flickered from hazel to a blazing orange, glowing with fury like a relentless fire.

"Sir, are you all right?"

"You don't seem like yourself."

He walked closer to the children, now frozen with shock. The swords of the adolescents became cushioned on the grass as they dropped them.

"You were never great at fighting," the instructor said to Callaghan, his voice grumbling deeper than usual.

"Excuse me?"

"You are no better than the squires and peasants, you insolent fool!"

His fist launched deep into the abdomen of the young man. Callaghan's knees buckled, his breath shortening in shock with his teacher's hand breaking through his skin. The black of the man's glove became shades of red when he retracted it, clenching the student's stomach that clung desperately for life, intestines slowly breaking away from it.

"Your form was always so atrocious!"

Blood spat out of Callaghan's mouth, sputtering onto the grass like a fountain along with the urine that trickled down his leg. He fell to his knees, shedding a glance of defeat to his friend who stood petrified amid his demise. Before Callaghan could react, Winston lunged forward, his movements fast. His fist connected with the boy's stomach again, and Callaghan crumpled to the ground, clutching his abdomen. Winston stood over him, his expression cold and merciless as he admired Callaghan's eyes becoming more vacant.

"R-Run," Callaghan said softly.

Phineas ran as his friend planted his face in the pool of his fluids. He ran deep into the bushes, trying to find a safe spot. The surrounding turf became darker with each second, only about a couple of feet in front of him to see. The greenery began to close in on him like a dooming hedge maze, scratching every exposed inch of his skin. His calves screamed in agony with each second as he sprinted in every direction the foliage would allow him. Tears streamed down his face as he whispered little prayers for protection.

"Please don't do this."

The hedges stopped and the fog lightened. A meadow-like space filled with vines that sprawled up high along the iron fence. A lone tree stood mighty in the center, cradling two ropes that fastened a plank of wood. Upon the swing sat another shadow; the hem of their cloak floating in the air as the body moved hypnotically like a slow pendulum. Launching itself into the air, the silhouette planted their feet into the mossy turf; the hood of the cloak fell back.

Phineas froze again; his tongue getting thicker, dryer. His hand trembled around the handle of his sword.

The person glided closer to him, flirting with his mortality by swinging Callaghan's sword like a cheerleading baton. The blade whipped through the air, echoing inside the young man's ears.

"Please, don't do this."

The tip of the blade swiped over the middle of his neck. Blood drained out of his body like a waterfall. His hand was slippery when he clenched his Adam's apple to stop the flow. His eyes rolled to the back of his head before his body planted itself onto the squishy ground. The boots trembled as the last ounce of his lifeline was nourishing the landscape.

DOMINIC AND GRETEL wandered through the courtyard; their shoes soaked from the damp grass. They had been searching for what felt like hours, but there was no sign of Callaghan or Phineas. Each moistened step on the grass brought frustration on their mood. Dominic's heavy feet wanted to rest in the bed, wrapped in the comforting fibers of silk.

"This is stupid," Dominic muttered. "Maybe they were just messing with us."

Gretel sighed, her shoulders slumping. "Maybe you're right. They were just being punks."

Dominic placed a comforting hand on her shoulder. "At least we tried, right? That's something."

"Yeah," she murmured, her voice heavy with disappointment.

As they turned to leave, a faint rustling caught their attention. Dominic glanced over his shoulder, his stomach knotting with unease.

"Let's go," he said, quickening his pace. "We need to get back inside."

Gretel nodded, and together they hurried back toward the castle, unaware of the blood-soaked horrors that had unfolded just out of sight. They paced up each step, ignoring the exhaustion of their heavy muscles that craved desperately for some rest. The food in their stomachs was settling into the lower chambers of their intestines, needing some hydration before moving further.

"I'll tell you what, though. If they showed up tonight, I would've cut their throats and watched them bleed to death."

Chapter 37

Sebastian stirred awake as the first light of dawn seeped through the intricate curtains of his room. But today, unlike most mornings, he allowed himself the luxury of staying in bed. The plush mattress seemed to cradle every aching muscle in his body, offering a rare reprieve from his usual routine of waking before sunrise to tend to the farm. No hauling hay bales or shoveling horse droppings today—a break he hadn't realized he desperately needed until now.

As the minutes passed, he stretched out, the satisfying crack of his bones echoing softly in the spacious room. The cold breeze slipping through the open balcony door coaxed him to his feet. Unconcerned by his lack of clothing, Sebastian stepped out onto the balcony. He let the chill sweep across his skin, refreshing him as he gazed down at the bustling town beyond. Familiar faces moved about the cobblestone streets, preparing for the day. Vendors set up their stalls, and families greeted each other warmly as they went about their morning routines.

A pang of gratitude washed over him. These were his people—the ones he had worked alongside for years. But now, thanks to Ella's leadership, life for many of them had improved drastically. No longer were they subjected to the cruelty and neglect of her stepmother. The farm was no longer a place of endless toil and meager rewards; it had become a sanctuary of fairness and care under Ella's watchful eye.

Sebastian's thoughts lingered on those darker times. The stepmother's harsh words, the daughters' entitled sneers, and the long, hungry nights when the workers who toiled to maintain the estate were denied food while it was reserved for lavish parties all remained in his memory. And yet, despite the horrors those women faced after being driven away—the birds that had gouged their eyes and the life of destitution they now endured—he didn't feel guilty for their downfall. It wasn't vengeance; it was justice. They had lived so far above everyone else, treating the people beneath them as nothing more than tools. Perhaps now they understood what it was like to be on the other side.

Was it wrong to feel relief at their suffering? That thought lingered in his mind longer than he wanted to admit.

AFTER SAVORING THE calm of the morning for a little while longer, Sebastian dressed and ventured out for a walk. The fresh linen from the nightshirt was loose, letting the hairs on his muscled chest breathe. The air was crisp, carrying the scent of dew and blooming hydrangeas. Each step seemed to pull the tension from his body, and the aches and stiffness from days of cramped hiding began to fade.

He was halfway down the garden path when Ella's cheerful voice broke the quiet. "Good morning!" she called out, her tone bright and melodic as ever.

"Good morning, Queen," Sebastian replied, smiling as he turned to greet her. It was always refreshing to see Ella so full of life, especially knowing how much she had overcome.

"How did you sleep?" she asked, walking beside him.

"Wonderfully," he answered honestly. "Best sleep I've had in ages."

"I'm glad to hear that," she said, her smile widening. "You deserve it."

The two strolled off the cobblestone path, their boots brushing against the wet grass. The morning light danced across the hedges, highlighting tiny beads of dew clinging to the leaves. Ladybugs crawled across the foliage, oblivious to the humans passing by.

"Thank you for letting us stay," Sebastian said after a moment. "It means a lot to us."

"You're welcome here anytime," Ella replied, her voice as warm as the sunlight filtering through the trees.

He chuckled softly. "You know I can't take you up on that offer. The farm needs me."

"Ah, yes," she teased, her gloved hand covering a laugh. "You and your work. You're more dedicated to those horses than most people are to their own families."

"I just do what I can for those who need me," he said with a shrug. "Right now, it's the horses."

"And Dominic?" Ella's eyes sparkled with approval. "You've taken a liking to him, haven't you?"

"It's not about liking," Sebastian replied, his tone thoughtful. "It's about seeing someone who's lost and knowing I can help. He needs guidance. He needs someone to have his back."

"And I think he's lucky to have you," Ella said, her voice gentle. "He's what we need to vanquish the Concealment."

Sebastian frowned slightly. "Do you really think so?"

"I do," she said firmly. "He's not what anyone would expect in a savior, but that's what makes him special. There's a light in him—a fragile light. It could grow into something powerful if nurtured properly. Or, if neglected, it could turn into something dark."

"Well, I won't let that happen," Sebastian said, his voice steady with resolve.

"I know you won't."

Their walk led them into a secluded garden nestled behind a cluster of tall hedges. Vines climbed the iron gates surrounding the space, and at the center stood a grand tree. Its gnarled branches stretched wide, one holding an old swing that swayed gently in the breeze. Time seemed to pause, mesmerized by the tranquil perfection of its beauty.

Ella stepped forward, her gown brushing against the mossy ground as she approached the swing. "This place reminds me of my mother," she said, her voice tinged with nostalgia. "She used to sit in tranquil places like these for hours, finding peace in the smallest things."

Sebastian watched her as she seated herself on the swing, her golden hair catching the sunlight as it escaped her tidy updo. She began to sway, the train of her gown fluttering behind her like the tail of a cloud. The smile on her face reflected innocence from the days on the farm.

"Your Majesty," he said, breaking the silence, "did you ever think about fighting back against your family?"

Ella's movements slowed as she looked at him, her expression soft but curious. "What do you mean?"

"I mean, when they treated you so horribly, didn't you ever want to do something? To make them pay for what they did?"

Ella tilted her head, considering his question. Then, with a small push, she resumed swinging. Her voice, a tranquil pool, reflected her composed state as she responded, "There were times I wanted to. But I realized that wouldn't make me any better than them. Darkness tests you, Sebastian. It tries to consume you. But I chose to nurture my light instead of putting it out."

"That must've been difficult," he said with admiration.

"It was," she admitted. "But I had people like you to support me. And that made all the difference."

Sebastian stepped closer, his hand grasping the ropes of the swing to slow her momentum. Ella looked up at him, her cheeks flushed from the cool air and the motion of the swing. Her eyes held the same warmth and resilience that had always inspired him.

"I would do it all over again," he said softly. "For you."

Ella's smile widened, and for a moment, the world around them seemed to fade away. In that quiet garden, beneath the sturdy tree that had weathered countless seasons, the bond between them felt unshakable—a testament to the light they had both chosen to protect and share.

Chapter 38

FROM THE PAGES OF THE STORYBOOK
Ella

STEPPING INTO THE COOL morning air, a wicker basket of chicken feed rested against my hip. The kernels sifted through my fingers like tiny bits of hail, scattering across the yard as my flock of feathered children raced to claim their share. Their clucks and flutters brought a faint smile to my lips. The dogs dashed around them, barking playfully, their exuberance filling the grounds with life.

I couldn't help but watch them for a moment, letting their carefree innocence wash over me. It was bittersweet. They reminded me of how my sisterhood could have been if Aurelia and Evangeline had ever chosen kindness over cruelty. Instead, their coldness ensured my childhood was a lonely one.

A steady clopping of hooves caught my attention, pulling me from my thoughts. A familiar horse rounded the corner, its tail swishing as Sebastian followed closely behind, his hand brushing the animal's coarse mane. He guided the mare toward the stable, his touch calming the animal's hunger-driven impatience.

"Sebastian," I called, my voice low with concern as I walked toward him, "you're not supposed to be here. They let you go."

He shrugged nonchalantly, ushering the horse inside. "I know. I just miss them, that's all," he replied, his voice light despite the weight of the truth.

"Don't let Stepmother catch you," I warned, glancing over my shoulder toward the house. "She'll be furious."

Sebastian gave a scoff, wiping his hands on his trousers. "Like she pays attention to what goes on outside. She's too busy fussing over the festival tonight. All three of them are."

I hesitated at the mention of the festival. "Yeah," I said softly, my tone heavy. "The festival."

Sebastian's brow furrowed as he turned toward me. "Are you going?"

I shook my head, the weight of disappointment settling over me. "I can't. She won't let me."

"That's not fair! All eligible maidens in the land are invited."

"Tell her that," I said bitterly. "Besides, even if I could go, I have nothing to wear."

"You must have something," he insisted, stepping closer. "What about one of your mother's dresses?"

I thought of the old gown tucked away in the corner of my trunk. It was beautiful once, a pale blue trimmed with delicate pink lace that she had me help her sew when I was younger, but years of neglect had left it threadbare in places. "There is one," I admitted, lowering my voice as I noticed Aurelia's shadow in the upstairs window. "But it's too worn. It needs repairs, and I don't have time. Stepmother has me running errands in town all day."

Sebastian folded his arms, his expression defiant. "Forget your chores," he said firmly. "The house will survive one day without your elbow grease."

"I don't know..." I hesitated, the thought of disobeying stepmother enough to make my stomach twist.

"You deserve this, Ella. Just one night. You're not asking for much."

He was right. It wasn't much to ask for—a single evening of freedom, a chance to feel alive again. My mother had always told me to embrace the joy in life's fleeting moments, to find beauty even in the darkest days. One time, a massive storm ruined a lot of our garden and caused one of our trees to fall on the side of the house, creating a monstrous hole. She persuaded me that it could always be worse; we could end up with no house at all. Silver linings were always a part of her approach, and she tried her best to instill it into me.

"Okay," I said finally, the resolve settling in my chest. "If I work quickly, I can manage. But I'll need to hurry."

"That's the spirit!" Sebastian grinned, his enthusiasm infectious.

THE MARKET BUZZED WITH life as I made my way through the streets, the hem of my dress sweeping up the dust of the cobblestones. Vendors called out to passersby, their voices blending with the clatter of carts and the laughter of children. As usual, I kept my interactions brief, focusing on the tasks at hand. Most townsfolk treated me kindly enough, though I knew their pity lingered just below the surface. I had overheard their whispers about my gaunt frame and threadbare clothes, the way they shook their heads when they thought I couldn't see. It didn't bother me much anymore. Pity was a small price to pay for survival.

I ducked into the seamster's shop, the doorbell jingling softly as I stepped inside. My eyes were immediately drawn to the rainbow of fabrics lining the walls, bolts of silk and satin stacked neatly alongside spools of thread in every imaginable color. Every color of lace brought reminders of Evangeline's whining since she was so obsessed with lace. The smell of freshly dyed cloth filled the air, tinged with the faint metallic tang of sewing tools.

Mister Gloomis emerged from the back, his face shiny with sweat as he carried an armful of gowns. "Pickup?" he asked, barely glancing at me.

"Yes, sir," I said, folding my hands neatly in front of me.

"Ah, Mirelle's order. Give me a moment."

While he disappeared into the back room, I let my fingers graze over a bolt of pale pink fabric near the counter. It was soft, delicate—perfect for a sash, or maybe a small embellishment for my mother's dress. It called to me, tempting in its simplicity.

When the seamster returned, he was dragging three enormous gowns, their trains trailing behind him like waves of silk. "Here you are," he said, depositing the dresses onto the counter. The intricate stitching and embroidered rosettes took my breath away. Each one was a masterpiece.

"And the payment?" he asked, wiping his brow.

I placed the coins on the counter, hesitating for a moment before gesturing to the fabric I had admired earlier. "Could I purchase half a meter of that as well? Just enough for a sash."

The seamster glanced at the fabric, then back at me. "I'm afraid not. Mirelle made it very clear her money is only for these dresses."

My heart sank. "I can pay for it separately," I offered quickly. "Please, I just need a little."

He shook his head, his expression apologetic but firm. "She warned me not to sell you anything extra. If I do, she'll see to it that my shop is shut down."

"I understand," I said quietly, gathering the gowns in my arms. The silks slipped against my skin, cool and smooth, but they felt heavier than they should have.

I left the shop with my head held high, though my chest ached with frustration. My mind raced as I walked back toward the carriage, the weight of the gowns pressing down on me. Could I truly manage it all? The chores, the errands, the repairs to my mother's dress? It seemed impossible.

But I had to try. For one night, I wanted to be free. Just one night.

Chapter 39

FROM THE PAGES OF THE STORYBOOK
Evangeline

LOOK AT HER. THAT PATHETIC excuse for a servant.

I couldn't believe Mother allowed her to stay in my house. Every time I laid eyes on my stepsister, all I wanted to do was vomit. The way she carried herself, like she was some kind of martyr, feeding the chickens as if they were her adoring subjects. This morning, she had been talking to them like they could actually respond. Could you imagine? A grown girl, chattering away at thin air.

It made me sick.

I had seen the way her father used to look at her before he died, all doting and sentimental. It was so weak. The love in his eyes, the way he let her get away with anything—it was pathetic. Mother would never do that to us. She had always known the value of discipline. Everything Mother had done, every single choice, had been for us. Even marrying Cinderella's father was for our benefit.

Too bad the man turned out to be a horse's ass. He wasn't even as rich as he made himself out to be! Now we've been stuck here, trying to survive on the scraps of what he left behind. He didn't even come back with that gift he promised Mother. Some special treasure or trinket? He didn't even bring me my lace! Just empty words like the rest of him.

It made me so angry, being stuck here on this filthy farm. It's humiliating! Sometimes, the frustration bubbled up so much, I just had to do something about it. And if that had meant making messes for her to clean up, so be it. If I suffered, so would she.

While she was outside feeding her precious little chickens this morning, I went straight to the stable, shoveled a bunch of horse droppings, and dragged it all over the foyer floor. Not so shiny now, huh? That'll give her something to keep busy with.

And those bruises she tried to hide? Oh, those were Mother's work, but I'm the reason they're there. I knew exactly how to rile Mother up, how to whisper just the right things to get her temper flaring. Every shard of broken ceramic on the floor? That was because I tipped over the vase. Every tear in the velvet curtains? My stepsister's tailoring shears cut those, with my hand holding them. Every smear of filth on the walls? That was me, too.

Did I care if it was gross? Not really. A little mess never hurt anyone—except her pride, of course.

And now, the ungrateful little rat had actually thought she could go to the festival tonight? My festival. The one chance I have to meet a man who can finally get me out of this godforsaken place. She will not ruin this for me. I won't allow it. Aurelia better not mess this up either, but at least she's my sister. Blood is thicker than water, after all. I could never do to her what I've done to Cinderella.

Aurelia and I used to be close. When we were little, we'd play together with the finest toys Father could afford. We shared dresses, secrets, and laughs. Back then, even Mother would smile at our happiness. Those were the days.

If we played princesses, he became our king. If we were bandits, he made himself our sidekick. We became the center of his world, leaving Mother to fight for scraps of his attention.

And when he died, everything fell apart.

Mother couldn't cope. She stopped smiling altogether. Instead, she started focusing on making us perfect—powdering our faces, tightening our corsets, telling us we were too fat before our hips and breasts had even fully formed.

I had been starving for love ever since.

Mother's love has been the hardest to earn, but I'm determined to get it. I would do anything. If I had to be the perfect daughter, so be it. If I had to excel at the arts, I would do it. If I had to sabotage Cinderella at every turn, well...that's hardly a challenge.

Tonight is my chance to secure my future. To prove to Mother that I should be worthy of her pride. That I'm better. And I won't let anyone, especially her, take that from me.

Not tonight. Not ever.

She thought she could fix up some rags and call it a gown? She thought she could charm her way into a world she didn't belong in? She has no idea what I'm capable of. I should get back to the kitchen, anyway. That pot of porridge is about to spill. Maybe I'll even "accidentally" ruin her supper while I'm at it.

Let's see how she handles that!

Chapter 40

WHAT THE STORYBOOK MISSED...
Aurelia

I'VE BEEN COUNTING the days until this festival, and now it's finally happening. My stomach has been a tight knot ever since Ella read the invitation aloud. I've imagined this night so many times, not for the chance to prance around in some grand dress or to charm a prince, but because this could be my escape. A way out of this torturous house, away from my mother's suffocating grip and my sister's mischief.

Don't get me wrong—I love them. I really do. But love doesn't erase everything that's happened since Father passed. Something changed in our house that day, and I don't know if it's just them or if it's me, too. Maybe it's all of us. Either way, things haven't been the same, and I've felt more alone with every passing year.

I think back to the night my father died. It's a memory I try to bury, but it's always there, creeping into my thoughts at the worst times. I'd had this horrible nightmare that a dragon had burst into our home, torching everything—me, Evangeline, the curtains, the beds, our toys. When I awakened, my nightgown was soaked with urine. I was mortified, so much so that I didn't even want to leave my bed, but I forced myself to. I remember thinking that Father wouldn't judge me. He was always so kind, so understanding. That's why he was the best person in the world.

I crept downstairs that night, clutching the banister, and found him sitting by the fire. The room was warm; the flames cracking as they devoured a dry batch of wood. For a fleeting moment, I felt safe again. Mother was there too, standing behind him, holding a teacup in one hand with her fingers lightly grazing his shoulder. She looked calm, which was rare for her. I almost smiled, thinking maybe things were starting to get better.

Then I saw the little black bottle. It disappeared into the pocket of her robe so quickly I almost thought I'd imagined it. My heart started to race, but I didn't know why. Then Father took a sip of his tea, and everything went wrong. His face twisted in pain as he gagged, his throat constricting, his body convulsing. I wanted to scream, to run down and help him, but I was frozen. I couldn't move. All I could do was watch.

And she just stood there. No, worse than that. She laughed. I couldn't believe it. She kissed the bottle like it was a treasure; her smile growing wider as Father collapsed in his chair, gasping for breath. I wanted to save him. I wanted to yell at her to stop. But I was a coward, too afraid to do anything. And then he was gone.

That was the night I learned what she was capable of. Since then, I've been walking on eggshells, doing whatever I can to stay in her good graces. Evangeline, on the other hand, seems to have leaned into it. She's practically her shadow now, mimicking her cruelty, feeding off her approval. I've tried to get close to her, to remind her of the sisterly bond we used to have, but it's pointless. Every time I think I can trust her, she does something to ruin it.

Like the way she treats Ella. It's disgusting. She breaks her family's heirlooms, cuts up the curtains, smears...things on the walls. And she doesn't even try to hide it. She actually seems proud of it. Meanwhile,

I'm stuck cleaning up the messes, trying to make things right behind the scenes without drawing attention to myself. I've learned to move quickly and quietly, fixing what I can before anyone notices. It's the only way to keep Ella from getting blamed for things she didn't do. I am only one trying to keep up with my sister; there are some things that Ella will have to clean. I wish it wouldn't come to this, but it could be much worse with all the extra work she could be bombarded with.

Poor Ella. I don't know how she does it. She's been through so much, yet she's still so kind, so forgiving. It makes me sick to see how Mother and Evangeline treat her. She deserves so much better than this. I wish I could be brave enough to stand up for her, but I'm too scared. If I make one wrong move, I could end up like Father.

That's why the festival is so important. This could be my chance to escape. If I can find someone—anyone—who can take me away from here, I might finally be free. I don't care if it's the prince or some nobleman's son. I just need someone who can give me a new life, one where I don't have to pretend to be someone I'm not. Maybe then, I could find a way to get Ella out of here and take her with me.

CLANK.

Of course. That sounded like the porridge pot. And there it is—Evangeline's signature cackle echoing through the house. I swear, that girl creates chaos just to amuse herself. I sigh and push myself out of my chair. Time to clean up her mess before Ella gets home and has to deal with it.

Again.

Chapter 41

Dominic

A SOFT BREEZE WHISPERS across my skin, creeping up my legs and teasing my bare thighs. My stomach presses into the mattress, which cradles me like I'm floating on a cloud. For once, the aches in my body, the ones that usually nag at me like old scars, fade into a distant memory. Every fiber of my being is relaxed, savoring the quiet, uninterrupted bliss of sleep.

It's rare for me to sleep this peacefully. Night terrors are usually my nightly companion, dragging me down into a pit of dread as soon as I close my eyes. But tonight, something is different. I find myself dreaming of an open field, vast and untouched, glowing in a spectrum of emerald greens and soft pewter blues. The sunlight dances across the blades of grass, making them shimmer like jewels.

There's a woman there—gentle, nurturing, with a smile so warm it could melt the frostiest of mornings. She holds my hand, guiding me through a sea of wildflowers. The petals brush against my legs with every step, a soft, ticklish sensation that only adds to the dream's serenity. Above us, birds sing in harmony, their notes weaving together like a perfect melody in a traveling chorus. It's the kind of peace I didn't know existed, and I could stay in this dream forever, wrapped in the innocent joy of it all.

Even the butterflies seem to be in on the magic, flitting gracefully around us. One lands on my nose, its delicate wings brushing against my skin. I laugh—actually laugh. It's light and carefree, a sound I haven't heard from myself in years. Everything feels perfect, like the world has been sculpted to be this one, serene moment.

But of course, perfection can never last.

A shadow appears, small at first, just a blot on the horizon. I barely notice it, lost in the dream's beauty. But it grows, stretching taller and darker, until it looms over us like a monstrous specter. The woman's hand tightens around mine, her comforting smile faltering as fear creeps into her eyes. And then, before I can even process what's happening, a sword—a gleaming, brutal thing—bursts through her stomach.

Her face contorts in pain, the light in her eyes dimming as she gasps for air. I can't move, can't scream, can't do anything but watch as the blood begins to pool around her feet, staining the flowers red. The chorus of birds falls silent and butterflies scatter. The dream unravels into a nightmare, sharp and vivid, the kind that clings to me long after I've woken up.

And just like that, I'm yanked back to reality.

The first thing I feel is the heaviness in my chest, the ache of my breath catching in my throat. My eyes blink open, adjusting to the faint light spilling through the curtains. The bed beneath me is soft, almost too soft, but it's no longer comforting. The echoes of the dream linger, and the image of her pain burns into my mind.

So much for a peaceful night. Too bad.

Chapter 42

Dominic rose slowly, savoring the lingering softness of the bed, which allowed him to take his time getting dressed. The cool air from the open balcony brushed against his skin, and he allowed himself a brief moment of indulgence, standing there without a care. The view below was a tapestry of early risers, townspeople bustling about in their mundane routines. A wry smile crossed his lips, a flicker of mischief coursing through him at the thought of his bare form unwittingly exposed to their oblivious gazes.

He made his way downstairs, navigating the hallways with a newfound ease after last night's unexpected escapade. The castle felt different in the daylight; its grandeur seemed amplified. Sunlight streamed through tall windows, illuminating vibrant tapestries and intricate paintings. Dominic admired them as he walked, marveling at their colors and precision.

Monet, eat your heart out, he thought. *Even Van Gogh wouldn't hold a candle to these.*

When he entered the dining hall, Calypso was already there, perched on the table and invested in a bowl of food. The cat's tail twitched enthusiastically, and porridge clung to his chin.

"Morning," Calypso said between bites, unbothered by his lack of decorum.

"Good morning," Dominic replied, shaking his head with a smirk.

The air was thick with the aroma of freshly baked bread, warm and doughy. Dominic's stomach growled in response. He slid into his seat and reached for the teapot, pouring steaming water into a delicate teacup.

"No coffee?" he muttered under his breath, swirling the tea leaves with a spoon. He wasn't expecting a Starbucks, but a good cup of coffee would have been a welcome start to his day. Tea would have to suffice.

Gretel joined him moments later, plopping down at the table with a heavy sigh. Her hair looked like a pair of neglected bird nests, and the dark circles under her eyes gave her a haunted appearance.

"Rough night?" Dominic asked, blowing gently on his tea.

"I don't think I've had a good night's sleep in years," Gretel replied, stifling a yawn. She reached for a biscuit and began tearing it apart absentmindedly.

Dominic raised an eyebrow, intrigued by her comment. "Do you not get much rest where you're from?"

Her expression hardened as she glanced at him. "Let's just say my living situation has been less than ideal."

Dominic took a sip of his tea, feeling the hot liquid soothe his throat. "I can relate. I've been without a proper home since getting evicted right before landing in this place."

Gretel snorted, her gaze fixed on the torn biscuit in her hands. "Try being without one for years."

Dominic froze, his cup halfway to his lips. "Years? Seriously?"

"Yeah." She set the biscuit down with a forceful thud. "And no, I couldn't stay with my brother. That's not an option."

"What happened?" Dominic asked, hesitant but curious.

Gretel's nostrils flared, and her body stiffened. "He's dead to me," she said sharply, cutting off any further questions.

"Got it. Sorry for asking," Dominic said, raising his hands in surrender.

"It's not just him," Gretel muttered, her tone softening. "People don't know the truth about me, but they think they do. Lies are easier to believe than the truth, especially when they're loud and convenient."

Dominic nodded, understanding more than he cared to admit. In his world, all it took was one viral post or a well-placed lie to destroy someone's reputation. Social media had turned into a weapon, allowing people to tear each other down from behind screens, free of consequences. The parallels between his world and hers weren't lost on him.

Before he could respond, the door to the hall swung open. Queen Ella entered with Sebastian close behind, their silhouettes framed by the morning sunlight. Ella's gown billowed gracefully, with chiffon fluttering across the floor.

"Good morning," Ella greeted, her voice like honey. "I hope you all had a restful night."

Sebastian smiled in agreement, his posture relaxed and easy.

Dominic nodded, his own mood lightened by their presence. "It was great, thank you."

Ella's smile widened. "I'm sure you already heard, but I wanted to personally invite you to our annual festival this evening. As our guests, I insist you attend. It's a special occasion for the kingdom, and your presence would mean a great deal."

Dominic's heart skipped a beat. A festival? With royalty? He would not turn that down. "We'd be honored," he said, trying to sound composed from being included.

"Wonderful!" Ella clapped her hands together. "This event is about bringing the people together and celebrating who we are. It's a tradition I hope will strengthen our bonds as a kingdom."

"It sounds like a beautiful cause," Dominic replied, impressed by her dedication to her people.

"My husband and I want to do all we can for the kingdom," Ella continued. "He's especially looking forward to conversing with you more, Dominic. He's quite fond of the stories he's heard."

"Fond, huh?" Dominic mused.

Well, if the king is into shoes, who knows what else he might like?

Finishing his tea, Dominic pushed back his chair with a smile. "I'd better head into town and pick up my clothes. The seamster should have them ready by now."

"I hope you're happy with what's been prepared," Ella said warmly. "I can't wait to see you all tonight."

Dominic smiled, but a flicker of anxiety crept in. His jacket was with the seamster—a piece that meant the world to him. If anything happened to it, he might not keep his temper in check. It may be Dominic that would get Mister Gloomis before any Concealment would if his most valuable item was destroyed. For now, though, he focused on the promise of an extraordinary evening ahead. One that he will hopefully never forget.

Chapter 43

Dominic sat slumped in the carriage's corner, head tilted against the wall, drifting in and out of sleep. It wasn't easy finding rest in this world, but he took whatever moments he could get. His body sagged with exhaustion, his mind still wrestling with thoughts of home and the chaotic events that had brought him here. Calypso, perched beside him, was grooming himself, completely unbothered by the bouncing of the carriage as it rolled through the streets.

Sebastian sat upright, gazing out the window at the scenery—a sea of people that admired the intricacy of the carriage. Gretel, however, kept her focus inward, her hands fidgeting with the daggers at her waist. Her gaze darted toward Sebastian whenever he glanced her way, but she quickly looked elsewhere, avoiding his eyes. She hadn't told him about last night, about the incident with the students. She knew his disapproval would be swift and uncompromising.

"So, how did you two sleep?" Sebastian asked, noting the exhaustion on Dominic's face.

"Very well," Dominic responded as he stretched his arms.

"Slept through the entire night? Or did you do anything exciting?"

Dominic fought the urge to look over at Gretel, who adjusted a tattered headscarf over her hair to protect her identity. His eyes looked directly into Sebastian's, sensing that he could see through his lies. The longer he hesitated, the further Sebastian's eyebrow perched closer to the top of his bald head. He couldn't come up with the excuse of being on his phone and scrolling through social media or streaming the newest episode of *Law and Order* on the royal television to justify his late night.

"No, we just slept."

As the carriage creaked to a halt in front of the seamster's shop, Dominic stirred awake and Sebastian's mouth tightened. His neck felt stiff, and he rubbed it absentmindedly as he glanced outside. Townspeople bustled about their day, their gazes occasionally wandering toward the group. He noticed some of them looking at him, their expressions blank, and some were vaguely envious. It was such a sharp contrast to the sneers and judgmental glances he was used to back in New York. Here, for once, he didn't feel like an outcast.

A young girl, no older than ten, caught his eye. She smiled shyly at him before letting out a small giggle that flushed her cheeks. Dominic couldn't help but smile back, a brief warmth spreading through his chest. It was an odd sensation—to be looked at with curiosity or admiration instead of disdain. It reminded him that not everyone was so quick to judge.

A cozy warmth infused the seamster's shop, a gentle embrace of dye and linen. The floor was littered with loose threads and stray pins, remnants of the flurry of work that had overtaken the place. Several girls bustled out of the shop, laughing as they carried their gowns for the evening's festival. The sound of their chatter faded as they disappeared into the street.

The seamster emerged from a back room, his face etched with exhaustion. His children scurried behind him, their small hands gripping spools of thread and scraps of cloth.

"You're here," he said with a tired but polite smile.

"Busy night?" Sebastian asked.

"That would be an understatement," the seamster replied. "My entire family's been working around the clock to finish everything in time for the festival. If my two-year-old could pick up a needle and thread, I would make them help too!"

"I can imagine," Sebastian said with sympathy.

Dominic stayed quiet, observing the piles of fabric bolts lining the walls, though he couldn't help but notice how much emptier the shelves seemed now compared to his last visit.

"Well, your jacket was worth the effort," the seamster added, a spark of pride lighting his weary expression. "Let me fetch it for you."

Dominic's stomach churned as he waited. He hadn't stopped thinking about the jacket since the moment he handed it over. It was one of the few things he had left from his old life, and the idea of it being changed had filled him with equal parts excitement and dread. When the seamster returned, carrying the finished garment, Dominic's breath hitched.

"Here we are!" the seamster said, laying the jacket on the counter with pride.

Dominic stepped forward, his hands hesitating as he reached out to touch it. Baroque patterns climbed up the sleeves, and vibrant hues of yellow and black adorned the bodice. Each seam, each panel, a vibrant tale woven in color and texture.

"Well?" the seamster asked expectantly. "What do you think?"

Dominic stared, unsure of how to respond. Part of him marveled at the artistry and sheer boldness of the design—it was the kind of flamboyant statement he used to dream of wearing without fear. But another part of him froze with trepidation. He could already hear the mocking voices of his past, the judgment of strangers. The thought of standing out so brazenly made him feel exposed.

"It's...beautiful," he said softly. "It's just..."

"Just what?" the seamster asked, his tone edging toward irritation.

"It looks great," Sebastian said, his lips tightening.

Dominic floundered for words, his palms sweating. He glanced at Sebastian, whose expression had shifted from supportive to displeased. Gretel, meanwhile, seemed captivated by the jacket. Her eyes sparkled like twinkling snowflakes as she admired the vibrant colors and intricate patterns, her fingers brushing over the fabric with childlike fascination.

"Don't you think it's a bit much?" Dominic blurted out.

"Dominic!" Sebastian's voice was sharp, cutting through the room like a knife. "What are you talking about?"

"I don't know," Dominic said defensively. "It's not exactly...subtle. Didn't you say you wanted me to blend in?"

The seamster bristled, his tired face tightening. "This is exactly what you asked for."

Sebastian crossed his arms, his jaw tightening. "Put it on."

Dominic hesitated, but under Sebastian's stern gaze, he complied. Slipping into the jacket, he found it fit perfectly, the sleeves snug but comfortable, the bodice tailored to his frame. He stepped in front of a trio of mirrors, his reflection multiplying into a kaleidoscope of color.

Turning, he noticed how the sunlight illuminated the fabric, making its patterns shimmer. For a moment, he let himself admire the craftsmanship, but self-doubt crept back in. "I look like Elton John," he muttered.

"Who's Elton John?" Gretel asked, her head tilting in confusion. "Is he a grand wizard?"

"Something like that, but never mind," Dominic replied with a faint smile.

"You look great," Sebastian said firmly. "The back is especially well done."

After comparing the outfit to Elton John, he knew he couldn't use a Bette Midler and Lily Tomlin reference in *Big Business*. He found it difficult to articulate his aversion to its gaudiness. Dominic turned to see the back, where a flare of salvaged denim formed a stylish peplum. He had to admit, it wasn't bad—actually, it was incredible. He gave a small, self-conscious twirl, the peplum flaring out like a dancer's skirt.

"It's...different," he conceded.

Sebastian's patience seemed to snap. "Different? Dominic, I saw the clothes you arrived in. That jacket is a masterpiece!"

"I think you look fantastic," Gretel interjected, cutting the tension. "Now, let's go. We've got a festival to get ready for."

The seamster offered a pile of additional garments, altered to complement the jacket. "Take these as well," he said, waving them off. "They are some little pieces I had my children practice on."

Dominic thanked him with a soft nod as they left the shop. Back on the street, Dominic glanced around, his wandering eyes expecting stares or whispers. But no one seemed to notice him. The townspeople were too busy with their own lives to care about his flamboyant jacket. He even found a woman whose regal bearing rivaled the New York customer's; her haughty expression gave way to admiration for his frock. Dominic's blood boiled with the memory of her hatred. He only recalled the strain on his heart from the management's disbelief in him, accusing his character and work ethic while he simply aimed to survive.

"Excuse me," he said as he got closer to her.

"Good afternoon," she said meekly.

"Look who's better now?" he asked, slapping her hand away from the apple she reached for on the fruit cart.

"I beg your pardon?"

Even though the woman knew nothing about Dominic, all he could think about was every person in the store or on the streets that would roll their eyes at the sight of him. Every time somebody sneered for just looking less privileged made his blood boil.

"You know what you did. I'm sure you're about to be rude to this person too, like you were with me!"

"I don't even know you," she said, her eyebrows furrowing.

"You didn't know me when you got me fired, you tired old hag!"

The crowd gasped as they stopped their activities. Children flinched at the sight of his disdain. The woman's friends gathered in front of her, creating a wall of protection to protect her sadness. The vendor took their wagon, his lip curling as he pushed away from them.

"Dominic!" Sebastian said as he turned back to him, his face full of surprise with his arms out in disbelief. "What are you doing?"

Sebastian's stomps toward him shook the wagons. The sharpness in his voice brought a wall around him. As Dominic watched the woman walk away, he caught his reflection in a window. The person he saw now differed from his memory of them. This jacket revealed a newfound confidence; his worries vanished, unnoticed by those around him.

"What was I so worried about?" he murmured to himself. As the peplum swished behind him with each step, he began to walk a little taller, his confidence growing with every stride.

He passed by another shop, looking into the windows and noticing a vast selection of headdresses and hats. The primary display featured a bycocket; the felt was a vibrant fuchsia with a long, blaze-orange feather billowed behind it in a dome shape.

"No, *that* would be too much."

MISTER GLOOMIS BRUSHED stray threads from the counter, his hands moving with practiced ease despite the weariness in his posture. A long, satisfying sigh escaped his lips as the end of his rush loomed closer. Nearby, his once-energetic children now shuffled their feet, their small bodies weighed down by exhaustion as they approached the curtain for a much-needed respite.

"Daddy, can we go outside and get some fresh air?" one of the younger children asked, their voice tinged with both hope and fatigue.

The seamster hesitated, his brow furrowing as he glanced at the mountain of work they had barely conquered. "I don't know," he replied with a cautious sigh. "How are the other orders coming along?"

"We finished everything for the festival tonight," the child said, their words edged with pride.

"And the rest? Have you started on those?"

A tiny groan bubbled up from the child's throat, their shoulders sagging under the weight of his expectations. A tear glistened from the corners of their eyes, threatening to spill. "But Daddy," they whined, their voice rising with a hint of desperation, "we need some fresh air!"

He sighed heavily, rubbing the bridge of his nose. "I could use some fresh air too, but you don't see me taking any breaks. That's the reality of running a business."

"But it's not our business—it's yours!" the child cried, their frustration boiling over. "All we're asking for is a little break!"

Mister Gloomis blinked, startled by the raw emotion in their voice. The glimmer of unshed tears and the sorrow etched into their small face struck a chord deep within him. Memories of his own childhood surfaced—how his father had pushed him endlessly, never allowing a moment of rest. He softened, his rigid exterior cracking just enough to let in a sliver of empathy.

"Fine," he said at last, his voice gentler. "One hour."

The child's face lit up like a sunbeam breaking through storm clouds. A chorus of whispered thank you's tumbled from their lips as they scampered outside, their laughter echoing as the door swung shut behind them.

Left alone, the seamster turned back to his work, reorganizing the stacks of parchment that represented his remaining orders, which caused him to let out an overwhelming sigh. His chest swelled with a flicker of pride as he realized how much progress they'd made—what had once been an insurmountable pile of requests was now reduced to a manageable fraction.

"I hate this time of year," he muttered under his breath, though there was more relief than bitterness in his tone.

Above the door, a tiny bell jingled, a sound nearly lost in his humming. A dark figure entered the shop, their voluminous black cloak seeming to drink in every ray of sunlight as the shop dimmed. Stray threads, pins, and fabric scraps clung to the torn train as it dragged across the floor. Flipping the shop's wooden sign from "OPEN" to "CLOSED," the figure shut the door behind them with a deliberate flick of their gloved hand.

"Good afternoon!" the seamster called out, startled as he looked up to find the figure standing in the shadows. His pulse quickened as he took in the imposing silhouette.

"I—oh, I wasn't expecting you this late," he stammered, a nervous laugh escaping him. "If you're here about an order, let me check...I see nothing under your name, but perhaps it's listed differently?"

The figure remained silent, their presence heavy and unnerving.

"No matter," the seamster continued, trying to mask his unease. "It feels like it's been ages since I last saw you. It's always nice to catch up, you know—"

The figure's head gave a slight tilt, their gloved hand disappearing into the folds of their cloak. When it reemerged, they held a pair of shears. Gleaming, brass-handled fabric shears. The blades caught the faintest glimmer of light as they gripped them.

"Oh," the seamster said, his voice faltering. "You found a pair of my shears. Did you need—"

Before he could finish his sentence, the shears hurtled across the counter with a deadly precision. They pierced the seamster's neck, embedding deep into the flesh. His body jerked, and blood erupted from the wound in a bright crimson spray, splattering the vibrant fabrics surrounding him.

His hands shot up, clawing at the shears as his throat emitted a sickening gurgle. He stumbled backward, his legs buckling as his boots slipped in the rapidly growing pool of blood. His vision blurred, the vibrant stripes and polka dots of his shop's fabrics twisting into grotesque patterns—chevrons where there were none, stars where there had been circles.

The back of Mister Gloomis's head struck the floor with a sickening crack, and he felt the warmth of his blood pooling beneath him, soaking into his once-pristine cotton blouse. His fingers twitched feebly, unable to stop the flow of life draining from his body. As his vision darkened at the edges, his desperate focus only multiplied the reflections of his assailant in the surrounding mirrors.

Above him, a sharp, unyielding silhouette loomed as the light faded. The world he had painstakingly built—a world of color, texture, and artistry—collapsed into blackness, consumed entirely by the shadow of the Concealment.

DOMINIC'S LUNGS BURNED as he pushed through the growing sea of people clogging the streets with the noon hour at its threshold. His legs pumped furiously, but he could feel himself slowing, the crowd growing thicker with each step. Townsfolk bustled about, their faces a blur of determination and routine. The commotion swallowed his shouts; the chaotic symphony of laughter, chatter, and clattering carts drowned him out.

"Sebastian!" he yelled, his voice raw and desperate.

The backs of Sebastian and Gretel grew smaller with each second, their figures vanishing into the mass of bodies. Dominic stumbled as a group of children darted in front of him, giggling and weaving through the crowd like fish in a stream. He staggered, narrowly avoiding a merchant's crate of fruit that almost grazed his side. A few apples tumbled to the ground, and he muttered an apology, barely sparing a glance back. He couldn't stop now. He had to catch up.

The noise was overwhelming. Voices overlapped in an unrelenting tide, and the sharp scents of roasted nuts, horses, and sweat clogged his senses. His temples throbbed, and a dull ache bloomed behind his eyes. The heat of the crowd pressed in on him, and he found it harder to breathe with every passing moment.

Finally, he broke free, veering into a narrow alleyway where the noise receded to a distant hum. The contrast was jarring, and Dominic leaned against the rough brick wall of a building, gasping for air. His forehead rested against a jagged protrusion, its cool surface grounding him for a moment. His fingers trembled as they raked through his damp hair, trying to collect himself.

"You look a little lost," a voice said softly.

Dominic started, his head snapping up. The voice belonged to a woman, standing just a few feet away at the mouth of the alley. Her tone was gentle, almost soothing, but there was something about her presence that sent a shiver down his spine.

"Is it that obvious?" he replied, his voice still shaky as he tried to regain his composure.

"Not to everyone," the woman said, her lips curving into a faint smile. "But I could hear it in your breath. Fear has a way of announcing itself."

Dominic's gaze flicked to the cane in her hand, tapping rhythmically against the cobblestone. Her other hand moved in slow, deliberate motions, as if brushing away invisible cobwebs. He noticed the milky hue of her eyes and felt a pang of unease with the scarred scratch marks around her sockets.

"Are you...blind?" he asked, his curiosity outweighing his caution.

"Is it that obvious?" she replied, a hint of humor in her voice. Dominic let out a short laugh despite himself, the tension in his chest easing slightly.

The woman stepped closer, the tapping of her cane steady and deliberate. "You seem like you could use a reprieve," she said. "Why don't you come with me? The crowd will thin soon enough. There's no sense in fighting it now."

Dominic hesitated, his gaze darting back toward the street. The chances of finding Sebastian or Gretel seemed slim at best. Despite proximity, shouting proved futile amidst the chaos. He bit his lip, weighing his options. His instincts told him to keep moving, to stay vigilant, but his body was screaming for a moment's rest.

"I wish these people had phones," he muttered under his breath as he dreaded the thought of his no longer working.

"Sorry, what was that?" the woman asked, tilting her head slightly.

"Nothing," Dominic said quickly, shaking his head. He looked at her again, taking in her calm demeanor. There was something disarming about her, despite the oddness of the situation. He sighed. "Sure. I'll come with you. I'm Dominic, by the way."

The woman's faint smile widened, revealing teeth that were uneven and discolored. She extended her free hand, groping the air until Dominic stepped forward to clasp it. Her grip was firm and cool, her fingers bony but steady.

"Evangeline," she said. "It's a pleasure to meet you."

Chapter 44

WHAT THE STORYBOOK MISSED...
Evangeline

LOSING MY FATHER WAS the moment everything changed. It wasn't just the grief; it was the way the air in our home seemed heavier, the way the light from the windows didn't feel as warm and bright. His passing left a hole in all of us. Mother withdrew into herself, becoming colder and harsher than she'd ever been. My sister was inconsolable. There were nights when her sobbing pierced through the silence, making it impossible for me to sleep. Sometimes I tried to comfort her, but she would push me away, retreating into her sorrow. We both lost him, yet her sadness felt so loud it drowned out my own.

Grieving wasn't a luxury we could afford for long. Next thing I knew, Mother announced she had found a new suitor. A man she claimed would save us. I still remember the day she told us. Our home was crumbling, literally falling apart. The servants were long gone, dismissed to save money. Aurelia and I were left to maintain the house, scrubbing floors and washing linens, all while surviving on scraps that barely filled our bellies.

Manual labor was not something I was made for. I loved beautiful things—the intricacy of fine lace, the delicate pastel hues of embroidered parasols. But those days of luxury were gone. Now my hands were chapped, my fingernails cracked, and my once-soft skin was rough and coarse. Mother, in her distant cruelty, never referred to us as her daughters anymore. We were her helpers, her tools for survival, and she wasn't shy about making her disdain for us known.

One day, Aurelia and I were hanging the laundry on a windy afternoon. The gusts were relentless, whipping the damp clothes out of our hands and sending them tumbling down the street. My arms ached from wringing out the sheets, the muscles in my forearms screaming in protest.

"I hate this," I said, glaring at the linens as the wind pulled them from my grip.

"It's fine," Aurelia replied quietly, pinning a pair of knickers to the line.

Her calmness infuriated me. Aurelia seemed to find solace in the work, using it as a distraction from reality. If there was dirt on the floor, she was scrubbing it. If someone threw eggs at the house, she was out with a brush before the yolks even dried. But this wasn't right. We weren't born to live like this.

"Don't you want something more out of life?" I pressed, shaking my head as I wrung out another sheet. "You used to hate this kind of work."

Aurelia didn't answer, just sniffled quietly as she worked. The wind gusted again, and this time it ripped a petticoat right out of my hands. I cursed under my breath as it tumbled down the cobblestone street. Nobody even noticed or cared. Merchants kept shouting their wares. Children darted through the streets, and everyone seemed oblivious to my struggle.

As I chased after the runaway fabric, a hand suddenly appeared, catching the petticoat before it could tumble further. A man stood before me, his mustache curling at the ends as he smiled warmly. The feather in his hat swayed in the breeze, and the edge of his cloak revealed the string of a bow strapped across his chest.

"*Looking for this?*" *he asked, holding out the damp cloth.*

"*Thank you,*" *I said breathlessly, taking it from him.*

"*It's no trouble,*" *he replied, his voice soothing and kind. He lingered, studying me as if he could see straight through to the heart of me.*

"*I see sadness in your face,*" *he said.* "*You've lost someone, dear, haven't you?*"

His words struck something deep within me, and my eyes filled with tears. "*Yes,*" *I said softly.* "*My father.*"

"*I'm sorry for your loss,*" *he said, his voice heavy with sympathy.* "*The heartbreak must have brought a darkness into your life.*"

Darkness? The word lingered in my mind. I supposed he was right. Life had felt dimmer since Father's death. There was no more light, no more laughter, no more joy.

"*Yes,*" *I admitted.* "*It feels like there's nothing left.*"

"*You feel unloved, don't you?*" *he asked gently.* "*As though no one truly cares for you.*"

The tears I had been holding back finally slipped free. He had voiced the ache in my heart that I couldn't bring myself to say aloud. Mother's coldness, Aurelia's withdrawal—there was no one left for me.

"*What if I told you there's a way to change all that?*" *he asked, stepping closer.* "*A way to turn your misery into something magnificent?*"

I blinked up at him, unsure of what he meant. "*What do you mean?*"

"*People like us,*" *he said, his voice dropping to a conspiratorial whisper,* "*deserve more. We deserve lives of luxury, of power. And you can have that, too. You just need to embrace the darkness inside you.*"

"*Darkness?*" *I repeated, the word tasting strange on my tongue.*

"*Yes,*" *he said, his smile widening.* "*Your pain, your sorrow—these are strengths. If you give yourself to the Concealment, you can transform your life. No more sadness. No more struggle.*"

I hesitated, the promise of a better life tempting me like nothing else had. "What would I need to do?"

"Let go of everything holding you back," he said. "Your grief, your family, even your sister. Let the darkness consume you, and it will give you the power you deserve."

"My sister?" I whispered, the idea of losing Aurelia piercing through my thoughts. "I can't lose her."

He scoffed. "What has she done for you? Has she lifted you up or held you back? Think about it. If she truly cared, why hasn't she supported you the way you want her to?"

His words were sharp, cutting through my doubts like a blade. Deep down, I knew he was right. Aurelia hadn't been there for me, not really. And yet, the thought of abandoning her felt like betraying myself.

"I...I don't know," I stammered.

"Think about it," he said, his fiery orange eyes locking onto mine. "I can tell that you're not ready yet. When you're ready to give up what you need for the life you deserve, I'll find you."

"Wait!" I called as he began to walk away. "Who are you?"

He paused, his silhouette disappearing into the shadows of the alley. "You can call me Robin," he said, his voice echoing faintly as he vanished.

I stood there, clutching the damp petticoat to my chest, my heart pounding. The idea of embracing the darkness both terrified and intrigued me. Could I really give up everything for the life I wanted? For the power I craved?

I want to, but I don't know. Only time will tell.

THE TREK TO OUR NEW *home was excruciating. Every bump and tilt of the carriage jolted me like a rag doll tossed around in a child's tantrum. The wheels were uneven, so it rocked with every*

agonizing roll forward. My stomach churned as if it were being wrung out by some cruel hand, and the stench of manure clinging to the countryside air clawed at my senses, driving a headache deeper into my skull.

This was not the life I imagined.

When the carriage finally lurched to a stop, I peered out at what was to be our new home. It was sprawling, the kind of estate that might be considered peaceful to someone who didn't have to think about the endless maintenance it required. To me, it was a prison in disguise. The sheer size of the place practically screamed work.

The doors opened, and a small gathering of servants stood ready to greet us. Relief flooded through me when I realized I wouldn't have to do everything myself. I glanced over at Aurelia, whose face was still stained with tears. Her sleeve was damp from constantly wiping them away. She looked miserable, broken even, and for once, I wished I could comfort her. But what could I say? This was as much of a loss as it was a gain.

At the door stood the man who had taken us from our world into his. He was dressed sharply, his formal attire pristine and regal. Beside him stood a girl about my age. Her hair was golden, shimmering in the sunlight, and her skirt bore the marks of grass stains and dirt. It was clear she wasn't afraid to get her hands dirty.

"This is my daughter, Ella," the man said with pride in his voice. "She is your new stepsister."

Ella smiled at us, warm and genuine, her hands folded politely in front of her. There was nothing contrived about her. I hated her for it. Her father's pride in her was so evident it turned my stomach. How could he love her so openly and unashamedly? It was a strange concept. Mother never looked at me or Aurelia that way.

"Pleasure," Aurelia said stiffly, her voice flat.

She didn't mean it.

Neither did I when I gave a half-hearted nod in return. My new stepsister continued smiling, oblivious or determined to pretend she didn't notice our disinterest.

"May I help you to your room?" she offered sweetly.

I nodded again, unsure of how to respond. As much as I hated the idea of this new life, part of me craved the warmth Ella and her father exuded. It was different, unsettling, and I didn't trust it for a second.

We climbed the stairs, the steps splitting off in two directions. At the landing, a bay window offered a view of the countryside. It stretched endlessly, a lush expanse of tall grass, wildflowers, and swaying trees. A gentle breeze brushed the petals, and butterflies flitted among the blooms, carefree and vibrant. For a fleeting moment, I felt my chest lighten, my heart steadying in a way it hadn't since Father's death.

This place had potential. It could be a home, a sanctuary.

But sanctuaries don't last. I knew better than to get comfortable.

Mother and our new stepfather disappeared up the opposite staircase, their footsteps echoing faintly. He spoke with animated joy, but her responses were curt, dismissive. She followed him like one would follow a host rather than a husband. It struck me then how temporary this all felt. Mother had no intention of staying. She was here for the convenience, for what this man could give us until she found a way to take it all for herself.

I turned back to the window, trying to distract myself from the thought. That's when I saw him.

Leaning against the stable, half in shadow, was Robin. His white teeth gleamed as his feathered hat tilted slightly in the breeze. The sight of him jolted me back to reality, grounding me in a way the butterflies and flowers never could.

This isn't permanent.

This isn't real.

The life Ella and her father offered might seem nice, but I knew it wasn't for me. It would lull me into complacency, rob me of my drive, and make me weak. Robin's words echoed in my mind. He had warned me about the light—how it tempts, how it deceives. I couldn't let myself be seduced by it. I had to stay strong, stay focused on what really mattered: my ambitions, my desires, my power.

Ella interrupted my thoughts with a soft, hopeful question. "What do you think of the house? Isn't it beautiful?"

I hesitated, her bright eyes searching my face for approval.

"What an awful place this is," I said, my voice sharper than I intended. I ran my fingers along the floral wallpaper, feigning disgust. "Did you decorate this yourself?"

Her smile faltered. "N-no. This was my mother's doing."

The gagging sound I made wasn't entirely fake. "Such horrible taste," I sneered. "No wonder she took ill."

Ella's face crumbled, her jaw trembling as she struggled to process my words. Aurelia froze, her expression torn between shock and disappointment.

I didn't care.

Or at least, I told myself I didn't.

Aurelia turned and climbed the stairs silently, retreating to the safety of her room. The look in her eyes stung more than I expected. She didn't understand. She couldn't see that I was doing this for us—for her.

She needed to trust me, though. I was only doing this for her. I knew that once I allowed the Concealment to take over, we would have nothing else to worry about. She needed to let me do what I had to do to change our lives. And if she didn't like it, then I guessed that Robin might be right and that I could only watch out for what was best for me and that I would have to rely solely on myself to make it in this world.

I hope not.

If I allowed myself to fall for this false sense of family, we'd be no better off than we were before. I had to stay strong, had to embrace the darkness Robin had spoken of. Ella might think her kindness could change me, but I knew better. Kindness doesn't lead to power. It doesn't protect you.

I glanced out the window again, but Robin was gone. His words, however, lingered.

I could't let anyone in.

Not Ella.

Not Aurelia.

Not anyone.

Chapter 45

Dominic followed the woman deeper into the alley, her hand fluttering in a gesture to guide him along. The further they moved, the livelier the main streets sounded behind them, their chatter and laughter reduced to a faint hum. Around him, cats prowled through piles of debris, their whiskers twitching as they hunted for scraps. Loose cobblestones shifted beneath his boots, and he stumbled, his foot catching on a jagged edge.

"Where exactly do you live?" Dominic asked, brushing dust off his pant leg as he steadied himself.

"Not much further," Evangeline replied, her tone confident despite the cautious sweep of her cane in front of her. Her other hand rested against the wall, using it for balance as they continued down the narrow path.

The sunlight dimmed as they pressed on, the tall buildings on either side casting long shadows. The alley seemed to swallow the light, leaving them in a haze of grays. Dominic's nose wrinkled at the sour scent of mildew and damp fabric. Figures huddled in the darkness, their hunched forms barely visible. Their clothing hung in tatters, with stains smeared along every seam. The smell reminded him of the underpasses back home, where homeless communities gathered around trash can fires for warmth and survival. His stomach lurched, and his steps faltered.

"Shouldn't someone like you live in better conditions?" Dominic asked, glancing at Evangeline as she paused briefly to adjust her grip on the cane.

"Some of us don't have much of a choice," she said softly, her voice laced with bitterness.

They stopped in front of a large piece of canvas fabric that flapped weakly in the occasional breeze. Evangeline shifted it aside, revealing an opening barely illuminated by the faint flicker of candlelight from within. She stepped through, gesturing for Dominic to follow. He hesitated, his breath catching at the stench that hit him—a pungent blend of unwashed bodies, waste, and stale air. The oppressive scent made his eyes water.

"This is it," Evangeline said. She pulled out a few burnt, misshapen loaves of bread from her cloak and tossed them onto a crate in the center of the room, nearly toppling the lone candle resting on top.

"Mother, I'm home," she called out.

Dominic's gaze swept the dim space, where straw was scattered across the floor, forming what passed as bedding. A pig trough in the corner reeked, its pungent stench telling it was repurposed as a makeshift toilet. The walls were damp, their surfaces streaked with grime. The room felt suffocating, the air thick and unmoving.

In one corner, an older woman lay sprawled on a bed of straw, her frail body barely moving. Her hair was a greasy, matted mix of salt and pepper, tangled into thick clumps like neglected ropes. She groaned softly, fumbling for a walking stick and disturbing a rat that had been rummaging nearby. The rodent squeaked in protest before scurrying off into the shadows.

"Do you need help?" Dominic asked, his voice tentative as he tried to mask his revulsion.

"That would be lovely," Evangeline said as she settled onto an overturned bucket, her cane resting against her knee. "Mother can't speak or see."

Dominic winced. He wasn't sure what to make of this revelation. He stepped forward and slipped an arm under the older woman's shoulder, helping her into a seated position by the crate. Her bony frame was light, but the effort still brought an ache to his muscles. He noted with some pride that his strength seemed to improve; the heavy physical exertion of recent days had clearly had some effect.

"Can I ask what happened to you two?" Dominic ventured, curiosity mixing with unease as the candlelight illuminated the scarring over their eye sockets.

The older woman paused, her trembling hands tearing off a chunk of bread. Crumbs fell onto her lap as she chewed with slow, deliberate motions. Her movements seemed fragile, as though the simple act of eating required all her remaining strength.

"We were attacked by the Concealment," Evangeline said.

The older woman froze mid-chew, her expression tightening. Tears welled up in her milky eyes as she sniffled, her lips trembling.

"Our servant quit on us," Evangeline continued. "And then, out of nowhere, a white cloud of flour coated us. Before we knew it, the room was swarming with darkness."

Dominic's gaze flicked to the older woman, who groaned and gestured weakly as if trying to add to the story. The scars on her tongue-less mouth were a chilling sight, and Dominic looked away quickly.

"It felt like needles stabbing into my eye sockets," Evangeline said, her voice cracking. "And I can't imagine the pain Mother felt when they ripped out her tongue."

Dominic's stomach turned. "I'm so sorry to hear that. It must've been awful to lose your home and your vision all at once."

Evangeline's face twisted with bitterness. "The worst part is that the servant didn't deserve the life she got. She was ungrateful for everything we gave her, and they repaid us with betrayal. I don't understand how good things happen to people who don't deserve them."

"If they were such a bad employee," Dominic asked cautiously, "why didn't you let them go sooner?"

"It's complicated," Evangeline snapped.

Dominic held up his hands in a placating gesture. "I see."

Evangeline's expression softened slightly, but her tone remained sharp. "We could've had more, you know. We deserved more. My sister prevented us from having the lives we deserved."

"And where is your sister now?" Dominic asked.

Evangeline scoffed. "Hell if I know. I suppose one benefit of losing your sight is that I don't have to see her anymore."

The bitterness in Evangeline's voice made Dominic's skin crawl. Her words hung in the air like a sinister fog, thick and suffocating. He opened his mouth to respond, to say something—anything—that might defuse the growing tension, but before he could speak, the older woman suddenly gripped the edge of the crate with an unexpected ferocity. Her frail, bony fingers, trembling a moment ago, now curled around the fork she had found. The dull, rusted tines glinted in the dim light as she clutched it tight, her knuckles whitening with the effort.

Dominic took a step back, his heart thudding violently in his chest. "I-I think I should go now," he stammered, his voice shaky. He could feel the sweat gathering at the nape of his neck, cold and clammy. "I don't want to intrude on your dinner."

Evangeline's head tilted at an unnatural angle, her long, greasy hair spilling over her face as her lips stretched into a smile—too wide, too predatory. Her eyes, though devoid of sight, seemed to bore into him with an unnerving intensity.

"Don't be silly," she hissed, her voice dripping with malice. "You *are* the dinner."

Dominic's stomach dropped. His mind scrambled for a response, but before he could process her words, the force of a violent flip sent the crate before him crashing to the floor. The crude wooden structure slammed into his chest, knocking him backward onto the cold, hard ground. The weight of it pinned him down, forcing the air from his lungs into a wheezing gasp.

Before he could fully comprehend what was happening, the older woman was on him. Her bony knees dug into his arms, pinning them down as her claw-like fingers raked at his face. Evangeline followed, her wiry frame pressing against his legs as her hands scratched at his shoulders. Their breath was hot and rancid, a nauseating stench of decay that made Dominic gag.

"They say stress makes the meat more tender," Evangeline crooned, her voice mockingly sweet. She leaned in closer, her cracked lips brushing against his ear. "We'll let you panic a little longer before we dig in."

Dominic's screams ripped through the small room, raw and desperate. "Help! Somebody, help!" His voice echoed against the walls, but there was no reply—only the cruel laughter of the women above him.

Evangeline threw her head back, her cackling filling the room like a chorus of nightmares. "Nobody's coming for you," she sneered, her nails digging into his skin as he squirmed beneath her. "Nobody cares about people like us. Just like they didn't care about the others."

"Others?" Dominic's voice cracked, his chest heaving as he struggled against their weight.

"Oh, yes," Evangeline purred, her tone almost vibrato. "So many others. Children, travelers, anyone foolish enough to wander into our little corner of the world. They were all so tasty! Could've used a little salt, but can't be picky!"

Her mother nodded wordlessly, her mouth twisted into a grotesque grin. The sharpened teeth that Dominic had previously thought were a trick of the dim light now gleamed menacingly as her chapped lips curled back. Her head dipped toward his exposed throat, her breath hot and sticky against his skin.

Dominic thrashed beneath them, his panic escalating as he realized how helpless he was. His mind raced, frantically searching for a way out, a weapon, anything he could use to defend himself—but there was nothing. His screams grew louder, more strained, until his voice became hoarse.

Then, like a crack of thunder, a deafening *thud* silenced the chaos.

Evangeline's body was yanked off him with such force that she hit the ground, sprawling across the filthy floor with a startled cry. The blow lessened the weight on his chest as it struck the older woman with such force that she stumbled backward, her head snapping to the side as she hit the wall.

"Let him go!" bellowed a voice, deep and commanding.

Dominic turned his head, his vision blurred by tears and sweat. Standing over him was Sebastian, his broad shoulders heaving as his fists clenched and restrained fury. His face was a mask of anger, his eyes burning with a fire Dominic had never seen before.

Sebastian didn't hesitate. He drove his fist into Evangeline's face as she scrambled to her feet, sending her crashing onto the overturned crate. The older woman lunged at him, her fork raised like a weapon, but Sebastian caught her wrist mid-swing. With a furious growl, he twisted her arm, forcing her to drop the makeshift blade. Another strike to her jaw sent her crumpling to the ground.

Dominic scrambled to his feet, his body trembling as he tried to regain his balance. His gaze darted to the corner of the room, where a heavy tarp had been dislodged during the struggle. What it revealed made his stomach churn: Bones. Piles of them. Some were small, belonging to children. Others were splintered and broken, as if gnawed upon.

"Oh my god," Dominic whispered, his hand flying to his mouth.

The older woman let out a guttural wail, crawling toward the pile of bones as if to protect them like prized possessions. Blood dripped from her split lip, staining the already filthy floor. Evangeline whimpered in the corner, clutching her bloodied nose as she glared up at Sebastian with pure hatred.

Sebastian didn't spare them another glance. He grabbed Dominic's arm, his grip firm but not painful. "We're leaving. Now," he said, his voice cold and unyielding.

Dominic stumbled after him, his legs shaky and uncooperative. His heart pounded in his chest, adrenaline still coursing through his veins as they fled the dark, oppressive alley. The cries of the two women faded into the distance, replaced by the eerie quiet of the now-deserted street.

Sebastian's boots echoed against the cobblestones, the sound steady and deliberate. Dominic dared a glance at his rescuer, but the look on Sebastian's face made him shiver. His jaw was clenched, his eyes dark and unreadable. He exuded an air of controlled rage, his shoulders tense with barely contained energy.

"Thank you," Dominic said weakly, his voice barely audible. "I-I didn't know they were going to attack me like that."

Sebastian didn't respond. He marched forward with unwavering purpose, his silence more chilling than any scream. Dominic kept his head down, his thoughts a chaotic swirl of fear and gratitude as they disappeared into civilization.

EVEN WITH THE AMOUNT of people passing by during their trek, the streets were eerily quiet, a stillness that Gretel hadn't experienced since she'd first fled to this town. The usual cacophony of merchant calls and clinking coins had faded, leaving only a dull hum of the occasional passerby. It felt like the town itself was holding its breath, waiting for something to break the fragile peace. The pause seemed to bring gratitude to the merchants, although their relief was tainted by unease over the lack of business.

Two children skipped down the road, their laughter carrying through the still air like a melody. They were inseparable, holding hands as they hopped over cracks in the cobblestones. The girl twirled a sticky lollipop in her free hand, brandishing it like a wand. It caught the sunlight, trapping a stray insect in its sugary coating.

"I hate candy," Gretel said as she curled her lip.

A loud clatter from an alleyway interrupted the calm as a pile of discarded crates exploded onto the street. Out stumbled Sebastian, his movements hurried and almost feral. His eyes were wide, pupils blown, giving him a manic look that sent shivers down her spine. A moment later, he barreled into the little girl, sending her sprawling to the ground. The lollipop shattered, its sticky remnants clinging to the cobblestones. Her brother rushed to her side, offering her a piece of saltwater taffy to console her while inspecting the scrape on her knee.

Gretel's stomach twisted as she watched. *I wish my brother had done that for me.*

She shook off the thought and focused on Sebastian, who was storming down the road with a fury she didn't recognize. Gretel quickened her pace, weaving through the thinning crowd to catch up. Her boots thudded against the uneven cobblestones, each step drawing her closer to him. Her lungs burned as she pushed herself, dodging carts and sidestepping strangers with a precision honed through years of survival.

For a brief moment, the town seemed to dissolve around her. The faces of the people blurred into shadows, and the mundane surroundings felt almost surreal. This wasn't the first time she'd been running through streets like this, her heart pounding as if she were being chased by something far more sinister.

She finally caught up to him near a fence at the edge of town, the sound of her boots scuffing against the ground, breaking the tense silence between them. "Sebastian," she called, panting, "are you okay?"

"I'm fine," he grunted, his tone sharp and unconvincing.

"You don't seem fine," Gretel pressed, trying to steady her breath.

He didn't answer, didn't even look at her. His shoulder nudged against a wooden cart as he passed, causing a loud creak that startled Calypso, who was busy grooming himself near the edge of the street. The cat darted into Dominic's arms as he caught up with them, his owner's face pale as a sheet. Gretel glanced back at him briefly before returning her focus to Sebastian.

"Did something happen to Dominic?" she asked, her voice laced with concern.

Sebastian finally stopped, his hands gripping the top rail of the fence that the wood groaned under the pressure. His fury seemed to ripple through the air, unsettling the horses grazing nearby. "Of course, something happened to Dominic," he snapped. "Something always happens to Dominic."

Gretel bristled. "What's that supposed to mean?"

Sebastian turned to face her, his eyes blazing with anger. "It means he's a walking disaster. It's like trouble follows him everywhere he goes."

Gretel frowned, her own temper flaring. "You and I both know the Concealment is after him. He doesn't control that. And besides, we need him—he's the one who's supposed to save everyone."

"I don't have a problem with that," Sebastian spat, his voice rising. "I have a problem with how ungrateful he is. Do you know how much you've done for him? How much I've done?"

Gretel hesitated. She knew what he was referring to—the shop, the stolen jewel, Dominic's less-than-gracious reaction, and his behavior toward that innocent woman. "So, he made a mistake or two," she said carefully. "We all make mistakes. It's not the end of the world."

Sebastian let out a harsh laugh. "Mistakes? Gretel, he used stolen goods to pay for clothes! Goods that you risked your life to steal! And what did he do? He complained about it!"

"It wasn't like that—" Dominic's voice cut in from behind them. He was close now, clutching Calypso like a lifeline. "I didn't mean to come off that way. I just...I didn't know how to act. This is all new to me."

"Well, maybe it's time to figure it out," Sebastian snapped, his frustration boiling over. "This isn't some dream you can stumble your way through. People are dying out here, Dominic. Real people. And it's about time you woke up to that."

Dominic flinched, his face reddening. "I'm trying," he said, his voice trembling. "I didn't ask for this, you know. I didn't ask to be dragged into some medieval death match with magic and monsters. I'm just trying to survive."

"That's your problem," Sebastian said coldly. "You're focused on surviving instead of fighting. You're so wrapped up in your own head, you can't see what's at stake."

"Sebastian, stop!" Gretel interjected, stepping between them. She'd seen anger before, but this was different. His anger wasn't just frustration; it was heartbreak.

Sebastian turned away from them, his fists clenching and unclenching at his sides. The wood of the fence cracked under his grip, startling the horses into whinnying protests. "I can't do this anymore," he mumbled, his voice barely audible over the commotion.

Dominic froze. "What do you mean?" he asked, his voice cracking.

"I mean, I'm done," Sebastian said, mounting one of the nearby horses with practiced ease. "You're on your own. Gretel can take care of you."

"Sebastian, wait!" Dominic's voice was frantic now, tinged with desperation. He reached out, his fingers brushing the fabric of Sebastian's sleeve, but he pulled away.

"No." Sebastian's tone was final, his expression unreadable. "I'm going back to the people who actually appreciate the small things in life."

And with that, Sebastian tapped his heels against the horse's sides, urging it into a gallop. The sound of hooves faded into the distance as he disappeared over the hill, leaving Gretel and Dominic standing in stunned silence.

Dominic's shoulders sagged as the tears he'd been holding back finally spilled over. Gretel watched him, unsure of what to say. She wasn't used to comforting people; she'd done more than her share with Dominic. But as Dominic clung to her, trembling with quiet sobs, she placed a hand on his shoulder, awkward but sincere.

"It's going to be okay," she said softly, though she wasn't sure she believed it herself. As she looked out toward the horizon, where Sebastian had vanished, she couldn't shake the uneasy feeling that their little group was falling apart. This may be the start of the savior falling apart.

Chapter 46

FROM THE PAGES OF THE STORYBOOK
Ella

I WAS EXHAUSTED.

After an early morning of chores and a trip to town, I was still far from done. Keeping this house in order was a never-ending battle, especially when it came to cleaning up after the messes my stepmother and stepsisters left behind. I still couldn't understand why anyone would intentionally make things harder by smearing filth everywhere. Who does that?

The only bright spot in my day so far had been a brief moment at the market when a little girl passing by smiled at me. Her innocent joy and the light in her eyes reminded me that good people still existed in this world. It was a fleeting moment, but it gave me hope—something I desperately needed.

By the time I arrived home, my legs felt like lead. My body ached from the hours spent in the saddle, even though I made the ride to the village regularly. Today felt different. The heat of the sun had been relentless, pounding down on me the entire time. My feet dragged across the gravel as I led the horses back to the stable. Even they were huffing with exhaustion. The persistent drone of cicadas filled the air, trying to liven the silence.

"You better hurry up and get your work done," Sebastian joked as he snuck from the back and took the horse from me to guide back into the stable. *"I want to see how beautiful you'll look tonight."*

I wasn't looking forward to the work waiting for me inside.

When I opened the front door, I stopped short. The floors sparkled under the sunlight streaming through the windows. The wood gleamed with a fresh polish and smelled faintly of citrus. Everything was pristine—every plate perfectly aligned on the dining table, not a speck of dust to be seen.

How?

"Cinderella, have you returned from the market?" my stepmother's voice echoed sharply down the corridor.

"Yes, Madam," I answered, still trying to process what I was seeing. *The house hadn't looked this immaculate since...well, ever.*

"Do you have our afternoon biscuits ready?"

I froze. "J-just a moment! I'll get those started now."

"Ugh!" She groaned loudly, her dissatisfaction palpable even from another room.

I quickly hung the gowns I'd picked up at the market on the hat rack, making sure the hems didn't touch the floor. My hands were trembling as I rushed into the kitchen, half-expecting to find chaos waiting for me. Instead, I was greeted by the sight of steam rising from a boiling cauldron and the warm aroma of baking biscuits.

What in the world?

The fire was toasting the biscuits to a perfect golden brown, and every dish was already in its place. The tea cups sat clean and ready on the counter. It was as if some invisible hand had done all the work for me.

That's impossible.

Was it? My heart skipped a beat. For a moment, I thought of the farm animals that often seemed to take an unusual interest in my tasks. But no, this couldn't be their doing. It just didn't make sense.

I pulled the biscuits from the fire, setting them on the table along with the tea. The setup was ready in record time, a small miracle given my state of mind. I tugged on the bell cord to summon my stepmother and stepsisters, though my hands still shook slightly from confusion and exhaustion.

The three women entered the dining room in their usual fashion. Mirelle and Evangeline took their seats with their usual air of dissatisfaction, while Aurelia dragged herself to the table and slumped into her chair. Her face was pale, her movements sluggish—something was off with her.

"Did you retrieve the gowns for tonight?" my stepmother asked, her voice as sharp as ever.

"Yes, Madam," I replied.

"Very good," she said curtly, breaking a biscuit in half with her fingers. Steam rose in lazy tendrils, but her expression didn't soften.

"You better not have gotten mine dirty," Evangeline snapped, wincing as she burned her tongue on her tea.

"Or mine," Aurelia muttered weakly, barely glancing up as she poured water into her cup.

"You're dismissed," my stepmother said briskly, waving me away. "Now go finish your chores. I don't want any distractions while we prepare for the festival."

I nodded and gave a small curtsey before leaving the room. I wandered up the stairs, expecting to find a mountain of work waiting for me, but as I looked around, I realized something strange. The yardwork was done. The laundry was finished. Every animal had been fed and their stalls cleaned. Even the rugs had been beaten and looked brand new. The entire house was spotless.

What was happening?

I paused at the window overlooking the yard. The horses were calmly grazing, their coats shining in the afternoon sun. The chickens pecked contentedly at the ground. Everything was peaceful, serene—perfect, even.

I returned inside and checked the corridor, half-expecting to find some hidden mess I'd missed. But there was nothing. Every surface was polished to perfection. There wasn't a speck of dust on the remaining porcelain pieces that hadn't been sold. For once, the house was completely, utterly silent.

There was nothing left to do.

I climbed the stairs to my room, my legs burning with each step. The weight of the day—and the weight of my life—pressed heavily on me. When I reached my small, drafty room, I was greeted by the cool breeze blowing through the broken window. I paused, looking out at the castle in the distance. It shimmered in the sunlight like something out of a dream, a world so far removed from my own.

Carriages rolled up to the castle gates, their passengers preparing for a night of splendor. Ships docked at the nearby port, unloading goods for the royal celebration. The sight sent a thrill through me, filling me with a longing I couldn't suppress.

I must go. I must be part of that world, even for just one night.

Motivated, I turned to the chair where my mother's dress sat. But as soon as I looked at it, I froze.

The sash was already stitched to the bodice.

The seams had been repaired flawlessly.

The hem was perfectly even.

My dress was finished!

I picked it up, my hands trembling. Holding it against my chest, I twirled around the room, imagining how I'd look wearing it tonight. For a brief moment, as I caught my reflection in the cracked mirror, I saw my mother in myself. Her warmth, her grace—it was there in the glow of my skin and the spark in my eyes.

The birds outside chirped a joyous melody, as if celebrating this moment with me. My heart swelled with hope. Tonight would be a night to remember. But first, I needed to rest. My body ached, my limbs heavy with fatigue. I sank onto my straw mattress, propping myself against the lumpy pillow. As I gazed out the window, the dream of dancing and freedom felt closer than ever.

Just one night. One night to feel alive.

There was a little guilt for taking some time for myself, but then again, when did I ever take a moment to relax? For now, though, I let my eyes drift shut, savoring the first moment of peace I'd had in what felt like forever. A moment I truly deserved.

Chapter 47

Returning to the palace proved difficult. Gretel sat across from him, her sharp gaze flickering to his face every so often, her silence heavy with unspoken questions. Calypso had curled up near Gretel instead, avoiding Dominic as if sensing the tension radiating from him. Even the townspeople they passed seemed to look at him differently. Before, he had been a curiosity, an oddity to be glanced at but ultimately ignored. Now, their stares felt sharper, judgmental, as if they could see the shame clinging to him like a shroud.

The thought made Dominic's stomach churn. He tried to convince himself it was all in his head, but the lump in his throat grew heavier with each passing second. When the carriage rolled to a stop in front of the castle, he was the last to step out. The grandeur loomed over him, its spires reaching for the heavens, but instead of being awestruck as he had been on his first arrival, he felt small and out of place.

Walking through the grand hall, the place was isolating with everybody focused on getting the space ready for the festival. Dominic's body tried to relax on one of the benches, letting the people pass by. Servants balancing platters of hors d'oeuvres, teasing his stomach with the options passing by. Through the nearest door, Sawyer followed by an assistant, taking a taste of lamb for quality.

"Everything okay?" Sawyer asked as he covered his mouth to finish his bite.

"Yeah," Dominic said quietly, boots scuffing on the floor.

"You don't look okay."

"I am."

Sawyer tilted his head, noticing Dominic's lack of eye contact. "I know when somebody is in trouble. Tell me what's wrong."

"I'm just struggling with this place," he answered, his eyes becoming sensitive from the formation of tears.

"What's wrong with this place? This castle is beautiful!"

"No, it's not this castle. It's this world."

"Oh, I'm sorry. What are you struggling with here in Golponia?"

"I think I'm losing myself here."

"Oh."

Three servant women passed by. Broomsticks scratched on the floor as they dragged them on their way to the ballroom. Two children chase each other, weaving around the pillars with soft giggles that struggled to put a smile on Dominic's face.

"Yeah. I feel like I don't know who I am."

"Well, you're Dominic."

Looking at Sawyer's confused expression made Dominic ponder for a moment. The realization had hit him that some people in his storybooks existed as supporting cast from the start to the last page. Remembering Ella as one that was full of pain and longing was the only thing he could recall. There was nothing in the story about Sawyer and what made him happy or sad. It was always about what the stepfamily did and nothing to do with royalty.

"What makes you happy?" Dominic asked with curiosity.

"Well, my queen makes me happy," Sawyer said, his eyebrow furrowing.

"I mean, what else makes you happy. Do you have any hopes and dreams? Hobbies?"

The king glanced around the castle. He tried to force a smile as he looked at every prized possession. The décor that was chosen by his parents, the chachkas displayed from family, the animal pelts laid out—he couldn't recall when any of this sparked joy. There wasn't a book in the grand library that he's picked up to read, not a single adventure he allowed himself to be immersed in fiction.

"I don't know," Sawyer answered blankly.

Sawyer got up from his seat, hand covering his mouth in disbelief. The rush of helpers passing by him made his eyes flutter. The doors opened with sunlight blinding him.

"I think I need some air," he said in a frantic panic.

"Wait! I don't mean to make you feel that way," Dominic said. "I was just saying that I was feeling a little lost here. I didn't mean to make you feel that."

"But you're right. I don't know who I am."

"You're a king. A king who loves his wife. And you're an amazing leader for your people!"

Sawyer stopped himself, his smirk tight as he took in the flattery.

"Please don't let my struggle wear off on you. This is my battle, and you have nothing to worry about."

"Okay," Sawyer said as he took a deep breath. "I think I'm going to get some fresh air."

As the king made his way out into the courtyard, the air wisped in Dominic's face. Watching Sawyer's defeat brought a heavy weight in Dominic's chest, noticing that his problem has now become someone else's. He thought about what he could've said to make it less of a strain. The same look of despair on Sawyer's face was one that was similar to another. The more he reflected on it, his words had been heavy on someone else, someone of value to him.

Sebastian.

DOMINIC SAT ON THE edge of his bed once he got to his room, staring at the ornate suit spread out before him. His mind churned as he replayed Sebastian's sharp words over and over, each syllable cutting deeper than the last. He'd made mistakes—plenty of them—but this time, it felt like the consequences were more than he could bear. He couldn't shake the weight of failure pressing down on him.

Dominic tried to clear his head with a hot bath. The steaming water soothed his aching muscles, and the dirt and grime of the past few days melted away, swirling in the tub. But no matter how much he scrubbed, he couldn't wash away the lingering shame. He stared at the bubbles popping on the surface, their brief, fragile existence oddly reflective of how he felt—always on the verge of bursting.

Wrapping a towel around himself, Dominic stepped to the window. The evening light bathed the bustling palace grounds in gold. Below, guests were arriving in ornate carriages, their laughter and chatter floating up through the open air. Women in voluminous dresses with skirts as wide as carriage wheels paraded up the steps, their jewels catching the sunlight like tiny stars. Men in tailored suits with polished shoes escorted them, their movements as refined as their attire.

But Dominic's gaze drifted past the opulence to the horizon, where the tiny silhouette of the farmhouse sat nestled in the countryside. It looked so small, almost insignificant against the vast landscape, but it loomed large in his thoughts. That little farmhouse had been his first connection to this strange new world, the place where he'd found safety and kindness when he'd needed it most. It was where Sebastian had taken care of him, had fought for him, had believed in him even when Dominic struggled to believe in himself.

Sebastian's words from earlier stabbed at his heart again. Dominic couldn't understand how things had gone so wrong. All he wanted was to make things right. But how? How could he even begin to mend the damage when Sebastian had walked away so definitively?

The soft purring of Calypso, who had returned to claim his spot on the bed, interrupted his thoughts. The cat sprawled across the intricate suit laid out there, his tiny bowtie skewed from his earlier antics. Dominic reached over to adjust it, earning a lazy swipe of the tail in response. At least Calypso still had faith in him—or so he hoped.

With a sigh, Dominic began dressing for the festival. The trousers were tighter than anything he'd ever worn, cinching around his waist in a way that felt both unfamiliar and restrictive. The shirt was a challenge, the delicate ruffles catching on the loops of the buttons as he fumbled to fasten them. He glimpsed at himself in the mirror and grimaced. This wasn't him—not the Dominic he recognized, at least. But then, who was he anymore?

KNOCK! KNOCK!

The soft click of the door opening pulled him from his thoughts. He turned, expecting to see Queen Ella, but froze when Gretel stepped into the room. Dominic's breath caught in his throat as he took her in. The mustard-yellow and teal layers of her gown shimmered in the fading sunlight, the tulle flowing like liquid gold with every step she took. Two polished buns contained her usually unruly and wild hair; not a single strand was out of place. She carried herself with an elegance he'd never imagined, her usual sharp edges softened by the glow of the evening light.

"You look...beautiful," Dominic said, his voice barely above a whisper.

Gretel's cheeks flushed, and she glanced away. "Thank you," she mumbled, her tone uncharacteristically gentle.

"I barely recognize you."

"I hope the rest of the people won't then either," Gretel said sarcastically.

Dominic couldn't take his eyes off her, but she seemed determined to avoid his gaze. Instead, she crossed the room and picked up his suit jacket, holding it open for him with an air of casual determination.

"Here," she said. "Let's get you ready."

He hesitated for a moment before slipping his arms into the sleeves. The fabric felt heavier than he'd expected, the weight settling on his shoulders as if reminding him of the expectations placed upon him. Gretel adjusted the collar and smoothed the mint-green lapels with careful precision, her fingers brushing against the intricate gold trim. Dominic caught a faint scent of lavender as she worked, a detail that only added to the surrealness of the outfit.

"You clean up well," Gretel said, a smirk tugging at the corner of her lips.

"Thanks," Dominic replied, his voice tinged with uncertainty. He glanced at himself in the mirror, half-expecting to see a clown staring back at him, but instead, he saw someone he barely recognized—someone who almost looked like he belonged in this world.

"Shall we?" Gretel asked, extending her hand.

Dominic nodded, taking her hand as they left the room together. Calypso trailed after them. His periwinkle bowtie straightened and his tail held high as if he, too, were ready to make an impression at the ball.

As they walked down the long corridor, Dominic's thoughts drifted back to Sebastian. The farmhouse was gone from view now, hidden by the castle's imposing walls, but it lingered in his mind. He couldn't shake the feeling that he was leaving something behind. Not just a place, but a part of himself. For now, though, he had to focus on the night ahead. The festival awaited, and with it, a chance to prove—to himself, to Gretel, and maybe even to Sebastian—that he was more than just a lost soul fumbling his way through this strange new world.

Chapter 48

FROM THE PAGES OF THE STORYBOOK
Ella

I WOKE UP FEELING LIGHTER than I had in weeks. Two hours of rest wasn't much, but it was enough to breathe new life into me. For once, the weight pulling at my eyelids was gone. The dark shadows under my eyes had faded, and I didn't even need to resort to slicing a cucumber from the garden to cover them up. That would've raised too many questions anyway.

I gave myself a quick sponge bath, blotting away every trace of dirt and pollen clinging to my skin after the day's chores. Each pass of the damp cloth felt like wiping away the weight of my responsibilities, leaving only anticipation behind. My hair, a tangled mess of golden knots, slowly unraveled as I brushed it out to its full, shining glory. It reminded me of the times my mother would brush my hair to get me ready for bed. Humming softly, I let a familiar melody escape my lips—a lullaby my mother used to sing to me. The tune filled the air, carrying with it a sense of calm and bittersweet joy.

With my shoes in hand, I grabbed a scrap of cloth and spit onto it before polishing them vigorously. The layers of grime that had built up from days of cleaning and walking around the yard surrendered under my effort. By the time I finished, the leather gleamed like new. These shoes weren't much, but tonight they would be good enough. Everything about tonight had to be perfect.

"Ugh! I already have this lace!" screamed Evangeline.

From downstairs came the sound of grunts and strained breaths, followed by sharp gasps of irritation. My stepsisters were tugging on each other's corset strings, pulling them as tight as possible. No doubt they were trying to create the smallest waists imaginable to grab the prince's attention. The thought made me roll my eyes. It wasn't the shape of a person's body that mattered—it was their heart. But I wasn't naïve enough to think everyone shared that belief.

When I stepped into my dress, a feeling of warmth and comfort washed over me. The soft pewter silk hugged my figure, and the flowing fabric fluttered gently around my legs like a wisp of smoke. The ruffled hem reminded me of flower petals—delicate, intricate, and full of life. I took a deep breath, imagining my mother's hands smoothing the fabric over me. Her spirit seemed to linger in the air, giving me a sense of lightness and courage I hadn't felt in so long. She always said that beauty wasn't about how you looked but how you felt, and tonight, I felt radiant.

But something was missing.

My fingers instinctively searched for the loose floorboard in the corner of my room. Carefully lifting it, I retrieved the tiny wooden box hidden beneath. Inside were treasures—small, precious things I had collected over the years, both before and after my parents passed. Among them was the necklace. The soft blue beads shimmered faintly, catching the last rays of sunlight before the night fully claimed the sky. It had belonged to my mother, and I was certain it had been passed down through generations before her. I'd kept it safe, hidden from my stepmother, who had already sold off so many of my mother's belongings to pay off her debts.

I fastened the necklace around my neck, the cool beads resting gently against my collarbone. It was perfect. Taking one last look in the mirror, I hardly recognized myself. This wasn't just me—it was a reflection of everything my mother had taught me, a glimpse of who I could be if I held on to hope. I felt beautiful, and for the first time in years, I felt free.

I couldn't resist giving the dress a little twirl. The fabric swirled around me, and my imagination ran wild. The walls of my small, dusty room melted away, replaced by the grandeur of a ballroom. In my mind's eye, the polished hardwood floor shimmered like glass, and I was gliding across it as if dancing on air. An orchestra played somewhere in the distance, their music blending perfectly with the melody of birdsong outside my window. I blushed when I saw my Sebastian, his smile glowing when he saw the dress pressed against my body; I knew he would approve.

My heart swelled with excitement. Tonight, for just a little while, I wouldn't be Cinderella, the servant. I would be Ella, the girl who dared to dream of something better.

I couldn't wait any longer. Tonight would be my night.

THE RHYTHMIC CLATTER *of the horses' hooves echoed against the stone pavement as the carriage rolled to a halt in front of our door. My stepmother and stepsisters rushed to gather the elaborate bustles of their gowns, lifting them delicately to avoid tripping as they moved through the foyer. I could hear my stepmother's clipped tone as she barked out final instructions, polishing their mannerisms for one last time before they were to present themselves to royalty.*

"Wait!" I called out, my voice breaking the stillness with a surge of enthusiasm.

Their movements froze at the doorway, and three pairs of eyes turned toward me, wide with surprise. I caught a glimpse of Evangeline stumbling slightly on the steps, her balance faltering from the sudden halt. Slowly, deliberately, I descended the stairs, allowing the soft ruffles of my dress to flutter with each graceful step. The faint sound of silk brushing against the air accompanied me like a whisper of reassurance.

Mirelle's lip curled in open disgust, her pencil-thin eyebrows arching dramatically as if framing her disdain. Evangeline's powdered cheeks flushed an unbecoming shade of red, her irritation breaking through the layers of makeup and powder. But Aurelia...she didn't react the same way. Her face softened, her lips curving into a smile so genuine it caught me off guard. Her eyes glistened as if she were looking at a work of art.

"Isn't it beautiful?" I asked, spinning gently to show off the full ensemble.

This was my moment—my chance to honor my mother's memory in the dress that once belonged to her. I could almost feel her spirit in the delicate fabric, and for a fleeting second, I imagined myself in the open fields, dancing with the breeze the way she once had.

"Cinderella," my stepmother hissed, stepping closer with narrowed eyes. "Where did you get this dress? I told you not to spend any of our money."

"This didn't cost you a thing, Madam," I said evenly, summoning every ounce of courage I could muster. "It was my mother's."

Her lips parted, and for a moment, she said nothing. I watched as she struggled to find a retort, her sharp tongue momentarily silenced. Behind her, Evangeline tugged at my sleeve, leaning in to whisper a hurried complaint. "She can't come with us, Mother. She'll ruin everything."

Aurelia, still standing apart from the others, watched quietly. Her expression was unreadable—part admiration, part sorrow. I wanted to believe she understood, that she was on my side. But I couldn't tell; it's hard to tell with them.

Stepmother moved toward me, closing the distance until her breath, hot and acrid, brushed against my exposed shoulders. Her sharp gaze swept over the dress, lingering on every detail. I felt her scrutiny, like a weight pressing down on me.

"Such a beautiful dress," she said finally, her voice laced with icy politeness.

"Well, I think it's awful!" Evangeline spat, her eyes darting toward the staircase as if searching for someone else to validate her claim.

"Now, now," Stepmother continued, her tone mockingly sweet. "We wouldn't want to disrespect her mother's memory. That would be so unfortunate."

Something was wrong. My chest tightened, and my heart began to race. Her words sounded kind, but the malice beneath them was unmistakable. Her gloved fingers reached out, brushing against the delicate sash at my waist.

"However," she murmured, her fingers curling into the fabric, "it's disrespectful to wear something so...damaged."

I barely had time to process her words before she yanked the sash free. The tearing sound was deafening, a cruel rip that echoed through the room. The sash fluttered to the ground, lifeless and discarded.

"No!" I gasped, my hands clutching at the bodice, desperate to hold the dress together.

"Oh, how unfortunate!" she exclaimed with feigned sympathy.

Evangeline seized the opportunity, stepping forward with a wicked grin. Her hands grasped the delicate layers of silk and ripped them apart with alarming ease. Shards of fabric fell around me, pooling at my feet like the tattered remains of my hope.

"Stop it! Please!" I cried, my voice breaking.

Behind her, Aurelia froze, her face pale. Her hands trembled as they hovered over the beads at my neckline, her hesitation palpable. Her eyes flicked between me and our stepmother, torn between obedience and guilt. But when Stepmother's glare darkened, Aurelia's fingers tightened. With a swift tug, the necklace snapped, and the beads scattered across the floor like tiny, glittering tears.

I stumbled, my foot catching on the torn hem of the dress. As I fell, I was swallowed by the layers of shredded fabric that now bore no resemblance to the gown my mother had treasured. Laughter filled the air—cold, cruel, triumphant. I looked up through watery eyes to see Stepmother and Evangeline walking away, their skirts swishing with smug pride. Aurelia hesitated for a moment longer, her face crumpling with shame before she turned and followed them.

"You can't go to the festival looking like this," Stepmother called over her shoulder, her voice dripping with mockery. "It would be such an embarrassment to our family."

I was left alone in the silence. My hands shook as I tried to gather the ruined fabric, but the tears blurred my vision. I couldn't hold it together—not the dress, not my composure, not the fragile hope that had carried me this far.

I stumbled to the fireplace, staring into the flickering flames. The warm hues of orange and yellow should have been comforting, but they only mirrored the chaos inside me. My tears sizzled as they hit the glowing embers, and little sparks of despair snuffed out as quickly as they appeared. I couldn't breathe. The walls felt like they were closing in, suffocating me. I needed air.

Fleeing the house, I ran to the one place that had always brought me solace—the tree by the meadow. My legs burned with the effort, but I didn't stop until I collapsed against the familiar boulders. The earth beneath me soaked up my tears, grounding me in its quiet embrace. I had nothing left. My mother's dress was destroyed, her memory tarnished by people who took joy in my suffering. My strength, my resolve, my kindness—everything felt hollow. I was empty.

The fireflies appeared slowly at first, their tiny lights blinking against the darkness. Then, all at once, the branches surrounded me, their leafy forms swirling in a magical dance. My breath hitched as a human silhouette formed along the trunk, so luminous. Tree bark covered the lower part with exposed roots looking like a voluminous hem. Exposed bits of tree looked like skin with cracks that contoured curves of breasts.

"No more tears, my child," she said softly, her voice soothing as a lullaby with leaves growing from an etched face like short hair.

I rose to my feet, my knees trembling. "Mother?" I whispered, my voice barely audible.

The figure smiled gently, shaking her head. "No, my dear. I wish I were. But I'm here to help you all the same."

"Who are you?" I asked, my voice catching in my throat.

"You can call me a friend," she said, her eyes filled with warmth. "My name is Hazel. And tonight, I'm here to change everything."

The words hung in the air, strange and almost too fantastical to grasp. I blinked, unsure if I'd heard her correctly. A tree guardian? For me? Magic was nothing unusual in this land, but the idea of a guardian who dedicated her power to helping someone as insignificant as me seemed impossible. Where had she been when my parents died? When I endured years of torment and neglect? And why now, when everything felt so hopeless?

But still, a part of me—a small, trembling part—wanted to believe.

"What are you doing here?" I asked, the moonlight glowing on her body.

"I'm a fae of the woods," she said, her voice melodic, her gown billowing around her as though caught in an unseen breeze. "I've been watching you since you were young. Watching you care for your parents over the years has brought so much respect to the land. I appreciate what you've done for them and their legacy."

"Well, it's the least I can do," I said, my tears starting to creep back in once again.

"You've done so much and gotten so little. You deserve more."

"I feel like I do. I guess I'm not destined for it this time."

"Then when else?"

The words clung to me. When else would I get the opportunity to treat myself. All I asked for is one night. One night to dance the night away and feel the freedom from this place. I want to drop my identity and be like the nobles. I want to get a taste of what they have. I want to touch the finer things, see the noble people, I want to stand under a fancy roof.

"What if I told you that I could make that happen for you?" Hazel said, bits of bark showed from her mouth to form teeth.

"What do you mean?"

"What if I told you that I'm here to take you to the festival!"

My heart leapt at her words. "Really?" I stammered, my breath catching in my throat.

"Yes, really," she replied with a warm smile. "Are we ready to go?"

I looked down at myself, at the torn remnants of my mother's dress clinging to me like a second skin. My hands instinctively moved to cover the shredded fabric. "I can't go looking like this," I admitted, my voice shaking with a mix of embarrassment and defeat.

"Oh, right you are," she said, her tone bright and reassuring. "Let me fix that for you!"

Her enthusiasm was infectious, but my confusion lingered. "Fix it? How?"

"*With magic, of course!*" *she exclaimed, her eyes twinkling.* "*But before we begin, I must ask if you are ready to embrace this magic fully.*"

"*What do you mean?*"

"*You need to believe for it to work,*" *Hazel encouraged, her branch arm waved at me with a flourish.*

I didn't understand her question. What did she mean by embracing it? All I wanted was to look presentable—to feel human again. If that meant using magic, then so be it. "*Sure,*" *I said, shrugging off my doubts.* "*Whatever it takes.*"

"*Good,*" *she said, her expression softening.* "*Now, let the emotions inside you—the hope, the despair, the yearning—flow through your veins. Let them fuel you before letting go.*"

"*Um, okay,*" *I muttered, unsure of what I was supposed to feel or do. But I closed my eyes and tried. My breath slowed as I focused inward. At first, there was nothing but the echo of my own heartbeat. Then, faintly, something stirred. A pulse, strong and insistent, thrummed in my wrists and coursed through me like a melody waiting to be sung.*

"*Perfect,*" *she said, her voice a lilting hum. From her branches, leaves fluttered like excited fingers and a trail of glittering sparks fell from the tips, illuminating the grass at her base.* "*A flick of my leaves will do the trick!*"

She waved the leaves with a graceful flourish, and suddenly, the fireflies erupted into motion. They swirled around my feet, their tiny lights sparkling like jewels. I gasped as a shower of golden sparks cascaded over me, warming my skin and filling the air with an enchanting glow. The tatters of my dress shimmered, mending themselves stitch by stitch. Threads wove together as if guided by invisible hands, the fabric growing richer and more luxurious with every passing moment.

The pale blue of the gown deepened, transforming into a stunning shade of gold that shimmered like sunlight on water. The skirt billowed out, full and regal, and a sash of vibrant teal encircled my waist, the silky material flowing effortlessly as if it had always been there.

I turned in awe, watching as the dress came to life around me. My reflection shimmered in a small puddle nearby, and I barely recognized the woman staring back. My hair, tangled and lifeless, had been swept into a cascade of polished curls that framed my face. My skin glowed, the weariness of years erased in an instant. I couldn't help but twirl, the fabric of the gown rippling like a dream brought to life.

"This is incredible!" I exclaimed, the words bursting from me in a rush of gratitude and disbelief.

Hazel smiled at my joy. "We're not done yet."

Her branch dipped toward the ground, and I felt a strange, tingling sensation at my feet. When I glanced down, my breath caught in my throat. My worn, mud-streaked slippers had vanished, replaced by delicate heels of bronzed gold. Intricate vines, studded with tiny green stones, wove their way across the shimmering surface. They sparkled in the moonlight, perfect in every detail.

"You're too kind to do this for me," I said, my voice trembling with awe.

The wood guardian stepped back, her satisfaction growing. "Before you go," she began, her tone growing serious, "there is something you must know."

"Yes?" I asked, my heart pounding with anticipation.

"Like my leaves, the life of my magic only has a small life. This magic will only last until the stroke of midnight. When the clock strikes twelve, everything will return to how it was. You will be back here, as you were before."

The words hit me like a sudden gust of wind. Midnight. So little time. But it didn't matter. I nodded quickly. "That's more than enough," I said. "Thank you."

Her expression softened, and she placed a branch over her heart. "Some magic is fleeting," she said, "but the strength and purity of your heart—that will last forever."

I didn't know what to say, so I simply nodded. My heart felt full, brimming with an emotion I couldn't name. Gratitude? Hope? Perhaps a bit of both.

"Now, are you ready?" she said with a gentle smile.

"I've never been more ready," I replied.

She fluttered her leaves one last time, and with a flick and a swirl of glittering light, the world around me dissolved. A mist rose from the ground, curling around my feet and enveloping me in a cocoon of silvery fog. My breath caught as I felt the earth shift beneath me. For a moment, I was weightless, floating as though carried by an invisible current.

Then, as quickly as it had begun, the fog dissipated. My feet touched down on smooth stone, and I blinked in surprise. Lush hedges surrounded me, their neatly trimmed edges glowing faintly in the soft light of the moon. The sound of a fountain reached my ears, its gentle trickle calming my racing heart. Beyond the hedges, fireworks painted the sky in bursts of vibrant color, each explosion more dazzling than the last.

The path ahead was lit with lanterns, their golden glow leading to a grand staircase that stretched toward the palace. I could see figures moving gracefully up the steps, their gowns trailing behind them like cascading waterfalls of fine fabrics. The air was alive with music, laughter, and the soft rustle of fabric.

I was here. I had made it.

I'm actually at the festival!

Chapter 49

Sebastian slammed the door behind him, and the entire house shuddered. The vibrations rattled the fragile antiques on nearby shelves, their trembling glass and porcelain mirroring his barely contained frustration. Even the wiry silver whiskers on his chin bristled, standing on edge as though mimicking his mood.

Everything in the house seemed to shrink back from him, but he barely noticed.

From the corridor upstairs, a group of women emerged, their shoes clicking softly against the floorboards as they descended. These were the servants, though tonight they looked nothing like their usual selves. They had traded their simple work attire for elegant but modest dresses, their outfits designed to retain a quiet dignity without veering into ostentation. The fabric of their dresses, though not extravagant, carried an understated charm that softened Sebastian's heart, if only for a moment.

Agnes was in green, Giselle in blue. Both looked radiant, their gathered skirts poofing gently with each step, the cotton fabric swishing as they moved. The simplicity of their beauty reminded him of better days, of a time when laughter filled these halls and there was no weight of grief, no looming shadows of guilt or regret.

"You both look wonderful," he said, his voice tinged with quiet admiration.

The women beamed at the unexpected compliment, their smiles glowing with a genuine warmth that dulled the edges of his frustration.

"Thank you, Sebastian," Agnes said, dipping her head in gratitude.

"Ella made them for us a while back," Giselle added, her fingers brushing the fabric. "Aren't you coming?"

The question hit him like a spark to dry tinder, igniting the conflict within him. He rubbed the back of his neck, glancing down at the sweat-streaked shirt he still hadn't changed out of. "No, I don't think so," he replied gruffly.

"But you have to come!" Giselle said, her tone tinged with concern. "We've all been looking forward to this night for weeks."

"You've been looking forward to this for a year!" Agnes joked.

"I know," Sebastian muttered, his gaze fixed on the floor. "I just...I'm not feeling up to it."

"Sebastian," Agnes pleaded, her voice softening, "you deserve a break. Just one night. Let yourself enjoy it—for us, if not for yourself."

He hesitated, guilt and doubt warring within him. "I can't," he said, the words heavy with finality.

"This is supposed to be our night!" Giselle hissed, her face flushing pink. "Get your butt upstairs and change."

Sebastian's palms became sweaty. He could feel his heart beating through his chest. The sweat beading on his forehead grew the more he stared at the antagonizing smirk across Giselle's face.

"This isn't our night!" Sebastian said, teeth gritting.

"What about us?" she asked, appalled.

"You ended us years ago when you left me for Theo! I will always love you as family, but we're over."

"No!"

Slippers slapped along the marble floor, echoing along the empty space. Her scream made the curtains tremble at the top of the grand staircase. Sparrows resting outside the windows scurried away, the screech of her despair was too much for them to bear.

"Everything okay?" Agnes asked, ushering Giselle away from him.

"I'll be fine," he said with vacancy as Giselle went to take a seat in the den.

"I'm not convinced. What's going on?"

Sebastian hesitated to pour out his feelings. The idea of saying anything negative about Dominic to Agnes after all the times that he'd spent convincing the others that he meant well made his stomach lurch. He wasn't ready for Giselle to smile with satisfaction, knowing that she was right.

"I'm just struggling today, that's all," he answered somberly.

"Let me guess. The chosen one?" Giselle hollered, her voice echoed on the stone floor.

Sebastian's mouth tensed, knowing his thoughts about her reaction was correct. Agnes rubbed her hand across his shoulder, the warmth from her palm moving across his back.

"He's just not what I thought he was."

"How can you be so quick to think that? You were so certain of him," Agnes asked.

"I dunno. Maybe I'm just naïve."

"Or maybe you're not embracing every side of him."

"What do you mean?"

"Someone I've known ever since they were a little kid has shown me many sides of him. One thing he's taught me over the years, and especially recently, is to trust every part of them."

Sebastian shed a little smirk, his hand reaching for hers, "I think it's more complicated than that."

"Is it? Or are you the one that's making it complicated?"

The sound of hooves clattering on the cobblestones outside announced a carriage's arrival. The women exchanged glances, their excitement rekindled by the thought of the evening ahead.

"We should get going," said another servant who had joined them. "The festival has already started."

Sebastian nodded, managing a small, bittersweet smile. "Go on. Have the best night of your lives."

"Remember to trust yourself just as much as I am supposed to trust you," Agnes concluded, her hand grazing his cheek before shedding a wink.

Agnes and Giselle each gave him a small curtsey before stepping outside with the others, with Giselle's being weak and insincere. Their skirts rustled as they crammed into the tiny carriage, bits of fabric peeking out like tufts of stuffing from an over-packed suitcase. The wheels squeaked in protest as the horses pulled them away, their excited chatter fading into the distance.

And then, silence.

Sebastian stood alone in the foyer, the faint crackle of the fire in the hearth his only companion. He moved toward the flames, drawn to their warmth but finding no solace in their light. The orange and yellow tongues danced and twisted, their chaotic beauty a stark contrast to the stillness of the room.

As he stared into the fire, something caught his eye—a glint of light from a tiny hole at the base of the wall. Kneeling down, he peered into the opening, his fingers brushing against the rough wood. The hole was just big enough for a family of mice to call home, and judging by the faint scuffling noises, it seemed they had made themselves comfortable.

Reaching inside, he dislodged a series of small, round objects. One by one, they rolled onto the floor—blue beads, smooth and shining like tiny droplets of the sky. At first, there were only a few, but with each motion of his hand, more spilled out until he had nearly a dozen in front of him. He held one up to the light, turning it over between his fingers. It was simple, yet beautiful. The idea suddenly struck him: perhaps these beads could be made into a necklace for one of the women. It wouldn't undo his absence tonight, but it might be enough to show them he cared.

Pocketing the beads, he stood, the weight of them pulling at the waistband of his trousers. As he turned back toward the fire, another glimmer caught his attention—this time from within the flames themselves. Squinting against the heat, Sebastian saw five larger objects nestled among the ashes. They were too big to be beads, their surfaces uneven and glinting in the flickering light.

Curious, he reached into the hearth, wincing as the residual heat prickled his skin. The objects tumbled out, landing with soft thuds on the hearthstone. They were unlike anything he'd ever seen—translucent, grayish-white, and veined with delicate patterns that resembled cracked glass. Their shape was irregular, almost like teardrops, and the sharp edges pricked his fingers as he held them.

"What are these?" he murmured to himself, his voice barely audible over the crackling fire.

Light flickered from the glass, winking at him with life. The intricacy in the veins were filled with shades of red and orange. The longer he looked at them, the more comfort he felt as he cradled the warmth in his hands.

"Strange."

The oppressive heat felt suffocating, as though the room itself was shrinking. Smoke stung his eyes, blurring his vision and forcing him to cough. Gasping for breath, Sebastian stumbled to his feet and made his way outside. The cool night air hit him like a balm, soothing the tightness in his chest and the rawness in his throat.

He stood in the yard, his hands on his knees as he gulped in fresh air. The crickets sang their nightly tune, and the tall grass swayed gently in the breeze. Ahead of him, the old tree loomed in the moonlight, its branches stretching over the two tombstones nestled beneath it. Sebastian straightened, his eyes fixed on the spot where Ella's parents lay at rest. The quiet dignity of the land offered a reprieve from the storm raging within him. He exhaled slowly, his shoulders loosening as he made his way toward the tree. No, he wouldn't be at the festival tonight. Here, beneath the tree's vigilant branches, he could finally find the peace he longed for.

Chapter 50

Dominic

MY HANDS SHAKE.

I can't stop them, no matter how tightly I clench my fists. The beat of my heart pounds in my chest, heavy and uneven, like a drumline with no rhythm. I've felt nervous before—at block parties back home, or when I'm asked to speak in front of my classmates for a presentation—but this is different. This is bigger, deeper, a kind of anxiety that wraps around my chest and twists my stomach into impossible knots. It's not just butterflies; it's like my stomach and intestines have tangled themselves into a mess.

The grand doors creak open, pulling me out of my thoughts. A wave of music sweeps over me, soft and elegant, the sound of violins sliding their bows in perfect harmony. The space beyond, the same vast hall where I've been training just days ago, is unrecognizable. The emptiness has been transformed into a breathtakingly lavish space.

The light from crystal chandeliers pours over the room, catching on the vibrant silks and satins of the gowns swirling across the floor. Women glide past in dresses with skirts so puffy and wide they seem like floating circles, their hems brushing against the polished marble as their male partners guide them through the dance.

I freeze in the doorway, my breath catching in my throat.

This isn't just a party. It's something out of a dream. The delicate lace trims, the soft candlelight flickering in golden sconces, and the gentle hum of voices mingling with the music create a visual of such elegance that I can barely process it.

Beautiful. That's the only word that comes to mind.

I swallow hard, the lump in my throat refusing to budge. I want to move forward, to step inside and join this magical world, but my feet stay planted. My nerves do their best to convince me I don't belong here, that I'm out of my depth. My palms are slick with sweat as I wipe them against my trousers, trying to collect myself.

This isn't home.

It's not the gritty streets or parties I'm used to. This is a different league entirely. But something about it—about the shimmer of the chandeliers and the swell of the music—calls to me, urging me to take that first step inside.

Chapter 51

The chandeliers illuminated the ballroom, flames flickering like tiny dancers in perfect rhythm. Dominic's hands trembled as he stepped further into the space, his breath catching at the sight of the transformed hall. It wasn't the stark training ground he had grown to dread—it was alive now, vibrant and buzzing with laughter, music, and movement.

Across the room, Dominic caught sight of Giselle, giggling as she exchanged coy glances with one of the merchants. He couldn't help but smile. Even in a room as grand as this, the familiar faces helped ground him, reminding him he wasn't entirely out of place.

The queen stood at the center of a growing cluster of guests, her attention split between welcoming new arrivals and engaging in animated conversation with a well-dressed couple. Her gown shimmered as she curtsied, the soft layers deflating gracefully with every movement.

"Queen Ella!" Dominic called out, more to steady himself than anything else. He wasn't sure how long he could stand frozen by the sheer weight of the moment.

Gretel hovered beside him, just as uncertain as he felt, her posture stiff and her eyes darting around nervously. Dominic knew he had to take the lead towards the queen—for both their sakes. Calypso, on the other hand, had no such concerns. His tail disappeared into the crowd as he bounded off toward the decadent banquet table.

Dominic let out a small chuckle. "Of course. Food first. Food always."

"You've known me for years, Dom!" Calypso said, his voice fading amongst the chatter.

As they approached Ella, the scent of roasted meats and spiced pastries wafted through the air, mingling with the hum of conversation and the lilting notes of the orchestra.

Ella's eyes lit up when she saw them. "Oh, you both look so radiant!" she exclaimed warmly. "You really do clean up nicely."

"Thank you," Dominic and Gretel murmured in unison, their voices barely audible over the chatter of the room.

"Where's Sebastian?" Ella asked, her gaze flicking past them, scanning the room for the one face she had hoped to see.

Dominic's chest tightened. "H-he couldn't make it," he replied hesitantly, trying to keep his tone casual. He didn't want to drag Sebastian's frustrations into this night, nor worry the queen with the tension that had unfolded between them. She had enough to think about without their drama weighing her down.

"That's unfortunate," she said softly, a note of sadness in her voice.

"I'm sure if he wanted to be here, he would," the king added, resting a comforting hand on Ella's shoulder. His attempt at reassurance was genuine, but it did little to lift the awkward weight hanging in the air.

"So, this party is very nice," she said, her voice stiff but earnest as she cleared her throat, an obvious attempt to change the subject.

Ella's smile returned, brighter and more genuine this time. "Isn't it darling?" she said, gesturing to the room with pride. "I never imagined in my wildest dreams that I'd be hosting one of the biggest celebrations in the land."

Dominic couldn't help but smile. "I'm sure you didn't," he said, knowing all too well how far she had come to get here.

"After everything, I made it my mission to bring light to people's lives, even if only for one night," she continued. "Everyone deserves a moment to celebrate, to forget their troubles."

The king's arm slid around her waist, pulling her closer. "That's one of the many reasons I fell in love with her," he said, his eyes shining with admiration.

Dominic raised an eyebrow. "Because she's a party animal?" he teased, smirking.

Ella laughed lightly, and even Gretel cracked a small smile, though her laugh still had a nervous edge.

"Not quite," the king replied, his tone more serious. "Because of her strength—her ability to find light even in the darkest places. She inspires me every day."

Dominic's gaze shifted to Ella, who stood radiant and confident, embodying the resilience he spoke of. It was admirable, but it also struck a nerve. Dominic couldn't help but think about how often he struggled to find that same strength in himself.

Before he could dwell too long on his own insecurities, the music shifted. The orchestra softened, the violins leading a new melody as the crowd parted to clear the center of the floor. Ella and Sawyer stepped forward, drawing every eye in the room. Dominic watched as the king took Ella's hand, his other hand resting on her waist as they began a slow, graceful waltz. Her gown twirled around her like a shimmering cloud, catching the light of the chandeliers and casting sparkling reflections across the marble floor.

Other couples began joining them, moving in time to the music, leaving Dominic and Gretel standing frozen by the wall. The room felt smaller now, the thinning crowd exposing him in a way that made his nerves spike all over again.

"Do you think we should join them?" Gretel asked, her arms folded across her chest.

Dominic hesitated. He wasn't sure if he wanted to be part of this or if he could even muster the courage to try. Memories of middle school dances flashed through his mind—standing alone, unsure, watching others pair off while he lingered on the sidelines.

"I-I guess so," he said, his voice uncertain.

Gretel extended her hand, and Dominic took it reluctantly. They stayed close to the edge of the floor, avoiding the center where the most confident dancers swirled. He placed his hand lightly on her waist, his fingers brushing against the thick fabric of her skirt. His movements were clumsy at first, his feet bumping into hers as he struggled to find the rhythm.

"Relax," Gretel whispered gently, her voice softer than he was used to. "You're doing fine."

Dominic met her gaze, and for the first time, he saw something other than judgment or expectation in her eyes. There was kindness, understanding. It steadied him, and slowly, his movements became more fluid. The music carried them, and before long, they were moving with an ease that surprised them both.

The tension in his chest eased, and for the first time that night, Dominic allowed himself to enjoy the moment. His heart still ached for the absence of Sebastian, but for now, he let the music drown out the weight of everything else. Every star twinkled so bright like the flash of a camera. It was so beautiful, like it was coming straight from a romantic painting. One big circle of an untouched moon at its fullest, with stars that were scattered all around it, and bordered with purplish-red clouds that grew with each step.

Chapter 52

FROM THE PAGES OF THE STORYBOOK
Ella

THE PALACE WAS BREATHTAKING!

As I stepped inside, my eyes were drawn to the intricate carvings on the archways and the gold-framed paintings lining the walls. Every surface sparkled under the glow of enormous chandeliers, their light reflecting off polished marble floors and creating an air of opulence I had never imagined. It was overwhelming. I couldn't help but pause to take it all in, despite my best efforts to keep moving and not look out of place. This wasn't my world, and yet here I was, standing in the middle of it.

Eventually, I made it to the grand doors leading into the ballroom. My heart raced as I watched the guards open them with a flourish, their movements synchronized like a performance in itself. The moment the doors swung wide, everything changed. The music stopped mid-note, and the low hum of chatter ceased. Every head in the room turned in unison, and all eyes locked on me.

I froze.

The weight of their stares was suffocating, my stomach tightening into painful knots. For a moment, I wanted to turn and run back the way I came, but I couldn't. My feet were rooted to the spot, caught between terror and awe. Even the king, seated high in the balcony with a goblet in hand, had stopped mid-bite to look my way.

My first step forward felt impossibly heavy, my legs trembling beneath me. The stairs leading down to the ballroom seemed endless. I focused on placing one foot in front of the other, praying I wouldn't trip. The sound of my heels clicking against the marble echoed through the silent room, amplifying my anxiety. The chandeliers overhead cast a golden glow across the space, illuminating the rows of finely dressed nobles who continued to watch my every move.

And then I realized. They weren't judging me.

They were admiring me.

Their eyes were wide with something I couldn't quite place—wonder, maybe? Awe? My dress shimmered under the soft light, the rhinestones catching and scattering the beams like a kaleidoscope. I felt a flush of warmth spread across my cheeks, a mix of embarrassment and exhilaration.

Over by the platters was a familiar face, their face blended with the bushels. The vines surrounded an opening in the plants, creating a face that framed the smile that was so encouraging. I worried for a moment if anybody else could see Hazel standing within them, but they didn't. It was as though she blended in as she raised her goblet to toast to my arrival.

My stepsisters stood among the crowd, their faces frozen in shock. Mirelle's lips curled into a sneer, her delicate features twisted with jealousy but confused with a glare that couldn't tell it was me. Evangeline looked ready to combust, her powdered face turning blotchy and red. But it was Aurelia's expression that surprised me most. Her lips parted in a faint smile, and her spring green eyes glistened, as if she couldn't decide whether to cry or applaud.

The music resumed, the violins picking up where they had left off, their soft, lilting notes filling the air and easing some of the tension in my chest. Conversations gradually resumed, though quieter and more fragmented than before. Still, one gaze lingered on me, unwavering and intent.

The prince.

He stood near the center of the room, dressed in a royal blue suit with gold epaulets gleaming on his shoulders. His dark hair framed a sharp, handsome face, and his piercing amber eyes never left mine. My breath caught as he began to move, his steps measured and deliberate, closing the distance between us.

Before I could process his approach, a tantalizing aroma drifted into my senses. My stomach growled audibly, reminding me that I hadn't eaten all day. Between the morning chores, running errands, and preparing for tonight, there hadn't been a single moment to stop and eat whatever was left over. The smell of roasted meats and freshly baked pastries was irresistible. Without thinking, I veered toward the banquet table, unable to resist the feast that awaited me.

The spread was more extravagant than anything I had ever seen. Platters of delicacies stretched as far as the eye could see—roast lamb seasoned with herbs, flaky pies stuffed with fragrant fillings, and towers of pastries dusted with sugar. My mouth watered as I reached for the nearest dish, grabbing a morsel of something buttery and savory. I barely tasted it before reaching for another, and then another. Hunger overrode my manners, and I shoveled bite after bite into my mouth, savoring every flavor. The idea of pacing myself didn't even cross my mind.

"Excuse me," came a soft, polite voice.

I froze mid-chew, the pastry half still in my hand. Slowly, I turned toward the source of the voice, my heart sinking as I realized who it was.

The prince.

He stood mere feet away, watching me with an amused smile. His expression wasn't mocking, but it didn't make the situation any less mortifying. My cheeks burned as I realized how I must have looked—cheeks puffed with food, crumbs on my lips, and a smear of sauce dangerously close to the neckline of my dress.

He chuckled lightly, the sound warm and genuine. "The cooks will be delighted to know their work is appreciated," he said, his tone laced with humor.

"I-I'm so sorry," I stammered, hastily swallowing and wiping my mouth with the back of my hand. My face felt like it was on fire, but his kind demeanor eased my embarrassment just enough for me to manage a weak smile.

"No need to apologize," he said, his gaze steady and kind. "I haven't seen you around before. Are you new to the kingdom?"

"I don't get out much," I admitted, my voice barely above a whisper.

"That's a shame," he said, extending a hand. "Would you care to dance?"

For a moment, I couldn't speak. My heart raced, and a thousand thoughts tumbled through my mind. Was he serious? Me? Dance with the prince? I glanced nervously at the crowd. People were watching again, their gazes filled with curiosity and, in some cases, envy. My stepmother's glare was practically boring a hole into my back. Despite the fear curling in my chest, I knew I couldn't say no.

"Yes," I said softly, placing my hand in his. "I'd love to."

The crowd parted as he led me to the center of the ballroom. My pulse thundered in my ears as the orchestra began a new song, a waltz that was both elegant and intimidating. The prince placed one hand on my waist and held my hand with the other. I tried to follow his lead, but my nerves got the better of me. My feet stumbled, clumsily colliding with his, and I winced in embarrassment. All the nights of practice couldn't prepare me for the real thing. Even though my dreams made me feel like an expert, my dancing made me look like a beginner.

"Relax," he said gently, his voice low and soothing.

Somehow, those simple words worked. His calm presence steadied me, and I began to move with more confidence. The music seemed to flow through me, guiding my steps as we glided across the floor. The ruffles of my gown swirled around us like clouds, and for the first time in years, I felt weightless.

I forgot about my stepmother, my stepsisters, and the life of endless chores waiting for me back home. At that moment, there was only the music, the prince, and the joy of the dance. This was freedom. This was magic. This was the night I had always dreamed of.

Chapter 53

Dominic felt the warmth of the chandeliers as they cast a golden glow across the ballroom, their flickering flames reflected in the polished marble floors and the dazzling array of gowns and suits swirling in time to the music. He tried to focus on the rhythm, his nervous energy slowly giving way to something lighter as he danced with Gretel. Each spin, each step, helped ease his apprehension, and he noticed Gretel smiling more freely than he'd ever seen before.

The music shifted into a more vibrant tempo, and for the first time in years, Dominic allowed himself to relax. His anxieties regarding his difference amongst strangers vanished. It was an unfamiliar feeling, but one he found himself savoring. Gretel seemed just as unburdened, her movements light and graceful as they flowed together.

"Mind if I cut in?" a voice asked.

Dominic turned to the king, his amber eyes glinting under the soft light. A comforting warmth shone from the king's eyes and voice.

"Sure," Dominic replied, stepping back to let him take Gretel's hand.

But the king didn't move toward her. Instead, he extended his hand toward Dominic.

"No, I want to dance with you."

Dominic blinked, stunned. "Oh?"

It wasn't something he was used to. Back home, no one had ever approached him like this. And on the rare occasions when someone did, it was usually in dimly lit clubs, where alcohol clouded intentions. And when he was dating Marcus, neither one of them felt comfortable enough to dance together in a more intimate setting. Dancing, especially in public, had always felt fraught with risk and judgment. Yet here, in this grand ballroom filled with strangers, he was being asked by the king, of all people.

"Okay," he said, slowly taking the offered hand with trepidation.

As Dominic and the king moved together in rhythm with the music, Gretel stepped away, heading toward the refreshments table. She still had a spring in her step, carrying the joy of the moment with her. Dominic, meanwhile, struggled to focus. The king's movements were confident and practiced, and Dominic did his best to keep up from memory of watching *Dancing with the Stars* and practicing in his living room.

"I've been thinking about what you told me," Sawyer said.

"About that," Dominic quickly interjected, his footing stumbled. "I'm sorry."

"What are you sorry for? You gave me a lot to think about."

"But everybody has their own battles to fight. I didn't mean to create one for you with my own issues," Dominic said with guilt.

"I don't think that you did that!" he said with a chuckle. "I just wanted to say that your thoughts have given me some time to reflect."

"I hope it wasn't too much reflection."

Sawyer's teeth glimmered in the light when he smiled, "Just enough for me to try and learn more about myself."

"That's great. I hope you find what makes you happy."

"Thank you. I know I will once this festival ends."

Dominic found his gaze drifting over the crowd, scanning the faces for any sign of discomfort or judgment. The fear of standing out was hard to shake. Old memories tugged at him—moments of feeling like the odd one out, of whispers and stares in places that didn't quite feel safe. Even here, among a seemingly welcoming crowd, the habit lingered.

"What are you looking at?" Sawyer asked, his tone light but curious.

"Nothing," Dominic replied quickly.

"Doesn't seem like nothing," the king pressed, his steps never faltering.

Dominic hesitated, his words catching in his throat before he finally admitted, "It's just...I'm not used to this. Where I come from, people like me rarely get to dance with each other. Not without someone noticing or judging."

The king tilted his head slightly, his gaze sweeping the room as if searching for what Dominic was describing. Sawyer's expression softened when he looked back. "I see nothing different," he said simply.

Dominic blinked, startled by the response. Sawyer was right. Laughter, music, and movement filled the room. No one seemed to pay them any special attention. Couples danced freely, their joy undiminished by the dynamics of who they were with or how they moved. For the first time in a long while, Dominic felt his walls begin to lower.

"You're right," Dominic said quietly, a small smile creeping onto his face. "I don't either. And I guess if they did, you could punish them."

They shared a laugh, the kind that felt light and genuine. For a moment, Dominic let himself believe that this was a place where he could belong, where no one cared about labels or expectations. A place where he didn't have to spare people's feelings and not make someone uncomfortable at their sacrifice. A place where people compromise their true selves and happiness to avoid upsetting others.

As the music picked up, Dominic grew more comfortable, his movements becoming smoother, more confident. His hand lingered a moment too long on the king's shoulder, then crept lower. Sawyer immediately slowed their pace, his hand tightening on Dominic's arm.

"Hey," the king said evenly, "I'm married to Ella."

Dominic's face burned with embarrassment. "Oh, I'm sorry," he stammered, stepping back. "I guess I got carried away. I just...where I'm from, anyone who asks to dance usually means..." He trailed off, unsure how to finish.

The king's expression remained calm, his posture relaxed. "It's okay," he said, his voice steady. "I just noticed you didn't seem happy. I wanted to change that."

Dominic's shoulders eased at the king's words. He hadn't expected such understanding, and it left him feeling both chastened and grateful. "Thank you for that," he said softly.

A sudden hand interrupted their moment on Dominic's shoulder, the grip strong and unsteady. He turned to find Giselle, her cheeks flushed and her eyes unfocused.

"Hey, you!" she slurred, her grin lopsided.

"Hi, Giselle," Dominic said, steadying her as she swayed on her feet.

"I'll leave you to it," the king said, giving Dominic a nod before slipping into the crowd with the effortless grace of someone used to navigating chaotic spaces.

"Are you having a good time?" Dominic asked, his voice tinged with concern as he held onto Giselle's arm to keep her upright.

"Oh, the best time!" she exclaimed, her enthusiasm unfiltered by her obvious intoxication. "Thanks to you!"

"What's that supposed to mean?" Dominic asked with an uncomfortable chuckle, gently guiding her away from the center of the room.

Giselle leaned in, her face full of intrigue. "Sebastian doesn't love me anymore."

Dominic rolled his eyes, looking at Gretel who hid behind her hand with laughter as she observed her unsteady stance.

"Because of me?"

"Yes," she slurred. "Before you came along, he wanted a family. He only cared about me and the horses."

"You clearly don't know him as much as you think you do," Dominic said, composed. "He's not someone you toss to the side and only care about when it's convenient to you."

"Hogwash!"

"If you took a moment to realize how much of a great person he is and attentive he can be to those he cares about, then you would actually appreciate him instead of having him as your fallback!"

The music stopped and the dancers bowed and curtseyed. Chatter roared through the silence with Giselle's face flushing with anger. Her slipper tapping echoed in the space before being interrupted by the violins starting the next song. One man walked by, his shoulder an inch from touching Dominic's, caught his attention. His attire was not one of a noble, but one similar to the workers. The polish in his black, pulled-back hair showed cleanliness, preparation for a night away from labor.

"Excuse me, sir," Dominic said, his smile tight. "Have you come with anybody?"

"Why, no, sir," he responded nervously. "I haven't."

"Wonderful!" Dominic said with fake enthusiasm. "I would like to introduce you to my friend, Giselle. Giselle here is so kind and loves to have fun and get to know people."

Giselle's stance teetered once again, the anger boiling inside caused her to lose focus with Dominic. She couldn't think of the right words to say, trying to let the gentleman down so she could finish her argument.

"Well, that's wonderful," the gentleman said. "My name is Olio. And I must say that you are quite beautiful, Giselle."

Giselle's frantic huffing slowed down, taken back by the compliment, "Really? You think so?"

"Absolutely! Your face has the delicate beauty of a porcelain doll."

Giselle bit her lip, leaning upon Dominic for a moment to take it in. Dominic ushered her toward Olio, her resistance was nonexistent as she embraced his arm with ease.

"I was just about to explore the castle. Would you like to come?" Olio asked.

"Some fresh air would do some good for you," Dominic said, sending a wink of encouragement.

"I guess you're right," she replied, waving a hand with a little flourish, forgetting everything she said moments ago. "This palace is full of secrets, and it's guarded by the best soldiers. What could go wrong? Would you like to join us?"

"I think I'll stay here, thanks," Dominic replied with a polite smile. "Besides, I'm starting to get hungry."

"Suit yourself, party pooper," she said, stumbling away toward the far end of the ballroom. Her movements were clumsy, and she bumped into nearly everyone in her path, drawing amused or irritated looks from the crowd. Agnes looked at her from the other end, her head shaking before resuming conversation with her group.

Dominic sighed as he watched her go, then turned back to the room. The king slipped into the crush of swirling dancers, the sparkles of adornments flashing before vanishing in a tangle of silk and music. Gretel leaned toward a cluster of guests by the appetizer table, her hands sketching lively shapes in the air as laughter spilled from her lips. For the first time that night, Dominic felt a moment of stillness, a chance to reflect. He wasn't sure what the rest of the evening would hold, but for now, he let himself enjoy the rare feeling of being part of something bigger—a celebration where he truly belonged.

GISELLE AND OLIO DESCENDED the spiraling staircase, each step carrying them further into the castle's unseen depths. The air grew colder as they went, the faint light of the flickering torches above giving way to dim, sporadic glows from sconces affixed to the walls. The flames barely pierced the darkness, casting long, erratic shadows that danced on the crumbling stone. Curiosity urged her on, yet Giselle moved with uncertainty, her steps faltering as the passage grew narrower.

"It's so different down here," Giselle murmured, her voice softer than usual. It was almost as though she feared the walls themselves might listen.

Olio nodded as he walked beside her, though his features were hard to discern in the gloom. "I haven't seen this part of the castle either. It's not a place many would go."

Despite his words, his pace never faltered. He moved with an unsettling certainty, his steps measured and deliberate as if he already knew where they were going. Giselle drew closer to him, her hand brushing against his. Her fingers grazed his thigh in an unconscious bid for comfort, though she hesitated to outright cling to him.

"You think this leads to the dungeons?" she asked, a slight tremor in her voice betraying her attempt at nonchalance.

"It's possible," Olio replied, his tone even. He reached for a torch along the wall and handed it off to Giselle, but it barely offered enough light to make out anything more than the immediate stones ahead of them.

Cobwebs clung to Giselle's face, sticking to her eyelashes and brushing her nose. She wrinkled it in disgust, swiping her hand through the air to clear them away. Each step forward brought more of the spider-silk curtains, their sticky threads seeming to multiply with every movement. Her chest tightened with each passing moment, her unease growing stronger.

The once-smooth walls of the staircase gave way to rough, uneven stone. The finely crafted masonry transitioned into a decrepit tunnel, the blocks cracked and eroded by centuries of neglect. Drips of water echoed in the distance, each droplet magnified in the eerie quiet, creating the sensation of something far larger lurking just out of sight.

The corridor tightened further, the walls nearly brushing their shoulders. A damp, earthy smell filled the air, tinged with mildew and decay. The faint flame of the torch highlighted ancient tapestries hanging in tatters, their gothic images almost unrecognizable. Figures loomed in the designs—gaunt, skeletal creatures with hollow eyes, their twisted forms seeming to writhe and shift in the torchlight.

"What was that?" Giselle whispered, freezing in place. Her voice cracked as she peered into the shadows ahead. The faint sound of footsteps echoed in the distance—heavy and deliberate, yet too far to pinpoint their source.

Olio didn't answer. She turned her head toward him, expecting reassurance, but his figure had become little more than a silhouette in the weak torchlight.

"Did you hear that?" she asked again, louder this time. Her heart began to race.

Still, the man said nothing.

Giselle's hand tightened on his arm, but it slid down to grasp only air. The realization hit her like a slap—she was alone. He was gone. Her breath caught in her throat as her pulse thundered in her ears. The darkness around her seemed to press in, suffocating and disorienting.

"Where did you go?" she called, her voice trembling. Her words echoed back at her, mocked by the emptiness of the corridor. She spun around, searching for him, but the torchlight seemed to dim with each passing second. Her steps faltered as she tried to retrace her path. The shadows danced mockingly, offering no clear direction.

"Looking for me?" Olio whispered, close enough to brush her ear. Giselle flinched, her heart hammering against her ribs.

"Y-yes," she stammered, her body stiff with fear. "I can't see you."

"Let me help you see the way," Olio said again, now softer, almost coaxing.

Relief washed over her momentarily. "Yes, please."

Then came the pain.

A sharp, searing pressure burst against the back of her head, just above the nape of her neck. Claws dug deep into her scalp, their razor-sharp tips piercing her skin with precision. Giselle's scream filled the corridor, but her breath hitched in her throat, stopping it abruptly. Blood trickled in warm streams down her neck, pooling at her collarbone and soaking into her dress.

Her eyes widened in horror as the talons thrust forward. A sickening squelch accompanied the talons as they tore her eyeballs from their sockets, erupting in unbearable agony. Dark, blurry shapes filled her vision before all went black. Blood poured from her empty sockets, her body trembling violently as a metallic taste filled her mouth. She collapsed to the ground; her legs had buckled. Crimson stains marred her once-pristine dress, its ruffled petticoat clinging to her trembling form like a shroud.

Olio's presence loomed over her. She could feel its breath, hot and putrid against her face. It whispered something incomprehensible, the words curling around her ears like a vile incantation. Her mind barely registered the sound as her consciousness slipped away.

The cold stone floor pressed against her cheek as her body fell limp. Her final thoughts were fragmented—fear, confusion, and regret mingling in a haze of pain. She barely felt the talons release her; her form discarded like a broken doll.

The corridor returned to silence. The faint drip of water echoed once more, accompanied now by the soft scraping sound of something heavy being dragged into the shadows, with only orange eyes glowing in the darkness.

Chapter 54

Sebastian sat beneath the oak tree atop the hill, the trunk's rough bark pressing into his back like an anchor grounding him to the earth. He sat with his legs drawn up, his elbows braced against his knees, and his chin resting in the palms of his hands. A hollow weight settled in his chest, heavier than anything he'd felt in years. The wind whispered through the tall grass, carrying with it the faint sound of music from the palace far away—soft, distant, and mocking. Ella's mother's gravestone stared at him, antagonizing him for absence.

He could see the glow of the festival from where he sat, its golden light spilling through the palace windows like a beacon. Inside, people were dancing, laughing, living a life of freedom and joy that seemed worlds apart from his own. That should have been him here tonight. He should have been beside Dominic and Gretel, celebrating this brief reprieve from the darkness. But instead, he was here, alone, spiraling further into the mess of his own mind. His fists clenched against his knees, his knuckles pale as he stared at the distant lights.

"Idiot," he muttered to himself, his voice low and hoarse. The sound of his own voice startled him—it sounded like someone he didn't recognize. Someone angry, bitter, and utterly lost.

Sebastian was adept at suppressing his feelings. He'd spent years wandering through life with a void in his chest, pretending he didn't need anyone or anything to hold on to. He told himself he was strong for it, for keeping people at arm's length. It had become second nature. And then Dominic had shown up—confused, broken, desperate—and for the first time in years, Sebastian had truly felt needed.

But now everything felt like it was slipping through his fingers. Dominic wasn't the same person he had met. He was reckless now, impulsive, like he'd already given up on himself. And Sebastian hated it. Hated the way Dominic's change made him feel helpless, as though he was watching someone drown just beyond his reach.

"What am I even doing here?" he whispered, his voice nearly drowned out by the rustle of the wind through the leaves. The words were bitter on his tongue. "I'm no hero. I'm nothing."

His head dropped forward, his forehead pressing into his hands. Memories came flooding back, uninvited and relentless. He remembered what it was like to wander, utterly alone. He felt aimlessness, despair, and a gnawing feeling in his gut that something greater than himself had abandoned him. How many years had he spent drifting from place to place, afraid to stop for fear of confronting the truth of his emptiness? How many nights had he sat beneath a sky just like this one, cursing the stars for shining when everything inside him felt so dark?

"Hard night?"

The voice came so softly, so unexpectedly, that Sebastian's head snapped up in alarm. His shoulders tensed as his eyes darted to the source of the sound. Standing a short distance away was a woman—her silhouette carved against the moonlit sky. She wasn't old, but there was a weariness in the way she carried herself, as though time had worn her down more than it should have. Her cloak fluttered in the breeze, the edges lifting like black wings.

Sebastian's eyes narrowed. "Who are you?" he demanded, his voice low and wary.

The woman stepped closer, the moonlight spilling across her face, illuminating the gray streaks in her oily red hair. Her features were delicate with eyes that were covered in dark circles, looking older than she appeared and lips pressed into a gentle, sad smile.

Sebastian frowned, the name sparking recognition. "Aurelia?" He paused, realization dawning.

She nodded, her gaze drifting toward the palace beyond as she held the tattered and filthy hem bottom of her olive-green dress. "That's me."

Sebastian looked her over, confusion knitting his brow. "But you're...you're not blind," he said bluntly. The words tumbled out of his mouth before he could stop them. "You look just fine. I was told that all three of you were attacked by the birds."

Aurelia gave him a humorless smile, folding her arms around herself as though warding off the cold. "No, I'm not."

"Why?" he asked, his voice sharp with disbelief. "Your mother and your sister, they're—"

"Blinded," she finished for him. Her voice was calm, but her expression twisted with guilt. "That was their punishment. Not mine."

Sebastian stared at her, waiting for an explanation. When none came, he pressed further. "Then what happened to you? Why aren't you—"

"I was cast out," Aurelia said softly, her eyes fixed on the distant palace lights. "While my mother and Evangeline were left to live with their blindness, I was sent away. Exiled to the woods to live out the rest of my days alone."

Sebastian blinked. "Alone?"

She nodded. "Isolation was my punishment. A life with no companionship, no home—only the sound of my own thoughts. My mother believed it to be fitting for Ella when she wanted to kick her out." Her lips trembled as she spoke, but she quickly masked it with a breath. "I suppose she was right."

Sebastian's jaw tightened as he processed her words. "So, you were punished for what *they* did?"

Aurelia let out a bitter laugh, though there was no joy in it. "Not for what they did. For what I didn't do. I stood by and let it happen. I watched as they tore Ella down, as they made her life unbearable. And I said nothing. I did nothing. I only added to her misery."

Sebastian was silent, staring at her as though seeing her for the first time. There was something haunting in her voice—a depth of regret that echoed inside him like a hollow note.

"I thought it would be easier," Aurelia continued, her voice trembling. "To stay quiet. To avoid their wrath. But silence is its own kind of crime, isn't it?" Her gaze turned back to him. "You would know."

Sebastian flinched, her words hitting closer to home than he cared to admit. "What's that supposed to mean?" he muttered defensively.

Aurelia tilted her head, studying him. "You're angry, Sebastian. I can see it. You're angry with the boy I saw you with in the forest, aren't you?"

Sebastian's jaw clenched, his hands tightening into fists at his sides. "This isn't about him."

"Isn't it?" Aurelia pressed gently. "He's not who you thought he was, and it bothers you."

Sebastian didn't answer. He turned his gaze away, staring out into the night. "He's different," he said finally, his voice rough. "Reckless. Distracted. He's not the same person I—" He stopped himself, his throat tightening. "He's not the same."

Aurelia nodded, as though she understood. "Maybe that's because he's still lost, just in a different way."

Sebastian turned to her sharply, her words cutting through him like a knife. "And what's that supposed to mean?"

"It means people change, Sebastian. And sometimes they need the space to figure out who they really are." She paused, her gaze unwavering. "You should know that better than anyone."

Sebastian swallowed, his heart pounding in his chest. "You don't know me."

Aurelia hesitated, her arms tightening around herself. Her voice dropped to a whisper. "I know more than you think."

Sebastian turned to her, confusion knitting his brow. "What do you mean?"

She looked at him for a long moment, her face pale in the moonlight. Finally, she spoke, her voice trembling. "Don't you ever wonder where you came from?"

"Yes, but I've given up a long time ago."

"All those years of guessing why you were left at that tree. Not a single idea on who would do such a thing, or why?"

The words hit him like a physical blow, knocking the breath from his lungs. He froze, staring at her, his mind refusing to process what he'd just heard. "What are you trying to say?" he whispered.

"When I saw you for the first time, your eyes twinkled like the day she left you," Aurelia said, her eyes welling with tears. "I hated her for it. I couldn't believe she would do such a thing."

"What?" Sebastian said, his heart racing horribly with growing anxiety.

Aurelia took a moment to compose herself. Her chin quivered with fear as the breath of the wind sent a chill down the nape of her neck. The tree branches rattled, reaching closer to Sebastian for comfort as he realizes his new identity.

"Ella, she had more than two stepsisters. She had a stepbrother, too."

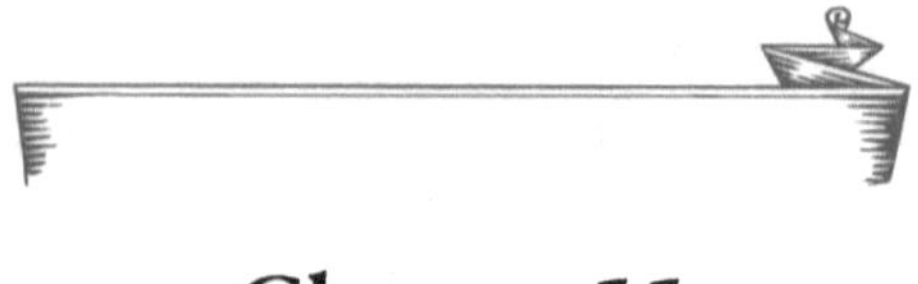

Chapter 55

WHAT THE STORYBOOK MISSED...
Mirelle

I USED TO DREAM OF more. A better house, a better life, a better version of myself that didn't ache with exhaustion at the end of every day. I'd sit in the quiet, staring at the cracked edges of our ceiling, the peeling wallpaper curling like taunting little whispers. All I could think of is if this was all. Is this what I've worked so hard for?

The truth is, I was never meant for this life of drudgery. I knew it the day I married my first husband. His promises had been sweet back then—honeyed words of a man who thought he could do better but never did. He tried, I'll give him that. But trying isn't enough when the house is falling apart around you and the debts pile higher than the chimney. Now I carried the weight of it all. I was the glue, the sweat, the fuel that kept this family together. And it was killing me.

"Momma?" Aurelia's small voice broke my thoughts.

I looked down at her, her bright, curious eyes reflecting nothing but innocence. She was always watching, always trailing after me like a shadow with that hopeful smile. She thought I was perfect, even in my apron that never stayed clean and hands worn raw from scrubbing the floors. Perfect.

How little she knew.

"Yes, dear?" I said, softening my voice for her.

She grinned up at me, missing a tooth already at the age of four. "Can I help you today? I want to help."

I pressed a hand to her cheek, ignoring the pang of guilt that hit me. She didn't deserve this life. None of us did.

"Not today, love. You and Evangeline go play. Stay close to the house."

Her little face lit up as if I'd handed her the moon. She turned to run off, her laughter like bells in the dead silence of the house. Evangeline appeared a moment later, a smaller version of Aurelia with her knotted blonde hair and scuffed shoes. She said nothing, only gave me a look that said she'd follow her.

"Go on, then," I murmured, waving them off.

I waited until the door shut behind them and let the air leave my lungs in one long, slow breath. The girls were the only source of joy in this miserable place. They were all I had—two bright lights in the dim reality of my existence. I loved them more than anything. And I wanted them to have more.

"More," I whispered to the pile of dishes in my empty kitchen.

That word had consumed me for months now, lingering at the back of my mind like a ghost. It haunted me in every room—reminded me that this life of scraping by, of working myself to the bone just to keep us afloat, was not enough.

My husband didn't understand that. He didn't understand the hunger I had for something grander. He thought love and loyalty were enough, as if they could put food on the table or sew the holes in my girls' clothes. But I knew better. I had seen it with my own eyes—the other families in the village, the ones with their grand houses, proper servants, and pretty daughters who were whisked away into wealthy marriages like a dream.

That was supposed to be my life. That was supposed to be my daughters' lives.

I wanted Aurelia and Evangeline to rise above this squalor, to have lives where their hands stayed soft and clean, where the only effort they would have to make was choosing which gown to wear to the next festival. That's what mothers do—they give their children the future they couldn't have themselves.

I thought of that constantly. I could see it so clearly it ached: Evangeline in a silk gown, her face painted with rouge, admired by noblemen with their golden rings and purses full of coin. Aurelia, with her charm and sweetness, the apple of someone's eye. Yes, I wanted it for them, but it wasn't enough. I wanted it for myself.

I slammed a pot onto the stove, the clang echoing through the room. My hands trembled as I gripped the handle, staring at the rusted bottom. The silence of the house filled my ears again. The emptiness swallowed me whole. No, I couldn't let this be my legacy. A life spent scrubbing floors, dragging buckets of water from the well, only to have nothing to show for it but calluses.

"Mirelle," my husband called from the parlor, his voice muffled.

I stiffened, gripping the pot tighter. He had a way of interrupting my thoughts right when I needed them most. For all his kindness, for all his sweet words, I couldn't help but resent him. Resent him for being satisfied. For dragging me into this life where we were stuck.

I stepped into the parlor to find him sitting on the threadbare chair, the journal opened neatly in his lap. He looked up at me, his eyes warm but tired. They were always tired these days.

"Come sit, Mirelle. You've been working all morning."

I bit back the retort that sat on my tongue. I didn't need his pity. "There's too much to be done," I said instead, my voice clipped.

He let out a sigh. "Sit for a moment. Please."

I hesitated, the ache in my feet winning over my stubbornness. I perched on the edge of the chair opposite him, folding my hands in my lap as he watched me. He was silent for a long time, and it made me nervous. When he finally spoke, his words hung heavy in the air.

"I've been thinking, Mirelle." He paused, searching my face. "Perhaps we should try for another child."

My breath caught. My hands froze. "Another child?"

"Yes," he said softly. "A son, maybe. Someone who can help me when he's older. Or another daughter...a sister for the girls."

The words settled like stones in my chest, the weight of them both thrilling and suffocating. I had always wanted another child; another daughter if I could help it. A third girl to complete the set, one more chance to raise a girl who could marry well, who could bring us the fortune we so desperately needed. My husband thought of children as a blessing—as simple extensions of love. But to me, a child was an opportunity. A chance. A future.

"Yes," I said finally, my voice barely above a whisper. I looked at him with carefully crafted softness. "Yes, I think...I think that would be lovely."

He smiled at me then, the kind of smile that reminded me why I had loved him once, a lifetime ago. A time where love was pure and before the cracks began to show. Before I started to resent him for his small dreams that weren't practical in this life or the next.

He reached for my hand, his fingers warm against mine. "We'll be all right, Mirelle. I promise. Things will get better."

I nodded, forcing a smile. But as he sat there, his hope filling the room, I felt nothing but a slow, gnawing bitterness. Things wouldn't get better on their own. They would only get better if I made them better.

I looked out the parlor window where Aurelia and Evangeline played in the yard, their laughter carried on the wind. For now, they were innocent. Unburdened. But one day, they would know the truth. They would understand what it cost to survive in this world. And they would thank me for it.

One more daughter. One more chance.

I would not let them suffer the same fate as me. I would make sure of it.

NINE MONTHS.

Nine months of carrying the weight of both my body and my husband's hopes. The strain had been unbearable, a constant pressure lodged in the pit of my chest. He'd been insufferable with his eagerness, hovering over me every moment, as if his prayers for a son might take physical form and usher themselves into my womb.

"A son will help us," he said, again and again, like a mantra he believed will shape the future. "A son will carry on my name. A son will give us strength."

Strength.

The word made me bite my tongue nearly to blood every time I heard it. As if the strength of a daughter was worth less than a son's, as if daughters had not already been the only light in this miserable life we live. Aurelia and Evangeline were bright, beautiful girls. Daughters could change the fate of a family just as much as any son. They could rise. They could marry into wealth. They could bring me the life I deserved.

But my husband refused to see it.

"Let's just hope," he murmured at night, pressing his hand to my swollen belly. He said it so often, I thought he was trying to convince himself, or perhaps me.

"Mama?" Aurelia asked one morning, her voice small and sweet. "When are we going to meet the baby?"

Her question tugged at me in ways I couldn't explain. Both girls had been giddy for weeks, delighted at the idea of another sibling. I envied their innocence. They didn't know what it meant to hope and be disappointed. To fight against the gnawing reality of this world.

"Soon, love," I replied softly, brushing back the loose strands of her hair. "Very soon."

Evangeline clapped her hands together, her grey eyes wide. "I hope it's a sister! I'll let her play with my doll."

I smiled, a tight curve of my lips. "Me too. We'll see, Evangeline."

THAT MORNING, I DECIDED to take Aurelia to the market while my husband watched Evangeline; one child to take to the village was more than enough. The house had been suffocating, the walls closing in on me as if they knew the baby was coming soon. The air outside was heavy with the scent of fresh rain, but at least it was cool, a reprieve from the sweltering heat that had made my pregnancy feel unbearable those past weeks. The walk to the market was slow. My belly was like a boulder strapped to my body, every step forcing me to carry its weight forward. Aurelia skipped ahead of me, her laughter light and free. I couldn't help but think how lovely she looked—how both of my girls were so perfect.

The market was bustling when we arrived. As always, the townspeople bustled about with their fine linens and heavy baggage, their noses turned up as if the air was only clean for the privileged. My presence here, swollen and tired, drew glances I'd grown used to over the years—disdainful sneers, pitiful nods, the whispers behind gloved hands.

"Poor woman," someone muttered just loud enough for me to hear.

"How does she even manage?" another voice cut in.

I gritted my teeth. I didn't have time for their judgment. They didn't know what it took to survive in this life. They didn't know how hard I'd worked to keep my family together.

"Stay close," I told my girl as I made my way to the produce stall. The merchant didn't even look at me as he counted his coins and bagged a turnip for someone else, someone more important. I took an apple into my hand and hold it up, waiting.

"Two bronze bits," the merchant said curtly.

"Two? Last week it was one."

"Prices change."

I wanted to argue, to claw into his smug face with all the frustration I'd been holding inside, but before I could open my mouth—

A sharp, searing pain shot through my belly.

I froze. The apple rolled from my hand, clattering onto the cart. My breath stuttered. Another pain gripped me like a fist, tight and unrelenting, spreading from my abdomen to my back.

"Mama?" Aurelia's voice was suddenly near me, soft with worry.

I didn't have time to respond. I took one unsteady step back, and then I felt it—hot liquid running down my legs, soaking the hem of my dress.

My water had broken.

"Sweetie, come here," I said quickly, trying to keep the fear out of my voice. My hands were shaking as I grabbed her wrist, guiding them away from the crowd. Eyes were on me again—more whispers, more judgment, but I didn't care. My body was on fire, and the pressure building inside me was unbearable.

"We're going to the alley," I said. My voice sounded distant even to myself, as though I'd detached from the reality of it all. "Hurry."

I didn't know how I made it to the alley, only that I did. My back pressed against the cold stone of the wall as I lowered myself to the ground, wincing through another wave of pain. Aurelia froze nearby, her eyes wide as she witnessed my anguish. The horror I saw in my child's face was one that motivated me to remain strong and calm, but it was difficult.

"Mama? Are you okay?" Aurelia whispered, her voice trembling.

"Stay there," I said, my teeth gritted. "Just stay there."

The pains came faster, each one ripping through me like a lightning strike. My breath was ragged, sweat pooling at the base of my neck and dripping into my eyes. I'd done this before, twice, but nothing prepared you for the raw violence of childbirth. I pushed, and I screamed through clenched teeth, trying not to frighten my girl, though I knew she was already terrified. My dress was soaked, stained dark with sweat and blood. My body felt like it might tear apart at the seams.

Finally—finally—there was a sharp release, a cry cutting through the air like a blade.

The baby was here.

I slumped back against the wall, trembling with exhaustion as I gathered the child into my arms. I couldn't see it clearly in the shadows, but I felt its warmth against my chest, heard its tiny cries. Aurelia moved closer, peeking nervously from a distance.

"What is it, Mama?" Aurelia asked softly. "A sister?"

I looked down at the baby, cradling it carefully as I shifted to see its face. The sunlight caught on its tiny, scrunched features, its delicate hands curled against its chest with a mark so unique on their knee. I blinked once, twice, trying to process what I was seeing.

It's a boy.

The disappointment hit me like a punch to the gut. My chest sank, the flicker of hope I carried for nine long months snuffed out in an instant.

A boy.

I stared down at him, my arms stiff. He wailed in protest, so small, so fragile, and yet I felt as if I'd been handed a weight I can't bear.

"What is it, Mama?" Aurelia asked again, her voice tinged with hope.

I swallowed hard, forcing myself to find words. "It's...it's a boy."

Aurelia's face fell, folding her arms across her chest, pouting. "I wanted a sister."

I said nothing. I didn't trust myself to speak. I wanted a sister too—a daughter. Another chance. Another opportunity. A son wouldn't change our fate. A son wouldn't lift us out of this life.

The baby stirred in my arms, his cries quieting into small hiccups. I looked down at him again, my heart twisting. He was innocent. He didn't ask to be born into this world. And yet, I couldn't stop the bitter taste from creeping up my throat.

I closed my eyes, my body shaking as I clutched him tighter.

"Come on," I whispered finally. "We need to go."

THE BABY WOULDN'T STOP *crying.*

His wails echoed through the narrow alley, bouncing off the cracked stone walls and straight into my skull. I cradled him in my arms, holding him tighter as though it might calm him, but his cries only grew louder, more desperate. My dress was soaked through, heavy with fluids, and my legs ached with exhaustion. I had no time to linger here.

The evening was creeping upon us, the sky turning to a bruised shade of purple, and I knew we had to leave before someone found us. This wasn't how I imagined this day, and yet here I was—sitting on the filthy ground with my third child, a boy who felt like the unraveling of my entire plan.

I scanned the alleyway for anything—anything to wrap him in. A small pile of discarded fabric lay near an old crate, its edges dirty and frayed, but it would do. I set the baby down for a brief moment, ignoring his cries, and snatched the cloth. When I wrapped him up, the fabric looked more like a shroud than a swaddle, but I had no choice. His limbs calmed down with the fabric covering him, and I noticed the crescent moon on his left knee. It took everything in me to ignore the unique beauty.

"Come, Aurelia," I said flatly, hoisting the baby into one arm while grabbing my eldest daughter's hand with the other.

Aurelia stared up at me, her face pale and streaked with dirt. She clutched her little hands to her chest, still trembling from what she had witnessed. "Mama...he's so small."

I didn't answer. My voice was caught somewhere in the pit of my stomach, buried under a tangled mess of shame and fury.

The market was far behind us now, the cobbled streets turning into uneven patches of grass and dirt as we trudged toward the fields. I had no destination in mind—only away. My shoes sank into the soft earth with every step, my skirts dragging like dead weight. The baby had stopped crying for a moment, lulled by the rhythm of my walking, but Aurelia wasn't so quiet.

"Mama, I'm tired," she whined, tugging at my arm. "My feet hurt."

"You can rest when we're done," I snapped.

"But I'm hungry," she continued, her voice breaking into sobs. "Please, Mama..."

I paused, my shoulders tense. The sun was dipping lower, painting the field in deep hues of amber and gold. I glanced down at Aurelia, her little face red and streaked with tears, her legs wobbling under the strain of our walk. Her exhaustion clawed at my nerves, but when I looked at her—truly looked at her—my heart softened, if only for a moment.

She's just a child, I reminded myself.

I looked at the bundle in my arms, at the face of my son—small, innocent, untainted by the world that awaited him. He was asleep now after a bit of feeding, his tiny mouth slack, his fists curled tightly against his chest. For the first time since he was born, I allowed myself to look at him, really see him. And in that moment, I felt something twist inside me.

This boy—this child—wasn't to blame for the life I'd been forced to live. He's blameless, pure in his ignorance. But that didn't matter. His innocence wouldn't feed us. It wouldn't change the fate of our family. It wouldn't get me out of this wretched, suffocating life. I took a deep breath, steadying myself as I tightened my grip on him.

"Mama, where are we going?" Aurelia asked, her voice trembling with uncertainty.

"We're almost there," I muttered.

The tree stood ahead, its branches wide and twisted, casting shadows that stretched across the ground like long, grasping fingers. A farmhouse was just beyond the rise of the hill, a small silhouette against the dying light. This would be it. The place where my burden would end.

I knelt at the base of the tree, setting the baby down carefully upon the grass. The earth here was soft, the air thick with the smell of hay and distant cattle. My fingers lingered on his swaddled body for a second too long and I felt my throat tighten.

"Don't do this," a voice inside me whispered. "Take him back. He's yours."

But I knew I couldn't.

Aurelia stood close to me, watching with wide, fearful eyes. "Mama?" she said softly. "Why are you leaving him here?"

I didn't answer her. I couldn't. Instead, I stood up, brushing my hands against my skirts, and turned my back to the tree.

"Mama!" Aurelia cried, louder this time. "We can't leave him! He's my brother! He needs us!"

Her words stung, sharper than I was ready for. "He doesn't need us, Aurelia," I said, my voice cold. I could feel the detachment in every syllable, as though I were speaking through someone else. "This is for the best."

"No, it's not!" she wailed, her face crumpling into tears. "I don't want to leave him. He's our family! I—I'm fine with having a brother. I was going to show him how to play, and—"

"Enough!" I snapped, spinning around to face her. The fierceness of my voice stopped her in her tracks. She blinked up at me, trembling, her sobs caught in her throat.

"Listen to me," I said, my tone sharp as a blade. "You will not speak of this to anyone. Do you understand me?"

Aurelia's lips quivered as more tears spilled down her cheeks. "But Mama..."

"If you tell anyone what happened here, you'll regret it," I said, stepping closer to her. I could see the fear in her eyes now—the fear I knew would bind her to silence. "Do you understand me?"

She nodded slowly, her shoulders shaking.

"Good," I said flatly. "Because this is how it has to be. If Daddy or Evangeline asks, the baby died in childbirth."

Aurelia nodded again, her lips trembling in fear.

I turned away again, leaving the baby at the base of the tree without a second glance. His soft cries began to rise behind me, blending with the rustling of the grass and the distant sounds of the farm. I didn't look back. I couldn't. Aurelia trailed behind me, sniffling quietly, her sobs swallowed by the wind. Each step I took away from that tree felt heavier than the last, as though the earth itself were trying to drag me back. But I refused to stop.

This is for the best, *I told myself again and again.*

This is how I survive.

As the sun dipped below the horizon and the shadows grew long around us, I felt something inside me harden. The softness, the hope, the warmth that once lived in me—it all began to fade, replaced by a cold resolve. This world was tough, and the only way to get what you wanted was to not let anyone or anything get in your way.

I thought of my husband and the life I wanted, the life I deserved. There was no room for weakness. No room for softness. If I had to claw my way out of this miserable existence, I would. And nothing—not a son, not a daughter, not even my own heart—would stand in my way.

This is who I have to be.

Aurelia walked beside me, silent now, her face streaked with tears. She didn't understand yet, but she would. One day, she would see the truth.

And so, step by step, I let the tree and the baby fade into the distance. And I let the last of my softness die with them, along with my husband, who eventually found out the truth. Every sip of the poison was another wall placed over the heartbreak I felt for the poor boy.

Chapter 56

Sebastian sat stiffly on the hillside, his arms crossed tight over his knees, staring down at the endless stretch of golden fields as though they could offer some kind of answer. All he felt was cold, one that started deep in his chest and clawed its way outward.

Her son.

The words echoed in his mind, ricocheting like arrows shot into stone. Mirelle's son. His mother—the one woman who had caused so much pain to others. Who tormented Ella. Who raised Evangeline and Aurelia to become shadows of her. And now Aurelia stood before him, claiming this nightmare was his truth. He shook his head, his jaw clenched so tight he thought his teeth might break. It couldn't be true. It couldn't be.

In the distance, the horses grazing at the bottom of the hill let out forlorn cries, their mournful sounds carrying on the wind like an extension of his own thoughts.

I can't be her son. I won't be.

Behind him, Aurelia stood silent and still, watching him from a distance. Sebastian refused to turn and meet her gaze. He couldn't bear to see the sympathy on her face.

"Sebastian," Aurelia said finally, her voice hesitant but steady. "I know it's hard to believe—"

"Hard to believe?" he snapped, the words leaving him before he could stop them. His head whipped around to face her, his dark eyes burning with a mix of anger and disbelief. "You think it's hard to believe? It's a joke, Aurelia. A sick, cruel joke!"

Her face fell, and she took a small step forward, holding out her hands as though trying to calm a wild animal. "It's not a joke. I wish it were, but it isn't."

Sebastian shot to his feet, the grass flattened beneath him. He spun away, gripping his temples as though trying to force the thoughts out of his head. "You're lying," he said harshly. "You're trying to trick me—maybe to mess with my head or use me for something. Because there's no way that she could be my mother."

Aurelia flinched at the venom in his voice. "Sebastian...I don't want to hurt you. I'm not lying."

"Are you kidding me? You guys hurt people. Why should I believe you? And why would she abandon me?" he shouted, whirling around to face her. His hands trembled as his voice cracked. "Why would she just leave me out there like I was nothing?"

"Because that's what she did," Aurelia replied softly, the regret in her tone stinging worse than any accusation. "She didn't see you as a person. She saw you as a problem. A mistake. You were never a part of her plan for a perfect life. That's the kind of woman Mirelle was."

Sebastian felt like the ground was shifting beneath him, tilting at an angle that left him unsteady. The rage boiled in his chest, a hot and uncontrollable force. His fists clenched tighter, nails digging into his palms as he glared at her.

"Stop!" he shouted, his voice breaking. "Stop saying that! You don't know me. You don't know my life!"

Aurelia's eyes softened, but she didn't back down. "I do know you, Sebastian. I remember the day you were born. I tried to push it out of my memories, but I can't."

His breath hitched, and a cold wave passed through him, leaving him frozen. "What are you talking about?"

Aurelia took a cautious step closer, her voice now gentle, almost pleading. "You have a mark, don't you? A small crescent moon, just above your left knee."

Something struck Sebastian. He took a step back, staring at her as though she'd grown a second head. His throat was dry, and his voice came out hoarse.

"How do you know that?"

"I saw it," Aurelia replied, her eyes glistening with emotion like fresh raindrops falling on swamp water. "I was there when you were born. You were so small, Sebastian. And you have our father's eyes. The same color. The same shape. The same sadness."

Sebastian staggered back, his breath coming in shallow gasps. He didn't want to believe her—he couldn't believe her—but the pieces she described fit too perfectly. That mark. His eyes. All things he'd carried his whole life, unnoticed and unexplained.

"No," he said weakly, shaking his head. "You're lying!"

His hands shook violently now, his body betraying him as a strange heat spread under his skin. It started in his fingertips, a crackling warmth that pulsed and grew.

Aurelia reached out a hand. "Sebastian, listen to me! I know it's a lot to take in—"

"Stop!" he roared, jerking away. Sparks erupted from his hands, sputtering and hissing as they coiled around his fingers like threads of golden light. Sebastian stared at them in horror, the flickers illuminating his pale face.

"It's magic," Aurelia breathed, her voice trembling as she watched the light dance from his skin. "Sebastian, it's magic."

Sebastian's heart pounded, the magic swirling in his hands building, growing louder and brighter than he's ever seen from his general sparks. The ground hummed beneath his boots, as though responding to the power surging through him.

"No!" he shouted, the light bursting outward in a blinding shockwave. Aurelia stumbled back, shielding her face as the air vibrated with raw energy. Sebastian collapsed to his knees, his hands still smoking as the sparks fizzled out.

The sky overhead darkened, a deep red bleeding into the clouds like ink dropped into water. Sebastian looked up, his chest heaving as dread clawed at his throat. The air became colder with horror weighing down on them.

Aurelia's voice was small, trembling. "It's them. The Concealment."

Sebastian followed her gaze to the horizon. Silhouettes appeared at the edge of the field—dark, shifting shapes moving with a predator's grace. The wind whipped around them, carrying with it a chill that sent shivers down his spine.

"What do they want now?" he asked, though he already knew the answer.

Sebastian clenched his fists, ignoring the faint sparks still crackling at his fingertips. Confusion, anger, and exhaustion weighed heavily on him, but he shoved it all down. Now was not the time for answers. Now was the time to fight.

"Get behind me," he ordered, his voice cold and steady with focus.

Aurelia hesitated for a moment before obeying, retreating as the red sky darkened further.

Sebastian planted his feet, his gaze fixed on the approaching darkness. Magic pulsed faintly in his hands, the power feeling less strange now, less uncontrollable. He didn't understand it—didn't know where it had come from or what it meant—but he knew one thing for certain.

He wasn't going to let the Concealment take him.

Sebastian's breathing grew heavier as the dark figures at the edge of the field crept closer. The crimson clouds overhead bled into the horizon, staining the fields in hues of blood and shadow. The air felt colder, thicker, as though the approaching darkness was swallowing all the warmth from the world. Aurelia stood close behind him, her breath shallow and quick as it tickled the back of his neck. She tried to mask her fear, but Sebastian could feel it—sense it—like the tremor in the ground beneath his feet.

Then they emerged.

Silhouettes stepped into the light, no longer just vague shadows but people cloaked in black, their faces obscured beneath heavy hoods. Their presence felt wrong, so unwelcoming. One figure stepped ahead of the others, his movements casual, confident, like a predator that knew its prey couldn't escape.

Robin Hood.

Sebastian's hands clenched into fists as sparks sputtered faintly along his fingertips, the warmth of his magic barely controllable. Robin Hood stopped a few paces away, his cloak fluttering in the chill wind. The hood obscured most of his face, but his grin shone through, wicked and sharp as a blade.

"Ah, so the boy has a little spark in him," Robin said mockingly, his voice smooth and taunting. "A beginner's magic, but magic nonetheless." He cocked his head to the side. "Is that all you've got, lad? Your mother would be proud."

Sebastian felt his blood boil at the sound of Mirelle being mentioned. "Don't talk about her," he growled. His voice cracked, but the sparks in his hands flared brighter.

Robin let out a soft laugh, slow and deliberate, as though savoring Sebastian's anger. "Touchy, are we? You're so much like your mother, you don't even see it. Quick to anger. Quick to deny what's offered to you." He stretched out his arms, the shadows around him writhing like living things. "I'll make this easy for you, boy. I'm here to offer you a choice. Join the Concealment. Both of you. There's still time to embrace the darkness that's flickering deep inside."

Sebastian glanced back at Aurelia, who froze in place, her eyes wide with fear but determination bubbling just beneath the surface.

Robin took a step closer, his shadow stretching far across the grass. "Don't be a fool, Sebastian. This is your last chance. You don't want to end up like Evangeline, do you?"

Sebastian stiffened. "Evangeline?"

Robin chuckled. "She was so eager, so full of potential. And she let it all go to waste. A shame, really. She could've had everything, and now...well, you've seen what became of her. A mockery of what we are about." He gestured toward the horizon. "Do you want to make the same mistake? Do you want to squander your power?"

Sebastian took a step forward, his hands crackling with faint ribbons of energy. "I will never join you!"

Robin's grin widened. "Such a pity. You're just as stubborn as she was." He lifted his hand, and the wind picked up, carrying with it a deep, resonating hum that shook the ground beneath them. "If I can't have you, I guess I'll have to give your friend a try without you in the way."

Sebastian's eyes widened. "What are you talking about?"

He fought the urge to allow his fingers to tremble. The more the trees quivered, Aurelia clenched onto his arm, nails digging into his skin. Dark fog surrounding them made his heart race with worry.

Robin Hood's body dissolved into darkness, his cloak unraveling into wisps of shadow. "I suppose you'll see for yourself soon enough." His voice echoed as he vanished, leaving nothing but black tendrils curling in the air. "Enjoy the reunion."

A deafening rumble shook the earth beneath their feet. Aurelia screamed as the field quaked violently, cracks splintering across the ground. The farm beyond—the once peaceful expanse of land—was suddenly alive with chaos. Animals cried out in terror, horse hooves pounding against the earth as they fled from unseen forces. The farmhouse creaked under the tremors, the windows rattling as though they would shatter at any moment.

Sebastian staggered, barely keeping his balance. "What's happening?" he shouted.

"Look!" Aurelia said, pointing toward the tree, her hand trembling.

Sebastian's gaze snapped toward the graveyard just beyond the hill. The tombstones nestled beneath the old oak began to crack and crumble. The earth bulged upward, dirt spilling over the edges as something pushed free from the ground. A hand shot up, skeletal and grotesque, its skin gray and rotting. Another hand followed. A low, guttural growl echoed through the field as the figures clawed their way out of their resting places.

Sebastian's blood ran cold.

From the earth emerged two bodies, their forms twisted and corrupted by dark magic. Ella's parents had become something monstrous. The last of their skin hung in loose, sagging folds, gray with death and decay. Their eyes glowed an unnatural orange, and their mouths curled into hideous, jagged smiles. Dirt and worms clung to the tattered remnants of their deteriorating clothes.

Aurelia gasped, stumbling back. "No...no, it can't be."

The creatures that had once been Ella's parents turned their heads in unison, locking their glowing eyes on Sebastian and Aurelia. A guttural, distorted voice hissed through the air. Rust scraped against his sheath when the father took out his sword, causing Sebastian's throat to thicken.

Sebastian raised his hands, sparks flaring back to life in his palms. "Stay back!" he shouted, his voice steady despite the fear pounding in his chest.

The two monsters stepped forward, their movements jerky and unnatural, as though their bodies resisted the magic holding them together. The ground trembled with every step.

Sebastian turned to Aurelia, his voice low but urgent. "Get out of here. Go!"

"What about you?" she shouted, panic breaking through her voice.

"I'll hold them off!"

Aurelia hesitated, her eyes flicking between Sebastian and the approaching horrors. "You can't fight them alone!"

"I don't have a choice!" he snapped, his magic flaring brighter. The heat coiled in his veins again, sharper this time—angrier. He turned back to face the creatures, his fists crackling with energy.

The monstrosities lurched closer, their mouths twisting into mocking smiles. One of them tilted its head and rasped, "You will join us...in death."

Sebastian gritted his teeth, his hands glowing with light as he prepared to fight. His pulse thundered in his ears, but this time he didn't let the fear consume him.

"I won't let them win."

Sebastian stumbled back as the skeletal figure of Ella's father lunged at him, the man's decayed, sinewy arms swinging a rusted blade inches from Sebastian's chest. Sebastian pushed him away, his strength was a struggle to match to the fiend. The bones scratched his face as he punched him, causing waves of pain to radiate. Outnumbered, Sebastian ran toward the stables, trying to ignore their screams that pierced his ears.

The sound of the blade scraping against the stable's wooden beams sent chills down his spine. He ducked, barely evading a blow, and retaliated with a shove that sent the creature crashing into a pile of hay. The firelight from the house caught the grotesque glint in the father's hollow eyes, his face an unnatural blend of bone and rotting flesh.

The rancid stench of decay filled Sebastian's nostrils as he grabbed a pitchfork lying against the stable wall. With every ounce of his strength, he swung the tool like a club, striking the father across his torso. The impact sent a sickening crunch through the air, but the creature barely stumbled.

"You think you can stop us?" the father rasped, his voice guttural and echoing with malice. "You're nothing but a coward. A failure. Even your own mother didn't want you!"

Sebastian gritted his teeth, trying to block out the taunts. His hands trembled, sparks sputtering at his fingertips, but his magic faltered under the pressure of his panic. The mother's decomposed figure crept closer, her nails clawing through the air as she hissed, "You're just like the others, weak and undeserving."

"Shut up!" Sebastian roared, thrusting the pitchfork toward her, but she moved with unnatural speed, dodging the blow and raking her talons across his forearm. Pain flared as blood seeped through his torn sleeve.

He stumbled backward into the stable doors, his breathing ragged. The father took advantage of the moment and swung his blade again, nicking Sebastian's shoulder. The sharp sting burned, but he didn't have time to dwell on it. He dropped the pitchfork and dove for a length of chain hanging from a beam. Grabbing it tight, he turned back toward his attackers.

The mother lunged for him, and he swung the chain with a desperate grunt. It wrapped around her wrist, and he pulled with all his might, dragging her into a trough of stagnant water. She shrieked, thrashing as water splashed everywhere. The father charged at him again, his blade aimed for Sebastian's torso. Sebastian ducked just in time, causing the blade to lodge against the stable wall.

"Nice try!" he growled, grabbing a wooden plank and slamming it into the father's back. The creature let out a guttural growl, spinning around to knock Sebastian off his feet with a powerful swing of his arm.

Sebastian crashed to the ground, the wind knocked from his lungs. The father's skeletal form loomed over him, his hollow eyes filled with malicious delight. "You really are just like your mother," he sneered, his voice dripping with venom. "Weak. Selfish. Worthless."

The words cut deeper than Sebastian expected, and his grip on the chain slackened. The mother emerged from the trough, water pouring from her decayed frame as she cackled. "You don't stand a chance," she taunted, her voice a screeching shrill. "I'll be your mother once you give up!"

Sebastian scrambled to his feet, adrenaline coursing through him as he grabbed a broken rake from the floor. He flailed it, keeping them at bay as he retreated toward the house.

Inside the house, shadows danced across the walls as the father and mother pursued him, their hollow eyes glowing in the dim light. The cramped quarters worked against him; every table, chair, and cabinet seemed to block his path as he maneuvered through the space. In the kitchen, Sebastian grabbed a cast-iron skillet from the table and swung it at the mother, catching her across the side of her head. The impact sent bits of bone and decay flying, but she barely reacted, her grotesque grin widening.

"Is that all you've got?" she hissed, her clawed hands reaching for him.

The father grabbed a chair and hurled it across the room. It splintered against the wall, narrowly missing Sebastian's head. "This is where it ends," he growled, his voice low and menacing.

Sebastian's back pressed against the kitchen table, cornering him. His chest heaved, and his magic sparked at his fingertips, but it wasn't enough. The two creatures closed in, their malicious laughter filling the small space.

Suddenly, a loud crash echoed through the room. Aurelia burst through the doorway, holding a chair she had snatched from the dining room. Her face was pale but determined, her eyes blazing with resolve.

"Get away from him!" she shouted, charging at the mother.

Aurelia pushed the legs of the chair with surprising strength, slamming it into the mother's torso. The chair pushed the mother backward, causing her to stumble over the scattered biscuits. Her body plummeted to the floor, her head collapsing into the empty fireplace. Aurelia flinched with surprise as the corpse combusted with flames growing around her remaining bits of hair. The flames licked at the decayed fabric of her gown, and the smell of burning flesh filled the air. The mother let out an ear-piercing screech as the fire consumed her, melting her grotesque form into a puddle of sludge on the kitchen floor.

Sebastian staggered to his feet, clutching his bleeding arm. "Aurelia..."

"Don't just stand there!" she snapped, shoving him toward the father to protect herself, the lone eye gazing at her with vengeance.

The father roared in fury at the loss of his wife. He lunged at Aurelia, swinging his rusted blade with reckless abandon. She ducked and rolled away, grabbing a heavy candelabra from the table and hurling it at him. Sebastian joined the fray, grabbing a fire poker from the hearth and jabbing it at the father. Together, they fought with a frantic desperation, dodging his wild swings and striking back whenever they could.

Finally, Sebastian and Aurelia worked in unison. Aurelia grabbed the father's arm, holding him in place as Sebastian delivered a powerful blow to his chest with the fire poker. The father stumbled backward, his skeletal frame teetering on the edge of the hearth.

"Now!" Aurelia shouted.

With a final push, they shoved the father to the floor. The fireplace roared with another burst of fire. Flames exploded, with one landing on Aurelia's hand, and she retreated in pain. He thrashed and screamed as the flames consumed him, his decayed flesh and brittle bones melting away into ash. The room fell silent, except for the crackling of the fire. Sebastian and Aurelia collapsed onto the floor, their chests heaving as they tried to catch their breath.

As the fire disappeared, Sebastian's eyes caught a faint glimmer in the fireplace. He leaned closer, squinting at the glowing object nestled among the ashes. Carefully, he used the fire poker to retrieve it. It was a tear-shaped gem, smooth and gleaming with an eerie light, with orange crackling like a burnt piece of wood.

"I've seen this before," Sebastian murmured, holding it up for Aurelia to see. "There were more of them."

Aurelia's eyes widened as realization dawned on her. "Ella," she whispered. "She cried here—she cried so much, and her heartbreak...it must have created these tears in the cinder."

Sebastian stared at the gem, its soft glow reflecting in his eyes. The weight of their discovery settled heavily on his shoulders, but he knew there was no time to dwell on it. Through the window, the sky burned into a deeper crimson, the color spreading like wildfire across the heavens. The low hum of impending danger vibrated in the air, sending chills down Sebastian's spine as Aurelia placed the beads in her pouch.

He pushed himself to his feet, his eyes locking onto one horse outside. "Come on," he said firmly, his voice steady despite the lingering tremor in his hands. "We need to get to the castle."

Chapter 57

The festival was in full swing, the grand hall brimming with life and splendor. Strings of violins carried a melody that danced through the air, weaving seamlessly with the hum of laughter and the soft clinking of glasses raised in celebratory toasts. The chandeliers above cast a warm, golden light over the room, their crystals shimmering like scattered stars.

Dominic leaned against the polished wooden railing of the balcony that overlooked the dance floor. Below him, a sea of nobles twirled in synchronized patterns, their brightly colored gowns and tailored suits moving like a living kaleidoscope. For the first time since arriving in this magical land, Dominic felt something close to belonging. The grandeur of the evening, though strange, wasn't oppressive—it was intoxicating.

Beside him stood Ella and Sawyer. Ella's laughter was a symphony of its own, clear and melodious, as she recounted a childhood memory to the group. Her eyes sparkled like the gemstones embroidered on her gown, and her cheeks flushed with genuine joy. Dominic smiled along, drawn into her warmth.

Sawyer leaned on the railing, his posture relaxed but still carrying the dignity of his royal lineage. His navy blue suit, adorned with gold epaulets and intricate embroidery, contrasted sharply with his approachable demeanor. His presence added a sense of calm to the festival, and Dominic felt less like an outsider with him there.

"Dominic," Sawyer said suddenly, his tone shifting from lighthearted to thoughtful. His voice carried a subtle weight, like the faint echo of something unspoken. "It's refreshing to have someone new at court. Most of the nobles I deal with...well, they're predictable, to say the least. All they care about is status, alliances, and wealth."

Dominic chuckled softly, raising his goblet to his lips. The wine inside was rich and velvety, the finest he'd ever tasted. "Trust me, I'm about as far from noble as it gets," he said, his tone light but honest. "But I appreciate being included."

Sawyer's lips curled into a faint smile, though his expression didn't fully mask the wistfulness in his eyes. Dominic noticed his gaze drifting across the room to where the king's throne sat, elevated on a marble dais at the far end of the hall. Though the festivities swirled around it, the throne remained untouched, an imposing symbol of authority and loss.

"My father..." Sawyer began, his voice softer now, tinged with a melancholy that seemed to weigh heavily on him. "He was a complicated man. Stubborn, proud, and deeply rooted in tradition. When I told him about Ella, he didn't approve. He thought I was throwing away my duty to the crown."

Ella, standing between them, reached for Sawyer's hand. Her touch was gentle, grounding, and filled with quiet reassurance. "He came around in the end," she said, her voice soft yet steady.

Sawyer's jaw tightened, his grip on her hand firm. "On his deathbed," he continued, his tone laden with both sorrow and pride. "When he realized the throne would soon be mine, he finally admitted that true love matters more than lineage. That I was right to choose someone who brought light into my life."

Dominic fidgeted, unsure how to answer such a personal disclosure. Words felt insufficient in the face of such raw vulnerability. "I'm sorry for your loss," he said, his voice sincere.

Sawyer nodded, his gaze still fixed on the empty throne. "Thank you," he said, his words simple but heartfelt. "I miss him every day, but tonight...tonight is about celebrating life, not mourning the past."

Dominic looked between the couple, their bond so apparent it was almost tangible. There was something profoundly human about the king's story, a reminder that even in this magical world, people faced the same struggles and joys as back home.

The music swelled, the violins joined by the deep hum of cellos. Laughter echoed from the far side of the room as a group of nobles toasted to some jest, their goblets raised high. At that moment, Dominic allowed himself to relax. The weight of his journey, his uncertainties, and his self-doubt faded into the background, replaced by the simple joy of being part of something beautiful and meaningful.

DESPITE THE LIVELY music and chatter in the main hall, Gretel stood near the grand buffet table, arms tightly crossed. Her sharp eyes, narrowed in suspicion, watched the room as the flickering chandeliers cast shifting shadows across her features. Calypso, perched on the edge of the table next to her hip, twitched his ears and flicked his tail, his unease mirroring her own.

"Something's wrong," Gretel muttered under her breath, her voice barely audible over the laughter and clinking glasses of the nobles. Her gaze drifted toward the towering windows that lined the hall, their ornate frames now casting ominous reflections of the outside world.

The night sky, once a tranquil deep blue, had transformed into something unnatural. Streaks of crimson bled into the clouds, swirling and spreading like veins, casting an eerie glow over the landscape. The air itself felt heavier, charged with an energy that set Gretel's nerves on edge.

Calypso hissed, his fur bristling. "I can feel it in the air, too," he murmured, his voice low and wary.

"I'll say," Agnes said as she stood by Gretel, her pulled-back gray hair showing every sunspot and wrinkle.

"Oh, are you having a wonderful evening?" Gretel asked, tentative as she noticed the cold expression on her face. "You're looking beautiful."

"As are you," she responded. "The evening would be better if we had Sebastian here with us."

"I know. It's unfortunate that he chose not to come," she said with guilt.

"But he was so committed to being by Dominic's side."

"I know."

Agnes's eyes squinted when they focused deeper into her soul. Ever since she faced the witch head-on, Gretel hasn't been this intimidated by a woman's stance. Calypso reached one of his paws toward her, pulling on her skirt.

"I just want to tell you that Sebastian is a very sweet boy," Agnes said with a firm tone that was sharp through the noise. "I've seen this boy happy since he was a toddler. He has been sad far too many times in his life, and I'll be damned if I let you or your friend make him that way."

"I-I see that he's told you," Gretel stammered. "I think this is just a big misunderstanding. Once he gets a chance to cool down, everything will be just fine."

"Don't talk to me like you know him!"

"I don't know him as much as you do," Gretel said, noting Agnes's furrowed eyebrows. "But I do care about him."

"Care about him enough to let him go?"

"Well, somebody has to keep watch over Dominic."

"And yet again, Sebastian is hurt. And here you are, keeping up with your reputation and hurting people."

"Agnes, with all due respect, he just needed to take a breath. You don't know me."

"You're right. I don't, nor will I ever."

Agnes disappeared within the crowd. The strings were scratched by the bows violently, causing Calypso's fur to stand up. Gretel grabbed a goblet from the buffet and downed its contents in one swift gulp. The wine burned her throat, but it did little to calm the growing knot of dread in her chest.

"What the hell was that all about?" the cat asked in confusion. "I'm sorry you had to deal with that."

Placing the goblet back with a clink, she squared her shoulders. "We need to find Dominic," she said, already moving toward the balcony where she had last seen him.

The cat leaped from the table, weaving through the throngs of twirling dancers and chattering nobles as Gretel pushed her way through the crowd. Her boots clicked against the polished floor, a determined rhythm against the backdrop of music. The red-streaked sky loomed in her peripheral vision, an ever-present reminder of the approaching threat.

"I love your dress," said one woman to another as Gretel passed by.

"Thank you," said the other. "Yours is nice too."

"It's not the one I had in mind for the festival. The damn seamster didn't finish mine in time!"

"Really? Mister Gloomis is usually great with deadlines."

"Well, that worm closed his shop early. Didn't give us the chance to pick up!"

"He never closes early!"

Before she could reach the balcony, a firm hand clamped down on her arm, pulling her off course into the shadows of a side hallway. The sudden motion sent her instincts flaring, and she spun around, half-drawing her dagger. But the sight of Sir Winston stopped her short. His grip was unyielding, his expression twisted into something unfamiliar. An unsettling smirk marred his usually calm and composed face, and his eyes glowed orange like embers smoldering in the dark.

"Sir Winston," Gretel said sharply, her voice laced with suspicion. "What's the meaning of this?"

He didn't answer right away, his silence dragging uncomfortably. Calypso crouched low, growling deep in his throat, his claws sinking into the plush rug beneath them.

"Let me go," Gretel demanded, her hand tightening around the hilt of her dagger.

Winston's lips curled into a sinister grin. "Oh, but that wouldn't be any fun," he said, his voice low and dripping with malice.

Before she could react, he shoved her forward. Gretel stumbled, catching herself just as she crossed the threshold of a dimly lit room. Calypso darted in after her, his fur standing on end. The heavy wooden door slammed shut behind them with an ominous thud, and Winston's imposing frame blocked the only exit.

The room was suffocatingly quiet, the air thick with a strange, metallic tang. Gretel's heart pounded as she stepped back, her eyes fixed on Winston. That faint orange glow in his eyes had intensified, and realization hit her like a blow to the chest.

"You're Concealment," she spat, her voice cold and accusing.

Winston's laughter filled the small space, low and menacing. "And you're far sharper than I gave you credit for," he said, stepping closer with slow, deliberate movements. "A pity. You could've been a valuable asset."

Gretel's grip on her blade tightened, and she yanked it free of its sheath in one swift motion. But Winston was faster. Before she could raise it, he lunged, grabbing her wrist with a strength that was far beyond human. His grip was like iron, and the blade slipped from her fingers, clattering to the floor.

She struggled against him, kicking and twisting, but he held her in place with unnerving ease. "Don't bother," he said, his voice a purr of mockery. "You've walked right into the lion's den, my dear. And your little hero? He's too preoccupied with coming to your rescue. Not this time."

Calypso snarled, his eyes glowing with defiance as he leaped at Winston, claws outstretched. Winston swatted the cat mid-air with a force that sent him skidding across the floor. Gretel cried out, her anger surging, but Winston only laughed, his eyes blazing like fire.

"Such spirit," he sneered. "It's almost a shame to crush it." His words filled with horror as he loomed closer, the oppressive weight of his presence suffocating the room.

Gretel's mind raced, searching for any opening, any weakness. Her pulse thundered in her ears, but she refused to let fear take hold. Whatever was coming, she would have to face it head-on.

Chapter 58

Sebastian

THE WIND WHIPS AT MY face as I urge the horse faster, its hooves clattering loudly against the cobblestones. Aurelia clings to me, her arms wrapped around my waist like a lifeline. This is the closest embrace I'll probably have with any of my family. I barely notice her grip, though—I'm too lost in my own thoughts, my mind swirling with the weight of what I've just learned.

Mirelle. My mother.

The word feels strange, like it doesn't belong in my head. I want to deny it, to shove it back into the recesses of my mind where it can never resurface. But the truth clings to me, inescapable, like a thorn burrowing into my chest.

She left me.

My teeth clench as the thought burns through me like fire. I'm not just abandoned; I'm discarded like I'm nothing. Left at the base of a tree, no more valuable than a forgotten trinket. And now, after all these years, the truth about my identity feels like a curse. A chain I can't break.

"Sebastian," Aurelia calls over the rush of wind, her voice muffled against my back. "We're almost there."

I nod tightly, though I don't say a word. My eyes lock on the silhouette of the castle rising in the distance, its spires cutting sharply into the crimson-streaked sky. The red clouds churn ominously overhead, and a chill runs down my spine that has nothing to do with the wind.

The town we pass through is eerily silent. The streets, usually bustling even at night, are empty. Windows are shut tight, their shutters rattling against the breeze. Even the taverns are quiet, their doors barred as though the very life of the place has been snuffed out. Shadows stretch unnaturally long, creeping along the walls and pooling in the alleyways like ink.

I tighten my grip on the reins, my knuckles white. The horse snorts, its ears flicking nervously as it senses the unease around us. I can't blame it. The air itself feels heavier, charged with something dark and heavy.

As we approach the castle gates, I slow the horse to a trot. The courtyard is deserted, the usual guards nowhere to be seen. The torches that line the pathway flicker weakly, their flames barely clinging to life. The shadows here are thicker, almost tangible, writhing like living things against the stone walls.

"Something's wrong," Aurelia murmurs, her voice tight with tension.

"No kidding," I mutter back, my eyes darting around. My pulse quickens as I urge the horse forward, the sound of its hooves echoing hollowly in the stillness.

We dismount near the entrance, and I tie the reins to a post with shaky hands. Aurelia stays close, her wide eyes scanning the courtyard as though she expects something—or someone—to leap from the shadows.

The grand doors to the ballroom loom ahead, light spilling out through the cracks. Music and laughter filter faintly into the night, a stark contrast to the oppressive air outside. I take a deep breath, steeling myself, and push the doors open. The warmth and light of the ballroom hit me like a wave, almost disorienting after the cold darkness of the courtyard. The sight of the crowd—nobles in their finery, twirling and laughing—feels like stepping into another world entirely. For a brief moment, I hesitate, my anger and confusion about my identity colliding with the surreal normalcy of the space.

"Sebastian, you made it!" Agnes says, her warm smile cut short. "And what on earth are you doing with that wretched woman? She is banished, and you should not be with her!"

"Where's Dominic? Where's Gretel?" I ask, my breath hitching as my eyes wander around every part of the room.

"You don't need them. They hurt you, and you don't deserve any more of that pain tonight," Agnes dismisses. "And I'm sure Aurelia will do the same to you."

"They need me!" I hiss with irritation. "Where are they?"

"Oh, they went with your friend, Giselle," says a man, his confidence standing out from the exhaustion within the crowd. "I can take you to them if you'd like."

"Who the hell are you?" Aurelia asks, her hand reaching for something to protect her.

"Oh, I'm sorry. Where are my manners! My name is Olio. Your friend introduced me to Giselle, and we've found this lovely room in the castle. One that's quiet and less crowded."

The overabundance of people makes my mind race. I can't think, and part of me feels like I can't breathe. I need to find the people I feel like I'm meant to be with. I need to protect those who I care about the most. If Agnes isn't going to come with me as I find Dominic and Gretel, then I can't waste time to convince her.

"Right this way," Olio continues, his hand grabbing onto Agnes's arm to usher her.

But then the light dims.

A collective gasp ripples through the room as the chandeliers flicker, their flames sputtering as though struggling to stay alight. Shadows creep across the floor, pooling at the edges of the room and stretching toward the center like long, grasping fingers.

"Ladies and gentlemen," a voice booms, smooth and mocking. My blood runs cold as I turn toward its source.

Robin Hood.

He stands at the far end of the room, his figure illuminated by the faint, flickering glow of the remaining light. His cloak billows around him as though stirred by a wind that no one else can feel, and his eyes gleam with a sinister orange light that sends a chill down my spine.

Behind him, more figures materialize from the shadows—cloaked, their faces obscured, but their intent unmistakable. The Concealment. They spread out, encircling like predators closing in on their prey.

"Apologies for crashing your little soirée," Robin says, his lips curling into a mocking smile. "I was sad that I didn't receive my invitation."

The crowd recoils, the once-lively space replaced by a palpable tension. I step forward instinctively, my hand curling into a fist at my side. Aurelia grabs my arm, her grip tight with fear.

"Sebastian," she whispers urgently, "don't—"

"I'm not standing here and letting him do this," I snap, shaking her off. My anger boils over. The weight of everything—the revelation about Mirelle, the dark magic in my veins, the intense shadows—fuels the fire inside me.

Robin's eyes land on me, his smile widening. "Ah, there you are," he says, his tone dripping with mockery. "The son of the bitch."

His words hit harder than I expect, but I don't falter. My jaw tightens, and I step closer, my voice steady despite the rage bubbling beneath the surface.

"Please, don't do this. Leave these people alone."

Robin looks at me, his eyebrow furrowing with pleasure. Weapons slowly unsheathe underneath the black robes, the sound of metal screeching into my ears. The people scurry toward the window, their blood flowing heavy like the veins in the sky, with the curtain revealing the sign of their presence.

"Start the music," Robin says softly. "It's time to dance."

Chapter 59

The atmosphere in the castle had shifted, but Dominic found comfort in the quieter halls away from the bustling ballroom. He walked alongside Sawyer, the faint hum of controlled music trailing behind them. The two strolled down a long corridor lined with tall windows that framed the moonlit gardens outside. Ornate family portraits adorned the walls, each one illuminated by the soft flicker of sconces.

Dominic's gaze lingered on a painting of a stately man with piercing blue eyes. His pose was regal and full of power, standing tall even though he looked less than five feet tall with a pudgier shape. His expression unreadable with a silver mustache that was waxed to a point beyond his cheeks. The darker hairs on his beard camouflaged the roundness in his face.

"That's my father," Sawyer said, following Dominic's line of sight. "King Aldred. He commissioned that portrait shortly after his coronation."

Dominic nodded, studying the details. "He looks intimidating."

Sawyer laughed softly, his tone tinged with nostalgia. "He could be. My father was a man of tradition—unyielding, proud. He did prevent me from making my own choices. But he had his moments of softness. Toward the end, at least."

"I'm sure he was a great father," said Dominic.

"He was. I just don't know who I was apart from being a prince because of him."

Trying to steer the conversation, Dominic said, "He probably did it for good reason."

The king gestured for Dominic to follow, and they moved further down the hall. Sawyer stopped in front of a glass display case, its contents illuminated by a warm, golden glow. Inside, perched on a velvet cushion, was a single golden slipper.

Dominic stared, the artifact capturing his full attention. "The shoe."

Sawyer smiled, nodding. "Yes, Ella's slipper. The one she left behind."

Dominic leaned closer, taking in the intricate detailing of the shoe once again. "I can't imagine how stressful it must have been to find the person who fit that."

Sawyer let out a chuckle. "Stressful doesn't even begin to cover it. My father thought it was a foolish endeavor before he passed, but I was determined. Ella had this spark—this light—I couldn't ignore. I knew she was the one, even before I found her."

Dominic straightened, turning to Sawyer. "And what about her family? You must've seen how they were to her."

Sawyer's expression darkened as he thought back. "Mirelle and her daughters, you mean?" He sighed, shaking his head. "They were desperate, I think. Clinging to whatever hope they had for a better life. But that desperation turned sour. When they realized Ella had caught my eye, they tried to overshadow her in every way possible. I shouldn't complain about not being able to do much when she couldn't do anything at all."

He paused, a flicker of something like guilt crossing his face. "I didn't see it then, but I should have known how much Ella was enduring under their roof. She never complained, never spoke ill of them. And then...well, the birds."

Dominic raised an eyebrow. "Oh yes, the birds."

Sawyer grimaced. "An accident, really. Ella told me the servants were baking in the kitchen, and somehow flour got involved. It spilled everywhere, and the next thing we knew, flocks of birds had stormed the room. They pecked, they clawed...Mirelle and her daughters were caught in the chaos."

"That sounds awful."

"It was," Sawyer admitted, his tone somber. "But it was also a wake-up call. Ella's stepmother and stepsisters were more concerned about their appearances and social standing than anything else. The moment revealed a lot about their character, and Ella's resilience."

Dominic absorbed the story, glancing once more at the golden slipper. The weight of its history felt tangible, the symbol of a fairy tale that had brought joy and hardship alike.

Sawyer placed a hand on Dominic's shoulder, breaking the reflective silence. "Come," he said with a small smile. "I want to show you something."

They made their way down the corridor, their footsteps echoing softly in the grand halls. Sawyer led Dominic through a side door, and the cool night air greeted them as they stepped outside. Moonlight bathed the garden. Flowers of every color lined the paths, their petals glistening with dew. Trees stood silent without a whisper of wind to tickle their branches. Cicadas greeted them with a symphony accompanied by grasshoppers and crickets.

"This," Sawyer said, gesturing to a secluded corner of the garden, "This is where I brought Ella after I found her at the festival."

Dominic followed him to a stone bench nestled beneath a sprawling willow tree. A small fountain bubbled nearby, its water sparkling under the moonlight.

"We sat here for what felt like hours," Sawyer continued, his voice quieter now. "Talking, laughing. It was the first time in my life I felt completely at peace."

Dominic took it all in; the serenity of the space, the history it held. "It's beautiful," he said simply.

Sawyer nodded, his gaze distant. "It is. I come here a lot. And it's a reminder that even in the darkest times, there's always a place for light."

Dominic looked at the king, noting the sincerity in his words. Though the wind tickled his body, he remained uncaring. The garden felt like a sanctuary—a moment of stillness with no worries bothering him.

SUFFOCATING AND THICK with tension, the air in the dimly lit room pressed down on Gretel as she faced Sir Winston. His glowing eyes pierced into her soul. He stood tall, his frame imposing in the shadowy space. A cruel smile played on his lips, his confidence radiating with every calculated step he took toward her.

"You've always been a fighter, haven't you?" Sir Winston sneered, his voice a chilling mix of mockery and menace. "But no matter how hard you try, you can't escape your past."

Gretel tightened her grip on her dagger, her jaw clenched. "I've faced worse than you," she said, her voice steady despite the storm building inside her.

"Have you?" Winston tilted his head, his expression almost amused. "What about Hansel? Your dear brother. Do you remember how he looked at you after the witch was gone? How he blamed you for everything that came after you killed her?"

Gretel's breath hitched, her chest tightening. She tried to push the words aside, but they wormed their way into her mind like venom.

"And the witch," Winston continued, his voice twisting into something high-pitched and cruel, mimicking the cackle that haunted Gretel's nightmares. "Oh, the way she laughed when she saw your weakness. You were so small, so helpless. You still are."

"Shut up!" Gretel snapped, lunging forward with her blade. Winston sidestepped her with ease, his laughter echoing off the stone walls.

"Touched a nerve, did I?" he taunted, his movements fluid as he circled her. "Face it, Gretel. You've always been the weak one. Always dragging others down with you."

Her blood boiled, the taunts stoking a fire deep within her. She could almost hear Hansel's voice, sharp and bitter, echoing in her ears. The witch's laughter intertwined with his words, a cacophony of guilt and pain. But Gretel didn't back down. She channeled her anger, letting it fuel her movements. She struck again, her blade aiming for Winston's chest. This time, she grazed his armor, the sound of clanking metal ringing in her ears.

Calypso darted around Winston's legs, his fur bristling as he hissed and swiped with his claws. Winston's eyes chased the feline as Calypso's groans got louder, his smile growing from the challenge; the distraction gave Gretel the opening she needed. She feinted to the left before spinning to the right, her dagger slicing across Winston's arm. He let out a hiss of pain, his glowing eyes narrowing.

"You'll regret that," he growled, his voice dripping with malice.

He charged at her, his strength forcing her back against the wall. Gretel gritted her teeth, using her blade to block his strikes. Each blow sent shockwaves through her arms, but she refused to falter. Calypso leaped onto Winston's back, sinking his claws into the knight's shoulder. Winston roared, swatting at the cat, but Calypso clung on with feral determination.

Seizing the moment, Gretel brought her knee up, sharply catching Winston in the gut. He staggered back, winded. With a fierce cry, she swung her dagger, the hilt connecting with the side of his head. Winston crumpled to the ground, his glowing eyes dimming as he lost consciousness.

Panting, Gretel stumbled back, her heart racing. Calypso leapt to her side, his tail lashing. "Good work," she muttered, running a hand over his fur. The cat let out a low growl, his gaze fixed on the unconscious knight.

Gretel didn't linger. She sprinted out of the room, her dagger still clutched tight in her hand. The corridor was quiet, but as she approached the main hall, the distant sounds of chaos reached her ears.

Screams and shouts echoed from the ballroom, mingling with the crashing of glass and the guttural growls of something inhuman. Gretel's stomach churned as she crept closer, peeking around the corner. The ballroom was a place of terror. Figures in dark cloaks moved like shadows, their faces obscured as they unleashed their wrath upon the unsuspecting guests. Nobles cowered, their elaborate gowns and suits torn as they scrambled for safety. The once-elegant space was now a battlefield, the air thick with the acrid scent of fear.

Gretel's grip on her dagger tightened. She glanced at Calypso, who stared at her with unflinching resolve. "This isn't over," she whispered, her voice steady despite the dread curling in her chest.

With a deep breath, she stepped forward, ready to face whatever horrors awaited her.

THE BALLROOM DESCENDED into mayhem as the guests began falling victim to the merciless attacks of the Concealment. Blood stained the polished marble floor, pooling into sinister puddles that reflected the flickering flames of the chandelier above. Screams filled the air, mingling with the guttural laughter of the cloaked figures, their movements as fluid and predatory as wolves among sheep.

The brutality ripped the heavy curtains from their rods, leaving them soaked in blood as grim reminders. Nobles scrambled for the exits, but the Concealment had blocked most of the paths, herding them to their demise.

Aurelia, though not strong, refused to stand idly by. Her eyes darted around the room, assessing the chaos with a calculating sharpness. Spotting a group of terrified guests cornered near an overturned table, she grabbed a candelabra from a nearby wall sconce and hurled it toward the cloaked figures advancing on them. The heavy object struck one in the shoulder, disorienting them.

"This way!" Aurelia shouted, waving the guests toward a narrow hallway leading to the kitchens.

The nobles hesitated, their faces pale with fear, but Aurelia's determined expression spurred them into action. She continued to create distractions—knocking over chairs, throwing goblets, and tipping over the food trays to get their attention. Each clattering noise pulled the attention of the attackers just long enough for another group to slip away.

Looking at another exit, she noticed Agnes struggling, her skirt ripping at the grasp of Olio. The gentleman's eyes glowed orange, making Aurelia's blood flow cold as ice. Letting out a sigh, she expelled the fear and marched over to him, ignoring Agnes's cries for help.

"Let her go!" Aurelia said, voice shaking.

"Why would I do that?" Olio grunted. "I told you I'm taking her to a safe place. The same one Giselle is in, deep in the dungeons, along with the rats eating her insides."

Tears flowed down Agnes's face. The grunt of Olio's laughter made Aurelia cringe with annoyance. Her hand trembled from the amount of pain and anguish the people had experienced. She reached down to a nobleman's corpse. Metal screeched when she unsheathed the sword from their belt, hand trembled as she grabbed the weapon.

"And you're the one going to save her?" Olio chuckled. "You're so weak, even your mother and sister couldn't love you!"

"Stop it!" Aurelia hissed, the pain stinging with tears forming.

"At least your sister had the potential to become one of us. You don't have it in you to be good or evil!"

Aurelia thrusted the sword, hurling it toward Olio. The weapon flew past his face, causing his laughter to stop for a moment. Olio's laughter grew when he realized Aurelia was powerless once again, letting go of Agnes to compose himself with the satisfaction of his provoking. As Agnes scurried away, force plummeted on Olio. Metal clunked as the knight's suit of armor fell on top of him with parts crumbling on the floor.

Aurelia raced to grab the sword, letting out a guttural scream as she let the blade dig deep into its back. Blood pooled around the man, leaving his lips and dark presence drifting out of him. Every additional stab was a moment of regret Aurelia let out of her body, cleansing herself of the guilt that's weighed her down.

"Thank you," Agnes said, panting with a gracious smile.

Aurelia's focus ignored Agnes's shock at seeing this different side of her, and yelled, "Go hide!"

Meanwhile, on the ballroom floor, Sebastian squared off against Robin Hood. The leader of the Concealment exuded a menacing calm, his movements deliberate as he circled Sebastian.

"You've come far, boy," Robin said, his voice like silk laced with venom. "But you're still nothing more than a novice. Tell me, do you even know the true extent of your power?"

Sebastian growled, his fists clenched at his sides. "I know enough to take you down."

Robin smirked, the faint orange glow in his eyes intensifying. "Such arrogance. Just like your mother."

The taunt hit a nerve, and Sebastian lunged, his movements fueled by rage. He managed a solid punch that sent Robin staggering back, but the leader quickly recovered, laughing as he rubbed his jaw.

"Good," Robin said. "Let's see what else you've got."

Robin's strikes were precise, and Sebastian struggled to keep up, the pain from each blow radiating through his body. But with each hit, his anger burned brighter, igniting something deep within him. Sparks flickered at his fingertips, tiny embers that danced in the air.

Robin noticed and grinned. "Ah, there it is. The fire. But can you control it?"

Sebastian's hands erupted into flames, the heat scorching the air. With a roar, he hurled a fireball toward Robin. It struck him square in the chest, sending him flying into a decorative column. The fire spread quickly, licking up the walls and onto the plum curtains, turning the ballroom into an inferno.

Robin pushed himself up, his cloak singed and his smirk replaced with a snarl. But before he could retaliate, Aurelia appeared from the shadows. With surprising speed, she drove a dagger into Robin's side, twisting it for good measure. He howled in pain, his eyes blazing with fury. Above them, the grand chandelier groaned as the flames consumed its supports. With a deafening crash, it fell, shattering on the floor mere inches from Robin. The leader of the Concealment glared at Sebastian and Aurelia, his form flickering like a shadow.

"This isn't over," Robin spat before dissolving into darkness, vanishing into thin air.

Sebastian staggered, his chest heaving as the adrenaline coursed through him. Aurelia grabbed his arm, her face streaked with soot, but resolute. "We have to move."

The two raced up the grand staircase, dodging falling debris and leaping over smoldering remnants of furniture. They burst into the east wing, where Calypso's yowls echoed faintly down the corridor.

"Calypso!" Sebastian shouted.

The cat darted out from behind a toppled armoire, his fur singed but otherwise unharmed. Behind him, Gretel emerged, her blade in hand and her face set in determination.

"Took you long enough," she said, though there was relief in her tone.

"Where were you?" Sebastian asked, panting.

"It doesn't matter. We need to find Dominic!"

Together, the group made their way outside, the cool night air was refreshing compared to the blazing inferno behind them. In the courtyard, they found Dominic standing with King Sawyer, both deep in conversation. Sebastian glanced over at Gretel, who shared a mutual expression of confusion. Neither one of them was concerned about the chaos inside. But the further they stepped towards them, the visual of the night sky had changed. What was once covered in red clouds has now been cleared with pure midnight blue. Turning back to the building, there was no sign of smoke. No sign of screams. No sign of destruction.

"What happened to the castle?" Gretel asked, looking around the courtyard for any sign of distress.

"I dunno!" Aurelia said. "How can they not see it? How can they not hear it?"

Sebastian wasted no time. "Dominic, we need to go. The Concealment attacked the members of the festival. They're not stopping here."

Dominic turned, his expression guarded. "No they haven't. And besides, why should I go anywhere with you? After what you said—"

"This isn't about us," Sebastian interrupted, his voice firm. "This is about survival. You saw the red sky, right? You must know something's wrong."

"There is no red sky, Sebastian. Everything is fine."

Aurelia stepped forward, her voice steady despite the chaos around them. "He's telling the truth. The Concealment is stronger than ever, and they won't stop until they've destroyed everything."

Sebastian's gaze bore into Dominic's. "Please. We don't have time for this. You're part of this fight, whether you like it or not."

"You have to believe him, Dominic," Gretel pleaded.

After a tense stare, Dominic sighed, his shoulders slumping. "Fine. Let's go."

CLAP!

In an instant, Dominic and Sawyer froze in shock. Looking at the castle, they saw what the others have experienced. Clouds had suddenly appeared with bleeds of red consuming the blues. Shattered windows huffed out gusts of smoke. The cries of people made them cringe.

"What the hell?" Dominic asked, his heart jolted.

"See? I told you." Sebastian said.

"Oh, my goodness!" Sawyer said, his eyes looking around the courtyard. "We need to find Ella. We need to save my people!"

"Did you see here in the hall?" Dominic asked, his heart stopping.

"No, I was busy getting cornered by that prick, Winston!" Gretel answered.

"I didn't see her in the ballroom," Sebastian said.

"Me either," Aurelia added.

The group looked at each other, their eyes widening with concern. She hadn't been on anybody's radar for quite a while. Dominic thought back to the last time he saw her, disappearing into the crowd when she let him dance with Sawyer. When the night was getting more alluring, his focus on the hostess seemed to dissolve.

"Where the hell is my wife!" Sawyer said, his face flushing.

"Do you think the Concealment got her?" Aurelia asked.

The golden sparkles cascaded from the sky like falling stars, glimmering against the backdrop of the crimson clouds. Amid the shimmering rain, a figure emerged, her radiant, green gown flowing effortlessly as though woven from foliage itself. The woman's presence was almost calming, gliding with light-hearted ease with hydrangeas covering the top of her corset. The smile on her light green skin glowed as if she were oblivious to the chaos that had erupted moments ago.

"My, my," the mysterious woman said, her voice lilting with a sing-song quality. "What a mess we have here. But don't you worry, darlings. Hazel can fix all of this, just like I fixed dear Ella's life."

Sebastian's fists clenched at the mention of Ella, but it was Aurelia who reacted first. Her brow furrowed as her gaze darted between Hazel and Sebastian.

"You. You're the one who helped Ella?" she asked, her voice tinged with confusion and unease. "You're the one who blinded my family?"

Hazel chuckled softly, her laughter floating like a melody as her pine needle brows raised. "Oh, yes, my dear. It was I who gave her the life she deserved. The life she was meant to have." She turned slightly, her glowing figure casting a strange shadow over the group. "She embraced her inner self. That's the key, after all."

Aurelia's breath caught, her instincts screaming that something was wrong. "What do you mean, 'inner self'?" she pressed, stepping closer. Her voice wavered, the words trembling under the weight of suspicion. "What did you do to her?"

Before Hazel could answer, rustling in the nearby bushes drew everyone's attention. Emerging from the shadows, Ella appeared, her face pale and streaked with dirt. The ballroom's blaze had torn and ashed her once-pristine gown. Her wide eyes scanned the group, brimming with fear as they landed on Sawyer.

"Ella!" Sawyer exclaimed, breaking away from Dominic to rush toward her. He wrapped her in his arms, his protective grip shielding her from whatever unseen terror haunted her.

"I-I was hiding," Ella stammered, her voice barely above a whisper. "I saw...I saw what they were doing. The Concealment. They're everywhere."

"It's all right," Sawyer soothed, brushing the tangled hair from her face. "You're safe now. I won't let anything happen to you."

Hazel's smile widened, but there was an unsettling edge to it now. Her glowing form seemed to darken as she tilted her head, her orange eyes flickering. "Ah, but it's almost midnight," she said, her voice suddenly sharper, as if underlined with urgency. "And there's a job to do."

Sebastian's head snapped toward her. "What do you mean by that?" he demanded, his voice low and steady, though his fists still burned with residual magic.

As if in response, Ella's trembling stopped abruptly. Her breathing slowed, her shoulders straightened, and her fearful expression melted into something cold, something calculating. When she lifted her head, her eyes were glowing—burning with the same fiery orange as Hazel's, causing the bark-covered heels to illuminate.

"Ella?" Sawyer asked hesitantly, pulling back to study her face.

In one swift motion, Ella reached for the sword at Sawyer's side. She yanked it free from its sheath, the blade gleaming in the eerie light. Before anyone could react, she turned the weapon on him, pressing the tip to his throat.

"Ella, what are you doing?" Dominic shouted, stepping forward instinctively.

"Stay back," she hissed, her voice low and unnatural, layered with an echo that wasn't her own. Her gaze locked on Sawyer as her lips curled into a twisted smile.

"Sweetheart, you're hurting me," Sawyer said, his voice steady despite the blade at his neck. He didn't flinch, though his eyes searched hers desperately for any trace of the woman he loved.

Hazel's laughter filled the air, soft and melodic but dripping with malice, the leaves on her skirt bouncing. "Oh, my sweet, clueless king," she said. "She's not your Ella anymore. She belongs to the Concealment now. Just like she was always meant to."

"No," Aurelia whispered, her voice trembling as she took a shaky step back. "This...this can't be happening."

Ella's orange eyes glowed brighter as her grip on the sword tightened. "The clock is ticking," she said ominously, glancing toward Hazel. "We have a kingdom to take."

Chapter 60

WHAT THE STORYBOOK MISSED...
Ella

AS THE PRINCE AND I continued to move, his hand resting lightly on my waist, my fears melted away. He guided me effortlessly, his movements confident and sure. I had never danced like this before, had never been held with such care since the broom I waltzed with in the attic didn't have a mind of its own. Around us, the world blurred—the murmurs of the crowd, the glittering chandeliers, even the jealous stares of Mirelle and her daughters. It all faded until it was just us, spinning through a dream.

"You're a vision," he said softly, his words meant only for me. "I feel as though I've known you forever."

His words sent a warmth through me, but it was more than just flattery. There was something else stirring inside me, something I couldn't quite name. Was it joy? Hope? Or something...different?

My thoughts grew hazy, the magic pulsing faintly in my veins. For the first time, I didn't feel like the servant girl from the ashes. I felt powerful, beautiful, untouchable.

And it frightened me.

As the music swelled, I looked up into Sawyer's eyes, his kind and sincere gaze grounding me. But even as I smiled, a shadow flickered at the edge of my mind, a whisper I couldn't ignore. It wasn't just magic that had brought me here. It was something more, something deeper.

Hazel's words echoed in my memory: "Embrace your inner self."

But what if the self I was embracing wasn't the girl I thought I was?

The music slowed, and the dance came to an end. Prince Sawyer bowed, his smile genuine, and I curtsied in return, masking the unease growing in my chest. As he led me from the floor, I couldn't help but glance at the shadows flickering in the corners of the room, wondering if they were following me. Wondering if they were a part of me.

The dance floor seemed to blur around me, the light of the chandeliers shimmering like stars caught in a web of gold. Prince Sawyer held my hand with such gentle assurance as he led me toward the grand staircase. I could feel the warmth of his touch even through the delicate fabric of my glove, his presence anchoring me in a moment that felt increasingly surreal.

"I'd like you to meet my father," he said, his voice soft yet tinged with anticipation. "I think he'll find your spirit as refreshing as I do."

I nodded, though a nervous flutter stirred in my chest. The king. To meet him was an honor I could never have imagined, let alone deserved. But there was no denying the genuine kindness in Sawyer's eyes, and I allowed myself to trust in that as we ascended the steps to the balcony.

The king sat on an ornate chair draped in emerald velvet, a plate of hors d'oeuvres balanced precariously on the edge of a small, gilded table beside him. His presence was imposing, his graying beard framing a face carved with deep lines of experience. His sharp blue eyes flicked toward us as we approached, his expression neutral but observant through the sharpness of his pointy mustache.

"Father," Sawyer began, releasing my hand to gesture toward me. "I want to introduce you to someone."

I curtsied low, my heart pounding against my ribs. "Your Majesty, it's an honor."

The king regarded me for a moment, his gaze calculating. "You carry yourself with remarkable poise. Tell me, from what lineage do you hail?" he said, his voice deep and measured.

My stomach twisted. Lineage. Bloodlines. The words I'd been dreading. I glanced at Sawyer, but he had already excused himself, leaving me alone under the king's scrutinizing gaze. "I...my family, Your Majesty, is not of noble standing," I admitted, choosing my words carefully. "But we value hard work and loyalty above all."

The king arched a bushy brow, unimpressed. "Hard work, you say? Admirable, perhaps, but insufficient for one who seeks to stand beside my son."

His words stung, but before I could muster a reply, his plate tipped precariously, sending a few pastries tumbling to the floor. Without hesitation, I dropped to my knees, gathering the fallen pieces and placing them back on the plate. "Let me help," I said quickly, brushing crumbs from the carpet into my hands.

The king's eyes narrowed, watching me with an intensity that made my skin prickle. "Most women in this hall would have called for a servant to clean that up. Yet you act without hesitation."

I straightened, clutching the plate as I returned it to his table. "It's second nature, Your Majesty. I've always believed in doing what's necessary, no matter the task."

He didn't respond, but his gaze lingered on me, a flicker of something unreadable passing through his eyes. I tried to focus on his expression, but a faint whisper tugged at the edge of my mind, like a distant melody carried on the wind.

"Look inside your pocket."

The voice was soft, almost soothing, but it sent a chill down my spine. I tried to ignore it, but the whisper grew louder, insistent. My fingers twitched, seemingly of their own accord, as they brushed against the fabric of my gown.

"Look inside your pocket."

I hesitated, my heart racing, and slid my hand into the small pocket sewn into the folds of my dress. My fingers closed around something unfamiliar—a small velvet pouch. I drew it out carefully, my breath catching as I loosened the drawstring.

Inside was a tiny vial filled with a dark, viscous liquid. Poison.

"Kill him."

The whisper was no longer soft. It was a command, firm and unyielding. My hands shook as I stared at the vial, the words echoing in my head with increasing ferocity.

"No," *I whispered under my breath, clenching my fists around the pouch.* "I won't."

"He deserves it. He's standing in the way of your happiness. Of your future."

Tears stung my eyes as I fought against the voices, my grip tightening on the pouch as though I could crush it out of existence. This wasn't me. I didn't have a cruel bone in my body. I didn't—

"Pour it in the goblet."

I blinked, startled, as my vision swam. For a moment, the grand hall around me seemed to flicker, the bright light dimming, the elegant decor warping into shadowy shapes. My reflection in a nearby mirror caught my eye, and I gasped. My eyes—normally soft and blue—were glowing orange, a sinister gleam that felt entirely different.

No.

My body moved of its own accord, my hands loosening the vial and tipping its contents into the king's goblet as he turned to speak with a servant. I barely registered the movement, my mind screaming in protest as the dark liquid mixed with the wine, swirling into a venomous concoction.

"Ella," Prince Sawyer's voice broke through the haze. "Shall we?"

I snapped back to myself, nearly dropping the goblet in my haste to step away from the king's table. My heart pounded as I turned to face Sawyer, his warm smile a stark contrast to the turmoil roiling inside me.

"Yes," I managed to say, my voice barely above a whisper. "Let's go."

He took my arm, guiding me down the staircase toward the garden. I cast one last glance over my shoulder, my eyes locking on the goblet still sitting on the table. The voices in my head had gone silent, but the damage had already been done.

What have I done?

THE GARDEN WAS A DREAM painted in green and gold. Every leaf seemed to shimmer with its own light, every petal a masterpiece of nature's palette. I trailed behind Prince Sawyer as he led me through the winding paths, my breath catching at the sheer abundance of color and life around us. Roses in every imaginable hue climbed the trellises, while orchids hung delicately from branches, their petals dancing in the soft breeze. A canopy of wisteria draped over us, their lavender blooms swaying like chandeliers in the dim light of the moon.

"This place is beautiful," I said, my voice hushed in reverence.

Sawyer smiled, his gaze fixed ahead. "It was my mother's favorite place in the castle. She tended to every corner of this garden herself."

I glanced at him, noting the sudden weight in his tone. "She must have been an incredible woman."

"She was," he said softly, his steps slowing as we approached a small stone bench near a bubbling fountain. "She loved beauty in its purest forms—nature, music, kindness. But sickness..." He hesitated, his jaw tightening. "Sickness doesn't care about beauty."

I sank onto the bench beside him, my heart aching at the sorrow etched into his face. The same look that I had whenever I thought of mine.

"It's been ten years. Every year, I come out here to feel closer to her. To remember. Today's the anniversary of her death and every year it doesn't get easier."

A lump formed in my throat. "I lost both of my parents," I said quietly, surprising myself with the admission. "It was a long time ago, but the pain...it lingers."

Sawyer's gaze softened, his hand brushing lightly against mine. "It does. But it also shapes us, makes us who we are. You're strong. Stronger than you know."

His words sent a warmth coursing through me, and I turned away, embarrassed by the way his eyes seemed to see straight through to my soul. We walked further into the garden, crossing a small arched bridge that spanned a crystal-clear pond. The water was so still it reflected every detail of the sky above, every leaf and flower along its edges. I caught sight of our reflection and smiled, but the smile faltered when I noticed something behind me.

A shadow.

It moved quickly, its presence fleeting but undeniable. My heart raced as I felt a sudden weight in my pocket—a dagger. My fingers brushed the cool hilt, and panic gripped me.

Had Sawyer seen it?

I glanced at him, but his expression was unchanged, his focus on the water. My relief was short-lived as the voices returned, louder and more insistent than before.

"Kill him."

No.

"Do it."

I clenched my fists, my nails digging into my palms. I wouldn't. I couldn't. This wasn't me. The voices grew louder, drowning out the gentle hum of the garden, the trickling of the fountain, even Sawyer's words. My body tensed as the dagger seemed to burn against my skin.

"Ma'am?" Sawyer's voice cut through the haze. "Will you dance with me?"

I blinked, startled, as he extended his hand. The smile on his face was so genuine, so free of judgment, that I couldn't refuse. My hand slipped into his, and he led me to the center of the bridge.

The silence was profound, broken only by the soft rustle of leaves and the distant chirp of crickets. His hands found my waist, and I rested mine lightly on his shoulders. We swayed slowly, the rhythm dictated by the beating of our hearts.

But the voices wouldn't stop.

"Do it. Now!"

I fought to control myself, but my hand moved of its own accord, slipping into my pocket and wrapping around the dagger. Tears welled in my eyes as I raised it, every ounce of my will fighting against the pull.

Sawyer leaned closer, his voice a whisper. "You're trembling."

I was so close. Too close.

And then, the clock struck midnight.

The chime rang through the garden, clear and resonant. My grip on the dagger faltered, and it clattered to the ground before materializing into pure black smoke. My body shook as if a spell had been broken, and I stumbled back from him.

"What's wrong?" he asked, concern etched into his features.

I couldn't speak. Shame and fear gripped me, and without another thought, I turned and ran.

"Wait!" he called, his voice filled with desperation. But I didn't stop. I couldn't.

The bells continued to toll, their sound chasing me as I fled the garden, the palace, and him. My slipper caught on a stone, slipping from my foot, but I didn't dare pause to retrieve it. I needed to get away. The fog thickened as I reached the castle gates, wrapping around me like a ghostly shroud. The final bell rang as I crossed the threshold, and with it, the world shifted.

In an instant, I was back at the farm. My ball gown was gone, replaced by the tattered dress of a servant. The magic, the voices, the grandeur—it was all behind me. And yet, the weight of what I'd almost done lingered, pressing down on me as I fell to my knees in the dirt.

This was the night I've always dreamt of, but this was way more than I bargained for.

THE WEEK AFTER THE festival felt like a prison sentence, each day dragging on heavier than the last. The memory of that night lingered in my mind like smoke, suffocating me with every breath. I replayed every moment: the garden, Prince Sawyer's kindness, the warmth of his hand in mine. And then the voices. The dagger. The poison.

Two days ago, the heralds made the announcement I had dreaded the most.

"His Majesty, King Aldred, has succumbed to his illness."

Illness. That's what they called it. But I knew better. It wasn't illness that had taken his life. It was me. My hand had poured the poison into his goblet. My hand, guided by a darkness I didn't understand. My hand, tainted by something far more sinister than illness.

I wanted to tell someone, to confess, but the words were stuck in my throat like shards of glass. Who would believe me? Even if they did, what would they do? I wasn't just a servant girl now—I was a murderer. And worse, I didn't even know if it was truly me who had done it. I clung to that thought, desperately hoping it wasn't my fault. Yet the guilt was relentless, gnawing at me like a rat in the dark. And then, as if the week wasn't unbearable enough, another announcement came.

"Prince Sawyer has declared his intention to marry his true love, the maiden from the festival. He will visit every home in the kingdom to try the golden slipper left behind by the mysterious maiden."

The words sent a cold wave of dread through me. That slipper was mine. But claiming it meant more than stepping into a life of royal splendor. It meant facing Sawyer again, knowing what I'd done. Knowing what I'd become.

The clatter of hooves and the jingling of armor brought me back to the present. I peered out from behind the curtain as the prince's entourage approached the house. My breath hitched at the sight of him, sitting tall and regal on his horse, holding the gilded slipper with reverent care.

He looked so kind. So trusting. And I couldn't bear the thought of what he'd think if he knew the truth.

"Girls, quickly!" Mirelle's voice snapped like a whip, jolting me back. "Straighten your hair, adjust your gowns. We won't let this opportunity slip away!"

Evangeline rushed past me, fiddling with her bodice and muttering frantically. "It'll fit. It has to fit. It must fit."

Aurelia followed more slowly, her head bowed as if already resigned to failure. Our eyes met briefly, and there was something in her gaze I couldn't place—fear, perhaps, or maybe pity.

"Ella!" Mirelle barked, snapping her fingers at me. "To the kitchen. Make biscuits for the prince. He must be welcomed properly."

"*Yes, Madam,*" *I murmured, slipping away before she could say more. My heart thudded heavily in my chest as I stepped into the kitchen. I set the flour on the counter, but my hands trembled so violently that I knocked over the jar of sugar.*

That's when I felt it once again: the darkness. It crept into my mind like an unwelcome guest, wrapping around my thoughts and tightening its grip. I tried to push it away, but it only grew stronger.

From the sitting room, I heard Evangeline's frustrated cries. "It's too small! It won't fit!"

Mirelle's sharp voice followed. "Useless. Absolutely useless."

Moments later, she stormed into the kitchen, dragging Evangeline by the arm. My stepsister's face was streaked with tears, her makeup smudged. "Pathetic," Mirelle spat, shoving her toward the table. "You couldn't even do this one thing."

Evangeline collapsed into a chair, her sobs filling the room. For the first time, I felt something other than hatred for her. Something resembling pity.

"I'd like to try," I said softly, barely recognizing my own voice.

Both women turned to me in unison, their faces blank for a moment before twisting into sneers. Mirelle laughed, the sound cruel and cutting.

"You?" she scoffed. "You think the prince will let a dirty servant girl touch his bride's slipper?"

"She's delusional," Evangeline said, tears turned to bitter chuckles wiping at her eyes.

Their laughter ignited something in me. Outside the window, a familiar face appeared. One that was kind and helpful, whose smile was bright as she stared deep into my soul. Hazel's branchy wand waved in front of her, causing orange sparks to sputter and my stomach to turn.

"They're no longer of use to you. To us." The voice cried out from inside me again.

The darkness surged forward, filling every crevice of my mind. My hands moved without thought, tipping the bag of flour off the counter. A white cloud exploded into the air, blinding Mirelle and Evangeline as they screamed.

"What are you doing?!" Mirelle shrieked, her voice raw with fury.

The windows slammed open, and a cold wind howled through the room, scattering the flour like snow. My arms raised instinctively, and I felt the power surge through me—uncontrollable and wild. My hands trembled as I reached out, and the summoning began.

The birds came.

They swarmed through the open windows, a flurry of feathers and piercing cries. Crows, sparrows, ravens, doves, all of them drawn to the darkness within me. They filled the kitchen, their wings battering the walls as they descended upon Mirelle and Evangeline.

Mirelle screamed as a crow clawed at her face, its beak tearing at her skin. "Stop this, Ella!" she cried. "Stop it!"

Evangeline stumbled backward, her hands shielding her eyes as a raven perched on her shoulder, its talons digging into her flesh. "Help me!" she sobbed. "Someone help me!"

I wanted to stop it. I wanted to call the birds away. But the darkness had taken over, and my voice was no longer my own. Through the chaos, I caught a glimpse of my reflection in the window—the orange glow in my eyes, the twisted expression on my face. This wasn't me. But at the same time...it was.

Mirelle's screams turned into guttural cries as the birds relentlessly attacked, their sharp beaks tearing at her face. Blood streaked across her cheeks, staining the once-pristine fabric of her dress. She turned her gaze toward me, her icy green eyes wide with disbelief and terror until the vision faded entirely, her sight stolen by the feral swarm. My hand trembled as I reached for the dagger lying on the counter. An unknown strength surged through me, unnatural and terrifying, forcing me to move.

Before I realized what I was doing, Mirelle was pinned to the table, her weakened body trembling beneath my grip. My fingers dug into her jaw, forcing her mouth open as my other hand raised the blade. Every stroke of the knife cut deeper—not into her flesh, but into my own humanity. Each movement shackled me further to the darkness inside me, a darkness I couldn't seem to escape.

Evangeline's screams rose above the chaos. She clawed desperately at her own face, her cries blending with the cacophony of flapping wings and sharp caws. "Robin! Help me!" she shrieked, her voice cracking with desperation.

Through the chaos, I turned toward the window. Standing outside was the man in green. His piercing gaze met mine briefly before shifting to Evangeline's bloody, panicked figure. Disappointment etched itself into his expression, and he shook his head slowly, dismissively, as though she had failed some unspoken test. Then he turned and walked away, leaving her to her fate. Whatever she had going with this guy, it was too late for her now.

The door creaked open, breaking through the din of noise and panic. Aurelia stepped into the kitchen, her face pale with shock. Her eyes darted around the room, taking in the blood pooling on the floor, the specks splattered across pots and pans, and the grotesque sight of a severed tongue lying atop Mirelle's chest.

Her trembling hand flew to her mouth. "Ella?" she whispered, though it barely sounded like a question.

I froze, my chest heaving, the dagger still slick with blood in my hand. A part of me recognized the kindness in her, a glimmer of humanity untouched by Mirelle's cruelty. She didn't deserve this. She didn't deserve to be swallowed by the same darkness.

"Go! Get out! Never come back!" I said fighting the urges inside of me, my voice came out low, guttural, and unrecognizable.

Aurelia staggered back, her wide eyes locked on me for a moment before she turned and fled through the back door. Her silhouette disappeared into the open field beyond, her hurried steps blending with the rustle of the tall grass. The birds took flight, chasing her into the woods, their flapping wings a haunting reminder of the chaos I had unleashed. The kitchen fell eerily quiet. Mirelle and Evangeline lay limp in pools of their own blood, broken and blind. Their torment finally returned to them.

But at what cost?

They deserved punishment for the misery they caused. They deserved something. But this? This carnage, this loss of control? This was beyond anything I'd imagined, and I couldn't take it back. I couldn't undo what the darkness had made me do.

My hands shook as I brushed the flour from my frock, my movements mechanical, detached. I unfastened my bloodstained apron and let it drop to the floor, a small barrier between myself and the mess I had created. Slowly, I felt a semblance of calm returning, though it wasn't real—it was restraint, a leash tightening around the monstrous part of me that had taken over.

I stepped out into the den, my chest tight with dread. Prince Sawyer was there, his face lighting up as he recognized me. His warmth, his joy—it should have comforted me, but instead, it sent a chill down my spine. My heart stopped. The girl he knew was gone. The girl he saw now was a stranger—a new person born of darkness and regret. And yet, I smiled, a hollow mask to hide the storm raging within me.

A new chapter had begun, but I was no longer sure if I was its author, or merely a pawn in a tale I could no longer control. Whatever happened this past week, the memory of the magic and the horror has flushed out of me. I couldn't tell you what just happened in the kitchen. As much as I wanted to stop it, I couldn't tell you what the darkness did to my family.

Chapter 61

The air grew thick, suffocating under the weight of shock and disbelief. Dominic stood frozen, his mind reeling as he tried to process the horrifying reality before him. Hazel's gown sparkled, her twig wand shimmering like a beacon. She was nothing like the benevolent figure he had read about in stories. Her serene smile twisted with malice, and her glowing orange eyes burned with an unsettling intensity, causing the vibrant green foliage on her form to appear dry.

Ella stood beside her, her posture rigid, her grip on Sawyer unwavering as she held the blade close to his neck. Her glowing eyes mirrored Hazel's, her once kind and timid demeanor now consumed by something unrecognizable. Dominic's heart sank as he realized that the Ella he had known was gone, replaced by a puppet of darkness. Gretel held Sebastian's shoulder to help him fight the urge to protect his family; every blink brought a strain to his heart.

Sawyer's breaths came in shallow, uneven gasps, his muscles tense under Ella's grasp. "Ella," he mumbled, his voice trembling with confusion and heartbreak. "What's happening? What are you doing?"

Hazel's laugh rang out, light and melodious, but with an undertone that sent chills down Dominic's spine. "Oh, King Sawyer," she said, her voice dripping with mockery. "Your sweet Ella has simply embraced her true self. Isn't it beautiful? More beautiful than the flowers?"

Dominic studied the woman's features. Apart from the green complexion, the smile was gleaming like the woman in the marketplace. Her rosy cheeks still stood out and her black hair was cascading over her leafy dress. Her giggle was familiar with all the times he was caught in the woods, running away from the Concealment during the countryside ambush and encountering flue frogs. He couldn't believe it; she was there the whole time.

"That's not true," Dominic said, his voice shaky but defiant. "Ella isn't like this. She's kind, she's—"

"Kind?" Hazel interrupted, tilting her head as if amused by the notion. "Oh, she was kind, wasn't she? Kind enough to suffer quietly as her stepmother and stepsisters tormented her. Kind enough to smile through years of servitude while dreaming of a life she could never have."

Ella's glowing eyes flickered, and for a brief moment, Dominic thought he saw a glimmer of the girl she once was. But the darkness held firm, and her grip on the blade didn't waver.

"You're lying," Sawyer said, his voice gaining strength. "Ella would never do this. She's not capable of—"

"Oh, but she is," Hazel said, her smile widening. "Do you know what happens to a heart weighed down by envy, by despair? Do you know what happens when someone tastes what they've always wanted, only to realize it can never truly be theirs?"

Hazel stepped closer, her wand spinning in her hand. "Ella tasted that darkness the night of the festival. The moment she stepped into the hall, surrounded by beauty and opulence, she sank deeper. She envied them. She envied their freedom, their wealth, their happiness. And when she danced with you, her heart broke under the weight of a lifetime of longing."

Ella's voice broke the silence, low and unsteady. "I wanted to be like them," she said, her words trembling with both sorrow and fury. "I wanted to belong."

"You do belong," Sawyer said, his tone desperate. "You've always belonged. None of that matters to me, Ella. None of it."

Hazel chuckled. "Touching, but meaningless. You see, Ella embraced her darkness. And when she did, she became part of something greater—something eternal. She is Concealment now."

Dominic felt his knees weaken, but he clenched his fists, willing himself to stay upright. "Ella," he said firmly, trying to reach her through the haze of darkness. "This isn't you. You can fight this. You're stronger than it."

Ella's hand faltered for a fraction of a second before Hazel's voice cut through the tension like a knife. "Stronger? Oh, no, Dominic. She's finally free. Free to take what she wants, to strike back at those who wronged her. Free to kill off that worthless student and that seamster."

The words hung in the air, thick with implication. King Sawyer's expression hardened as he processed Hazel's statement. "What do you mean strike back?" he asked, his voice low and sharp.

Her smile turned sinister. "Oh, did she not tell you? Sweet Ella, so innocent and pure, wasn't quite so innocent after all."

"What are you talking about?" Sawyer demanded, his body rigid with tension.

Hazel waved her wand, and an image appeared in the air—a hazy, shimmering replay of a moment Ella had buried deep within her. It showed her standing on the balcony with the king, her hands trembling as she poured poison into his goblet. The image froze on the king taking a sip, his face contorting with pain as the poison started settling in his stomach. Sebastian stood with eyes widened and Aurelia jaw dropped. They knew of Ella as somebody not capable of such damage, and every piece of the puzzle revealing itself brought a whole new wave of shock.

"No," Sawyer whispered, his voice cracking. "No, that's not possible. Ella...tell me that's not true."

Ella's glowing eyes flickered again, this time with tears pooling in their orange hue. "I didn't want to," she said, her voice breaking. "I tried to fight it, but the voices...they wouldn't stop. They made me do it."

Sawyer's gaze filled with anguish as he looked at her, searching for the truth. "You...you killed my father?" His voice was barely audible, each word laced with devastation.

Dominic stepped forward, his heart pounding. "It wasn't her," he blurted, his voice firm. "It was Hazel. She manipulated her."

Hazel's laughter echoed again, cold and unforgiving. "Oh, Dominic. Always so quick to absolve guilt. But it was Ella's hand that poured the poison, her hand that silenced the king forever."

The weight of her words crushed everyone. Dominic clenched his fists, his mind racing. He couldn't lose Ella to this darkness. Not now. Not ever.

Hazel's sinister smile widened as she stepped forward, her glowing eyes casting an eerie light across the garden. The tendrils of darkness around her seemed to ripple with life. She waved her wand, and the very air around her seemed to pulse with a malevolent energy.

"Tonight must be the night," Hazel declared, her voice cold and resolute. "His heart is filled with sadness and is weakened by his mother's death. His heart—untainted by greed, cruelty, or selfishness—is the last beacon of light in this wretched land. The king's death will mark the final chapter of this kingdom's so-called purity. Once it's extinguished, the kingdom will fall into shadows where it belongs."

Sebastian's hands clenched into fists, flames flickering at his fingertips. "You're insane," he growled. "This kingdom has already seen enough suffering. You won't take more."

Hazel's laughter echoed mockingly. "Suffering is what fuels the world, dear boy. It's what fuels us all. Even your little Ella here couldn't resist it. That's what led her here. To me."

Ella stood frozen, the orange glow in her eyes flickering, as if the light of her true self fought to the surface. Her grip on Sawyer's arm loosened.

"Ella," Sebastian said, his voice softening, "this isn't who you are. I know the kindness you carry. I've seen it. That's stronger than anything she's feeding you."

Aurelia stepped forward, her voice trembling but determined. "Ella, you fought your whole life to be free, to find happiness. Don't let her steal that from you. Don't let her twist your pain into something you're not."

Ella's lips quivered, her grip faltering further. "I...I didn't want this," she whispered, her voice cracking. "But you failed your promise to protect me, and this is what you get!"

Hazel's expression darkened with both her and Ella laughing, her eyes taking in every second of Sebastian's defeat. "Enough!" she snapped, slamming the tip of her wand into the ground. "If you won't embrace your true nature, then I'll show you what happens to those who defy me."

The earth beneath them trembled. Vines shot up from the ground, twisting and curling as they grew into monstrous forms. Dominic and Gretel stumbled, losing contact with the group as foliage thickened, making a barrier between their party longer. The once-serene garden transformed as plants mutated into creatures with gnarled limbs, thorny appendages, and snapping jaws of leaves and bark.

Sebastian leaped back as a massive vine lashed out toward him, narrowly avoiding its barbed edges. Flames roared to life in his hands as he retaliated, sending a fireball straight into the creature's center. The vine hissed and writhed as it burned, but two more replaced it, advancing with eerie precision.

Aurelia unsheathed her dagger, slashing at the tendrils that lunged toward her. The blade cut through the vines, but they regenerated quickly, twisting around her arm and pulling tight. She gritted her teeth and yanked free, stabbing at the base of the plant to sever its connection to the ground.

"Sebastian, they're everywhere!" Aurelia shouted, her voice strained as she ducked beneath a clawed branch that swiped at her head.

Sebastian spun in a circle, flames erupting from his palms as he created a barrier of fire around them. The light from the blaze cast ominous shadows on the monstrous plants, their glowing orange eyes glaring through the flames.

"We have to take out the source!" Sebastian yelled.

Aurelia nodded, her dagger slicing through another vine as she advanced toward the larger clusters of plant creatures sprouting from the center of the garden. But the plants were relentless, their thorny tendrils striking with deadly precision. One caught Sebastian by the ankle, pulling him off his feet and dragging him toward a snapping maw of jagged leaves. He roared in defiance, a burst of fire engulfing the vine and freeing him.

As they fought, Gretel and Dominic emerged from an archway, drawn by the chaos of smoke coming from every direction. Dominic's eyes widened as he took in the fight: the monstrous plants, the glowing-eyed fae, and Ella, standing beside Sawyer with her expression torn between fear and anguish.

"Ella!" Dominic called out, his voice desperate.

But before they could reach her, a shadow loomed behind them. Sir Winston stepped into their path, his orange-glowing eyes narrowing with malevolence. His blade gleamed in the faint light of the flames, and his smirk was as cold as death itself.

"Not so fast," Winston said, his voice low and menacing. "You're not going anywhere."

Gretel stepped forward, her dagger at the ready, her eyes blazing with determination. "Get out of our way," she said, her voice steady despite the fear gnawing at her.

Winston chuckled, raising his blade. "I'd love to see you try to make me."

Dominic's hands trembled as he gripped the hilt of the sword he had just snatched from the wall. It was heavier than he expected, the weight pulling at his already shaky arms. Across the court, Sir Winston stood tall and menacing, his blade gleaming in the flickering light of the burning garden. His eyes locked onto Dominic with a predatory smirk.

"You're really going to do this?" Winston mocked, his voice dripping with disdain. "You can barely hold that sword properly. What hope do you think you have?"

Dominic swallowed hard, his throat dry. His pulse thundered in his ears, drowning out the sounds of chaos around him. The mocking laughter of his opponent twisted in his mind, intertwining with darker, deeper taunts that came from within.

"Why did your boyfriend leave you?" Winston's voice seemed to echo with a cruel edge that cut deeper than any blade. "Because you're weak. Helpless. No one stays with someone who can't fight for themselves. You couldn't even fight back against Jasper."

Dominic clenched his teeth, the words striking a nerve. His mind flared with memories—painful, raw memories of being left behind, of the crushing realization that he hadn't been enough. The walls seemed to close in as Winston pressed forward.

"And let's not forget," Winston continued, his steps slow and deliberate. "An orphan like you? No family. No home. You've been running your whole life, haven't you? Running because you know there's nothing for you."

Dominic's grip tightened on the sword, his knuckles white. His chest heaved with anger, fear, and something else—a flicker of defiance that burned just enough to keep him rooted in place.

"I'm not running anymore," Dominic muttered, though his voice wavered.

Winston's laughter boomed, cold and sharp. "Oh, this is rich. You think you're some kind of hero now? Let me show you just how wrong you are."

Winston lunged, his blade slicing through the air with terrifying precision. Dominic barely raised his sword in time, the clash of steel ringing through the courtyard. The force of the impact rattled his arms, and he stumbled back, his boots skidding on the polished floor.

"Dominic, watch out!" Gretel shouted, darting forward with her dagger aimed at Winston's side.

But Winston was faster. He sidestepped Gretel's attack and swung the hilt of his sword into her temple. She crumpled to the ground, unconscious.

"No!" Dominic cried, his fear momentarily replaced by rage. He charged at Winston, his sword raised in a clumsy arc. Winston easily parried the attack, his superior skill evident in every calculated movement.

Dominic was panting within moments, his muscles screaming in protest. Winston toyed with him, feinting and slashing in ways that forced Dominic to spend more energy than he had to spare. His arms felt like lead, his legs trembling as exhaustion set in.

"This is pathetic," Winston sneered, raising his blade for a final strike. "Goodbye, Chosen One."

Before the blade could fall, a blur of movement caught Winston's attention. Calypso leaped onto Dominic's shoulder, his small body bristling with determination.

"You can do this, Dominic!" the cat said, his voice sharp and urgent as his claws dug into his shoulder. "You're the chosen one for a reason. Believe in yourself!"

Dominic's breath hitched. Calypso's words ignited a warmth and fire deep within him, overcoming years of self-doubt and pain. The necklace started to glow, and the blue light burned brighter than any of the orange glowing within the darkness. The metal vibrated against his chest, causing his retreated self to awaken and stand up for himself. His grip on the sword steadied, his body straightening despite the fatigue.

Winston's blade descended, but Dominic moved faster this time, ducking under the swing with a newfound agility. His movements felt more fluid, more natural, as if something within him had clicked. A flash of light burst from Dominic's hand, the edge of his blade igniting with a faint flicker of fire. The light blinded Winston, who staggered back with a snarl.

"What...what is this?!" Winston growled, shielding his face.

Dominic didn't hesitate. He lunged forward, his blade slicing clean across Winston's chest. The knight let out a choked gasp, his eyes flickering and dimming. Dominic twisted the blade and pulled it free, watching as Winston staggered, his strength failing.

Winston collapsed to his knees, blood pooling beneath him. His sword clattered to the ground as his gaze lifted to Dominic, filled with shock and fury.

"This...isn't...over," Winston rasped, his voice barely a whisper.

Dominic took a step back, his chest heaving. The light in his hands faded, but the warmth remained, a comforting reminder of the power that had surged through him.

Winston's body slumped to the floor, lifeless. Dominic stood over him, his legs trembling as the adrenaline wore off. The glow of the pendant slowly fading away with his skin becoming cold once again. Calypso nuzzled against his cheek, his voice soft but proud.

"You did it, Dominic. You're stronger than you know."

Dominic nodded, his eyes fixed on the fallen knight. The reality of what he'd just done began to sink in, but there was no time to dwell. He turned toward Gretel, who was stirring, and helped her to her feet.

"Come on," Dominic said, his voice steady despite the chaos still raging around them. "We have to find Ella and stop this before it's too late."

Dominic crouched beside Gretel, shaking her shoulder. She groaned, her eyelids fluttering as consciousness returned. Blood matted her hair at the temple where Sir Winston had struck her, but her sharp resilience was already beginning to shine through as she blinked up at Dominic.

"Ugh, what...happened?" she muttered, her voice groggy.

"You got knocked out," Dominic said, his voice steady but urgent. "We don't have much time."

Gretel sat up slowly, wincing. Calypso darted to her side, his eyes glowing with concern. "Dominic, you need to go after the king. I'll stay with Gretel and make sure she's okay."

Dominic hesitated for only a moment, his gaze darting between Gretel and Calypso. "Okay," he said as he watched his cat licking her face. "Take care of her."

With that, he turned and sprinted into the chaos. The garden had become a nightmare, with plants twisting and writhing unnaturally, their thorny tendrils blocking paths and reaching for him like living creatures. Dominic hacked at the overgrowth with his sword, his breathing labored as he fought through the dense thicket.

In the distance, across the pond, he saw them. Sawyer knelt on the ground, his face pale and contorted with fear as Ella stood over him, her expression a twisted mixture of torment and malice. Hazel hovered nearby, her presence radiating a dark aura. Her laughter rang out, mocking and cruel, as she watched Dominic struggle to reach them.

"Ah, the chosen one," she sneered, her eyes gleaming with spite. "You stand alone, boy. Do you think you can save anyone? You couldn't even save yourself."

Dominic gritted his teeth, ignoring her taunts. He focused on clearing the path, his sword slicing through the vines and bushes with every ounce of strength he could muster. The plants seemed to grow back almost instantly, but he pressed on, determined.

As he drew closer, Ella raised the sword high above her head, the blade gleaming with intent. Sawyer's eyes widened in horror, his body frozen as if paralyzed by the weight of what was about to happen.

"Ella, stop!" Dominic shouted, his voice cracking with desperation. "Please, let him go!"

Ella turned her head toward him, her eyes narrowing. For a moment, it seemed as though she recognized him, but the darkness controlling her quickly swallowed any trace of familiarity. She gripped the weapon tighter, her body trembling as if caught in a battle with herself.

"Ella," Dominic said again, softer this time, stepping closer. "You're stronger than this. You don't have to do this."

Hazel's laughter grew louder, her expression twisted with glee. "Oh, but she does," she purred. "She's embraced the truth, the power within her. And soon, his life will be ours."

Just as Ella's arm descended, a blur of movement streaked through the chaos. Aurelia burst from the shadows, her expression fierce and determined. In her hand, she clutched the glowing Tears of Cinder.

"Ella!" Aurelia cried, her voice cutting through the din like a blade. With one swift motion, she thrust the Tears of Cinder into Ella's chest.

Ella let out a guttural scream, her body jerking as the tears glowed brighter, embedding themselves into her heart. A dark cloud erupted from her body, swirling into the air like ink dissolving in water. Hazel watched in anger as Ella forcibly expelled the darkness through her mouth, causing her triumphant smile to falter and her eyes to narrow.

"No!" Hazel screeched, her hands clawing at the air. "You wretched girl! You've ruined everything!"

Ella collapsed to her knees, gasping for breath as the orange glow faded from her eyes. Her hands trembled as she dropped the sword, the weapon clattering to the ground. Sawyer scrambled back, his face a mix of relief and confusion as he looked between Ella and Dominic.

Dominic reached for Ella just as she sobbed, her body shaking with the weight of what had transpired. "Ella," he said gently, kneeling beside her. "It's okay. You're free now."

Hazel's fury radiated in waves as she glared down at them. "You think this changes anything?" she hissed. "You think you've won? This is far from over."

She raised her hands, dark energy crackling around her fingers, but the ground beneath them rumbled. The plants around the garden began to wither and die, the power of the tears unraveling Hazel's control.

Sebastian and Gretel appeared at the edge of the garden, both bruised and battered but alive. They hurried toward the group, their weapons drawn, with Calypso climbing his way through the foliage.

Dominic helped Ella to her feet, his arm steady around her trembling shoulders. "You will not win," he said, his voice firm despite his exhaustion.

Hazel's lips curled into a sinister smile, but the flicker of uncertainty in her eyes betrayed her confidence. "We'll see about that," she spat.

The garden fell silent, the oppressive weight of Hazel's presence lifting. Dominic, Sebastian, Gretel, Aurelia, and Sawyer stood together, their breaths ragged as they took in the aftermath.

Ella looked at Dominic, tears streaming down her face. "I'm so sorry," she whispered.

The clock began to toll, its deep chimes reverberating through the night air. Midnight loomed closer with each passing strike, the tension so thick it was almost suffocating. Hazel's eyes burned brighter, her expression contorting with desperation and fury.

"No!" she shrieked, her voice echoing like thunder. "This is my last chance, and I can't let this slip away again! I can't!"

She raised her wand high, and a series of blinding, thunderous bolts erupted from its tip. The streaks of electric green surged through the air, crackling with lethal intent as they aimed for Sawyer. His eyes widened in terror, his body frozen as the deadly magic hurtled toward him.

In an instant, Aurelia stepped forward, her arms spread wide in an act of pure courage. "No!" she screamed, her voice breaking with emotion. She threw herself into the bolts' path, shielding the king with her body.

The electricity struck her, engulfing her in a blinding light. Her scream of agony tore through the garden, freezing everyone in place. Sparks danced across her skin, her body writhing in pain as the voltage coursed through her.

"Aurelia!" Ella's scream ripped from her throat, filled with anguish. She lunged forward, but Dominic grabbed her, holding her back. "No! Let me go!" she sobbed, struggling against him.

Aurelia's legs buckled, and she fell to her knees, her strength fading rapidly. Her breaths came in short, ragged gasps as the magic took its toll. Through the haze of pain, her gaze locked with Ella's. For a fleeting moment, everything else faded—the chaos, the destruction, and Hazel's looming presence.

Aurelia's lips curved into the faintest hint of a smile. "Ella," she whispered, her voice barely audible. "It's...okay."

Tears streamed down Ella's face as she shook her head, her heart breaking. "No! Don't do this! Please!"

Aurelia's gaze softened, her eyes filled with an unspoken peace. She looked over at Sebastian before giving a tiny nod, as though making amends for everything that had come before, who had a glint of a tear forming while he acknowledged her. Then, with one final, shuddering breath, her body went limp, holding one last tear in her hands as the fiery veins flickered.

The final toll of the clock echoed through the garden, signaling the arrival of midnight. Hazel's eyes widened in realization, her mouth twisting into a snarl of frustration. "No!" she screeched, the glow of her magic dimming as the clock sealed her fate.

"It's too late," Dominic said, his voice quiet but firm. He stepped forward, his hand steady on his sword. "You've failed once again."

Hazel's glare swept over the group, her orange eyes blazing with hatred like a growing fire. "This isn't over," she hissed, her voice venomous. "You think you've won? You think this is the end? You're wrong, fools."

She raised her wand, and a swirling cloud of darkness enveloped her. The grotesque shadow expanded, the wind whipping through the garden with a deafening roar. "You'll see me again," she snarled as her form began to fade. "And when you do, you'll wish you hadn't."

As the smoke disappeared, something else hadn't. Hazel looked at herself with disbelief, her wand flickering with the last bit of power emptied from its source. Laughter erupted from around her, with her body materializing into bits of sand.

"What's...What's happening?" she asked, her hands drying out like petrified wood.

"Looks like you ran out of chances," Sebastian said with a smirk.

"You're no longer of use to the Concealment if you can't carry out their task," Gretel added.

"No!"

With that, she vanished into the night with only traces of dust left behind, laughter echoing as the darkness dissipated. Only the soft wind and Ella's quiet sobs disturbed the silence of the garden.

Hazel's power is gone. The plants crumbled into lifeless heaps of vines and thorns. A somber gray now replaced the glowing red sky, and the once chaotic property was eerily calm.

Ella knelt beside Aurelia's lifeless body, her trembling hands reaching out to touch her stepsister's face. "Aurelia," she whispered, her voice breaking. "Why? Why did you do this?"

Sebastian approached slowly, his expression grim. He placed a hand on Ella's shoulder, his grip firm yet gentle. "She saved him," he said, his voice heavy with emotion. "She saved all of us."

Dominic stood nearby, his sword still in hand, his heart pounding as he took in the aftermath. He looked at the king, who had collapsed to the ground, his face pale and his body trembling. Sawyer glanced up, his gaze meeting Dominic's with gratitude. Ella reached out to her husband for support, grabbing each other tight as the realization that the festival was over. Dominic looked over at Gretel and Sebastian, their exhausted expressions telling each other that the madness had been silenced.

Chapter 62

The first rays of sunlight crept over the horizon, casting a pale tangerine glow across the ruined castle grounds. Dominic stood in the shattered remains of the garden, the once-lush greenery now trampled, burned, or tangled in lifeless vines. The silence was almost deafening after the chaos of the night. The only sounds were the faint rustle of leaves in the morning breeze and the distant call of birds, unaware of the devastation below. His sword hung loosely at his side, its tip brushing the dirt as exhaustion weighed heavy on his limbs.

Smoke curled from the remnants of the ballroom, the once-grand hall now a charred shell. Curtains that had once shimmered with opulence were now torn and bloodstained, fluttering weakly in the morning breeze through the shattered windows. Puddles of crimson streaked the stone floor, stark reminders of the lives lost during the chaos. Bodies piled along the floor that was once inhabited by dancing and life. It was a silent wasteland.

The townspeople gather around the gates, trying to look through the iron to make sense of the carnage. Ella knelt near what used to be the heart of the garden. Her hands trembled as they clutched Aurelia's lifeless hand, her body wracked with quiet sobs. Dominic didn't know what to say. He shifted, his shoulders locked as he watched her from a distance. Sebastian and Gretel were nearby, their faces etched with grief and fatigue as they began assessing the castle's damage. Calypso padded silently between them, his tail flicking with unease with the sun reflecting from his eyes.

Ella's voice broke the silence, soft but steady. "She didn't have to do this."

Dominic took a cautious step closer, unsure if she was talking to him or to herself. "She chose to," he said gently. "She wanted to save you, Ella."

Her shoulders shook, and she turned her tear-streaked face toward them. "After everything I did, she still thought I was worth saving. How is that possible?"

Dominic swallowed hard, kneeling beside her. "Because she believed in redemption. She wanted to make things right for you."

Ella nodded slowly, her fingers brushing Aurelia's face with a tenderness that made Dominic's chest ache. "I forgive her," she whispered. "For everything. The pain, the lies...all of it. She was brave. She was better than I ever gave her credit for."

He stayed quiet, letting her words settle in the morning air. She needed this moment, and nobody wasn't going to take it from her. Her freedom from the Concealment has brought a wave of realities. So many things out of her control had now come back into her memory.

Eventually, Ella's gaze shifted, her expression clouded with guilt. "Dominic, I killed him."

"King Aldred, I know," Dominic said quietly.

She nodded, her voice trembling. "I didn't mean to. I didn't want to. But the darkness...it took over. I couldn't stop it."

Before Dominic could respond, Sawyer approached them, his steps slow and deliberate. He crouched beside Ella, placing a hand on her shoulder. His face was pale, his eyes heavy with loss, but there was no anger in them. Only sadness.

"You weren't in control," Sawyer said firmly. "None of this was your fault, Ella. Hazel manipulated you. She twisted your pain and your desires into something you couldn't fight."

Ella shook her head, tears streaming down her cheeks. "But it doesn't change what I did. I took him from you."

Sawyer's jaw tightened, but his hand remained steady on her shoulder.

"You've been through so much, more than anyone should ever have to endure. That's what matters."

Dominic watched as Ella leaned into his words, her sobs subsiding into quieter cries. It was hard not to admire Sawyer's calmness, his ability to forgive so freely. If somebody took away the lives of Penelope or Alex, he's not too sure if he would be as lenient. With the sun climbing higher, long shadows casted over the castle ruins. Gretel joined them, her arm still nursing her head from the pain, but her posture resolute.

"It looks like you've got a lot of rebuilding to do," she said, her voice firm. "The castle, the kingdom, everything."

Sebastian nodded, standing a few steps behind her. His expression was unreadable, but determined in his stance. "We'll get through it," he said. "Together."

Dominic let out a breath, a flicker of hope stirring in his chest. They were battered, broken in some ways, but not beaten. There was still a chance to set things right. Ella placed a hand over Aurelia's, her lips moving silently in what could only be guessed was a final goodbye. When she stood, her shoulders were squared, her expression a mix of grief and resolve.

"We'll make it right," she said softly, her eyes meeting each of theirs in turn. "For Aurelia. For everyone."

Gretel and Sebastian approached Dominic, their faces still worn. Their body ached, every muscle screaming in protest, but they couldn't help but straighten up when they neared.

"You were incredible, Dom," Gretel said, crossing her arms but offering a faint smile. "Not bad for someone who thought they couldn't do it."

You called me Dom! Only my friends call me that! Dominic thought, his stomach fluttering.

Sebastian nodded, his eyes steady on him. "She's right. You saved us back there. You're a lot stronger than I gave you credit for."

Hearing him say that made something inside him twist uncomfortably. "Thanks," Dominic said awkwardly, scratching the back of his neck. "But I'm sorry for how I acted before. I wasn't exactly pleasant."

Sebastian chuckled, shaking his head. "Neither was I. For a second I didn't believe in you, and I should have. That's on me."

"I wasn't exactly making it easy to believe in me," Dominic admitted, feeling a flicker of guilt. "I was horrible to everyone."

Gretel smirked. "You weren't that bad. Just...frustrating."

"Thanks for the glowing review," Dominic muttered, but couldn't help but laugh a little.

"You were all great," Ella said as she wiped her tears. "Even you, Gretel."

Gretel's eyes widened as she let out a thick gulp. Her body froze in terror as she tried to think of a way to deter the queen back to her identity.

"You think some little name like Bernadette was going to hide who you were?" Ella asked with a little chuckle.

"T-Then why didn't you have me arrested?" Gretel asked nervously.

"Everybody deserves a chance at redemption. And after meeting you, I know for a fact that you are not the person people say you are."

The moment of levity was short-lived. Before they could continue, a sharp, metallic scraping sound made their head whip around. His armor was cracked and blackened, his movements labored, but his eyes burned with unrelenting rage. From the rubble of the collapsed garden wall, a figure emerged, staggering forward with a twisted grimace.

Sir Winston.

"You think this is over?" he snarled, his voice like grinding stones.

Dominic froze, his heart pounding so loudly he could barely think. "Not again," he whispered, gripping the hilt of his sword with trembling hands.

Sebastian and Gretel immediately moved to flank him, their stances defensive. But Dominic could feel their unease. None of them were in any condition to fight him again.

Sir Winston raised his blade, his strength clearly fading, but his determination as fierce as ever. "You won't leave here alive," he hissed, his eyes locking onto Dominic.

Just as he lunged, a blur of green shot across them. A swift movement, precise and calculated, intercepted Sir Winston's attack. The clash of steel echoed sharply in the quiet morning air. They all stumbled back, startled, as the figure—a person clad in a green cloak—spun gracefully, their movements fluid and effortless. A dagger gleamed in one hand, and in the other, a bow was slung across their back.

In an instant, Sir Winston was disarmed and driven to his knees. The figure's dagger slashed cleanly, and Sir Winston collapsed, his body crumpling into the rubble like a discarded puppet. The silence that followed was deafening. Dominic struggled to catch his breath with his heart thundering in his chest, the grip on his sword slackening as he stared at the green-cloaked figure.

"Robin Hood," Sebastian muttered, his voice low with apprehension.

Dominic felt my pulse quicken, dread creeping into his veins. Robin Hood. The thought was chilling. If this was him, what came next wouldn't be any better than what they'd just survived. The figure turned slowly toward them, their hood still up, hiding their face. Each step they took seemed deliberate, purposeful. Dominic's mouth went dry as he prepared himself for whatever came next.

But then they raised a hand and pulled the hood back.

It wasn't Robin Hood.

The person who stood before them was a woman, her olive-toned skin glowing faintly in the early light. Her dark brown, wavy hair was tied back, a few loose strands framing her striking face. Her sharp eyes scanned each of them with a mix of curiosity and calm authority.

"Who—" Gretel began, but the woman cut her off.

"I'm Maid Marian," she said, her voice steady and clear. "I was sent by Merlin."

Chapter 63

The tension in Dominic's chest eased slightly, but confusion quickly took its place. Merlin? An archer? Why now? And why them? The focus on her face made him uneasy. Dominic grew to know Maid Marian as a fighter, he didn't know how skilled she really was. It was more impressive seeing the skill and the accuracy in front of him, especially when it was to save their lives.

"Maid Marian?" Sebastian asked, brows knitting together. "Merlin sent you?"

She nodded, her gaze lingering on Dominic a moment longer than he liked. "He did. And it seems I arrived just in time."

They stared at her, stunned into silence. Only when she looked down at Sir Winston's body, verifying the creature was truly defeated with darkness oozing out of their open mouth, did she speak again.

"The darkness isn't gone," she said gravely. "It's spreading faster than we anticipated. Hazel's power may be broken, but worse things are out there than her."

You mean there's worse than her? Worse than Robin?

A wave of exhaustion crashed over Dominic. The weight of the kingdom, the Concealment, every battle they had endured—it was almost too much. "What do we do now?" he asked, voice trembling.

Marian's expression softened slightly. "You keep fighting," she said. "But we need to move quickly. There's no time to rest. Brone's army still has loyalists creeping through every shadow."

"Oh, so you know Brone?" Dominic asked, unable to hide his edge. "Seems like everyone only talks about Robin."

"Brone is the dark sorcerer who created the Concealment," she explained, her hazel eyes glistening with a forming tear. "Robin is just one of his right-hand men. We need you to defeat Robin—and the rest of Brone's people."

The idea of more henchmen in the world of twisted tales made his mind race. The endless possibilities of what else could be out there was overwhelming. The one time he stepped up to fight against the Concealment couldn't be enough to define him as the one to vanquish it.

"Brone has done so much damage to Golponia. Innocent lives have fallen victim to his greed. He will stop at nothing to take away the happiness out of every single person. We must stop those that have been consumed by his creation. If they are stopped, then they are no longer of use to him, just like Hazel."

Dominic hesitated, glancing at Sebastian and Gretel. "I can't do this alone," he said.

"You won't," Sebastian said as he placed his arm on his shoulder.

"Not when you have us," Gretel added.

Marian studied them for a beat, then nodded. "Can you trust them?"

"With my life," Dominic said, firm and without hesitation with a grin that glowed as bright as the sun.

Canaries chirped in his ears. The chorus of peace brought warmth back to his body. He may not have had his people back in Everside Valley to bring him ease, but at least he had Sebastian and Gretel with him to offer the comfort he craved. He'd met these people days ago, but it felt like he'd known them for longer with trust that was fortified through struggles.

"They're your chosen family," Ella said with a wink. "And they're mine too."

Sebastian stepped forward, tension tightening his features. "Ella, there's something I should tell you."

"Yes?"

"Aurelia told me where I came from."

"The tree," Ella said, placing a comforting hand on his arm. "Agnes told me about the tree."

"Yes. The tree that Mirelle left me at."

Ella froze, the realization striking her silent. The sunlight caught in the tears forming in her eyes. All those years of torment from her stepmother—and now the boy who had witnessed it all turned out to be her son. Dominic could see the pain behind her quiet gasp. The loneliness Sebastian had spoken of when they were younger suddenly had a name, a root, and it was bitter.

"I'm so sorry," she whispered. "I didn't know she brought pain onto you too."

"Thank you," he said, managing a tight smile.

"But look at it this way—you've always been like a brother to me. Now it's just official."

"And as your brother, I'll always protect you."

"I know you will. But right now, you need to protect the people. Do it for me. That's an order from your queen."

They embraced, arms wrapped around each other tightly. Dominic watched, a soft smile tugging at his lips. The tears sliding down Sebastian's cheek were a rare glimpse into the vulnerable side of someone usually so composed. It made Dominic like him even more.

When Sebastian pulled away, his concern shifted. "What about the palace? If we leave, there's nothing stopping another attack. Sawyer could be in danger again. Ella too."

Marian's mouth was a thin line. "Merlin will send his mages. They'll guard the kingdom and begin repairs. You have my word. They'll be safe."

One of the mages approached the side of the castle. Their canary-yellow robe fluttered in the wind as their arms rose above their head. Incantations chanted from their lips with forces moving from the air. Rubble floated around them, slowly piecing together on their missing base. The night's wrath began to become erased by the swish of fingertips. Dominic's stomach fluttered with admiration, watching the damage slowly repair itself, watching what would only be created in television happen before his very eyes.

Ella approached, her steps hesitant but filled with determination. "Thank you," she said softly.

She wrapped her arms around Dominic. He stiffened instinctively, an old fear brushing up against him—the memory of her possession by Hazel still fresh. But this embrace was real. She kissed his cheek, and a moment later he felt a soft thump in his coat pocket. Reaching inside, he found a faint glow—a cluster of smoldering cracks alive with flickering orange light.

The Tears of Cinder.

The beads sparkled in his hands. His palms felt the heat radiate into his wrinkles. A twinkle in his eyes gave him a glimpse into Ella's soul, the deepest and most vulnerable part of her soul had been encapsulated into the biggest part of her identity. Her heart was the strongest weapon, one stronger than any form of magic as the tales he remembered from his storybook flashed in his eyes.

"Just in case," she whispered with a wink.

Dominic's apprehension hadn't completely faded. Part of him wanted nothing more than to collapse into the soft bed they'd been given. But they were moving forward now.

He gave one final glance to the queen, whose eyes shimmered with gratitude as she handed them their belongings, salvaged by surviving servants from the blaze. In his pack, he found it—his denim jacket. Repaired by Mister Gloomis, it still felt new but still familiar. He slipped it on, catching Sebastian's faint smirk of approval. Looking at the patterns reflecting in the daylight brought a sense of transformation, something he didn't feel when he was in the shop.

This time, the jacket didn't feel like baggage. It felt like armor.

He caught his reflection in a pond nearby. The face staring back wasn't the same boy who'd entered this world. The battle had changed him. Maybe even the tacky pattern on the jacket didn't look so bad now. Maybe this was part of who he was.

A hero.

Chapter 64

HAPPILY EVER AFTER?
Dominic

I AM SO TIRED.

I don't know if I have it in me to leave this place. It's been a long night of dancing and fighting—something I usually don't do separately or together. Maid Marian wants us to leave right now, and all I want to do is rest. I'm sure she can see the exhaustion and pain across all of our faces; it shouldn't be that difficult.

"Here, take some of this," Marian says as she reaches inside her pouch.

She tosses a small bottle, the sunlight reflecting off the green glass. The liquid sparkles inside with twinkles of violet. At this point, I don't have any energy inside me to fight back or rebel. It could be poison for all I know, but I know she wouldn't do that to me. As I take a swig, warmth trickles down my throat. As the contents fill my stomach, a shot of energy surges through my body. The muscles in my arms and legs ease, and there's no more pain from the punches I endured. Watching Gretel and Sebastian take their turns, I notice the energy perk back into their bodies, and Gretel's wound on her head even closes up; it doesn't even need any stitches.

"What is this stuff?" I ask, my throat no longer scratchy as the dehydration fades.

"Vervain Elixir," she says as she reaches for the bottle from Gretel, placing the rest back inside her pouch.

I can't believe it. Vervain Elixir. I feel like I've slept a couple nights in a hospital. If only the people back home had some of this, there'd be a lot fewer sick people and so many without hefty medical bills!

"Are we ready to go?" Marian asks, her eyebrow cocked.

"Wait!" a woman yells from around the corner, passing by the mage.

Agnes paces along with Sawyer, whose shoes clap on the uneven cobblestone. Their steps avoid the carnage.

"I just wanted to give you a gift," Agnes says, as she takes out a bottle of her own.

What is it with these people and their bottles?

One drop into the opening of my messenger bag, and a cloud of smoke wisps out. My heart races as I imagine the possibilities of her setting my belongings on fire, but I know she wouldn't do that to me; she wouldn't do that to Sebastian.

"A little something we use to help us take fewer trips," Agnes says with a wink.

As I look at my bag, the volume is still the same, and the appearance looks filled. Once I look inside, it's a black hole. Where did my clothes go? Where did the cat food go? Calypso will have a fit!

"It gives you more space to store without feeling the burden of the weight," Agnes explains. "All you need to do is think about the item, and it will appear in your hand.

Another neat invention that I can take back home. I swear, these people are geniuses!

"I also owe you an amends," she continues as she makes her way to Gretel. "I shouldn't have made my assumptions about you."

Gretel sheds a tight smile, her shoulders sinking. "It's okay."

"No, it's not. I've heard so much about you, and it's wrong. If people could see the person that I see, they'd be so blessed to have known you."

Gretel tries to keep it together. Even though the Vervain Elixir works to heal us, the pain inside Gretel needs to hear that. A lone tear trickles down her cheek, her hand reaching toward Agnes with veins protruding from her tight squeeze. She hasn't told me the extent of her pain and why she landed herself in this situation, but she doesn't need to at this moment.

"And I'll make sure to watch the farm for you while you're gone," Agnes concludes with another wink as she touches Sebastian's cheek.

"I know you will," he says warmly.

"Are we ready to go?" Marian asks again, her clenched hand making the leather emit a crunch.

"Actually, can I have a moment with Dominic?" Sawyer butts in, and Marian lets out a frustrated sigh.

"Sure."

The king guides me through the bushels with freshly healed leaves repaired by the mage. The tree stands tall and proud as though his own mother is talking to him with relief that his life has been saved. I make my way to the stone bench at the end, interrupting the sparrows mingling along the edge.

"I wanted to personally thank you for everything you've done," he says to me, his tone soft and full of vulnerability.

"You're welcome," I say, unsure. "I did have some help."

"I know. But I wanted to thank you for your entire company. You've been so kind and open. It took my wife betraying me to appreciate the courtesy."

"Oh, it was nothing," I say, my fingers creeping under myself.

"I wanted to give you a gift for the road."

Sawyer reaches inside his jacket. A leather-bound book illuminates in the light with a golden ribbon hanging below the spine. The little book flutters its blank pages as I notice the lack of writing throughout the parchment.

"A journal? Thank you so much."

"Oh no, this isn't a journal," Sawyer says quickly. "Haven't you seen one of these?"

He gives me this puzzled expression, one I've had a number of times since I got to Golponia. I think he forgot that I am not familiar with this land or any of the tricks and gadgets that come with it.

"A book?" I ask with confusion.

The king lets out a little chuckle. "It's more than just a book. It's a simikope. They are enchanted books that let you write to each other."

So it's like texting? Maybe I won't need my phone after all!

"Everybody should have one of these. All you do is put a drop of the person's blood on the page, and it links to their simikope. I already linked mine with yours."

I don't know what else to say. That was very kind of him to think of gifting me this book. I don't know what I can talk to him about on my travels. I don't want to come across as rude, so I'm going to enjoy this book. And who knows, maybe we can be great penpals?

"Thank you so much for this," I say, catching a fresh breath as I let out a big smile. "I will surely write."

He's very kind to me—all of them are. The confusion on his face is endearing, especially when he gets caught up in my inner turmoil. In fact, he's making that same face again as he leans closer to me. I don't have a moment to react when his lips touch mine. The warmth of his kiss catches me off guard. I don't know what to do.

"Sawyer," I say, my eyelids fluttering like crazy. "What are you doing?"

Sawyer's eyes twinkle as he stares at me in a daze. "I'm sorry. I just wanted to say thank you one more time."

"Your wife?"

"I know," he says, knowing then that his mistake was made. "I'm just a little confused, that's all."

Confused is something we both can agree on.

"I-I just feel a little betrayed by Ella, if I can be honest with you. I know she was possessed by the Concealment, but she did kill my father."

I could see a tear forming in his eye. The crack in his voice made my heart ache for him. That would be a tough pill to swallow. I'm not sure what I can say to him that would take away his pain, especially with a wound that has been opened up and fresh once again. All I can think about are the words Ella told me before, ones I remember from her story that I hope would keep his happiness at bay.

"I know it will be painful to face her betrayal," I say carefully, knowing his tears are forming. "But remember how much she loves you. It was only her body that did the deed, not her will. Take it one day at a time, and maybe it will get you closer to forgiveness."

"Yes, forgiveness," he says solemnly.

I don't know if those words will work on him. I mean, it does seem like those two will have to start over. But a lot of these stories I read only had the prince or king fall in love after one encounter, so my hope is that it will work again with those two.

"Ella is a kind soul, and you know that. Give her a chance, promise me.

Sawyer lets out a little nod. He lets himself up from the bench, his nose letting out a sniffle of sadness as his hand reaches for mine.

"And I promise I will write to you," I assure him. I feel like I have no other choice now that he feels alone.

Sawyer lets out a forced smile, his hand squeezing mine. "Thank you."

As we make our way out of the garden, he takes one more moment to give me a hug. I can feel his heart racing against mine—it's so fast. I know he doesn't want me to leave. I don't know if I want to leave either. But it's fate that brought me here, and it's fate that is going to keep me going until I find my way home.

Once we let go, we walk back into the clearing where Marian stands impatiently. Her lips are tense as she taps her boot on the stone. Gretel and Sebastian hoist their bags, now enchanted with Agnes's gift. I readjust my jacket before looping the strap of my messenger bag over my shoulder, tucking my simikope inside, watching Sawyer grin as I do it.

"It's time to go," Marian says, giving me no choice but to stall any longer.

I give my new friends a wave goodbye. Ella's face flushes with tears, as does Sawyer's. Their hands hold on to each other's tight the further we make our way from Mynnshire Castle. I look over at Sebastian and Gretel, who have twinkles in their eyes, one similar to Alex and Penelope—it's one that's ready for adventure.

But am I ready for it?

Even with being away from my friends, I know that these two need me just as much as I need them. As we turn to leave, the sun rises in full over the horizon, casting golden light over the castle. The path ahead is uncertain. The battles aren't done. Not even close by the sound of it. But as we step into the forest, sunlight filtering through the canopy, something dawns upon me:

Fairy tales never warn you about the messy parts. About how complicated real heroism can be. How villains are made. How some things aren't what they seem. As cheesy as it sounds, this story is still being written, and I can't wait to see how it turns out with the people I care about most.

"*Can we please find something to eat?*" *Calypso's voice cuts through my thoughts, thick with exaggerated irritation. "I'm a hero cat, not a fasting monk."*

Gretel rolls her eyes. "Didn't you eat enough last night?"

"Doesn't count," Calypso argues. "That was pre-battle sustenance. Now I need a victory feast."

Despite everything, I laugh. The sound surprises me. It feels good.

This isn't the end.

It's just the beginning.

Acknowledgements

Writing *Tears of Cinder* came during a dark period in my life. The land of Golponia was born as an escape from life's obstacles—a place where magic works differently and familiar characters take on new forms from the stories we thought we knew. Growing up, I often imagined a world like this, and with this book, I wanted to create a story of triumph that has now blossomed into a full series I've completely fallen in love with.

Fairy tales have always brought me joy since childhood. Having written several books in the slasher subgenre, I wanted to challenge myself by blending the horror elements I love with this fantasy world I adore. I'm incredibly proud of this book and excited for the upcoming adventures Dominic and his friends will face in the next stories.

I must thank my husband, who has given me the freedom to live fully in my imagination and put my dreams on paper. He has been a guiding light in my darkest times for over a decade, and I am forever grateful for his unwavering support.

I hope you enjoy *Tears of Cinder* as much as I enjoyed writing it. It has been an absolute joy, and I can't wait for you to join me on the next adventure!

About the Author
Brady Phoenix

BRADY PHOENIX IS A self-published author. With a love for horror movies and fairy tales, his goal is to add diversity to the horror and fantasy genre through his work. When he is not writing, he enjoys long nature walks, hanging out with his husband and two cats, along with reading and supporting the self-publishing.

Facebook- @Brady Phoenix
Instagram- @AuthorBradyPhoenix
Bluesky- @bradyphoenix.bsky.social
TikTok- @AuthorBradyPhoenix
Website– bradyphoenixauthor.com

Also by Brady Phoenix

The Concealment Saga
Tears of Cinder

Standalone
Cardinal Rules
Nun Taken
Troll
Petals of Peril

www.ingramcontent.com/pod-product-compliance
Lightning Source LLC
Chambersburg PA
CBHW031734180726
48283CB00005B/1507